GLIMMER

THE BLACK SWAN FILES: 001

TRICIA CERRONE

This is a work of fiction. Names, characters, places, and incidents are either the products of the author's imagination or are used fictitiously. Any resemblance to actual events, locales, or persons (living or dead), is entirely coincidental.

Published by Stone Media, Inc.
This book is a first edition.

ISBN-10:1938258142
ISBN-13:978-1-938258-14-5

Cover and book design by The Killion Group, Inc.
www.thekilliongroupinc.com

DEDICATION

To Sydney, Olivia, and Kate

ACKNOWLEDGEMENTS

No book is completed without a lot of hours at your desk and a lot of support from the right people. I was fortunate to have several incredible beta-readers—Samantha Purvis, Maia Grace Tivony, Mia Speier, and Yuka McGrath—who took the time amidst their studies and other activities to give me my first critiques. Thank you for your insight and honesty! A very special thanks to my trusted critique partner, Janet Maarschalk—who also writes as Lynne Marshall—for a thorough and thoughtful story and character edit that made my book better. Additional thanks to The Killion Group, Inc. for the beautiful cover art, Heather Osborn Edits, proofreading by Joyce Mochrie of One Last Look, and map by Laci Jordan. I also want to thank the many strong, creative, and courageous women in my life who are an inspiration for the kind of girls and women I write about. Loving thanks to my parents, children, and all my family who are still my top fans. My deepest gratitude goes to Andrew Stone, who is my constant supporter and inspiration in life—all my heroes are inspired by you!

Most of all, I want to thank all the readers who have purchased, borrowed, or shared this book. It was written for you, and I hope you enjoy it.

GLIMMER

Camp Holliwell is a United States Government, Science and Military facility located in the Virginian mountains, specializing in solutions to humankind's greatest issues. Their motto: *Science, Technology, Service.*

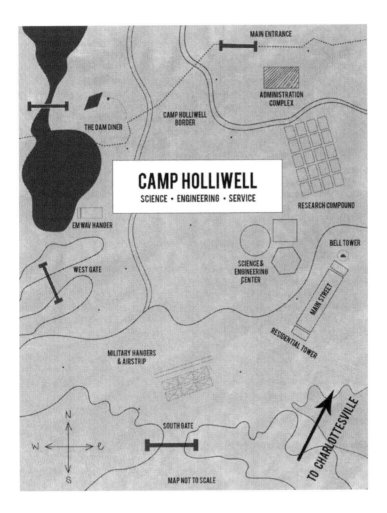

WHO'S WHO IN THE BLACK SWAN FILES

Jocelyn Esperanza Albrecht: a.k.a. Sunnie Cashus a.k.a. Project Sunday, TOP SECRET

Georgie: High school senior, super sleuth, and crusader for justice

Brittany: Georgie's best friend, expert in snark, and sustainable fashion designer

Lena: Computer scientist, passionate cryptologist, and pie connoisseur

Seth: Social outcast, smooth-talking survivor, and a new experiment at Camp Holliwell

Graeme: Software engineer, softhearted protector, and tenacious truth-seeker

Alastair: Georgie's cousin, former Army Ranger, and general badass

Richie: Al's Army buddy, mechanical genius, and Holliwell survivor

Medina: Jocelyn's military handler, fierce rule-keeper, and conflicted soldier

Sergei Baratashvili: Longevity scientist, nanotechnologist, and captive at Camp Holliwell

Laurence Cashus: Jocelyn's guardian, neuropsychiatrist, and lead scientist on Project Sunday

Dominique Wicker: Fearless geneticist, fiendish manipulator, and Laurence's competition

General Martin: Military Commander in charge of Camp Holliwell and Special Projects

Sarge: Leader of Jocelyn's military training

Megan: Jocelyn's assistant trainer and kinesiologist

Liz: Psychologist and neighbor to Jocelyn and Laurence

Jerry Ramstein: The President's top advisor and Secretary of Information of the United States of America, or SOI

PROLOGUE

Subject: Jocelyn Albrecht Lives

Message: My name is Jocelyn Esperanza Albrecht. I am the eldest daughter of Illeana Marques and Grayson Albrecht. At Camp Holliwell Research Facility, I'm known as Sunday Cashus –- Sunday, because that was the day I woke up after my family died in an accident, and Cashus, because I am the ward, patient, and test subject of Dr. Laurence Cashus. My parents were longevity scientists. The irony is that due to their scientific breakthroughs, I now have a life expectancy of twenty-one. I just turned seventeen. That leaves about four years. Three good ones...if I'm successful tonight.

Jocelyn lifted the pencil and shook her head, staring at the paper.

Too dramatic.

No one cared who she was. Even *she* wasn't sure who she was anymore—*or what she had become.* If she escaped tomorrow, what would be the final cost? After all she had done, was there any price she wouldn't pay for her freedom?

She released a controlled breath, careful not to make any noise that would activate the surveillance system. Hunched against the cool windowpane, eyes closed and invisible to the outside world, she could indulge in the fantasy of being known and remembered by someone. She could pretend she was important enough that someone still searched for her and that she had a family who cared.

With one more exhale, the moment was done.

She was not important. She was not remembered. She was not…she couldn't use the 'L' word without getting ill. She was pragmatic, and though she steeled herself to acknowledge it, no one cared about her. There wouldn't be anyone coming to rescue her from this prison.

Jocelyn opened her eyes and began to quietly and methodically shred the single piece of paper.

If her message got through security, the most important thing was her name and that she lived. She wasn't going to have time to write an obituary, much less an autobiography.

She turned the single stack of long paper strips horizontally and tore them into small squares, depositing each new stack in her mouth, then swallowing. Paper was nice for passing messages and organizing her thoughts, but the deleting process provided no nutritional value.

She worked up some saliva and stared out over Camp Holliwell. The condo she shared with her Uncle was one quarter of the top floor of the tallest residential building on camp. Her stark bedroom had a corner window in the front of the residential tower, with the best views of Main Street and the lights of the impressive Science and Engineering Center in the distance.

She used to adore the view, finding comfort in it. Here, in the Virginian mountains surrounded by beautiful forests, lakes, and rivers on all sides, lay a bastion for civilization. Science, Technology, Service—that was the motto of Holliwell, and ultimately, its mission.

Night or day, she'd been awed by the modern and sleek lines of the reflective Nanotech Tower, smiled at the stark-white whimsical bubble structure that made up the Biology Labs, and delighted over the optical illusions designed into the Optics Building. There were other structures filled with scientists, engineers, and researchers focused on the study of the senses, chemistry, genome mapping, and a variety of other pursuits that she'd been told were vital to national security.

From a distance, the layout of the S & E Center was a thing of beauty—what happened inside those buildings inspired her worst nightmares.

She'd been shielded from that for most of her time at Camp Holliwell. Her life had been limited to the pretty Main Street and the military training grounds. It might have been perfect, except for the hospital that took up the top floors above the storefronts of Main Street. She'd spent half her life in hospitals, and a large portion of it in that particular one.

Science, Technology, Service—it should be comforting. It wasn't.

A movement in the night caught her attention—a soldier being escorted to the civilian research side of the hospital.

A shiver of warning disrupted her focus. Her uncle worked late. If the soldier was being brought to Uncle Laurence, it was not a good sign.

She pressed against the glass looking down to the street, her eyes automatically filtering the darkness to get clarity on the target. There was something familiar about him—definitely one of the younger ones. She was able to note some of the victim's features from behind, but her soundproof chambers prevented her from hearing the conversation.

One thing was clear—though he sauntered along, he didn't go willingly.

She put the fourth stack of paper in her mouth, ignoring the familiar dryness on her tongue. She didn't have enough saliva to keep the paper soft, but continued swallowing the square piles with practiced discipline. There was a price for fantasizing.

There was a price for everything.

Hoping was not something she could afford to do—not with only three good years left.

At the side entrance of the hospital, one of the escorts reached for the soldier's arm and he shook it off, his elbow flicking up and out like a weapon—fierce, threatening, angry…and afraid. Jocelyn froze. She saw his face.

Medina!

Apprehension whizzed lightly over her skin, creating a warm current she still struggled to control. He was the one person who could testify to the abilities she'd been working diligently to hide. Her stomach contracted with fear.

The men disappeared through the hospital doors, and the streets were once again empty.

She put the final shreds of paper in her mouth and gulped hard, hiding the evidence and pushing away the last fantasies of love, hope, and family that remained.

The night sky sparkled with stars, and in the vast vision above, uncontrolled and unrestricted by physical boundaries, she could imagine what freedom felt like.

The weather promised to hold for the holiday weekend, security would be light, and her patience would pay off. It must.

Jocelyn pulled the dark beanie lower around her skull, ignoring the itchiness of the material on her hairless scalp. Slowly, she unfolded her legs, stretching them to prevent cramping before placing them on the floor and stepping strategically around the room to avoid triggering the sensors. She reached the bed and rested on her back, body straight, arms folded over her stomach, eyes staring at the ceiling fan above her as she visualized every step of her plan.

Finally, she closed her eyes for precious sleep.

She'd made one error. In twenty-four hours, she'd know if it was fatal.

If it was…then who she was wouldn't matter to anyone, not even herself.

CHAPTER ONE

Three months earlier…

This field trip had been doomed from the beginning.

The muzzle of a gun pressed to Sunnie's temple. It had been used recently. She could tell by the heat on her skin and the burning scent assaulting her nose. Her heart did a triple beat vibrating in her ears.

There had been other signs that pointed toward doom, but the gun definitely confirmed it.

She heard a young girl cry for her mother and breathed with control, surprised that all the years of meditation actually helped when it mattered. The girl cried out again. Sunnie heard and felt her terror. It was the only reason she wasn't safely in the elevator, heading to the truck. She would not be telling her uncle that part of today's misadventures.

Her uncle worked at Camp Holliwell, a high tech, high science, highly militarized zone secured deep in the Virginian mountains. Because of Sunnie's unique abilities, she was sometimes called upon to assist Uncle Laurence's colleagues. He called them field trips so as not to frighten her. And nothing had frightened her. She liked the opportunity to go somewhere, anywhere, off Camp Holliwell.

As she got older and the outings became more militarized, she understood them for what they were—secret missions. For her uncle's sake, she pretended they were still harmless field trips.

It was harder to pretend with a gun to your head, but she wasn't about to let one man ruin her chances to attend the next mission.

From the corner of her eye, she identified a ghoulish, full-face oxygen mask—another sure sign that things were about to get worse...and she was going to need that mask.

She might need the gun, too.

Sunnie wasn't allowed to carry weapons as a matter of policy, and a family rule. Granted, she'd never been on a field trip where she *really* needed a weapon. Her job, in general, simply relied on her super hearing and language skills. In a world where every room was scanned for listening, probing, and picture devices, non-detectable solutions were in demand. She had only to sit in the suite next door and repeat what was being said. Today, that amounted to conveying instructions about the transport of a high-risk "asset." Easy peasy, safe and breezy.

Only now, she wondered what that asset was. Apparently, a lot of people wanted it.

She swallowed the lump in her throat and held her hands up in surrender when her assailant pushed the gun harder against her head. She went through a visual picture of what she needed to do next. She tuned her ears into every sound, searching for clues in her surroundings to guide her. The heartbeat of the man next to her surfaced the loudest. It beat louder and faster than her own. Perhaps his mission was doomed as well. The thought reassured her and gave her courage.

A loud crash distracted her attention from the immediate danger.

Medina flew out the door of a hotel room, his body thudding hard against the wall on the other side of the hallway. Wood and plaster sprayed around him, making her think he might have actually gone through the door. Medina was her handler—a military protector who got her in and out of field trips. He wasn't supposed to be flying through walls or doors.

Lucky for him, she'd been delayed by her buddy to the right. Maybe this trip wasn't going downhill after all.

Using the distraction, Sunnie stepped sharply in reverse, tilting her head backward while her right hand moved lightning fast and grabbed the muzzle with forward motion. The flash of exploding fire and the bullet whizzing past her nose were synchronous with the explosion in her ears. She cried out in pain, and her eyes squeezed shut protectively, but she knew she had to fight now and recover later. Most fights are against yourself—that's how she'd been trained. You have to fight yourself from giving up.

She could do that.

Her heel crushed the top of the gunman's foot, while her right hand followed through pushing the muzzle down and against his thigh. She grabbed with her other hand, cracked the gun hard, breaking his trigger finger, and snatched the gun from his grip. Her elbow swung up at his chin, knocked the mask off kilter, and impaired his vision. She used the opportunity to kick out his knee and shoot his foot. The shooting wasn't deliberate. It just sort of happened. Probably why her uncle didn't want her using guns.

Her assailant cried in fury at the pain and lurched toward her with a punch. She ducked, then launched upward with a chop to his throat. She grabbed the mask, pulled him forward, and hit him on the back of the neck.

It was a blow that could kill or stun. She'd been careful to stun.

He fell to his knees and she ripped off the mask, turning to shoot the knee of the other masked gunman going after Medina.

The shot knocked him off balance and took his attention from Medina to her. She shot his gun arm next. It gave Medina time to secure his gun and pistol-whip his head. She winced as the victim flopped forward to the ground.

She'd been taught to shoot at the chest or head, but...she hadn't been planning on killing anyone today. Preferably never.

Bluish gas seeped out from under the hotel room door where the cries came. She went back and shot the door of the locked hotel room until the clip in the gun was empty. She tossed the gun and shoved the rest of the way with her shoulder.

Medina grabbed her arm and pulled her back violently.

"They need help," she said. The mask muffled her voice, so it wasn't clear he understood until he checked out the room, nodded, then stood guard.

Huh. Not so heartless after all?

The room was a large suite, and through the blue smoke, Sunnie spotted a woman unconscious on the floor with a little girl screaming, desperately pulling her woman's arm. Nothing in her last nine years prepared her for what happened next.

The memory rocked her. Sunnie lost balance and fell. Suddenly, she was seven again, trying to drag her mother through the gas and fire in their home, crying for help, and begging her mom to come with her. Her mother's eyes opened briefly and then she was gone.

Sunnie struggled to stay in the moment. She needed to act. Reality was a gas mask, hands and knees hugging the floor, seconds to save this woman and get to the truck.

She swallowed hard, clutching weakly at the carpet as she crawled to the woman. It took an act of will to keep going, to reach the girl and her mother against the heavy weight of memories threatening to crush her mind. The girl's crying became her own and nearly overtook her emotions. She reached the woman, and for a split second, thought she would turn the woman over and see her mother's face. But it was a stranger.

Sunnie snapped back to reality, found her breath and stood, compelling herself to pull the woman with her. It helped that she had super strength along with her super hearing. She put the woman over her shoulder and grabbed the kid with her free arm, charging out of the hotel suite toward the bank of elevators.

The doors dinged open, and she faced two tall men in business suits and a blonde woman in a business dress. They gasped in surprise, the younger man stepping in front of the woman defensively when Sunnie swung the kid to her feet in front of them, and dumped the woman into his arms.

"Gas leak," she spoke in French. "Please evacuate the building."

She reached in and pressed the first floor. The little girl stared silent and afraid. Sunnie wished she could have done more. She couldn't. She simply stood and held a frozen wave as the doors closed.

Medina called, and she turned to join him as another elevator opened and three armed men in black suits and gas masks stepped out. The mask she wore covered her identity, but the hotel uniform she had acquired to fit in must have warned them.

The instant it took them to assess was long enough for her to grab the four-foot-high decorative vase off the table and swing it like a baseball bat at the first man, sending him into the others. They, in turn, caught and flung the first man forward like a weapon. She stepped aside as the body flew into the opening elevator doors opposite and to the screams of another hotel guest holding her little dog. The dog's ears popped up, its eyes went wide, then it buried itself in the screaming woman's fur coat.

Sunnie spun, jumped, gripped the outside frame of the elevator, and hit the men with matching kicks to their chins. One of them held a semi-automatic that shot off randomly. The screaming woman behind her got louder and more frantic.

Sunnie secured the weapon and fired back into the elevator, crippling the men. Russian curses joined French curses and yippy barks.

The men moved, trying to get up.

The screams and barks got louder.

Sunnie winced at the noise, trying to think.

The first man lie half in the elevator behind her, while the Frenchwoman frantically pressed the close button, only to have the doors open again and again at the obstacle she continued to uselessly kick.

Sunnie didn't have time for a fight, and no one was watching other than a hysterical woman, so she took the easy way out. She put the gun in her belt, harnessed her energy, and swept the two men back hard into the elevator, holding them immobile with one hand while she grabbed the first man and threw him in with the others. She pressed the button for the lobby and didn't release her focus on the men until the doors shut. The delay would only give her precious seconds, but it was enough.

She pulled the firearm and ran down the hall to the other end of the building. Medina held the service elevator open with his body, gun aimed. Two more armed and masked attackers ran to the hall intersection separating her from Medina. They saw her. She stopped. They aimed. The gun in her hand choked on empty.

Survival her first instinct, she broke all the rules.

She sprinted toward them.

They wouldn't know why they missed.

Hand up, she created a shield to deftly deflect the bullets in her path, then ran up the side of the wall, flipped, and took them both out with a cartwheel kick, the heel of each foot connecting hard to their heads. She landed on her feet, low to the floor, one hand touching the carpet for balance, the bodies spread out behind her. When she looked up, Medina had his gun aimed between her eyes.

For a split second, she thought he meant to use it on her, but realized he was tracking the men on the ground.

He studied her, as if for the first time, then nodded to himself. Apparently, she passed his assessment.

He lifted his gun high and fired. She heard the sprinkler ding. Water sprayed everywhere, soaking her before she slipped through the elevator doors.

Medina grabbed her by the shirt and threw her forcibly behind him while he unloaded on the trio from the elevator, hobbling, but bearing down on them, nonetheless. She wanted to protect him or help him, but knew better. She never used her powers publicly. It was against the rules. And though Medina knew she had some skills, he didn't know the full extent.

She pressed against the elevator wall as they safely dropped to the lower levels. She'd broken a lot of family rules today. She bit her lip wondering what kind of trouble she'd be in.

Today had been a near disaster, but she wanted to do more field trips. Sometimes she got a glimpse of the outside world that she would tuck away for herself until she could figure out where she had been. She knew where they were today. She'd seen out one of the hotel windows earlier. The giant Eiffel Tower had been in her history book. It was a small reward no matter what happened when she got home.

She took off her mask when they reached garage level. Medina didn't speak, so neither did she.

At the garage, he wrapped their masks in his white room service jacket, and they walked casually to the awaiting laundry truck—Medina with his usual cocky saunter. He lifted the back sliding door, tossed in the masks, then "helped" her. She landed with a hard thud.

The driver took off. Medina patched them into HQ.

"Did we get the target?" she asked.

"Shut up." Medina pressed a code. "Don't say a word unless asked. You almost got us killed."

"I came back to help you."

"Didn't need your help." He said a few more choice words as they took a hard corner.

General Martin's voice came over the communication speaker. "Status?"

"Field trip complete. All students accounted for."

"Excellent. What was the hold up?"

"A third party showed up. Russians."

"Copy." General Martin asked another question. "Are we compromised?"

Medina looked thoughtfully at her, then the facemasks, before responding. "No, sir."

"Great. Get to base. Your flight is waiting."

"Copy."

The transmission was meant to be over, but Sunnie heard another voice interrupt. "I want to speak with her." There was some static before her uncle's concerned voice came over the line. "Sunday? Are you all right?"

Medina nodded for her to respond. "Yes, Uncle Laurence. It was no big deal."

"No injuries?"

"No, sir."

"Great." He didn't mute the microphone, and she heard his stern tone with General Martin. "That's the last time. This is ridiculous. She could have been killed."

"We can hear you," Medina said.

The communication went dead. Medina turned the Comm off and sat back, ignoring her.

Medina was in his early twenties, not that old. He'd been in the military six years, but his eyes held the wisdom and misery of a much older, long-suffering soul.

He raked a hand through a flop of thick, black hair. Most military had crew cuts, but the ones who did spy missions had to look more like ordinary people. Medina was anything but average, unless you compared him to an ordinary thug with an unnaturally high I.Q. On the job, she'd seen him go from thug to aristocrat in the course of a few minutes. His brown skin could be that of a construction worker or an Arabian prince who spent too much time on his yacht. He was a genius of disguise. Sometimes he wasn't bad to look at, and sometimes he was downright scary. She preferred the former. Unfortunately, with his current scowl, he was scary.

They drove in silence for twenty minutes before she broke. "Why are you always mad at me?"

"Stupid people make me mad."

She sighed and looked down.

"You were supposed to get in the elevator," he said.

"I know." She felt the heat of humiliation on her face.

"Our job was not to make contact."

"I know."

"You put my life and yours at risk."

"Well, that's a little over-exaggeration."

He lifted a heavy brow.

"I knew you'd have my back."

"Really?"

"Well, I hoped, because we're partners and you're supposed to." She smiled engagingly.

He stared back stone-faced. "We're not partners. I'm your handler, got that? I *babysit* you to make sure you don't do anything *stupid* outside the boundaries of our field trip."

Fine. She felt lame and stupid.

"Do you understand?"

"Yes."

"Yes, *sir*."

"Yes, sir!" she mimicked stubbornly.

"Don't do it again."

"Fine." She sulked. "Sir."

He was silent another five minutes before he deigned to speak to her. "Why did you do it?"

She shrugged. It's not like he would understand wanting to help a little girl crying for help. And she couldn't tell anyone about that flashback to her childhood. Her uncle would have her in psychiatry for weeks prying into her brain. Some things she knew to keep to herself. It made her uncle happy that she didn't remember her childhood or previous family.

Feeling sorry for herself, she finally offered, "Just lame and stupid, I guess."

"Got that right."

Her shoulders sunk. It was hard to stay upright when you felt so down.

"I'll have to report it."

And there went the last of her spirits. Her uncle would not like it—at all.

"There's a reason for following orders," he lectured.

"I know!"

"What's the reason?"

"Weak links get people killed. We don't know the full mission, but we have to trust the orders no matter what—even if they don't make sense."

"Right. You broke the trust."

She wanted to deny it. Breaking the trust was the ultimate failure on a team. "But we helped those people."

"You don't know who those people were. They could be enemies you helped to get away. Ever think about that?"

The mother and child could be enemies? If they were, she'd really messed up. She'd let emotion rule her. She went from feeling excited and successful to confused and miserable. Would the General trust her again? "Okay. I get it. Can we stop talking now?"

"You're the one who asked why I was mad."

She didn't say anything. This was her life. Whether it was the military team or the science team, there was a reason for everything.

It's just that lately those reasons didn't seem to make as much sense as they used to.

CHAPTER TWO

Graeme Rochester had never wanted for love or money.

His family enjoyed the luxury of a modern fortress in the former meatpacking district of New York. Real Estate had been cheaper there when his dad started the pharmaceutical company that later became A & R Technologies. Their first labs had been here, and today a newly- designed headquarters stood tall in its place.

His mom had made sure their home reflected the success of his dad's entrepreneurship and her various roles in government—in a way that was more classic than ostentatious. When it came to her four children and their bedroom suites, she allowed a certain amount of design freedom. In his case, that meant computer and mechanical clutter—a sure sign it was time to move out.

Graeme had grown up with privilege, but thanks to his parents, had learned the right way to take advantage of it. It also helped that he was naturally driven to excel when it came to figuring things out.

He adjusted the light exoskeleton against his little brother's arm. Benny and his sister Morgan were legally his foster brother and sister, but other than a different last name, they were loved and treated the same as Graeme and his older brother Rex. They were a tight family. One person's success was everyone's success. One person's loss was also everyone's loss.

These days, the stakes were higher than ever for everyone in his family to figure out a solution that would help his little brother. He prayed his dad came back from Paris with something that would lead to a breakthrough. In the meantime, Graeme continued to test a new material that might eventually be sewn into fabric and replace the current, less flexible exoskeleton attached to his brother with straps and screws.

Benny stood perfectly still—amazingly so for a ten-year-old— likely patience learned from being poked and prodded for years by doctors. The genetic neurodegenerative disorder that affected his strength and mobility had been diagnosed while he was still in the womb, so even before he was born, he'd been poked and prodded.

"One second." Graeme went to the other side of his bedroom suite and dug through a toolbox for a set of scissors. He came back and cut off a flyaway piece of metallic fabric. "How does the new material feel?"

"A little scratchy," Benny said.

Graeme nodded. "It's still in prototype phase, but it will get better."

"I don't mind."

Benny wouldn't. Not so long as it allowed him to move like other kids.

"Do you think we could make a body suit with this and get rid of my Exo?

"Eventually," Graeme promised. He weighed his commitments at the University. He would graduate in a few months, and the last semester was primarily final project work, so he didn't need to be there much. Benny's Exo-S was his main graduation project. He and some friends had already launched their first mobile game, and it was doing well—he ticked off a list in his head. He'd completed all the requirements of technology and entrepreneurship necessary for his degree. He could focus on this new material, but it would take more than his time to solve the next set of problems.

"Like in a month?" Benny encouraged, interrupting his thoughts.

The eagerness in his little brother's voice made him look up. "What's in a month?"

Benny shrugged his skinny shoulders and turned his dark brown eyes to the new Exo-arm attachment. It was thinner and lighter than the previous version and could more easily be hidden beneath clothes, at least in winter. Something tickled the back of Graeme's mind. Benny wore board shorts and a Star Wars t-shirt that said, "Judge me by size, do you?"

It reminded him of an earlier conversation they'd had. He glanced at his brother's serious face, then focused on the task before asking him nonchalantly, "Is that Poem's birthday party?"

Benny squirmed a little as Graeme tightened the back section of the brace. "Yeah."

"Well, this version of the Exo-S is still working fine, isn't it? You have enough strength for regular activities?" His brother's condition had gotten worse in the last year, so Graeme had slowly been adjusting the exoskeleton to make up for the gradual loss with an increase in responsive power. The first exoskeleton had been a bulky, mechanical nightmare, better for soldiers than little kids. He'd spent his college years improving it. Normally, he wouldn't mess with a good thing. His current version was lightweight, flexible, and sensed Benny's movements with ninety-five-percent accuracy. But Benny was growing while his body got weaker. A new solution was needed.

The new material was a revolutionary solution, and it might replace the exoskeleton altogether, living against Benny's skin and stimulating his muscles rather than being his muscles. Only it required testing and programming, and there wasn't a good way to adhere it to skin yet. For now, he was testing it on the inside of a redesigned portion of the skeleton from the shoulder to the hand. When that worked effectively, he might actually have something and could think about the next steps.

"This new material is going to be a work-in-progress for about a year." Maybe longer, but Benny didn't need to know that.

"Oh."

"But you never know."

"You're a genius," Benny said. "It'll be faster."

"Thank you for your confidence." Graeme smiled. "I have friends helping. You have your own team of brainiacs. We will do our best."

"Okay." Benny smiled and flexed his arm, testing it. "Anyway, it's better than wheels."

"Definitely better than wheels." Graeme finished with the settings, and sat back on the stool. "But even in a wheelchair, your charm is irresistible."

Benny patted his shoulder sympathetically. "Some guys are just born with it."

Graeme laughed out loud and ruffled Benny's hair. "You kill me sometimes, kid." Benny was curious, funny, bright, and ever the optimist. But that was the power of a childhood well lived and loved—even in his condition.

Benny believed in Graeme. It was a lot of responsibility. Of all the people he didn't want to let down, Benny was the top of the list. He just hoped that A & R Technologies would find a cure before it was too late. His dad's Paris meeting was with a scientist who'd had success with degenerative muscle disorders. If the serum showed as much promise as expected, a cure might be around the corner. They were hopeful, but until there was a cure, Graeme focused on quality of life.

"So what are you going to get Poem for her birthday?"

"A light saber."

"Cool."

"I know." Benny smiled, imitating the cocky look he'd learned from Graeme and their older brother Rex. He grabbed Graeme's shoulder with mock seriousness. "I need you to make me a real one—but the laser can't cut off limbs. I don't want Poem going to jail for bad form."

"Good call," Graeme said. "Just so happens I might be able to help you."

"Really?" Benny's voice squeaked with excitement.

"Yep."

"How?"

"I've got skills."

"Can you make two?"

"In the next month?"

Benny nodded, sheepishly. "I need one to battle her. I'll let her win," he offered. "At least…on her birthday."

Graeme chuckled. The kid had it bad. "You're a good man, Benny." He took out a piece of paper and began to draft a light saber. "Here's what I'm thinking...."

Benny tucked his little frame inside of Graeme's shoulder, his whole being enthralled. Graeme gave him a one-armed squeeze, his heart tightening a bit, and started to explain the options. As he began to draw, he thought there might be an opportunity to use similar technology to update his team's mobile game with real-world action.

But if nothing else...a great gift for young love.

He hugged Benny protectively. Young love might be all Benny would ever have.

CHAPTER THREE

Georgie Washington was not named after the first President, but rather her great-great-great-grandfather, Henry George Washington. She thanked her mother every day for dubbing her Georgie rather than using her first name—Henrietta.

"First Henry," as he was known in the family, had been part of the Underground Railroad and was instrumental in helping hundreds of African-American families find freedom in the time before and during the Civil War. His wife had been an educated slave whom he met on the railroad one fateful night, and after the war, Henry went to North Carolina to find Miss Mary and bring her home. They raised eight kids, started a school aimed at educating formerly enslaved people, and were advocates for ensuring human rights in America. Their children and grandchildren became lawyers, teachers, Senators—leaders in their communities. At least that was the story passed on to her by her proud father.

No pressure.

The truth was, she was proud of her family. Who wouldn't be? But the likelihood of her ever doing anything as important as fighting slavery, or leading a civil rights movement, was outside the realm of her imagination. Even if she didn't think it was dangerous, her overprotective parents would.

Her long, gold-brown braids fell around her as she put her head down on the steering wheel of her dad's car, waiting for Brittany.

She was taking the day off school to be with Brittany and pick out flowers for her aunt's funeral. Brittany's mom handled most of the arrangements, but Georgie suspected she wanted to give Brit something to do that could help contribute and get her out of the house.

Her friend finally appeared and hopped in the car clothed in something that smelled like wet straw. Georgie got one whiff of the dress and opened the windows.

"It's a new hemp fabric," Brittany said.

"Um-hmm." Georgie didn't want to open her mouth and have the smell become a taste.

"It's all natural and biodegradable, and the buttons are made from reclaimed wood."

Georgie nodded, taking a shallow breath.

"You should be more encouraging about my sustainable fashion designs."

"Maybe you can use it as kindling to start a fire next winter."

Brittany punched her arm lightly. "It was a test," she admitted.

"Sorry. It fits really nice." Georgie stuck her head out the window for air, then turned to give her friend a smile. "The smell is probably getting right into your skin."

She succeeded in making Brittany smile. Truth was, she loved seeing what her inventive friend came up with next in her quest for a sustainable life. And the tawny color of the dress suited Brittany's light mocha skin and long, dark, wild hair.

"Where to?"

"5521 Old River Road."

"That's not in town," Georgie said.

"It's my aunt's house."

"Oh." Georgie didn't know what to say. It would either be sad, creepy, or weird, but she wasn't going to let Brit do it alone.

"Do you need to get something?"

Brittany looked determined. "Something like that."

Okay.

They drove in silence until they were closer to Old River Road. Brittany gave her the directions, and they pulled up in front of a charming one-story white house with a long front porch.

"Do you want me to go in and get it for you?" Georgie asked.

Brittany shook her head, then opened her hand to reveal a small card from a local florist. "My aunt sent my mom flowers last week. They arrived last night."

"Oh." *Sad, creepy, and weird!*

"I think Aunt Nancy knew something, but she couldn't tell my mom. We can't talk when we go into the house. It might be bugged."

"Bugged?"

"Yeah. Like they were spying on my aunt."

"They?"

"Holliwell."

"Oh."

Holliwell was the Area 51 of Virginia. Everyone she knew who went in either didn't come out, or came out with problems. Her cousin Al, included.

"I know it sounds weird, but trust me."

"It's not that weird."

Brittany sat still for a moment. "I took the card off before my mom could see it."

"That's probably a good thing," Georgie said. *Or not. Would her mom want to know?*

"My mom doesn't want to know the truth. My aunt was trying to tell her something, but couldn't. That means her phone, her home, probably everything was under surveillance. Aunt Nance joked about it once, but when I think back...I don't think it was a joke. Holliwell owned her."

"But wasn't she just a nurse or something?"

"It's the 'or something' that I wonder about. She took care of special patients. That could mean anything, right?"

"Yes." Georgie dragged out the word, hesitant to overreact.

"Look. See these numbers." She held out the card. "I think these numbers on the card are either to a safe at her house, or a safety deposit box, or something like that. Right?

"Maybe. Then again, they could be her dress measurements." Georgie looked at the numbers. "If she had a really small waist and unnaturally large hips." She read the message out loud. "To my sister, a flower among flowers?" *Strange.* "That's a little...uh...flowery."

"I know. She had a really sweet side," Brittany said. Her eyes watered as she got out of the car.

Georgie saw the fresh tears and felt bad for thinking the expression odd. She gave Brit's arm a squeeze as they walked across the perfectly manicured lawn.

Brittany entered the side door into the kitchen and went to turn the alarm off. Georgie followed.

"Huh, it's not armed." Brittany stared at the alarm on the wall. "I thought we set this last night. It must not have worked."

The hairs on Georgie's arm shot up. Nancy *had* worked at Camp Holliwell. "What do you mean? Do you remember setting it?" One of the guys at the movie theater where they worked had told her and Brittany stories of Camp Holliwell—how you didn't quit the place, you just disappeared. He'd been a good storyteller. They'd been riveted—in the way you listen to ghost stories—appreciating the freakiness, but not really believing. Only this time, it was real. It was Brittany's aunt.

"Did your mom set it?" Remembering their plan, she typed into her phone and showed Brittany. *Does anything look out of place?*

Brittany looked around, a little nervous as well. The kitchen seemed fine. She went over to the counter where the flour and sugar were kept in jars with an orchid pattern on them. Brittany stared at the counter, then wiped a finger across it. She held up her finger, now covered with a layer of flour. She shook her head indicating something was not right. She looked in the jars and showed Georgie. Both were empty. Panic lit up her eyes.

"We made sweet tea last night before we left." She typed quickly into her phone. *The sugar was nearly full last night.*

Georgie held back her panic, and instead, looked in the trash can to see if anything had been dumped there. Nothing.

She went to the sink. It was wet. Perhaps recently used? She noted the water with her fingers.

Brittany looked more panicked. "Maybe my mom was here this morning," she said out loud. But they both knew that wasn't the case. It was a warning.

Georgie typed into her phone again. *A flower among flowers?* She pointed to the orchid on the jar of flour. Was it a secret message?

Brittany pulled her arm and spoke loudly. "Let's just get the dress my mom wanted for Aunt Nancy and go. Our florist appointment is in fifteen minutes. I don't want to be late."

Georgie's heart beat rapidly. What if someone *was* still here!

She backed out of the kitchen into the living room and moved carefully around the corner with Brittany behind her.

Neither of them saw the man until it was too late.

The morning humidity might have bothered her if she'd been standing still, but at speeds nearing thirty miles an hour, Sunnie didn't notice it. Mondays she did long runs. The schedule would be easy-breezy the rest of the week. Sunlight barely touched the trail as she jumped a four-foot boulder, easily clearing the stone and breathing in the nature around her to create enough transformable power to extend her jump into a short float. It was nothing beyond the usual for the cameras to catch, but just something for herself. The sense of gliding on air was freeing.

The landing slowed her down fractionally, but was worth it, especially after forty-eight hours in the oxygen room. Her uncle was neurotic about her intake of clean oxygen after she'd been exposed to "air pollution" on field trips. It was a small price to pay for the chance to see the world—even if it was just the inside of a building.

Sunnie focused back on the path, picking up speed. Most of her run had been in early morning darkness, but Uncle Laurence had promised something special if she broke her record today. She checked her watch. No problem—except that she was starving. She was always starving. The nurses said it was her teen metabolism.

She grabbed the water left for her at the last five-mile marker and slowed a little to drink before plopping it on the wood fence that guarded the trail. Golden sunlight filtered through the trees. She heard a Jeep on the nearby perimeter road. One glimpse of the vehicle, and she knew it was her uncle. She hurried to the overpass to cut him off, waving as she crossed. Excitement pushed her the last miles. Uncle Laurence rarely came out to her morning run. She sped up to impress him, racing against the Jeep. It slowed to keep pace with her, and the passenger window lowered. A stranger poked his head out and stared, eyes wide.

"Hi!" she called, waving.

The Jeep took off, but the man stuck his head out further to follow her, his hair sticking up in the wind. She waved again. Finally, he waved back, just before the Jeep disappeared around the bend.

Sunnie focused once again on the trail. Later, she would recall for the technicians how her body responded at each point in the run. Accuracy was required for her morning measurements, and she tried to be a good patient, grateful to feel healthy and cancer-free.

Running as much as she did, she instantly recognized the heat of her body burning through her shoes. Shoes didn't last long. She could feel the pebbles in the dirt path. It was time for new ones.

She left the cover of trees and spotted the group at the end of the open field. As usual, her Uncle Laurence stood tall and fit, his hands folded behind his back, a smile on his face beneath the receding hairline. The visitors stood around him, watching her curiously. Sarge, her military training specialist, held a stopwatch that she heard click distinctively as she passed—the click of the finish line.

Sunnie circled them in a small lap, her senses alive after the run. Nature always rejuvenated her, even if she was hungry. She slowed down enough to notice the bottom of her left running shoe flopping open.

Her training assistant Megan, a kinesiologist, handed her another water. Sunnie grabbed it while holding out the opposite arm for Megan. Megan touched the attachment on her smart phone to the inside of Sunnie's wrist and held it a few seconds to note her heart rate, blood pressure, and temperature. All of it was routine. It had been the same every day since age seven. Different people maybe, but all the same tests.

Megan reviewed the measurement then pressed Sync, to add it to Sunnie's file back at the hospital. She hopped on her bike and nudged Sunnie to complete her cool-down laps.

Ignoring Megan's signal, Sunnie jogged to her uncle. He didn't offer a greeting, probably because she was supposed to be obeying Sarge and Megan, so she waited politely at his side for an acknowledgement and introduction, curious about the strangers. One man looked a little younger than her uncle, early forties. She guessed he was a scientist. He lacked the muscle tone of a military man and the tan of a politician. He wore a suit, but the knot of his tie was slightly uneven, as if he didn't wear them often, or preferred the clip-on brand that some of the hospital workers snapped on when they had visitors.

Even without those clues, she would have known. The way he studied her gave him away. She'd seen it in the eyes of other scientists who'd been introduced to her over the years. It was an expression of awe mixed with hunger—as if he wanted to cut her open and see inside. Fortunately, she knew she was safe at Camp Holliwell—everyone loved her, and the density of military experts would scare off anyone. It was a nice place to belong.

She smiled and turned to the other two men. One was clearly military. The uniform identified him as a four-star General. His expression was more guarded, but he smiled. She offered a hand and he took it, his grip warm and strong.

"Miss," he greeted.

The third man offered his hand. It was cold and clammy. She stepped back, a little defensively, not sure what to make of him yet. He wore a nice suit and gave the impression of friendly efficiency...as though he would bulldoze her while smiling. She hadn't met anyone like him before.

"That was some run you just had," he said.

Sunnie didn't know what response was expected. She glanced at her uncle for guidance, but he merely grinned.

"Yes, it was nice, thank you." You could never go wrong with polite agreement. Her first tutor had taught her that.

"Sunday," Sarge said. "You're not done."

She looked hopefully at her uncle for a reprieve, but he shooed her off. "We'll wait."

He usually didn't, but went to Sarge anyway. She lifted her left foot in front of him, jiggling it playfully. He eyed the flip-flop of loose rubber and shook his head.

"I know," she agreed with his look of disgust. "They really should invent a rubber that doesn't wear out so easily."

"They wouldn't change the shoe even if they had better rubber," the clammy-handed man said.

Sunnie turned, interested, and waited for him to explain.

"They want you to buy more shoes."

"*What?*" She went through two pairs a month. "That's just wrong." How much money did a shoe company need? She flapped the shoe in front of him, earning a smile.

"Sun-day." Sarge's deep voice resonated from inside his large torso.

"But it's an injustice to my feet! And the feeties of millions," she said, playfully indignant.

"Sunday!" This time it was a commanding bellow. She turned to Sarge. He was big enough to be intimidating if you didn't know him. His stomach didn't ripple anymore when he shouted, so she guessed his diet was working —but it did nothing for his mood.

Sunnie reluctantly obeyed the command and followed Megan for the cool-down laps. She'd been pushing it with Sarge, but with guests there, she knew she could get away with it. "Okay, but how was my time?"

"Very good," he said.

"A new record?"

"Barely. You could have done better if you weren't jumping so much."

"I like jumping," she returned. "It's super boring otherwise."

She didn't wait for his response. It would just be a lecture on the benefits of keeping fit. Catching up with Megan, she said a quick "hi", while listening to the conversation behind her.

"How far did she run at that pace?" the stranger asked.

"Forty-five even."

"Forty-five minutes?"

"Forty-five miles," Sarge corrected.

Sunnie could tell he wasn't satisfied. He thought she could do better. She could have, but she wasn't going to tell anyone that. She liked her time alone and outside. The rest of the day was in classrooms or the hospital.

"That's phenomenal. What else can she do?"

Her uncle shushed him.

"Can she hear us?"

Sunnie turned her head in time to see her uncle give a slight nod. She sighed. So much for eavesdropping. She turned her attention back to Megan as they circled the loop at the end of the forest trail.

Megan rode her bike one-handed, reading off the day's schedule. "Are you listening to me now?"

Sunnie nodded and Megan continued.

"Zero-seven hundred hours—measurements, then breakfast."

That was now. "Thank you!" Starving didn't begin to describe what went on in her stomach.

Megan smiled and continued to read the updated schedule on her phone. "Zero-seven-thirty to zero-nine-thirty hours, we're doing some tests for our visitors. That's we, meaning you. Nothing too crazy. The pencil test, Ping-Pong balls, auditory sensing, and a physical. Sarge is going to set up something. Probably multiple attackers. He loves that stuff."

Sunnie nodded, wondering who these men were. They rarely did tests with outsiders watching.

"Classes will continue back on schedule at ten with Physics, Mandarin, lunch, Korean, Farsi, and defense strategies with practical training. Don't worry, there's a fifteen-minute break and protein shake before and after defense class. I'm also supposed to ask how your Russian is."

"Still good," Sunnie said.

Megan made a note. "Next week, we start training for a new field trip. You'll be partnered with Medina again. I don't know many details beyond that, except that the schedule is going to get busy.

Sunnie nodded. She'd had periodic field trips since she'd turned nine, but there did seem to be more lately. They were usually very easy and took a day to complete, but sometimes months to prepare. Her uncle wasn't going to like her doing another one so soon. Especially after the last one went a little awry. But it gave her something to look forward to, and helping others made her feel useful for a change.

The rest of her daily schedule was typical—calculus, weapons training, and this month's specialty—gymnastics.

Her days were very structured, but by dinner, the hard work was done. Then she had conversation time with Liz, Pilates or yoga, homework, meditation, and sleep.

Done with the cool-down, she went to her uncle. He came to meet her while Megan biked over to Sarge to give them a moment.

Uncle Laurence put his arm around her shoulders and led her away from the others.

"How are you feeling, Sunnie?"

"Good, as always." Only he never called her Sunnie except when he worried over something. And he hardly *ever* put his arm around her. "What's going on?"

"Nothing. Nothing," he hurried to assure her. "Periodically, our leaders review the program for funding and such, and these gentlemen are here to see our progress and report back. I'm confident they will be very impressed."

"And continue our funding?"

"Without doubt. Just do exactly as we tell you," he said.

She nodded. "Can I stop at Starbucks before my measurements?"

"As long as you don't drink anything until after."

"I never do."

"I know." He removed his arm and gave her a pat on the shoulder. "You're a great kid. I got lucky."

His praise and encouragement always made her feel warm and safe inside. She reciprocated with a smile. "So did I."

Sunnie watched him leave, hoping she did, indeed, impress the visitors.

Failure was not an option.

Without funding, her uncle couldn't provide the medicines needed to keep her alive.

CHAPTER FOUR

Sergei sat at the table in Starbucks with his hands around a coffee cup waiting for his sixty-five-year-old muscles to wake up. He was reluctantly impressed by the small town created exclusively for staff and soldiers at Holliwell. Across the street stood a bookstore and pharmacy, along with a sandwich shop, shoeshine stand, tailor, dry cleaners, a clothing outlet, optometrist, and more. At one end of the street was a small, square, grassy park with a clock tower that chimed the time just loud enough to hear within the two-block radius. At the other end was their hospital, research labs, and who knew what other scientific torture chambers. He would learn about that soon enough.

If this was what it was like to be a prisoner of war in America, life wasn't so bad. He looked to his military guards. "You got a cushy assignment here, eh?"

One of them, an imposing, broad-shouldered giant named Ruben, grunted his agreement.

The other one did most of the talking. "It can be nice when you cooperate. As a guest, there are many privileges—unlike at some of our other facilities."

The threat of being sent to a dismal prison had been made clear to him already. If he chose to assist the scientists here, he could have a very comfortable confinement. But it was still imprisonment.

He winked and smiled at the men, playing along. They could go to hell for all he cared. He wasn't going to help *any* government use science for their twisted goals. But he also knew he had a long stay ahead. He needed to at least seem cooperative.

The door whisked open, and a lanky teenage girl with dark hair and bouncing ponytail breezed into the shop. Sergei watched her, curious.

She lifted a foot to the barista, and her shoe flopped open revealing the white sock underneath.

"Another pair?" the man said.

"I know! Can you believe it?"

He laughed.

"A mango slushie, please, Lou. Put it on my tab."

"Sure thing, Sunnie."

She crossed to the delivery counter and spotted Sergei watching her from the table. Brilliant, unusual blue eyes targeted him, went to the other two men, then back to him. She walked over meeting his gaze with a welcoming grin.

"Hi, I'm Sunnie."

Sergei stared bemused before slowly accepting the hand offered. The guards seemed to think it was okay. He studied her. Even without makeup, the girl had a clean and classic beauty, primarily due to great bone structure and those stunning eyes. He tried to place her ethnicity and couldn't decide. Like all Americans, she was a mutt. He guessed there was some Spaniard and Northern European in her genes.

"I am Sergei." He released her hand with a sharp bow of his head.

She grinned even bigger. On closer inspection, her eyes weren't just blue—they were unique in a seemingly unnatural way. The ring around her irises was not a thin, dark ring, but thick and an even darker blue than the rest of her eyes. They were startlingly bright.

And innocent.

He wondered about her grin. "That's funny?"

"Is every Russian named Sergei?"

"I'm not Russian, I'm Georgian," he said. "We're much more civilized."

She looked immediately contrite. "Oh, I'm sorry. I didn't know. I never met a Georgian."

"Have you ever met a Russian?"

"Yes, my Russian tutor was Russian, so I recognized the similar accent."

"His name was Sergei."

"Yes." She beamed.

"You have lovely eyes," he said in his native tongue.

"Thank you," she responded easily in his language.

The man behind the counter called over, "Mango slushie." He slid the drink across the coffee bar.

"Oh, thanks!"

The girl, Sunnie, turned to get the fruity concoction. That's when Sergei noticed the very thin and faded scar on her arm. He touched his own arm in the same spot. It was recently bandaged and still tender. *Curious.*

She came back over to his table.

"What are you in for?" he asked in Russian, his eyes noting her arm.

She stared back. This time, the innocent eyes blinked—confused. Her Russian was not so good it seemed. He repeated his question in English.

"What are you in for?"

"I understood," she said, still confused. "I live here."

The barista frowned. "Sunnie, you're late. People are waiting on you."

She apologized to him. "I have to leave. It was nice to meet you, sir." To the guards, "Bye guys." As an afterthought, she looked at him. "Maybe I can help you with your English."

"Maybe," he said, amused at the idea.

He waved back as she lifted her hand to him, and watched her trot across the street in her military sweats and white tank top. His first impression had been she was a sweet kid.

But if she lived here, then, for the first time in a while, he must be wrong.

⁂

"I'll handle this today," a woman said, entering the measurements room and dismissing Sunnie's nurse.

Sunnie studied the new person. The woman didn't smile. Maybe she was having first day nerves, because she seemed really grumpy. Sunnie told herself to be patient, reminding herself of Liz's advice. *It's best to think positive about people.*

As she watched the woman, she decided it wasn't her first day. The woman knew her way around the room and what needed to be done. There was something very superior in her attitude as well. She was not the average nurse. She was used to commanding and being in charge. Even the curt way she motioned Sunnie to the scale said she demanded obedience.

Sunnie stepped off the scale and sat on the adjustable patient chair. "Where's Nancy today?"

"Transferred." The woman didn't look up from Sunnie's chart. "Swab."

"What?" Sunnie's chest tightened. It must be a mistake. Nancy had said she would be here forever. She would have told Sunnie if she was transferring. Right?

"Swab." The lady repeated the command, staring at her face.

Sunnie obeyed, putting on gloves, taking the swab from the box, opening her mouth and brushing cells from the inside of her cheek with the swab stick then handing it back.

She took off the gloves and threw them out. Sunnie knew she shouldn't get attached to people, but she did. Nancy had been part of her small family on the base, and always had a warm smile and encouraging words. She was one of the rare people who actually didn't ever want anything from her. Somehow, that had made their friendship special—at least to Sunnie. She couldn't believe Nancy would leave and not tell her. Her throat constricted, and her eyes started to burn. "Where did she transfer to?"

"Don't know. Finger." The new person held out the blood meter to take a prick of blood.

Sunnie wiped her finger with the provided cleanser, then put it in the plastic device nearly doing the test herself. She wouldn't let the heartless woman see her feelings. Not many people on the base talked to her—at least not about normal stuff. Nancy always made her feel normal. This woman made her feel like a freak who needed examining.

She pressed a wand to her temple. "One hundred and one," she noted.

Sunnie nodded. That was normal for her. "What's your name?"

The woman made a notation in the medical chart and didn't look at her when she finally spoke. "You can call me Nancy if it makes you feel better."

Sunnie's spine straightened. Was the woman being deliberately mean? Why would she be mean to her? Did she think Sunnie was stupid, or as Nancy would describe, emotionally unintelligent?

Suddenly, Sunnie was in a situation in which she didn't know how to respond. She was brought up to be polite in all things. She felt a rare surge of anger building but remained silent for the rest of the measurements.

When done, she got up, happy to leave. For some reason, she stopped and turned back. "Why would it make me feel better?"

The woman put the instruments back in place. "What?"

"Why do you think it would make me *feel* better if I called you Nancy?"

The woman didn't say anything. Worse, she studied her. A frisson of energy traveled down Sunnie's arms, and she took a breath. The woman continued to stare at her in silence as if waiting for some reaction to write down in the chart with the other measurements. That's when Sunnie realized she wasn't a nurse. She was a scientist. There was no doubting the devouring look in her eyes.

"Is your name Nancy?"

The woman didn't respond.

Sunnie waited. Silence. *What a mental case.* "Do you have trouble understanding English?"

Finally, the woman's lips lifted, as if a smile, only it didn't reach any other part of her face. Turning in her chair, she opened the drawer of the desk and put on the nametag she found inside. It said *Nancy*. She smiled again.

Sunnie didn't speak. That was Nancy's nametag. The woman baited her. But why? Sunnie felt the burn of anger in her chest build, but forced her face into something she hoped was expressionless. If the woman didn't want Sunnie to know her name, that was fine.

"I don't know what you're doing here, but I do know you're not a nurse or a technician."

She saw the blink of surprise. The woman really did think Sunnie was an idiot!

"And you'll never be a Nancy," Sunnie added. "She was kind, and she had class." Sunnie grabbed her smoothie and headed to breakfast. Her uncle would tell her where Nancy went. Maybe he could also get rid of this woman. Or Sunnie would be punished for being disrespectful. That was always a possibility. She straightened her back, determined not to care. Nancy had left without saying goodbye. She wouldn't care about that, either.

But it still hurt.

The last thing Georgie and Brittany expected that morning was an intruder. Either it was a coincidence, or Brittany's theory that her aunt had been murdered might have some credence. Either way, they weren't going to find out from the man charging them.

Georgie caught sight of someone in a blue maintenance uniform coming at her before being knocked backward into Brittany. They hit hard against a cabinet before tumbling over each other.

Georgie heard the screeching of a cat freaking out but was focused on the man, furious that someone would break in and attack them.

"Hey!" Georgie yelled instinctively and scrambled to her knees as he wrestled with the front door. She reached for a heavy, glass cat sculpture that fell when they hit the cabinet and hurled it at the man just as he got the door open. He yelped as it hit his leg.

She got to her feet, then rethought her strategy when the man reached for the thick sculpture. Brittany screamed in pain and panic behind her. For a split second, Georgie thought there might be another attacker.

There was.

Only it was a black cat on Brittany's back, clawing frantically at her hair and getting caught in her hemp dress. Georgie grabbed a decorative chair and knocked the man's arm as he launched the cat sculpture toward Brittany. The object hit the same cabinet sending more plates, glass, and china on top of Brittany and the cat, making their struggles even more frantic.

The man ran across the lawn to a car. Georgie chased hoping to get a license, but it took off as soon as he got into the passenger side. Realizing she probably hadn't made the safest choice, she ran back to the house to help Brittany.

Georgie's arm bled from the scratches, but it was nothing compared to Brittany's back.

Nancy's cat Whiskers had come out of nowhere and attacked in panic. Every effort Whiskers made to get free triggered a cry or curse from Brittany.

Georgie yelled for Brittany to be still so she could get the wild cat detangled. Finally free, the cat took off to another part of the house. Dress ruined, Brittany sat in pain and shock for a quiet moment before they stared at each other in relief.

"Oh my gosh. I thought I was being attacked by a Taser gun or something!" Brittany's eyes watered while she smiled. "Are there any more flying cats I need to watch out for?"

Georgie laughed, amazed her friend could find humor after being attacked by a man, a cat, and an assortment of home accessories. She helped Brittany up. "I think we should put something on your back. It's a mess."

Brittany found her phone and dialed 911. After a few rings and some information, she hung up. "On their way. There's a first aid kit in the master bathroom. I can change into some of my aunt's sweats." Brittany went and looked through her aunt's clothes, pulling out some options.

Georgie checked out the bathroom. It was well stocked with nursing supplies. She pulled out some disinfectant wipes and Neosporin, attending to her arm while she waited for Brittany. The bathroom was nice and had a full, built-in bathtub. There was a little decorative vase at the foot of the tub filled partially with blue marbles and a bouquet of faux flowers. Georgie stared a moment at them. There were white orchids surrounded by a mix of smaller purple and lavender accent flowers.

"Brittany," Georgie called to her friend. "What kind of flowers did your aunt send your mom?"

Brittany came into the bathroom. "Orchids."

"White orchids?"

"Yes," Brittany said.

"With little purple accents?"

"Yes." Brittany's eyes widened as it clicked.

Georgie went to the little vase, grasped the plastic stems, and pulled them from the marbles. At the bottom of one of the orchids was something wrapped in duct tape. Brittany pulled the tape off, and the two of them stared silently at the mini flash drive.

The silence of the morning became deafening in Georgie's ears. Eventually they heard the sirens. "The police are here."

Brittany clutched the flash drive.

"But," she nodded toward Brittany's hand. "I wouldn't mention that just yet."

CHAPTER FIVE

Sunnie sat across the table from her guests—the badly-dressed scientist, the Armani-clad businessman, and the crisply-cut General.

She felt calmer after food, her regular energy restored.

"Ready?" her uncle asked.

"Yes."

"It looks like you already have hold of the pencil." Uncle Laurence inclined his head to the center of the table where the pencil jittered.

It stopped moving instantly and froze—above the table.

The men stared, and Sunnie held out her hand to catch it, controlling the speed as it flew closer to her palm. She stopped it an inch from her hand, then clasped it. To prove it was an ordinary pencil, she wrote a message on the paper in front of her. She put the pencil on the paper and slid both objects over to the men using her harnessed energy. Three pairs of eyes widened. The men sat up in their chairs.

The scientist reached for the paper. "Paper test complete." Delighted, he looked at her, then the others. "Fantastic."

The businessman looked pleased as well. Only the General remained unsatisfied. His brows furrowed, more concerned than pleased or unhappy.

Her uncle explained what they were looking at. "Sunday has been able to control objects through her transmission and control of energy in her surroundings. One object is easy. More is a challenge."

Megan brought a basket of Ping-Pong balls over to the guests.

Her uncle instructed them. "Go ahead and check them out yourself. No strings."

The businessman took a handful, and watching her, threw them across the table.

Sunnie reacted quickly and relaxed her body. Multiple objects required her to be calm and pay attention to instinct more than direction. She let the energy from her body transform and held the Ping-Pong balls in place, casually calling dozens more from the basket. As the men watched, she began to spin them as a group clockwise, then counterclockwise.

"Simply fantastic," the scientist said again, a broad grin stretching his gaunt jaw. "What else?"

She moved the spheres into the form of a simple flower. Then a happy face.

"Can you do words or letters?" the General asked.

"No," her uncle explained. "What we think happens is that words engage the left side of her brain, and this talent seems to be controlled by the right.

Sunnie didn't contradict her uncle. He was correct, but she'd been working on that skill in her daily meditation sessions. Now was not the time to unveil it. She had a few surprises she was saving for his birthday.

The businessman reached out and took a Ping-Pong ball that formed an eye from the happy face. Static electricity caused his hair to float up. His arm reached back, and he tossed the plastic prop back at the floating image. Sunnie stopped the acceleration and arranged the white ball back in place.

"Brilliant," the General said. "But what is the purpose?"

The question surprised Sunnie. No one had ever asked for a purpose. Her talent just was—an unusual case of cancer mixed with large doses of the new chemotherapy her uncle had designed. This was simply a unique side effect.

"You can put them away, Sunday."

Sunnie sent the Ping-Pong balls back to the bucket with a graceful swirl in the air. Her uncle didn't look pleased. She sat and waited for instruction.

"There are many uses for this talent, sir. The amount only limited by the imagination."

He stood up to guide them to the next location. "Megan, bring Sunday down to the field. We'll watch from the viewing deck."

Sunnie followed Megan. Once outside, she asked, "Did I do okay? Uncle Laurence looks tense. Are we in trouble? What happens if they don't let us stay?"

Megan patted her shoulder. "Don't worry. You did great."

"What if they don't like me?" It was on her mind after the incident with the new Nancy. Life could be harder if people didn't like you.

"They don't need to like you," Megan assured. "They just need to want to make more people like you."

"What do you mean more people like me?"

Megan looked like she regretted her words.

"Are they trying to heal more people?" Sunnie thought about the opposite. "They wouldn't deliberately give anyone cancer, would they?"

"You can't give people cancer."

"Yes, you can. You can radiate them, and do lots of other things."

"Well, we're not doing that. I just meant if they see that some good can come from the research, they'll continue to fund the research."

"What would they do with more people like me?"

"Nothing! Sunnie, I didn't mean that the way it sounded. Forget what I said. You're one-of-a-kind. Trust me."

"Okay."

"Ready for the vision test?"

"Yes."

"They're up on the deck. Tell us what each has written on their pads.

The distance was about one hundred meters. Vision was not her strength. Sunnie spoke into Megan's phone to communicate the message each man had written in small type on their pads. "'E=mc squared.' 'What's the return on investment?' and—Sunnie smiled at the General's message— 'I come in peace.'" She warmed up to him. "Thank you, sir, so do I."

Megan took the phone and disconnected. "Good job. Now, listen to their conversation and tell me what they're talking about. I'll text it back to them."

Sunnie didn't waste time, but repeated everything she heard without identifying the speakers and changing her voice to mimic each man. "What should we talk about? Anything. That Megan woman is attractive. She's taken. Too young for you. Is Sunday her real name?"

"Okay, okay!" Megan typed as quickly as possible.

The conversation continued, and Sunnie kept repeating it. "Where does she come from? Does this space amplify sound? What happened to her parents? Her family passed away in a tragic accident. I think that's enough."

The last lines were from her uncle. He stopped the conversation. "We can go over all that later in the history debrief."

The phone rang and Megan got her next directions. She turned and started walking, explaining as she went. "We're supposed to go to the end of the field and wait for another racer."

Sunnie hurried to catch up. "Another racer? To run *against* me?" They wouldn't have a chance of winning. No one at the camp had ever beaten her. "Why?"

"Perhaps as a comparable," Megan explained. "The average speed of a healthy man versus you. That way they can appreciate how fast you are."

"Oh." Strange. "Can't they just use a stop watch?"

Megan sighed. "Yes, but they want to do this for some reason. I don't know why. Just relax. They'll be here in a minute."

Sunnie nodded silently. She didn't mean to annoy Megan. She just wanted to know what was going on. She'd run with other residents before, but not in many years. Did this other racer know he or she was being set up to lose?

Seth lay on the military bed staring at the ceiling. Prison couldn't be much worse than a military research facility, but he'd opt for prison now. At least there he'd know his exit date. Since arriving at Camp Holliwell, nothing had been as he expected. He corrected himself—Camp Holy Hell.

He traced the smooth skin of his freshly-bald head. He'd had nice, thick, blond hair that girls loved. He wondered if it would ever grow back…and if he would ever get out.

The only thing he did know for sure, whatever they had given him, it hadn't been a new growth hormone. He turned his head to the three empty beds in the room. And apparently, only one in four survived this kind of medical research.

He looked back at the ceiling then closed his eyes, dropping a weary hand over them. He'd had nothing to lose. Neither had Molly, Ryan, and MacKenzie. That's why they'd all agreed to sign on. *Nothing to lose, except cash in the bank.*

The empty beds told a different story.

They were kids from different cities with no family to miss them, no teachers to track them, no history recorded. The recruiters had done their homework—four runaways with nothing to lose but their lives.

"Three down, one to go," he said to no one. Outrage and determination lit a fire in his stomach. He wasn't going without a fight. As long as he was alive, he'd find a way out of this place.

The sound of automatic doors opening got his attention. Soft-soled shoes stepped methodically across the concrete floor. Footsteps stopped while the second, inner door opened. They'd really done their job securing him.

His nurse Betsy called to him. "Seth?"

He lay still, ignoring the call.

"Seth? You're up for testing."

One of his new military handlers walked past and stood at the foot of the bed.

Seth didn't move. Testing. Right. *Screw you.* What did they think he'd already survived? A medical trial?

His military handler added, "Dr. Wicker said if you're successful, we can consider it a sign of your good health and move up your release date."

His heart leapt, betraying him. He still had the ability to hope. Hell. What a sap he'd become. They weren't going to release him. Not soon, not ever. *But what if?*

He gave into the temptation. "How soon?"

"As early as next week."

Much better than indefinitely. He sat up and stared at the military handler. "What do I have to do?"

The man smiled. "Nothing much. A race. If you win, you're out by next week."

Seth stood. Next week? What a lie. *But what if?* He could leave this part of his life behind and disappear.

He pulled on his old beanie and winked at Nurse Betsy before nodding to the handler. "Lead the way."

They took him to a part of the base he hadn't seen yet.

Seth hopped out of the Jeep, curious. He'd not known there were more buildings and an Olympic-sized racing track. Another runner waited on the field stretching casually, dark hair tied into a ponytail. In the sunshine, he almost thought it had a bluish tint, but then it looked normal again. He glanced at Dr. Wicker to confirm she was the opponent. Wicker nodded.

A girl—outstanding—should be a quick race.

As if reading his thoughts, the dark-haired girl spotted him and came over, staring at him with interest. It made him feel like the freak he'd recently become.

Just as suddenly, she reached out a hand in cheerful welcome. "Hi. I'm Sunnie."

Seth stared at the hand, her smile, then back at her hand, before carefully accepting it. Her hands were noticeably warm. Her nails had a blue tint. At first he'd thought it was nail polish. But she didn't seem to have a hint of makeup or the usual girl enhancements. Her nails just looked cold, but her hands were warm. Strange. He studied her hair again. It *did* seem to have a blue hue in the sunlight.

Then there was the obvious. She was cute. Not just cute—hot. The blue eyes were freaky vivid but filled with wide-eyed, genuine welcome. If they'd been on the outside, he would guess they still raised girls in convents or something. The poor kid looked completely innocent.

Except, she specifically ignored Wicker. He thought he might have even caught a glance of dislike? Hmm. So she wasn't stupid.

Her skin was a very light olive shade. Soft-looking. Classy.

Dang. Why did he have to race her?

He looked down at his running shoes, suddenly self-conscious of his own less-than-stellar appearance.

"What's your name?"

He hadn't offered one. He'd been told not to talk. Best to step away now. Fortunately, his handler and another woman saved him.

"Sunnie," the woman said. "Line up."

The girl's eyebrows drew together in frustration or perhaps impatience, but she obeyed silently and they took their places on the track with Sunnie on the inside lane. Dr. Wicker and his handler stood by quietly—Wicker with a calculating smile on her face, a beast ready to devour her prey. It gave him the creeps. He suspected he was meant to crush Sunnie. Fine. For all he knew, she was one of them, the friendly smile yet another act.

He dug his right foot into the dirt, pressing back, ready to leave her in the dust. For the first time in his life, he wanted something. He wanted out. If winning this race was the answer, he'd do whatever necessary.

Sunnie's handler held a stopwatch. "Two laps, one-half mile total. Fastest time wins." "On your mark, get set...go!"

It was like he was in grade school again—only he ran much faster.

So did she.

To Seth's surprise, Sunnie was ahead, but not by much. He kept pace, pushing hard, feeling self-satisfied when she turned her head slightly after the first lap to see him on her tail. He smiled for the first time that day—she was a freak, too.

Apparently, the hair did grow back.

He focused on moving his legs faster, edging closer to her around the turn. He had no intention of losing, and with their talent mostly even, strategy and street smarts gave him the edge. Shoulder to shoulder they sped across the dirt, each pushing the other for top speed.

He timed his step and stretched his foot to the right—in front of her.

Her leg got caught behind his. He heard her surprised cry and felt a twinge of guilt, before his shoulder knocked her the little extra needed to send her flying at top speed across the infield grass.

CHAPTER SIX

Sunnie hit the ground with force, her shoulder jarring, her arm burning, and her hip banging against the packed surface. She slid and tumbled and slid again. For a moment, her brain rattled with confusion. She absorbed the pain while rolling back to her feet, brushing dirt and debris from her scratched arm. The entire right side of her body stung. In natural self-defense, energy transferred to the injured spots, easing the pain and speeding up her recovery. Regardless of her self-healing abilities, this was gonna hurt. It would be a couple of days before she was normal again.

She watched her competition cross the finish line, and Megan called "time" before looking over at her and giving a sigh of disappointment.

Surprise and fury hit at once. This was turning out to be a morning of outrages.

She walked to Sarge, barely holding her temper, catching a look from the other runner while fake-Nancy patted him on the shoulder. *No wonder.* Bad eggs stuck together.

"He cheated!"

Sarge continued to write in his digital notebook. "Uh-huh." He twirled the stylus between his fingers before sliding it into its holder, eyeing her. "But he won."

"But he cheated!"

Sarge shrugged.

"I didn't know you were allowed to cheat and push and knock people over. What about the rules?"

"It wouldn't be cheating if it were in the rules," Sarge said.

Point taken.

"There's always adversity," Sarge explained. "You need to learn how to handle it. I guess it's time we started to allow that."

Confusion hit. "Why?"

"There're no rules in war, Sunnie. Life is war. You go for it, or you don't."

"I see." *Life is war.* She thought on this ill-timed lesson and brushed a few more pebbles from her arm hoping for some sympathy.

He looked her over. "Luckily you heal fast."

Wow. Really? No sympathy? Was this a lesson in growing up today?

Finding no justice in her corner, she spun on her heel and approached the cheater, ignoring fake-Nancy and the annoying smirk on her face.

She held out her hand to the guy. He was about her age. When she'd first seen him, she'd been excited to meet someone her age. She'd even thought he was kind of cute. What a jerk. She smiled. "Congratulations on your win."

Reasonably cautious, he studied her, as if not sure what to make of her. Obviously, he'd never been taught sportsmanship.

He accepted her hand.

She shook it and held. "I'd like a re-match."

He tried to pull his hand free. She held tighter. He was strong. Unnaturally so. Their eyes met, and one side of his mouth lifted in a half-grin.

"You're strong…for a girl." He tightened his grip.

It was almost painful. Sunnie smiled brighter and squeezed tighter. "A re-match?"

He tried to out-grip her, but she could equal him in strength.

"Sure," he said. "Hope you like dust."

Sunnie grinned with relish—then zapped him.

He jumped back, his hand freed from her. "Ouch!" He shook it in the air. "You're hot!" He blushed. "You burned my hand." He looked at his palm, his face still pink.

"If you can't stand the heat, get out of the sun." She walked past him to the starting line.

"Freak." He followed, taking the spot next to her.

"Cheater."

"Just smarter."

Sunnie didn't continue the conversation. She was never angry! She hadn't even known what angry felt like—until now. Now…she was going to smear his body across the track with no remorse.

"Megan! Give us a start," Sunnie shouted to the woman while Sarge and fake-Nancy looked on curious, amused, and a little uncertain. If the government guys were still watching, she'd show them what happened to cheaters.

"How'd you get your mutant powers?" he asked.

She ignored him. Distraction was the child's play of warfare. Her martial arts training had taught her that. She'd just never brought it to the sports field.

Megan called out. "On your mark. Get set."

"Are you an orphan too?"

He succeeded in distracting her. A mere hint of sympathy in his voice connected with an emotion that tightened around her heart momentarily, stifling the energy in her body and stealing her focus. She turned her head to look at him, wondering what happened to his family.

"Go!"

He took off. Sunnie bolted a half second after him. He'd done it again!

But not for long.

Sunnie felt a rush of adrenaline spur her forward. She kept her distance from him, side by side, but an arms-length apart. At the second turn, she surged and got ahead on the inside track. She could feel him just to her left, but on her heel.

A perfect target.

And from this angle, no one would notice.

Seth didn't know what hit him. One second he was running. The next moment he stopped dead. No, not stopped dead. He hit a wall and bounced backward like a cartoon character until he landed spread-eagle on his back.

Temporarily stunned, Seth opened his eyes to the sky, waiting for his brain to stop knocking against his skull. Had he been unconscious for a moment? He coughed, dust from the track floating around him. The little brat. She learned fast. He grinned, slowly pulling his body up and resting his arms on his knees. He watched Sunnie slow to a trot around the track and cross the finish line with a less-than-restrained hop of triumph. Dr. Wicker and Megan ran up to him.

"Are you okay? What did she do?"

The wicked professor actually sounded worried. *And pissed.* She didn't like losing, either. Only, Seth actually felt bad about cheating the first time. Wicker didn't.

"I'm fine."

Sunnie and the guy named Sarge joined them.

"You two have enough yet?" Sarge asked.

The blue-eyed hellion smiled at Seth, knowingly. "I missed you on the second lap. Did you trip?"

"Yeah. I guess so."

Wicker didn't believe it. "What did you do?" she accused Sunnie.

The others turned and stared at her, waiting for some revelation. Seth thought the Megan chick looked ready to frantically write up a report on a new mutant power. Interesting. Perhaps Sunnie had secrets, too. Was she trapped here as well?

"Nothing," Sunnie said.

"That's not what it looked like."

"I was in front, so I didn't see what it looked like—*Nancy.*"

Wicker's curious expression became enraged. Seth didn't know her name was Nancy, but the second he saw the effect of her words on Wicker was the second Seth knew he was on Sunnie's side.

The girl stood quiet, but strong, against the increasingly livid Wicker.

Eventually, Wicker decided she wasn't going to get an answer. "Right. I'll find out when I dissect you."

Sunnie gasped, her skin losing color. Megan and Sarge gasped as well, both turning to Sunnie for signs of reaction. Seth didn't think that made them particularly nice people no matter what their relationship was. Didn't people have any common sense? Shouldn't they be standing up for their patient?

Sunnie trembled slightly and her blue eyes went bright as if with tears, but she didn't cry. He gave her credit for maintaining. If Wicker had said that to him, hell, he'd take her neck and crush it. It would be self-defense since dissection was exactly what Wicker wanted to do to them—after she finished all her experiments, of course.

He guessed between himself and Sunnie they could easily take on the three adults—it was the military force around the camp that was the problem.

"I'll tell you what she did," Seth said. He drew the attention on himself and caught Sunnie's worried expression.

Wicker waited, expectant.

"She stepped on my shoelace."

The others perked up with surprise, looking down at his shoe. The right shoelace had come loose and hung in the dirt.

"I don't know if it was deliberate or not, but that's what happened."

Sunnie grinned widely at him, obviously relieved. Damn, she really was hot.

"It was deliberate. Sorry." She offered her hand, and he gave it a wary glance before accepting. When she didn't burn the skin off but gave him a pull to his feet, he knew they'd be friends.

"Apology accepted. Sorry I made you nosedive like a sick bird."

She nodded. "It's okay. Apparently, I'm supposed to toughen up."

He laughed. She might be strong, but tough was the last thing she had going for her. They walked to the vehicles ahead of the others. He hurried forward so they could talk alone.

"Where do they keep you locked up?"

She frowned before answering. "I live in the penthouse at the edge of Main Street, with my uncle." She pointed to the group of men who'd been observing them the whole time.

"Your uncle?" Oh, hell. Was she one of them? Or was her uncle running tests on her? This place got freakier every day. "Where's Main Street?" Wonder what that was like.

She pointed to some buildings through the trees. "Maybe you can meet me at Starbucks in the morning."

"There's a Starbucks?"

"Uh-huh. Have you been there before? That's where Main Street is."

"I've been to a Starbucks before. It's a chain. They're all around the world. I've been to at least a couple dozen."

"Oh." She stared at him in awe. "I didn't know that. You've been to twenty-four?"

"At least," he bragged. Maybe she was a clone or a test tube baby who'd never left the confines of Holliwell.

"I have about fifteen minutes before morning measurements. They have slushies and coffee," she said.

He stared at her, not sure if she was for real or just completely brainwashed. Measurements? Is that what they called it on the civilized side of the camp?

"Right. Well, I'm in cellblock 24C of the Medical Detention Ward. Very military, very cold, very not fun. Definitely, no Starbucks."

She frowned. "I don't know that area. I mean, most of my classes are around the condo, and I'm in the hospital a lot for my daily check-ins. Are you in the military?"

"I'm a lab rat. I volunteered, and now they won't let me out. When were you last out?"

She stared at him a long time. "I have a lot of homework."

Seth got a sick feeling in his stomach. "Does that mean you don't get out much?" Her brows furrowed. "I'm allergic to a lot of stuff."

"You've never left here, have you?"

She didn't answer.

"I'll take that as a yes." He looked toward the Jeep he rode in on. His two guards, armed with more than just tranquilizers, approached to escort him back.

"They're supposed to let me out in a week. If I don't see you, good luck, Sunshine."

"It's Sunnie."

He eyed the guards on his right, and Wicker approaching from the left. He shook his head at her, disagreeing. "Not where I'm standing."

They drove away, but he kept his eyes on her as long as possible. She remained still and thoughtful, until her handlers ushered her into another Jeep. *And not where you're standing either, Sunnie.*

Seth finally looked away. He had enough to do taking care of himself.

CHAPTER SEVEN

Georgie and Brittany loaded the USB drive onto Georgie's laptop, but whatever was on the drive was either damaged or encrypted.

Georgie voted encrypted. "We need an expert," she said.

"Right. Where are we going to find an expert?"

"I was thinking Lena."

Brittany stared at her blankly.

"You know her, she's president of the Charlottesville chapter of Girls Who Code."

Brittany shook her head, expression blank.

"She's in our class! White-blonde hair. Super pale."

"Milk?" The description finally clicked. "The albino?"

"She not an albino," Georgie said. "Her family is Swedish or Norwegian or something."

"She looks like an albino."

"Have you ever *seen* an albino?"

"Yeah." Brittany nodded at the obvious. "Her."

"Well, regardless...." Georgie wasn't sure what to say about her color—or lack of it. "Regardless, she is super smart and she could tell us if this is corrupted or encrypted, or what."

"I don't know if I can trust someone that...transparent." Brittany hedged. "You think she can keep a secret?"

"I don't know, but she got early admission into the Computer Science program at M.I.T., so I think we could get her gut reaction about what this is, then find an expert."

"All right. Where do we find her?"

"Leave it to me." Georgie was already on it. "I can track anyone down."

For the first time, General Brody didn't feel comfortable in the Oval Office. It had been a long day at Holliwell, followed by arguments with scientists, bean counters, and military leaders—all over the direction of Project Sunday. Most of it made him ill. They were using children to fight their wars.

His Commander-in-Chief sat on the sofa across from him with the President's long-time friend, the current Secretary of Information Management—Jerry Ramstein. The scientist and economist who'd gone to Holliwell with him sat on his right. They were giving the debrief on Project Sunday. Brody listened with growing concern, realizing he had reached the highest level in his field, and it was all for nothing.

"You're quiet, Ray. What's your take on the whole thing?" The President interrupted his thoughts, his expression interested but with an air of objectivity that struck him as false. Ray was certain the President's mind had been made up for him before he entered the room. They wanted to keep the status quo and expand to a new facility in Colorado to continue the "testing."

Brody sat forward, elbows on knees. "There's no doubt the work being done at Holliwell is…remarkable. As are the girl's abilities. But whether or not she would make a useful military asset?" He lifted his hands skeptically and leaned back in his chair. "Much would depend on temperament, character, and personality. How does she handle stress? Can she adapt quickly?" He shook his head. "All that is unknown."

Ramstein was more bullish. "She's been doing ad hoc assignments since she was nine. Granted, mostly simple things, but she always kept her cool. She's shown a knack for figuring her way out of sticky situations. And she passed Ranger Training, so she's certainly levelheaded and competent," Ramstein said. "Not many men get through that, especially not at fourteen."

Brody nodded, "You're absolutely right, Mr. Secretary. And it's a good sign that she's pretty tough physically and has a certain amount of training behind her. My concern," he paused and looked at the men, neither of whom truly wanted his opinion. "My concern is she's sort of a sweet, happy-go-lucky kid who wants to please. Could we turn her into a fighting machine? Would we want to? Is there a need for her type of skills that we can't achieve with other people or technology? According to the report on her last field trip, when things went wrong, she didn't shoot to kill."

"She wasn't given permission to," Ramstein argued.

"True." Brody acknowledged Cashus had achieved a level of psychological control. "It all depends on your goals, Mr. President, and balancing that with any risks."

"What do you think are the risks?" the President asked.

Brody felt the two men on his right give him a hard look. They wanted him to support their evaluations. According to them, Sunday Cashus could be trained to perform a number of sensitive jobs, number one on the list being to infiltrate Sergei Baratashvili's lab, acquire his formulas for the miraculous cures he'd been credited with, and destroy the facility so no one else could get access to the medical intellectual property. Nations were fighting for IP, and this administration wanted to own nanotech, especially the kind that made soldiers and leaders stronger and smarter.

The scientists were also interested in the kid as an asset, but mostly for study, inspection, and dissection. It made his hardened skin crawl with disgust and self-loathing—he was part of this now.

The CIA had taken a girl captive to use as a test subject, and even if they weren't actively experimenting on her, they were still denying her freedom, normalcy, and the opportunity to know her family. What did that say for what was left of life, liberty and the pursuit of happiness?

He needed to be careful. The President had chosen to continue this program after he'd found out about it. There was also the new facility. State-of-the-art and designed for test subjects—specifically, not to let them out.

"I don't know enough yet to tell you the risks, sir. Our visit was very brief."

The President nodded, and the room went silent while he appeared to wage an internal debate. Finally, he nodded, coming to his conclusion.

"She's well cared for. And in the end, I have to weigh the thousands of lives such an asset might save—both in civilians, and our men and women in the military who risk their lives regularly. I'd like to proceed with the program and step up her military training." He looked Brody in the eye. "For evaluation only. As you say, there are a lot of unknowns. Don't want to send in an agent and find out she's more concerned about her shoes than the mission."

The men in the room chuckled appropriately.

"You can tell Cashus we'll release her from military duties when we have better data on whether or not she is best used as a military or scientific asset."

The group nodded agreement.

"Brody," the President said. "I want you on point. I need a leader in Colorado."

He knew this was coming. The moment when he'd have to decide between his career and crossing a line. This was a big line.

"I'm honored, Mr. President."

"Good."

"But—."

All eyes turned on him. He had a warrior's instinct that more things turned on him in that moment than just eyes.

"This is an assignment that needs time and attention. The truth is, I'm putting in for my retirement, sir. I'd hate to start this and not be able to follow through. It requires a consistent hand."

"Retirement? Damn it, Ray. You're too young to retire."

Brody agreed. "Tell that to the wife."

The room relaxed. Some tension dissolved.

"I'll send you some recommendations, sir."

The President nodded. "I can't tempt you?"

"I'd be insulted if you didn't try, sir." Brody was almost free. "But it's time for me to put my family first. The two youngest are nearly off to college."

"I understand, Ray. And I respect you for it."

Coward. He should fight them. Instead he was running away.

But a smart soldier knew when to retreat.

⸝ ⟍ ⸖

"Liz, I'm telling you, she's evil. I never met anyone who was evil, but I'm pretty sure *that's* what it is." Sunnie cuddled on the comfy purple sofa, letting the cushions envelope her. As usual, classical music played lightly in the background. The sound of a cello usually comforted her. Tonight it made her restless. Like there was something she didn't know or couldn't remember, and it was just on the edge of her consciousness.

"Dr. Wicker just wanted to get to know you better," Liz said.

Liz was a good neighbor, and in some ways, a visual complement to her uncle. She was a tall woman in her early fifties and always played the sounding board to Sunnie's thoughts, sometimes offering wise and motherly advice. Liz was also the only one who was always on her side, didn't take measurements, and didn't tell her what to do. Cocoa and conversation with Liz were a daily ritual during the week before tackling her homework.

Sunnie tilted her head and frowned. "That's her name? *Wicked?*"

"No, Wicker."

"That's what I said. Wicked." Sunnie almost grinned.

"Wicked, I mean Wicker!" Liz corrected again.

Sunnie laughed. Liz joined in.

"Well, you're obviously not a fan," Liz said.

"She put on Nancy's nametag! Is her first name Nancy?"

"No."

"What is it?"

"Dominique."

"Dominator, you mean. Wicked Dominator."

Liz shook her head. "I'm sure she's not that bad."

"She said she would dissect me."

Liz froze. "*What?*"

"Right in front of Sarge and Megan. I thought I was going to be sick. Maybe the cancer's back and my uncle didn't tell me and it's terminal, and she knows when I'm going to die and is here to *dissect* me." Thoughts that had run through her head all day came spilling out.

Liz observed her, thoughtful. "Is that what you think?"

Sunnie shrugged. "Hard not to have it on my mind. Why would someone say something like that otherwise?"

They stared at each other before speaking in unison. "She's evil."

Sunnie sighed with relief. She felt better knowing someone was on her side.

"You're not going to die. If you have any concerns, you should talk to your uncle. You feel well, don't you?"

"Yes, never better."

"Great. Just keep taking your medications."

She sighed. "I am."

"What about this Seth guy?"

Sunnie sat up. He'd been interesting. He'd lived on the outside. She thought he could tell her a ton about regular life. Not that she felt like she had missed anything, but she didn't really know what she missed. She held out her arm and displayed the red and purple bruises.

"He pushed me at forty-two miles an hour. I *slid* halfway across the infield!" Sunnie waited for a sympathetic cringe. Liz didn't disappoint.

"Did it hurt?"

Did it hurt? Sunnie stared at her neighbor. "Would you want to hit the hard ground at forty-two miles an hour?"

"No."

"Yeah," Sunnie said. "It hurt. Really bad. I thought my hip broke, it hurt so much. But they x-rayed me and nothing seems damaged. Just sore muscles and bruises. I was able to protect my face. Obviously, I have strong bones."

"Hurt pride?"

Sunnie thought. "I guess. But losing against a cheater doesn't mean much. And I beat him the next race."

Liz looked down at her tea and bounced her teabag up and down. "I heard you stepped on his shoelace and tripped him? Is that true?"

Sunnie watched Liz methodically wrap the teabag and put it on a tray next to her chair. Seth had lied for her today. Who knew what Dr. Wicker would do if she found out. Sunnie's instincts told her to be discreet. Everyone on camp knew everything. Liz might be her friend, but she worked with the rest of the scientists during the day.

She frowned. No, not discreet. Her instincts said to be cautious. Why was that? And if she couldn't trust Liz, who could she trust?

Liz continued to fuss with her teabag and adjust in her chair. At Sunnie's silence, she finally looked up.

"Sunnie?"

Sunnie shook off her thoughts. "Yes, I guess I cheated, too. He was nice about it."

"Did you two talk after?"

"No, not really. We walked to the car. He asked where on camp I lived. Said he was leaving soon, so I don't expect I'll get to see him again, unless we have another competition or training session scheduled this week."

"Would you like to?"

"It was cool having someone closer to my age around. I don't know if I would like hanging out with him. Or if I would like him," Sunnie shrugged. She hadn't had time to think about it yet. It would be nice to have a friend. She had one when she was little. They'd gone to kindergarten and first grade together. It was strange to think of it now. She couldn't remember her name. It frustrated her how memories lurked just beyond reach. She vaguely remembered her mother's hand reaching for hers to walk her to school. She had no photos of her mother or father, so even their faces had been mostly lost in the years gone by.

Suddenly the cello music was too much. She sprang to her feet and slammed the 'off' button for the speakers. The room fell into silence. Sunnie exhaled with relief as the memories tickling her brain stopped. She stood still, taking in another deep breath before going back to the sofa.

"What are you thinking?" Liz asked.

Sunnie shrugged. "Nothing. Just that I don't have any friends here."

"What do you mean? I'm your friend. Lou at the coffee shop. Your uncle."

"You're not my age. And everyone works here, so they have to be here. That's different from friendship."

Liz gave her a wounded look that she didn't take too seriously, but maybe her explanation hadn't come out exactly right. She didn't want to offend Liz, but the truth was, everyone had to be nice to her because her uncle was most everyone's boss. Sunnie checked the time. Something bugged her tonight, and she didn't want to talk about it with Liz. She certainly didn't want to talk about liking Seth. He'd pushed her. What did that say about Sunnie's taste in friends?

Though, he'd been good-humored about the payback. For that short walk, it had felt like them against the adults—and it felt real. She'd earned Seth's respect. He wasn't paid to be nice to her. In fact, he hadn't been at first.

When Sunnie looked up, she caught Liz staring at her, waiting. Liz smiled immediately, but not before Sunnie caught her look. She shivered, despite being warm, and hot goose bumps went down her arms standing the thin hairs on edge. For a split second, Sunnie thought Liz wanted to dissect her, too. Sunnie reached for her hot chocolate and shook the feeling off. Liz was just concerned and trying to understand. Sunnie sipped the tepid drink.

"Is it still warm?" Liz asked. "Do you want me to heat it up for you?"

"No, it's fine." Sunnie sipped again, then put it down. Cocoa didn't appeal to her tonight.

"Anything else happen today?"

"No, it was a busy morning, but the afternoon was normal. I drove a new assault vehicle the army is testing. That was fun. Sarge said we'd be doing some watercraft maneuvers this month, so I'll get to be out on the lake. *That* will be fun. Plus, it's the only class that doesn't have gobs of homework." Sunnie smiled. She wanted to change the subject. "How was your day? We always talk about me. Is your research going well? Did you get that new grant you wanted?"

"Yes, and yes. The grant was extended two more years."

"That's great. So you'll be here."

"Yes."

Sunnie nodded. That was good to know. "If you leave, you should at least tell me goodbye. Nancy didn't tell me she was transferring. It's strange too, 'cause she said her only family was in Charlottesville and they moved to be near her."

"She told you that?"

"Yes." *Wasn't it okay that they talked about stuff? Had Nancy gotten in trouble for that?*

"I see. Well, I'm sure she and her family made the decision together. That's what families do." Liz got up and took Sunnie's cup. "I'm going to heat this."

"Don't bother. I'm not really in the mood for cocoa." She followed Liz to the kitchen and sat on a barstool.

"What can I get you?"

"Nothing. I should start my homework."

Liz looked at the time. "We still have fifteen minutes." Liz put the cocoa in the microwave. "I'll heat this."

"I have a lot of homework."

"I met a new professor in Starbuck's this morning," Liz said.

Sunnie put her elbows on the counter and settled in. Maybe Liz was lonely. Fifteen minutes wouldn't kill her.

"Oh? A man? Is he cute?" Sunnie wondered if other women had the same thoughts she had about guys. No one talked about liking each other, but she'd seen some of the soldiers at the camp hanging out, and Megan flirted with them. She'd heard them make plans to meet after work.

"What?" Liz's eyes blinked in surprise. "No!"

"I was just asking. You brought it up. It's okay if you want to talk about it."

Liz laughed and shook her head. "Lou said I just missed you. I thought maybe you met him, too. Sergei?"

"Oh. Yeah. I saw him this morning." With everything that had happened today, Sunnie had forgotten. Liz stared at her again, waiting. A tinge of annoyance hit her. She was sick of people staring at her! If her uncle wanted Sunnie to practice conversation, it would be nice if the other people shared and conversed. Sunnie caught herself. Why was she so grumpy today? It must be Wicker. And Nancy leaving. Sunnie took a breath. Liz was just interested in her life and opinions. And she was motherly. In a place with no regular female other than Nancy and Megan, Liz was the one real warm human. So why was Sunnie irritated with her?

"Did you talk to him?"

"Not really. I introduced myself to be polite. I like his accent."

"That's it?"

"Do you like him?" Sunnie smiled at Liz, teasing. "Maybe I could get his number for you next time I see him."

Liz pursed her lips with disapproval. "That won't be necessary."

"Why not? You're old enough to be married." Sunnie wondered about that. "Have you ever been married?"

"Yes, I'm divorced."

"I forgot. Did you ever want kids?"

"No. Not really." Liz got the cocoa from the microwave and slid it across the granite countertop. "Sometimes people make a commitment to a bigger cause. Like your uncle," Liz explained. "If we didn't have at least some people willing to make a sacrifice, we wouldn't have the advancements we have in the world. Besides," Liz came to the other side of the kitchen bar and gave her a hug, "we have you."

She released her and added, "You're the best kid anyone could ask for. Kind, hardworking, thoughtful. Your uncle is very proud of you, and he knows you'll never let him down. That's important to people. Especially him."

Sunnie felt overwhelmed—partially with guilt. "I try." She'd not been so great today, with what she did to Seth, but her uncle didn't know, and the visitors had left impressed according to Megan. Just sometimes she felt frustrated by the restrictions. She had to remind herself everyone here had made a lot of sacrifices to keep her alive. Being a good student was the least she could do.

What are you in for?

Sunnie stiffened, a memory of the conversation coming back to her. He'd said it twice. His English hadn't been wrong; she just didn't understand the question. *What are you in for?* It had underlined her irritation with Wicker. That's what had nagged her all day. She touched the scar on her arm. It was barely noticeable, but Sergei had noticed. Did he know she had cancer? That must be what he meant. But Seth…he was angry. He didn't want to be here. That feeling came at her loud and clear. Not everyone wanted to be at Camp Holliwell.

It made Sunnie wonder again, what was she missing?

CHAPTER EIGHT

"Freeze the tape," Laurence commanded.

The camera caught Sunnie and Seth in full sprint, but it was a blur. "We need to upgrade the camera system outdoors," the surveillance officer said. "But even with what we have, it looks suspicious." He clicked frame by frame then froze. "Look at this."

They all watched as the video moved slowly tracking the second race. Sunnie's hand went down, palm back. The feet of the two runners moved in sync. Seth's laces looked loose, but at the moment when Sunnie might have stepped on them, the camera captured the briefest flash of light.

"It could be an anomaly in the tape," one critic offered.

The surveillance officer gave him a look to indicate the man was an idiot if he thought that. He clicked the tape through several more frames.

Seth's body stopped and flew back.

"That's not the trajectory of someone tripping on a shoe lace," the officer said.

Laurence Cashus stared at the image with the rest of his team in the daily debrief. He pursed his lips with both frustration and disappointment. "She's hiding something."

"She's at the age when she wants some privacy. She's a teenager," the nutritionist reminded them.

"I thought we were controlling her hormones," the neurologist joked.

"We are!" The endocrinologist jumped in defensively.

"We need to give her a perception of freedom," Liz Horten, her psychologist, continued. "Otherwise, we'll lose her trust.

I'm not sure it was good to expose her to Seth, but on the other hand, maybe we need to give her some controlled life experience that we can shape rather than let happen randomly." Liz looked at Dominique Wicker, clearly angry. "Nothing promotes safety and trust more in a *cancer victim* than someone threatening to dissect you."

Laurence agreed with that. He wasn't at all happy to have Wicker interfering in his work. But he had to play nice for now.

"Agreed. Dominique, if you want to be part of this team, you need to be on board with the rules. Sunnie will never trust you now."

Dominique lifted a brow. "We don't need her trust. We need her blood. And a few tissue samples would be nice. The rules are fine, but you've all"—she lifted a pen as if to make a point and rolled it in the air to encompass everyone at the table— "lost your objectivity regarding the subject. She is not *your* niece, Laurence. She is not even *your* science project. She is a government-funded ward of the state that you are allowed to study as part of a larger grant. I'm here to make sure that happens. It's become obvious that you're no longer able to make the hard decisions."

Laurence bristled with fury. "No one here questions my relationship with the subject. I saved her, I'm her guardian, and as such, I make all decisions regarding her future. I'm all she has, and I'm the touchstone of her very existence."

"My sympathies. But you've had sole access to her for over nine years, and you've not yet been able to replicate her parent's formula. I've been here two years and already have a success."

"And thirty-two dissections," Laurence pointed out.

"To your twelve," she defended. "Oh wait, eleven. Number twelve was a former employee you couldn't control." She looked down at the notes on her e-pad. "Yes, Bonnie Hill. Talented young woman no doubt. Perhaps if you had not been so slow to adjust, you would not be investigated now for wasted funds."

Sarge spoke for the first time. He looked upset at the conversation. "Sunnie is a human being whether you want to recognize that or not. One that potentially could be a tremendous asset to our country."

"Our country or our government?" Wicker said.

Sarge ignored her. "The goal has always been to teach and train her in a field of work that would make best use of her talents. She is also the only source of H-plus material that any of us has. It benefits us all to work together."

The group around the table agreed. It was a delicate balance. Laurence breathed a sigh of relief. Sunnie wouldn't be with them for long. He wanted to get as much as he could out of her.

Dominique nodded reluctantly as well. "If she is such an important science asset, why do you continue to allow the military to put her at risk? I'm sorry, Laurence, but it seems to me that you're in a losing battle with the military. They've sent her on numerous "field trips" in the last year, and General Martin is planning another. At what point do you turn her over to them, or they turn her over to you? The White House sent General Brody. What do you think he was assessing?"

"It's a balance and a compromise," Laurence said.

"If they get her killed, you'll have neither a balance nor a compromise."

It was nothing the team hadn't discussed before. Having the military and science community behind them had given some legitimacy to their work, but more and more Laurence needed to limit and control Sunnie. The older she got, the greater the possibility she would become more difficult to manipulate. Surely no one would take her from him. She was the source of his power and position. Without Sunnie, he wouldn't have the large team, the funding, the prestige, or even the ability to run tests to keep things moving. He liked his life and his position. That's also why Dominique irritated him. She was well-connected and moving into his space in more ways than one.

"We're not going to solve the military issue today." Laurence turned back to the big screen. "We have a teenager who might be more powerful than we know. How can we test that?"

The statistician pushed his glasses back up his nose and raised his hand. "Uh, I might note that in the time since her last field trip, she has selected cello music seventy-two percent of the time to complement her nightly meditation."

Laurence felt a chill run up his spine. The others stared at the man, silent. Cello music indicated a direct link between Sunday and her past—specifically her mother.

The memory expert glanced at her files. "I have her on the lightest dose. I can increase the suppressant, but we might want to investigate if she is recalling something. It might be related to her hiding things from us."

Megan, their PhD in Kinesiology, spoke. "I think there are some things she's not going to tell us. We're older. But there seemed to be a connection with Seth today. If he is on board, maybe he could become her new confidante." She turned to Liz. "No offense, Liz, but I also don't think she's going to talk to you about the rest of us. And that's the info we really need. If she doesn't trust us, someone like Seth might be able to find that out."

"But can we trust Seth?" Laurence didn't think it was a good idea. He didn't think introducing her to boys at all was a good idea, let alone a streetwise petty criminal. Only, depending on the report out from today's visitors, he might need to prove a phenomenal new talent to keep control of this project and his most important asset.

"I can get Seth on board," Wicker said. She nodded approvingly to Megan. "I'd be happy to work with you and Liz to develop a strategy for the team." She turned to him, as the ultimate decision-maker, paying respect. Finally. "It's up to you, Laurence."

He didn't think for a second she was doing anything other than biding her time. Even so, it worked. "Hold off on changing the memory suppressant dosage." He turned to Dominique. "Get the kid on board and we'll discuss it."

"Hey, Milk." Brittany called across the small downtown diner to the girl in the corner.

The blonde coder seemed to shrink as they approached. If she got any smaller, she'd slip off the booth and under the table.

Georgie glanced at Brit and told her to smile. Brit was all drama. Today, she was in yellow jeans with a multi-colored blouse she had designed with organic, non-toxic inks. She looked like a multicultural rainbow as she towered over the timid, uber-pale blonde.

Brit slammed the USB down next to the computer, keeping her hand over it. "We need your help."

Startled, Lena looked up at them through white-rimmed glasses. She wore a white short-sleeved shirt and light blue jeans with white Vans. She wasn't a total fashion foul, but nearly. Mostly, she was super plain. And as Brittany pointed out, white to the point of transparency.

Lena swallowed hard, straightened her back, and squeaked, "What do you need?"

Brittany lifted her cupped hand just enough to reveal the USB to Lena, then covered it quickly. "Top Secret."

"If you stole grades or exams, I'm not going to help you."

Brittany huffed with outrage, her hands going to her hips. "Listen here, Casper—."

Georgie intervened. "Sorry, Lena. Brittany's aunt died this past week, and she's really not herself. Brittany, sit." She pointed to the other side of the curved corner booth and Brittany obeyed.

"I'm sorry about your aunt," Lena said.

Brittany nodded. "I think she was murdered." She held up the USB. "And this—."

Before she could say another word, Lena's bony hand snatched the USB. "Is this a clue? Evidence? Where did you find it? Did she send it to you?"

Brittany blinked and Georgie froze while Lena started moving and talking a mile a minute, totally transformed. She attached the USB to her laptop, her eyes bugging out with excitement.

"We found it hidden in a flower jar at her house," Georgie said.

"Ohmigosh. This is the most exciting thing *ever*." The screen came up and the same garbled images appeared.

"Encrypted," Lena said. She typed furiously for a minute and pressed enter. Nothing happened. "Okay, not basic. I'll get it. Order pie."

"Pie?" Georgie asked.

"Or whatever you want. I like pie. Coconut cream with a glass of non-fat milk."

"Of course you do." Brit nodded to Georgie as if to point out she was right.

"I work better with sugar."

Georgie waved down a server and they ordered pie.

"I can't believe this. This is amazing. It's totally government, isn't it? You don't have to say. I can tell. I did an internship last year at the FBI.

"Wow." Georgie didn't know that.

"My dad works there."

"Oh. Still. That's pretty cool," Georgie said.

"They taught me lots of encryption techniques." She typed on the little keyboard, her hands moving like lightning. "But not the really good ones. I hacked my supervisor's computer to see what they really did, and there were all these super cool programs. I might have taken some." She lifted her head to look at them. "For studying."

"Of course," Georgie said.

"I totally got this." Lena cleared a screen.

"You do?" Georgie and Brit spoke in unison. Brittany crammed around the corner curve of the booth until they had Lena squeezed in the middle. Her screen cleared and revealed three folders.

"Ohmigosh! You did it! Ohmigosh!" They squealed a little too exuberantly then hushed each other, staring at the screen.

Three pieces of pie arrived. The waitress eyed them, then looked at Lena. "Everything okay?"

"Yes, thanks, Bea. I'm just helping them with their college applications," Lena said.

Brittany nodded in agreement. "The pie looks good. Thank you." The waitress left and they scooted back together.

Lena turned to both of them. "Are you sure you want to know what's on here?"

Georgie looked around to see if anyone was watching them. There weren't any cameras that she could tell. "You're not connected to the Internet are you?"

"Of course not." Lena's back straightened, offended.

"Okay, open it and let's see." She looked to Brittany for confirmation. Brit nodded.

Lena clicked on the first folder and another box popped up. She paused and blinked. "Oh."

"What?"

"Do you have a pin code?"

Silence.

"Or maybe it's a password? But it says enter number. So if you have one, that's a lot easier than me trying to figure it out."

Georgie spoke. "Brit, your aunt's measurements, remember? On the card."

"Yes." Frantic, Brit pulled the card from her wallet and read off the numbers. Lena typed them in and the folder opened. It was normal passcode stuff, but it felt like magic.

"That is so awesome." Georgie stared at the list of numbered files that appeared.

Lena clicked the first one. "It looks like it's a code plus a date. The code is probably the project name plus the agent in charge...or maybe, in this case, the scientist?" Lena opened the file. They stared in confusion a moment before Lena slammed the cover of her laptop. "I need pie for this."

Brittany pressed, but Lena was adamant.

They ate their pie.

"Do you know what that was?" Georgie asked.

Brittany answered. "I know what it was."

Lena's fork froze midair. "You do?"

"Don't look at me like that, Ghost of Christmas past."

Lena's cheeks turned pink, partially from embarrassment and partially because she had likely heard that description before.

"Just cause I'm into fashion doesn't mean I don't like science. Hello?" She lifted her bright, floral shirt. "Sustainable fashion design. The intersection of science and haute couture."

"Sorry. And my name is Lena. Like Lena Horne."

"Lena Horne was African-American. You're an—."

Georgie gasped about to stop Brit from saying albino. Thankfully, Brittany had the grace to shut up, mostly.

"Anyway…drink your milk."

Georgie tried to soften the conversation. "Lena, you've been awesome. Thank you so much for helping us."

Lena nodded and drank her milk.

"So what is it?" Georgie asked.

Brittany took another bite of blueberry pie. "Someone's DNA test."

Georgie pushed her pie over to Brittany to try while she took a bite of her blueberry. "How do you know?"

"I've seen them before." Brittany gave them a sheepish glance. "Okay, I had one done. I was trying to find my dad. Turned out, he wasn't my dad. Don't ever tell my mom."

"Whoa." Lena put down her milk and patted Brittany's arm. "You've got issues."

"Touché." Brit pushed her empty pie plate away and moved over. "Now, let's see what's in the other folders."

CHAPTER NINE

Graeme knew his mother would nag him later for not dancing with any of the exceptional debutantes at the evening's fundraiser.

He didn't care. Of all places for an assassin to catch him, this would be the worst. Death at the debutante ball…Okay, it was a fundraiser for cancer research, but a debutante party, nonetheless. His team would never let him live it down. He tapped the side of his gaming glasses and began to scan the room. Detection was something he had added to the program after everyone signed in. It was the same as tracking someone's phone. He assumed the remaining players were doing the same. All the survivors had made modifications—that's what leveled the playing field—brains over brawn. He just had to find the M.I.T. assassin before she found him. His detector had warned him—Melinda Stein—M.I.T. EECS graduate program. Mel had taken out most of R.P.I. Had to respect that. The Electrical Engineering Computer Science students were tougher players than you'd suspect for a bunch of introverted nerds.

He ducked around some token celebrities, running a hand through his hair rather than tearing it out. Somehow he'd been dragged along as a replacement for his older, worldlier brother who'd begged off to go clubbing with the latest supermodel. That would have been a way better scenario for public execution.

He spotted his dad at the bar with a Senator and a man who was likely a lobbyist. His father was CEO of A & R Technologies, so there was always lobbying going on, or people interested in their latest biotech breakthroughs. Another man, not far away, nursing his drink, eyed his father as well. His face was familiar, but he stood outside the group and didn't look particularly comfortable mingling with the rich and elite. This was a man who wanted to get his business done, and get out. Something about the look he gave his dad made the back of Graeme's neck tingle.

"Photo," he spoke discreetly, and watched the image of the man snap into the frames of the glasses and disappear. Just behind him a woman's dress fluttered. It was barely distinguishable. Players were required to wear digital overlays in the game. How good a person was at designing and mapping clothes to their body could be the difference between life and death. Her virtual red dress was barely distinguishable from the real one. Good, but not good enough. He spotted Mel Stein a mere nanosecond before she spotted him. He touched the side of his glasses over his ear and the game laser, which was not really a laser but a high frequency beam, hit her detector a mere second before he put up his virtual armor.

Their player glasses registered his kill and noted there were three remaining M.I.T. players to be assassinated. He pulled off the frames as she mouthed a curse as she approached. Likely his team would be texting him high fives once the kill was recorded.

"I wasn't expecting an assassination attempt tonight. Good game, Melinda. 207 kills." He grabbed two glasses of champagne from a passing waiter and handed one to her. "Here. I'd buy you a drink, but it's free."

"I hate you."

He laughed. "You'll learn to love me. Everybody does." He reached for her glasses. "You added the indoor-outdoor glass as well, I see."

"Yeah."

"The dress was a good idea. Made it hard to detect."

She smiled and pushed long, dark curls behind her ear. "I know. It's called strategy." She brushed a hand down the skirt of the long red dress and fanned it out. "Since I'm here, wanna dance?"

She was nice and smart. If he hadn't been distracted by the

man at the bar watching his dad, he definitely would have complied. He folded his own glasses and slid them inside his jacket pocket.

"A victory dance seems mean-spirited," he teased. "Actually—."

Graeme watched over Mel's head as his dad excused himself and went toward the men's room. His awareness heightened when the stranger put down his drink and followed.

Too weird.

"Sorry, Mel. I have to check on something." He handed her his champagne to hold. "I'll be back."

The man was definitely following his dad.

Graeme moved quickly, weaving between guests to catch up with his father. Two guests, both in real estate, caught him halfway to see what his plans were post-Rensselaer Polytechnic. He stopped politely, angling to keep sight of his dad, and chatted quickly about how he still needed to finish his senior project. His mother didn't approve of bragging, so he left the part out about his Zombie Master app exceeding twelve million in sales. Instead, he quipped that he'd be calling them for a job and left them laughing.

He hurried to catch his dad, a strange urgency burning in his gut far different than a college game of Assassin. The sensation intensified when he saw the attendant standing outside the men's room like a guard. His long strides quickened with sudden images of his dad trapped by a crazy man. The attendant's expression grew more stressed at his approach. Just as Graeme burst in, the stranger walked out.

Graeme nearly ran him over, but for a man of at least forty-five, he was built tough.

"Excuse me, sir." Graeme said instinctively.

The man nodded and left. Graeme hurried into the room to find his dad staring into the sink, rinsing the edges with water before washing his hands. A hint of something recently burned left a scent in the air. He glanced in the porcelain basin, but no evidence of whatever it was remained. When his dad kept washing, Graeme went to him and touched his arm. "Dad? You okay?"

His father nodded, but his eyes didn't see Graeme. Whatever had just occurred, it had shaken his father. And his father was pretty unshakeable.

"Who was that guy?"

Pause. "Who?"

"The guy who just walked outta here, all tough and serious looking."

His dad shrugged. "Don't know."

Graeme stared his dad down in the mirror, letting him know he didn't believe that for a second.

"Did he want money?"

That earned a smile. "Did you do something I should know about?"

Graeme let out a short laugh, feeling some relief. "No. I'm good. Rex and Morgan are the ones you should worry about."

"I worry about all my children equally. That's why I'm gray." He slapped Graeme on the back and led him back out to the party.

"So…the man? He was watching you really intently before you came in here."

"Oh?" Whether his dad was surprised that Graeme noticed, or that the man had allowed himself to be noticed, Graeme didn't know.

"You know I've got your back, Pop." Graeme thought through what it could possibly be. "Is it about Sergei Baratashvili? Did that man know something about what happened to him in Paris or where the formula and serum are?"

His dad blinked. "You've got a lot on your mind."

"He was Ben's hope. Mom took it hard. We all did. I just thought…." Graeme studied his dad's posture for a sign he might be right. His dad relaxed.

"It was nothing like that. Nothing even related to that."

Okay, then what?

"He was someone in a tough spot, trying to do the right thing." His father squeezed his shoulder and looked him in the eye. "You need to forget you ever saw him. I need you to do that, Graeme."

Curiosity and concern tore at him, but his father's seriousness won over. "Yeah. No problem. Everything okay, though? Have *you* done anything *I* should know about?"

That earned him a wide grin. "No need to worry. I'm scandal free. And if I weren't, your mother would be a very rich widow. In jail, but a rich widow."

Graeme laughed as his dad gave him a quick one-armed hug, but it didn't erase the feeling of unease in his chest, or the concern lingering in his father's eyes.

Something was wrong. Very wrong. He reached inside the breast pocket of his tux, touching his glasses protectively. Maybe he could run a visual match on the photo.

Once he knew the identity of the man, *then* he'd forget all about it.

"Georgie! Dinner!" her mom called up the stairs.

"'Kay!"

She texted Brittany a quick bye. The folders had contained DNA reports, blood and chemistry reports, and MRI brain scans. But there weren't any names of the patients. Just numbers. It was frustrating and it told them nothing. There was no proof it was even connected to Holliwell or Nancy's job. They agreed to let Lena send one of the files to a former mentor at the FBI to see if she could find a connection to a person who might have been at Holliwell as a worker or a patient. They might even be able to decode the file numbers and figure out what the project actually was. It would require accessing Holliwell's massive databases, so Georgie had her doubts about their success, but any lead would help.

She pocketed the phone to join her parents downstairs, passing walls covered with historic photos and memorabilia of the heroes and other notables in their family tree.

With her mind only half on the dinner conversation, it was no surprise she missed what her dad was saying.

"Georgie, what time is your shift Thursday? Will that work?"

"Will what work?"

Her dad's lips pressed together and his left brow lowered. The hairy eyeball. Uh-oh. How long had she been spaced out? The last time her dad had looked at her like this was when she'd asked about Alastair...but she knew better than to bring up her cousin's name anymore.

Her dad was great, but he'd perfected the art of intimidation. She'd been in his University office when the hairy eyeball made the bravest students falter at the threshold. She tried to guess why she was getting the look. She got straight A's, was last year's Junior Class President, was the current President of the History Club and Yearbook, and never got into real trouble.

He must be irritated about something else.

She'd seen this look more and more lately to get her attention when she overused social media or didn't respond politely at the dinner table. She put her fork down and took on an interested expression. "Huh?"

"Next week. If you drive me to the interview Thursday then drop me at the University before you go to work, I'll come home with your mom. That way you'll have the car to drive home."

"Oh." Georgie caught up. "Sure." She definitely preferred having the car to being picked up. Finally, her mind unraveled what her father had said. "What interview?"

Her mom smiled. "Your dad was selected to interview for a civilian position at Camp Holliwell."

"What?" Georgie sat straight in shock. "That's military!" And creepy, she started to add.

"The military has a rich history and tradition," her dad said. "Your great-great-great-grandfather was a Buffalo Soldier, highly honored. Your—."

"No, I mean...I mean, you know what they say about that place." She stopped him before the history lecture, which she was positive irritated him, as the hairy eyeball sunk even lower. "It isn't *regular* military, Dad. Al said guys who get assigned there never hang with their friends again. They get brain warped."

At the mention of her cousin Alastair, Georgie earned the rarely-sighted, double-hairy eyeball. *Great.* Time to spill those beans. "I picked him up, by the way."

"I heard he was released," her dad said, stabbing some chicken with his fork.

"Time off for good behavior," she quipped cheerily. "He's looking for a job."

"'Bout time." Her dad chewed the chicken slowly before adding, "That boy had plenty of opportunity, and he threw it all away."

"But we can't give up on him, right? You're the one who always says we can't give up on people, Dad."

"Uh-huh."

She had him. Alastair had served time for misdemeanor drug possession. She really hoped he stayed clean. She knew he didn't use it, but if he'd really been selling it was just as bad—worse, according to her dad. Her dad didn't want her near Al, for obvious reasons, but someone had to pick him up, even if he was a 'blight on the family name.'

"Anyway, supposedly they breed them crazy at Camp Holliwell. Super-hyper military commandos. No smiling allowed." Her dad lifted an arched brow at her, the hairy eyeball having failed to intimidate her. "*No* smiling. None. And you're a happy person!"

Her dad scooped a second helping of chicken onto his plate, a grin peeking through. "I think I can handle it."

"Brittany's aunt thought that, too. Now she's dead."

"Georgie." Her mother clearly wanted her to drop it. "That was an accident. She fell asleep at the wheel."

"At a dangerous part of the road as well," her father added. "They need to post better signs."

"Someone broke into her house!"

"A thief taking advantage of the situation," her mom said.

"Fine. I'm just sayin' it might not be a good idea."

Her dad went on. "It's only part-time and adds a thirty-percent increase to my current salary, and the University already approved it."

"But...." Georgie's stomach lurched uncomfortably. Her dad was a good guy, and tenured. There was a financial break for tuition for children of employees at the University, and she wouldn't go somewhere else unless she got a scholarship. Maybe that wasn't enough? "I can get financial aid, you know."

Her father's back straightened this time. "And there's no shame in that." Only, he wanted to pay for her college, and she'd just chipped his pride. Perfect. No winning tonight. She sighed, looking to her mom for help.

Her mother simply shrugged. "It's just an interview."

"That's right," her father said.

Georgie picked at her food. "Well, why do they want a history professor anyway?"

Her father responded with his usual history professor line. "So they don't make the same mistakes again."

"Uh-huh. So basically you don't know anything about the job."

"Watch that tone, missy," her mother warned.

Sometimes it sucked being the only kid. Her parents paid way too much attention.

"Sorry, Dad."

"Umm-hmm." He smiled at his plate. "You can drive me there and check it out yourself."

"Okay." Like that would help.

Then again…maybe she could do a little reconnaissance for Brittany.

CHAPTER TEN

Sunnie couldn't concentrate. Her body still ached from the fall a couple days ago, but it wasn't that. It was the nagging feeling. *What are you in for? You've never been out.* Two strangers in one day had managed to throw her entire world off balance. Coincidence? Her life was simple for a reason. She had to be careful of allergies and exposure to viruses and things that other people didn't have to worry about. *But weren't there precautions she could take?*

What was so different about the air at Camp Holliwell versus Charlottesville, where many of the doctors lived or went for weekends? Did cars make that much pollution?

She stared at the volume on her desk. The military battles of the Hundred Years War had lost her interest. Normally, the parts with Joan of Arc would have captivated her, but tonight, she felt captive.

How far was Charlottesville? Couldn't they go there for a drive? There must be a map somewhere in the condo. She straightened her books in an orderly fashion on her desk, smoothed her bedspread in case Uncle Laurence came to inspect, then left her room and proceeded to go through every drawer and closet in the condo. There were plenty of books— all schoolbooks from years past. She went into her Uncle Laurence's bedroom and checked his drawers, careful not to disrupt anything—there was very little other than clothes and a medical journal that rested on the nightstand, perfectly squared with the corner. He kept a minimum of toiletries. On the wall were some photos of them, similar to the one in the living room. He didn't keep photos of their friends. She wished he did. She would have liked to have memories of the people who were with them when she was younger. Everyone had become a series of names by the time she was ten. Nancy, her medical nurse, had been the only one in recent years that she'd liked. Megan was nice enough, and Sarge was a good man, but they were there to push her and make her better—not to be her friend. Maybe that's why she'd been so struck by Seth.

She stopped in front of her uncle's office. The carpet changed color from brown to blue. She wasn't allowed anywhere where the carpet was blue. She stood there, frozen, staring at the floor. As a child, she'd been taught never to go on the blue carpet. The one time she did, she'd been punished...severely. At least it had seemed severe for a nine-year-old who liked to be around people and was always hungry. She'd been assured, when they let her out, that twenty-four hours of solitary without food or water was lenient.

Still, the memory gave her pause. She stared at the plain blue carpet abutting the safety of brown. Her uncle always knew when she disobeyed. She thought it was some freaky psychic ability, but he said he could see it in her eyes.

She only wanted a map.

She wasn't up to no good.

What could possibly be in his office that would be dangerous for her at this age?

She lifted her leg, fighting the heavy feeling of resistance embedded in her after years of obedience. Her leg barely moved.

Biting her lip hard, half expecting an alarm to go off, she slowly forced one foot onto the blue carpet, hesitating before easing down her weight.

She breathed in hard, then brought the other foot over the border. Frozen, she waited. When nothing happened, no alarms or flashing lights, she swallowed, exhaled slowly, and debated. She should retreat, but the office door was within reach.

She took the step needed.

She'd seen his pin code but had never used it. Quickly she pressed it in. Nothing happened. She tried again. Same.

"Dang."

Guilt set in, and she hurried back to the brown side of the carpet, still staring at the office door.

She must have gotten the code wrong. Or he changed it more often than she realized. He *did* work on top-secret government projects. Changing the code was SOP—standard operating procedure.

If she had her own computer, she wouldn't need to get into her uncle's office. She resented not being allowed electronics. If only they weren't so expensive. But it seemed like everyone had them. How much could they be? Maybe she could cut down on classes and work at Starbucks. That would be fun. And less homework.

Sunnie checked the time. She was still standing in the middle of the living room. Uncle Laurence would be home in twenty minutes. Maybe she could use Liz's computer. She went to the front door and stopped again. She wasn't supposed to go out after nine. But she was just going next door to Liz's. That's where she went when she needed things. Sunnie reached toward the keypad. An inch from touching, she pulled back. Uncle Laurence trusted her not to go out at night. Should she commit two violations in one evening?

You've never been out.

Seth's words taunted her. She'd never been off Camp Holliwell alone. She'd never even been out and about Holliwell without her uncle knowing her schedule. Suddenly, she'd become daring and disobedient.

She'd never been disobedient. And before yesterday, she'd never cheated, either. But hadn't they encouraged her to be more resourceful? She made the decision. She'd be back before Uncle Laurence got home.

Sunnie pressed the code and hit enter.

Nothing happened.

She stood in front of the door and waited. The keypad flashed: "LOCKED." Frowning, she entered her code again.

Nothing.

She was stuck. How annoying. The system must be broken.

What are you in for?

Sunnie shook her head. She was a patient, not a prisoner. This was an error. It had happened before. Annoying, but technology came with a price.

She went to the phone and dialed the operator. A calm female voice answered.

"Camp Holliwell, please confirm your extension."

"1226."

"Hello Miss Cashus. How may I help you?"

"Hi, the code to unlock my door isn't working."

Silence.

"Hello?"

"I'm sorry, Miss Cashus, is that your front door?"

"Yes." Sunnie looked around. There weren't any other exterior doors other than the living room balcony.

"Okay, I'm noting the problem. Your uncle is on his way."

"Okay, but can you override the lock and open the door? Or is there another code?"

Pause. "Are you in trouble?"

This time Sunnie was silent. "I'm not sure. Am I? I'm locked in our condo and can't get out. What if there was a fire?"

"Is there something you need? We can arrange a nighttime delivery."

Sunnie blinked surprised. "What do you deliver?"

"Whatever you need. Coffee, socks, Band-Aids, Soda, Popcorn. You name it."

"Great, but how would I get it with the door locked?"

Silence. "I see."

"It's obviously a flaw in the system. Can you give me another code to reset it?"

"I'm sorry. The residents make their own codes. We don't have access to a master code. Those are only used for the security of the overall base. Your uncle should be coming up the elevator any minute. I'm sure his code will work. In the meantime, I'll make a note of your call. Thank you, Miss Cashus. Goodnight."

"Goodnight." The line clicked on the other side before she got the word out. Just then the automated door began to buzz. Sunnie stood to welcome her uncle.

She ran to him, stopping when he held his hand out palm down for a greeting. She quickly took his hand and kissed it, waiting for permission to speak.

"Hello. What's wrong?"

"The door was broken, and the unlock code wouldn't work, and I was trapped."

Uncle Laurence smiled reassuringly and put his briefcase by the door. "You weren't trapped. A hundred people could reach you in seconds if there was an emergency."

"Why didn't they?"

"Because this was a glitch in the door's system, not an emergency, and the staff on the base have other jobs they need to attend to besides your door lock."

Sunnie sighed.

"I know it's frustrating. I'll reset it now." He did as promised, pressing seven numbers, then putting in her code. "Now check your code."

Sunnie punched in her code. Of course it worked. "It works now because you reset it, but I needed it earlier." She stared at the door wanting a solution. "What's your reset code?"

"What?"

"What code did you use to reset the door? I can use that to reset my code when things mess up."

His lips thinned. "How about you make me a cup of tea and we discuss why you were trying to break your curfew."

Great. Now it was her fault.

"I wasn't trying to break curfew. I was going to Liz's to see if I could use her computer for a minute. I need a computer. How much do they cost?" Sunnie decided to plow ahead and try to change the subject. "I'm thinking I should get a job at Starbucks."

Uncle Laurence blinked several times. "Well." He nodded. "I definitely need a cup of tea."

Sunnie hurried to the kitchen and put on the kettle. "Lemon, chamomile, or mint?"

"Chamomile, please."

She grabbed a tea bag from the box and quickly straightened it with the description facing out, prepped the tea mug and separate saucer for him, then waited for the water to boil. "I know we can't afford one for me, but I could get a job."

Her uncle went to the cabinet, opened it, and straightened the box of chamomile tea. "You're in a rush," he noted. "A tidy home takes thought."

"Yes. I'm sorry." She clenched her fists for control. The box was exactly as she put it.

Sometimes he just liked to correct her. This was going to be one of those times. "The economy is a mess, and there's twelve point five percent unemployment in the state.

Her uncle sat on a barstool at the counter and she put a spoon, napkin, and the saucer in front of him.

"Everyone who has a job needs it, and anyone who hires wants to hire someone who really needs a job."

"But I do."

"Not as much as others. Be grateful for what you have."

The kettle buzzed. *And time's up. Shut down again.*

"I am grateful." She poured the water and walked the cup around to the other side of the counter to his right, placing it carefully in front of him.

"And with your condition, we never know what chemicals or environments could have an adverse effect on you. I'm doing my best to keep your environment controlled in order to keep you alive."

"I know." He'd sacrificed a lot already.

"It's not meant to be a punishment. The curfew, on the other hand, is a family rule, and I expect you to obey it. If I can't trust you with something small, how can I trust you with something important?"

"I know. I'm sorry."

He nodded. "I can trust you, can't I, Sunday?"

"Yes."

"Good."

Shoot. He knew about the carpet. Maybe she should come clean now.

He sipped his tea, and changed his tone. "Why do you want a computer?"

She shrugged. "It just makes it faster to look things up."

"Like what?"

She shrugged again. "Everything." Since he wasn't going to let her have one, and had already lectured her about safety, there was no way she was telling him she wanted to know how far the city was. "I should get back to my homework."

He patted the barstool next to him, indicating he had more to say. She complied, making sure her face maintained a pleasant smile rather than the frustration she felt inside.

"I was very proud of you this week."

She nodded.

"Our guests were happy. And looks like you handled yourself well with that kid. I told Sarge next time the rules change to let us know in advance."

"It was all right." She smiled, "After I recovered from my high-speed nosedive." She grinned a little thinking of how Seth described it as a sick bird. "Where does Seth live?"

"Seth?" Her uncle turned fully around in his stool, tea mug in hand.

"The guy I raced. He was fast. Like me."

"He lives on the other side of the base."

"How come?"

"What do you mean?" Her uncle frowned.

"Why does he live there and not over here by us?"

"Dr. Wicker is treating him, and her facilities are farther away."

Sunnie thought about that. It wouldn't be good to be stuck with Wicker and no Starbucks even. "What is she treating him for?"

"You're very curious tonight."

"You said that's how people learn."

"Hmm." Her uncle smiled. "I don't know what his diagnosis is, but he might be joining you for some sporting classes."

Her skin charged electrically, but she nodded casually.

"Would that be okay?" he asked.

"Sure." *Yes!* That would be fun. And she could ask Seth about the outside. "Did you know there are Starbucks all around the world? Seth's been to over a dozen of them."

"Impressive."

"I'd like to go to more Starbucks."

"They're all the same."

"You've been to others?"

"A few. We have the best."

"Oh." She'd still like to go see them for herself. Maybe someday she could do a Starbucks tour and visit all of them. "I better get back to my homework."

"Okay. Anything else you want to talk about?"

She got up. "No. Everything's great." She gave an extra smile to make up for complaining earlier, and avoided looking at the blue carpet outside his office as she crossed the room.

"Sunday," her uncle called out as she reached the door. She stopped. He knew. Slowly she turned around, half expecting an explosion. Instead, he tilted his head at her. "We're not done," he reminded. He held out his hand, palm down. "I love you."

She walked back to him, took his hand obediently and kissed it. "I love you, too."

He smiled. For some reason, tonight his smile looked triumphant.

Sunnie closed the door within an inch, as was the rule, and sat back at her desk. The frustrating thing was that her uncle could talk his way around everything. He always had a logical reason, and it always came back to her illness and taking care of her. Everyone on the base told her the sacrifices made to keep her alive and safe. Did it make sense for her to have feelings that could put her in danger? She just wanted to see what else there was on the outside.

She called a fresh pencil to her hand and caught it midair.

Then there was Seth. Sunnie twirled the pencil in her hand, a smile on her lips. She had a little time tomorrow morning. Maybe she would go to cellblock 24C and surprise him.

Just the thought of that cheered her up.

CHAPTER ELEVEN

Sunnie tapped her foot impatiently. Her morning measurements were nearly complete. Sometimes she wondered why it was necessary. Same room, same hospital, same measurements—every day. It *seemed* a waste of time.

"Okay, all done," the nurse said.

Sunnie jumped to her feet. "Thanks. Will you be here tomorrow?"

"Yes, I will."

"Okay, I'll see you then!" Sunnie smiled at the new nurse and hurried off. She was eager to get out. It was 06:40. That left almost fifty minutes for breakfast before her martial arts training. If she showed up late, no one would notice, as long as she was ready by 07:30.

She hurried out of the hospital and jogged casually to the end of Main Street, making a turn toward the military housing. The next street was gated to cars and had a guard shack, but she could easily pass through via the walking path. At the far end was the other section of research buildings. There were really beautiful modern buildings in the Science and Engineering Center, but that wasn't where Seth stayed. She kept going.

As Sunnie ran, the buildings got more and more depressing—giant cement blocks. She definitely lived in the nice part of town. The last section of buildings was numbered. She counted the buildings, then followed the numbers upward. Eighteen, nineteen…another runner came toward her on a morning jog and waved. She waved back. He wore similar gear. Gray sweats and a t-shirt. Built like a soldier. Though she'd had no cause to come down this way previously, Sunnie didn't feel particularly worried. She found cellblock 24. It was like the other buildings—a sturdy cement block with very few windows except in the front façade, which showcased a modern lobby, elevators, and matching stairs on either side. She entered and spoke with the guard on duty.

"Hi, I'm looking for cellblock 24C."

"Scan your ID, please."

Sunnie waved her hand wrist ID over the reader and waited while the guard identified her on the computer.

"Sorry, Miss Cashus." He didn't smile. "Dr. Wicker's team only."

He looked past her, and Sunnie turned to see two familiar guards escorting Camp Holliwell's most recent visitor—Sergei. They entered the building. Sergei looked up in surprise when she greeted him. She turned back to the guard.

"I'm here to see Seth. They told me to come to 24C to visit."

"I'm sorry, Miss Cashus, you're not on the schedule."

"How do I get on the schedule?"

"I don't know, miss. Perhaps contact Dr. Wicker's office."

Like that was going to happen.

The guard looked to the others behind her, wanting her to move along. "If you'll step aside, I'll help these gentlemen."

"I appreciate the compliment," Sergei said. "But you're being over-generous with these two buffoons."

Sunnie turned again, catching one of the guards elbow Sergei in the back. She frowned. The rudeness struck her as strange for a camp guard. She wondered how Sergei took the disrespect, but he winked at her.

She tried the guard one last time, a little disappointed. "Can you at least call his room and let him know I'm here?"

"I'm sor—," the lobby guard started to respond when a cry got his attention.

"Oh!"

Sunnie spun at the sound of pain. Sergei bent over, a hand on his abdomen as he expelled another cry.

The guard hurried to move him to a bench in the small waiting space. Sergei said something about some medicine in the Jeep outside, and the other escort ran out.

"Is there a bathroom?" he asked the lobby guard.

"Yes, over here. Let me get the key."

The guard grabbed a key behind the desk and walked to the far side of the lobby. Sergei reached out for the remaining guard and fell over the burly escort's arm. Both guards had their backs to Sunnie when Sergei made visual contact with her. His eyes darted toward the elevators. Surprised, she stared. He did it again. He clearly wanted her to make a run for it. He was helping her!

Sunnie watched as the lobby guard reached the bathroom door and inserted the key. A second later, she was past the desk and inside one of the six open elevators. She read the information for each floor, found the C group, and her heart pounding, hit the button. She heard more noise, as Sergei cried out. The elevator doors closed. Total silence but for the hum of the lights.

I am in so much trouble. If I get caught. Don't get caught. Don't get caught. Ohmigosh. I'm in so much trouble. What's wrong with me?

The elevator opened, and Sunnie thought for sure there would be guards ready to yell at her and bring her home. She peeked out into the sterile, white-tiled hall.

No one.

She checked the time. 06:55. Thirty-five minutes to get back. Workers would be arriving soon. This didn't seem like a good idea anymore. Maybe she should abandon the plan. She checked out the names on the doors anyway. Toxicology, Nano 1, Nano 2, Research A. Intrigued, she followed the hallway around the building. All the doors had keypad locks. Biology, Neurology, Research B, Research C, Patient Care.

She stopped.

She was almost around the building. Seth must be in the Patient Ward. She backed up and stared at the keypad. The ding of an elevator told her to make a decision quickly. Odds were, her own passcode would not work—but what about her uncle's? She'd just seen it last night when he reset their condo. As far as she knew, passcodes were consistent all over the campus. Oh man. Stealing a passcode. Her heart thudded unnaturally fast.

She should abandon this idea now. She could still—.

Several pairs of footsteps got closer. She heard Wicker's voice clearly.

"Dr. Baratashvili, I hope you'll find the tour interesting and informative. We would very much appreciate your assistance with our work."

Then again…no time like the present to impersonate her uncle. She pressed the seven-digit code and hit enter. It worked! The soft engine of the door buzzed steadily.

Definitely grounded from Starbucks…for the rest of her life.

Sunnie pushed the door open quickly, hurrying to see if anyone was on the other side.

Wicker continued, "Nowhere else in the world is anyone as close as we are—."

Sunnie shut the door, pushing until she heard the soft click.

Great. The Wicked Dominator was recruiting Sergei. That was either good, or really bad. What if he told on her? She checked the time again. Thirty-three minutes before she had to meet Megan. She hurried down the hall for any sign of what direction to go. It was a long hall, and every door had security locks. Where was Seth? Maybe he was joking about where he lived. Oh, no. Sunnie felt sick. What if he'd lied about that? He cheated easily enough. And really, what were the odds they kept a person in this depressing lab location under lock and key?

You're under lock and key.

She pushed the nagging voice aside. She'd made a big mistake believing Seth. The sound of the door buzzing behind her told her just how big. Who knew how many days of solitary her uncle would give her for something like this?

She inputted her uncle's code on the nearest door.

Nothing.

There was no time to run for the exit at the far end of the hall. Frantic, she looked around. The building was equipped with transports in the walls used to send samples to toxicology and deliver supplies directly to private labs. Relieved, she opened the outer metal door to the mini-lift. The compartment could be opened from three directions at any given time, but was usually accessed from inside labs for the convenience of the researchers. Her uncle had used these lifts many times.

She folded up the plastic interior with one move and squeezed herself into the square vehicle. It was tight. Really tight. Not like when she'd been little and thought they were elevators for kids. With the interior still open, she was able to reach the external metal door and pull it closed.

She could hear the footsteps approaching. Wicker passed her hideout within inches.

Sunnie froze her body, terrified the people in the hall could hear her heart thumping. She felt the hair on her arms stand on end and focused her years of training on finding her center. Panic subsided…temporarily. She almost started to laugh. Instead, she listened carefully. She could hear Wicker continuing her grand tour.

"We've had success recently with one of my patients. I'd like you to meet him later, but first I'll show you what your lab looks like."

"You have a lab set up for me? You're very confident, Dominique."

"This is the chance to see your work thrive, Dr. Baratashvili. I'm sorry about the circumstances that brought you here, but it was necessary."

"Kidnapping?"

"Secrecy," she said.

"So I am free to leave at any time. I was not aware of that."

"As far as I'm concerned, yes. I'm afraid my military partners might have concerns otherwise."

Someone punched in a code. Ten digits, not seven.

"Ah," Sergei said. "Such is life."

"Yes. This way, please," Wicker said.

The door closed and they entered a lab. Sunnie realized her feet were pressed against the specimen door leading to Sergei's lab, with her back to another lab behind her. She held her breath. She could hear them clearly, and it didn't require super hearing. She prayed no one sent lab samples any time soon.

"This is remarkable," Sergei said. "You've thought of everything."

"Good."

"But why me?"

"Why not? You're the foremost longevity scientist in the world, and your work curing muscular disorders is nothing short of miraculous."

"Eh."

Sunnie imagined Sergei shrugging.

"That was many years ago. My research became obsolete when others came along."

"But those breakthroughs were inspired by your work. Dr. Marques's, for instance."

Silence.

Sunnie listened curiously. Nothing. Then....

"Dr. Marques was my student, yes. I'm afraid whatever insights she and her husband had died with them years ago."

"Not completely."

"That's very mysterious, Dominique."

"They had three children, Sergei."

"Yes, but surely you don't think any of them were old enough to understand their parents' work."

"Not exactly. I think they *were* their parents' work."

"What?" Sergei sounded outraged. "That is a serious accusation."

"I don't mean they experimented on them. At the time of the accident, the children were infected."

Sergei didn't respond.

"Thankfully, they survived." Dr. Wicker added, "*All* of them."

"What do you mean?" There was a sense of surprise and horror in Sergei's voice. "I understood that only the younger children were saved."

"I mean, thanks to Dr. Cashus, *all* of them survived. Laurence's niece, Sunday...." She paused, keeping Sunnie on edge. "...is the daughter of Dr. Marques and Dr. Albrecht."

Sunnie's heart raced even faster. Albrecht? That was her family name before Uncle Laurence adopted her. She was his *only* niece, right? Her breathing went shallow. Her brother and sister were *alive?* The memories came back, vaguely. They weren't dead. Morgan and baby Ben. Oh, God. Oh, God. Alive! All this time. The metal near her arm began to shake. She closed her eyes and pulled her energy inward. *Do not get caught!* She must not get caught.

But Morgan and Ben. Where were they? Did her uncle know about this? Was Wicker hiding them? She almost burst out of the little compartment to demand answers, but her fear was greater than her curiosity.

"I see," Sergei said. He sounded supremely calm compared to the chaos inside her. "Sunnie Cashus is Jocelyn Albrecht. Dr. Cashus has taken ownership of her, so to speak, and you want me to help do what, exactly?"

Jocelyn. That was her name. She remembered it. The sound and shape of it on her lips triggered memories of her parents as she repeated it. Jocelyn. Jocelyn Esperanza Albrecht. She remembered her father teaching her how to write it out. How she practiced at the kitchen table before dinner while her parents cooked. Just her name brought back memories of her parents calling to her, instructing her, playing with her…loving her. She desperately tried to hold the memory, but it was pushed aside by the voices outside her container.

"Cashus has been studying her for over nine years, with no success. I've already been able to use her DNA to create a serum that mimics some of her abilities."

"Abilities?"

"Yes. Don't you know?"

"It seems between the kidnapping, prison processing, and GPS tagging of my body, that I've had little time to catch up on the local gossip."

"Of course." Wicker gave a short laugh. "My apologies."

Her voice was amused, not sorry. It didn't win Wicker any points. And there was that prison reference again. Obviously, if Sergei really had been kidnapped, he would be upset, but the idea of Holliwell being a *prison* seemed absurd.

"Start from the beginning please, Dominique."

"Ten years ago, when their lab was destroyed, the eldest child was in severe danger, completely exposed to gases and chemical spills in the home lab while trying to save her parents.

She was put in a government isolation facility to make sure there was no danger to others, and for nearly two months, hovered close to death. Dr. Cashus believes that it was in that time that the toxins, or you might say 'the brilliance of her parents' work,' incubated in her system. She awoke from the coma *extraordinary*, and by that time, Laurence had persuaded the authorities to grant him sole rights to study her—for the good of mankind and protection of the nation, of course."

"Of course," Sergei agreed.

Wicker continued. "So far, he has learned a remarkable amount of information about what she can do, but he's had no luck replicating the technology that has unlocked and altered her genetic make-up. She's an H-plus, Sergei. Actually, I'm not even sure how human she is anymore, but she's definitely enhanced. Wait until you see her brain activity," Wicker added, excitedly. "It's the stuff of fantasies."

"My fantasies run more to sandy beaches and cocktails served by exotic waitresses."

"You say that now. I have my first specimen—Seth. If I can repeat my success with others, I've been promised the funding and authority to harvest even more DNA."

"Harvest from whom? Miss Albrecht?"

"We need to get all the knowledge we can *soon*. There are deposits in her brain growing at a steady pace. We've got perhaps three to four years before she won't be of any use to us."

Deposits? In her brain? The pounding in her chest moved to her head. She curled her fingers into fists and made an even tighter ball of her body. Were the deposits cancerous? What was an H-plus?"

"That's very coldhearted, Dominique."

"It's not. Would you rather see her die in Cashus's care? Her life useless? Look around you, Sergei. We have everything we need here to crack the code. We can cure diseases, help people to live healthier, longer lives. This might be the answer to reversing Alzheimer's, dementia, Parkinson's—the possibilities are limitless."

Sergei cleared his throat. "And who determines who we save? We're in a highly secure military facility. What do you think the government wants to do with this knowledge, Dominique? Now you're part of a conspiracy to hold a young girl prisoner for scientific experimentation, to "harvest" her blood and DNA, and who knows what else. For what? She has a family. Do they know she is here?" He paused, then said more quietly, "This is not science. It's medical slavery."

Yeah! *Thank you, Sergei.* Where was her family?

"It's not like that. Even the President said we shouldn't let ethics get in the way of good science. She's cared for here and has everything necessary for a good life."

"Everything except her freedom," Sergei said.

There was a long pause.

"I don't know," Sergei added. "This was more than I expected."

A chair scratched against the tiled floor.

"You present a compelling case. And yes, you've done remarkable things with this lab. But...I have to think. I need a minute. This is all so much...is it possible I could have a drink of water or juice. Maybe a moment alone to absorb."

Another chair moved. "Of course," Wicker said, soothingly. "Take a moment, look around. This is state-of-the-art. And the new facility in Colorado is spectacular, with the benefit of fresh mountain air. We have a kitchen down the hall. I'll grab you a juice. Orange okay?"

"Thank you."

The door opened, then closed.

Jocelyn. She said the name silently on her lips. Not Sunnie.

Jocelyn didn't move. It was silent.

To her surprise, quick footsteps came toward her, and stopped. She stared in the darkness, and gulped in horror at the sound of locks and latches clicking on the other side of the transport door.

Without hesitation, the door popped open.

Blinding light poured over her scrunched knees and hands. When she looked up, she saw the face of Sergei Baratashvili frowning down at her.

Her entire being ached from the control she forced on herself before speaking. She finally understood his question.

"Now I know what I'm in for."

CHAPTER TWELVE

Minutes earlier, Sergei had listened with interest as the girl, Sunnie, tried to get past the guard. It seemed she didn't have the run of the place after all. From the little he'd learned, she was a VIP of some kind—but not the free kind if they had a tracking system on her. It made him sympathetic to her cause. A fake abdominal cramp that he explained as gas from the bad food they served seemed a small enough effort to help. It also allowed him to study her a bit more.

She'd snuck into the elevator. Ha. Good girl.

Only neither of them realized what they did in this building.

Human testing.

Big mistake.

Now he looked upon the white face of Jocelyn Albrecht, her legs falling out of the transport system, her posture defensive. The innocent joy was gone, replaced with confusion, disbelief, and terror.

"It's okay," he said. "She went to get a juice."

"I'm going to die?"

"Yes." By the look on her face, he'd failed the reassurance test.

The energy in the room seemed to switch instantly. The tremble of what he first thought might be an earthquake caused objects to jitter around him. He put his hand on a table for support, his brain rapidly analyzing the signs.

The floor didn't move, but jars on the shelves shuddered. A pen from the desk oscillated in the air. A current of energy surrounded him, making the hairs on his arms stand up straight.

Very strange. What caused this? Surely not....

Blue eyes shone brightly from her pale face. She breathed deeply and slowly, a sure sign of someone fighting panic. He made eye contact with her to make sure she was coherent.

"But not today. Everybody dies sometime. It's what you do with your time that matters." Maybe that was better. He was a scientist, not a therapist. Impromptu encouragement was not his forte. "Get your feet back in."

"I have to find my family. They're alive."

"Yes." He shoved at her fresh, new running shoes, pushing them in the lift, with a quick glance at the door. "There are cameras everywhere. They can track you, Sunnie."

"Jocelyn. My name is Jocelyn."

He studied her angry, determined face before responding. "Yes. Yes, your name is Jocelyn Albrecht. I know who you are."

She nodded with relief.

"But you can't let them know that you remember this, or that it matters. They will try to control you even more. You must keep your knowledge a secret for now."

Her glare was rebellious, but she nodded again.

"Don't let them find you here, and don't let them know you know *anything*. Trust *no one.*"

"But, Seth. He might be in trouble, too."

"Trust no one and get out."

He closed the door firmly and hit the button for the first floor. If they were lucky, the lab downstairs would be empty. He listened to the whir of the lift. The pen settled on the desk, then rolled onto the floor. He picked it up, studying it as the door lock clicked, and Wicker came back. He could still hear the whir of the transport lift. Would she notice?

"Thank you, Dominique." He twisted the cap on the orange juice and took a drink. "Now. Are you going to show me this patient of yours? I admit I'm very curious."

Her lips curved with the satisfaction of one who has caught their prey.

Fear and anger knotted in his stomach. As happy and cheerful as Camp Holliwell seemed on the outside, it was warped and dangerous inside.

The whirring stopped.

And now one more person knew it.

Jocelyn didn't move for a few seconds. It was silent all around. She debated closing her eyes and hiding in the dark in the hopes of becoming invisible. The thought was short-lived.

Her sister and brother were *alive.*

She nearly kicked the door open in excitement.

The lift opened into another lab, identical in layout to Sergei's. Most regular workers arrived at 08:00. She checked the time. 07:25! Just five minutes before Megan would be looking for her! She jumped out and made for the exit. In the hallway to the left was the security door to the lobby. She turned right to an emergency exit.

This was an emergency.

She ran to the door, stopping abruptly at the sound of voices. There was a small kitchen open on the left with early birds making coffee. She peeked in and found a target. A second later, a box of coffee pods tumbled to the floor, distracting the workers. Jocelyn ran for the door. Sunlight and fresh air hit her. For a second, she could almost believe the last minutes hadn't happened. Inhaling with relief, she started to jog away from the building. Two other joggers turned to the exit of the compound's boundaries. She picked up the pace, and the three passed the internal guard gate and lineup of cars beginning to enter.

Her stomach flipped crazily. She felt like she would be sick right on the side of the road, but she kept going. The joggers headed to the tree path. She headed to Main Street. Starbucks overflowed with morning coffee-goers. A few people read in the shade of Chestnut trees outside.

She stopped running. *Don't look guilty.*

There was a small clothing store nearby. It wasn't open, but she looked in the windows. She never shopped here. Her uncle said a uniform was best at her age. She saw her face in the window. She was only seven when the accident happened. Morgan was what? Six? What did she look like now? Dark hair like their mother? And baby Ben. He'd had wisps of blond hair. She didn't remember much of them, and only a little of her parents. Would her siblings recognize her?

Jocelyn Albrecht. Hearing her real name spoken out loud had been a shock. No one used it. She'd been Sunday Cashus for nine of her sixteen years. Her uncle renamed her so she could have a new life. At least that's what he'd told her. She murmured her name a few times. It anchored her. Truth was freeing. Powerful.

And frightening.

It meant she had to look at her life in a new way. Who else knew about this? What did it say about the people around her and their motives?

She looked down Main Street. Megan waved to hurry her along. Did Megan know? Jocelyn walked down the sidewalk to the woman chatting up a soldier outside the hospital. Did Megan know what was going on and who Sunnie Cashus really was?

"Ready?" Megan asked, as the soldier smiled farewell and returned to whatever he should be doing.

Jocelyn nodded.

Megan looked at her daily notes. "You skipped breakfast?"

Jocelyn stared at her. Megan already knew that much.

"That's not like you. Feeling okay?"

Jocelyn shook her head negatively. "No. I have a stomachache. I thought fresh air would help."

Megan frowned. "When did you last have a bowel movement?"

Jocelyn stared at her again, grasping at the ready explanation. "I don't know. That must be it." She clutched her gut to add credence to the lie. "I think I might need to go."

Megan nodded. "We'll get you some cranberry juice and more water today." She studied Jocelyn. "Do you want to use the restroom in the hospital lobby?"

"Yes, please." Jocelyn made her escape and darted for the women's room. It was empty. Everything was empty. Even her insides felt empty. She locked herself in the toilet stall and sat down. What could she do? Were there really cameras everywhere?

The lock on her condo! Oh, no. It all made sense now. It was just like on cellblock 24C. But that was their home. She breathed again, unable to believe she was locked up the same way Seth was. No. It was safe at the condo…except that she couldn't open the lock past a certain time. She would test that tonight. She couldn't believe her uncle was conducting tests on her. He was trying to learn about the cancer to stop it.

You don't have cancer.

Jocelyn took several more calming breaths. Okay, if it wasn't cancer, what was it? What had made her so sick when she first arrived here? And again when she was ten, twelve, and fourteen? She knew Wicker was psycho, but she couldn't believe that anyone else was. Not her uncle, or Megan, or Sarge. And Liz did totally different research from her uncle. She rested her head in her hands, feeling a brief sense of relief. Okay. She was safe. This was all a lie. She didn't even know Sergei. *But her mother had.* Were they friends? Why had he been kidnapped? Was he really a prisoner?

"Sunnie?" Megan called. "Everything cool?"

Jocelyn jumped in surprise. "Yep!" She flushed the toilet. "Much better." She exited the stall and washed her hands.

"Okay. Sarge is waiting. He doesn't approve of tardiness."

"I know. Sorry." She kept washing her hands, suddenly aware of the camera in the corner covered by dark glass. They were everywhere. Even in her living room. They always had been. Only right now, as she tried to hide a tidal wave of emotion, they felt very intrusive.

Megan smiled. "It's okay. Even superstars can get constipated." Megan put an arm around her shoulders and led her out. It was comforting—the arm around the shoulders and the constipated part. Maybe she didn't have to be perfect all the time.

Then again, maybe nothing was as she thought.

The Secretary of Information Management cleared the Oval Office.

"What is it, Jerry?" the President asked.

"General Brody, sir." Jerry waited for the President to take a seat behind his desk, then laid some photographs on the table. "He made a visit to New York. Was at an event attended by the Rochesters. It might not be anything."

The President glanced at the photographs, then away, not touching or looking too close. "I really liked him." He lifted a silver ball hanging from the Newton's Cradle on his desk. He let it go until the rhythmic click of balls repeated the soundtrack of ticking time.

The President put his elbows on the desk and stared at the desk toy. "I trust you have it all under control."

Jerry knew the President didn't want to know how they had this information or how to deal with it. It was an unspoken agreement that Jerry would handle the messy parts of their partnership. The President only had to look presidential, deliver his speeches effectively, and be charming to campaign contributors—all of which he did exceedingly and surprisingly well for someone who passed University with straight Cs, even in theater class. That was the power of "woo."

Jerry didn't have woo.

Jerry had a network of knowledge and ways of controlling it. In the end, that was where the real power lived. Truth and justice were outcomes that a select few decided. But compared to the average American, he was much better equipped to be making those decisions. Just like the President, no one really wanted to make the hard calls. Sacrificing a decorated General for the good of the nation was one of those calls.

"I have it under control," Jerry confirmed.

"With minimal mess, please. There are some important campaign donors in those pictures."

"Of course."

The President stopped the clicking balls, looked up, and smiled. "Perfect." He stood. "If there's nothing else, I have to get ready for my sports segment. Need to support the national pastime."

Jerry agreed. "People need distractions during downturns."

The President had his hand on the door leading to the secretaries' desks. He stopped and turned, a slight frown of concern marring his normally inoffensive features. "Jerry, that girl can never go home. You understand that, right?"

"Absolutely, sir. Don't worry," Jerry said. "She'll either become an asset to the state, or she'll peacefully serve her purpose to science. It's a win-win either way."

The President grinned and opened the door. "That's what I like to hear."

Graeme woke with a start as his head slipped from his hand and nearly crashed on the desk. Someone pounded on the door again.

"Just a minute!" he called, wiping drool from his chin and rubbing his face, still groggy. At the door stood his older brother, looking fresh and alert in clothes that reminded him they were supposed to play golf with their dad this morning.

"I knew you were going to be late," Rex said.

"What time is it?"

"Time to get your ass in the shower."

Graeme groaned. He hadn't slept much the last couple of nights, and he didn't like his sleep interrupted unless coffee was involved. "I wrote a new image recognition program."

"Uh-huh." Rex went to the large bathroom and turned on the shower.

"Actually, I modified one and made it better and faster. I can photo match a person to any image on the Internet—well, almost any—and it doesn't need to be just full frontal." The program was still running the photo he'd taken at the charity event. He looked at the timer. It had been three minutes. "The search takes time, but I think I can optimize that." Or it didn't work. But best to think positive. There were a lot more photos on the Internet than he realized that matched "white male military over forty."

"Dad's waiting."

"Okay, okay."

Rex plopped on the king-sized bed and grabbed the remote, turning on cable news. "You could just search their name. That's what regular people do."

"Yeah, but if you don't know their name...."

"You could—," Rex suggested with sarcasm, "—I dunno, ask?"

Graeme slammed the bathroom door and shouted back. "What if it's top secret?"

"You're using it for everyday spying?"

"Something like that."

"Doesn't the FBI already use something like that?"

"Yeah. But theirs is primarily for front and profile matches." That's the code he started with, but he didn't want to explain how he got that software. "This takes it several steps further."

Graeme took a fast shower, letting hot water stream over him one extra luxurious minute. He threw on some clean golf clothes from the adjoining closet and entered the bedroom again.

"Okay, let's go."

"Shhh!" His brother stared at the TV.

"What—."

At the raised hand, he closed his mouth and watched. Car wreckage was being pulled from a site outside Baltimore, Maryland.

His brother swore. "I can't believe it. General Brody died last night in a car accident. He taught my senior year at West Point. He was a great man."

A picture of a man in uniform came onto the screen. Graeme didn't know the General, but as he stared at the picture on the screen, recognition made his heart beat faster. He ran to his computer and checked to see if the program had finished.

It had.

The top fifty matches displayed on the screen—all General Raymond Brody. He swallowed hard, glancing at his brother across the room, riveted by the report.

What had General Brody wanted with his dad? What did it mean now that he was dead?

Graeme knew better than to ask. He shut down his computer, disconnected the Wi-Fi, and unplugged the cords for good measure. *Shit. They were screwed.* If his dad was being watched, Graeme's interest could have easily been tracked to their family home.

Maybe it was sheer coincidence?

He glanced up again at the news. The President had been notified and was making a statement of sympathy to the Brody family. His dad and little brother entered the room, checking on them. Little Ben immediately came over, his Exo-S poking Graeme's thighs. Graeme put his arm around Benny's bony shoulders and hugged him protectively.

"Ready to get schooled by the big boys?"

Benny grinned up at him. "I have a secret weapon today. We'll see who gets schooled."

Graeme laughed and ruffled his hair. The kid was learning guy communication.

"Shush," Rex admonished.

Graeme waited and watched. In any moment, his dad would see what had Rex mesmerized. And....

His dad's hand reached blindly for the bed, to sit.

Yeah. That was the moment. And the glimpse of shock on his father's face told him for certain—there were no coincidences.

Finally, his dad grabbed the remote and killed the broadcast. "Let's go, boys. Family time is precious." His eyes met Graeme's in warning.

As much as Graeme wanted to question his father, the set look on his face told him not to try, especially not in front of the others.

"Agreed. Come on, Rex." He slapped his brother's shoulder and squeezed briefly, in sympathy.

General Brody had retired to spend more time with his family, and now that had been cut short. He couldn't blame his dad for wanting to enjoy each day. But he also couldn't help his dad until he knew what the hell was going on.

CHAPTER THIRTEEN

After visiting cellblock 24C, finding out her family lived, and that she would die an early death, Jocelyn spent the next twenty-four hours in quiet paranoia trying her best to act normal.

To her surprise, it worked.

To her growing fear, she began to notice things—blinking camera lights, clicking sensor sounds, and a large number of doors with locks. This *was* a military research facility—so security made sense—but couldn't she have classes somewhere less…secure?

By dinnertime the next evening, her paranoia had grown. She was angry at all the restrictions and frustrated by the forced routine—especially as it related to food. Thursday dinner was chicken, green beans, carrots and broccoli—again. Pepper was allowed. Salt was not.

Her uncle sat across from her, eating in his slow methodical manner, completing each item before moving onto the next.

Jocelyn stabbed at her chicken breast and lifted it in the air over her plate. "I'm so sick of skinless chicken. How about barbequing it, or frying it? I've heard people talk about that, but we never get anything different."

"Frying isn't good for you. Clogs the arteries," Uncle Laurence said.

She plopped the chicken on the plate. "It tastes like they cook it in water."

"Yes, it's boiled."

"I hate it."

Her uncle paused. "I like it. And I think it's very nice that we have people to cook and bring our food to us." He put down his knife and fork. "What's really going on?"

"Nothing." She gave a fake smile. "Just sick of chicken. I think I'll learn to cook myself. Can we skip dinner and go shopping and make our own meal?"

"No." He looked surprised. "This one is already made. Maybe another night."

"Tomorrow?"

"I'll see how the schedule is."

"How about we eat dinner, then go shopping so we have our own food for tomorrow."

"You have homework."

"I can still get it done. Or I can skip it. I'm the only student. It's not like it matters."

"Of course it matters."

"Fine, I'll get it done. I just want to buy our own food."

"Food service is part of my deal."

"So? You have money, don't you?" He simply stared at her like the question was ridiculous. "We do have money, don't we?" He must get paid something.

"We have just enough to take care of our basic needs."

She stared at him, not sure if she felt disgust or disbelief. "How often do you negotiate your contract?"

"Why?"

"Maybe I should negotiate next time. Even the soldiers have money for their own food and entertainment."

"I'm taking care of two, not one."

Instant guilt. "That's why I should get a job."

"Are you upset about something, Sunday?"

She almost screamed that her name wasn't Sunday.

"Nope."

"No," he corrected.

Trust no one. Until she figured out what was going on, she was alone. And trapped. That would make anyone angry, wouldn't it?

They ate in silence until finally her uncle surprised her.

"You had a little adventure yesterday. Is that what this is about?"

Jocelyn almost choked on boiled chicken. She lifted an eye curiously at her uncle. He apparently forgot that her coach was a military man. Strategy and combat history had been part of the lesson planning. Not that she'd ever thought she would need it. It was just interesting. And Sarge liked to share stories. One thing she remembered about interrogations—you never offer information unless you want to lead the topic.

She cut her green beans. If he knew anything about the other morning, he'd have to tell her.

After two more bites, her patience paid off.

"I'm told you went to cellblock 24."

"Oh, yeah." She shrugged. "I forgot."

"Oh?" That seemed to surprise him. "You used my code to enter a classified facility. That's illegal, Sunday."

She skewered two more tasteless green beans and stared at him. "Illegal? Why is it illegal? Someone made a *law* about using other peoples' codes?"

"Well, there's no law—."

"I didn't think so." She returned to eating the green beans, stabbing them with a little too much triumph.

"We sign a contract when we get our camp codes."

"I didn't sign anything."

"I signed for you, since you're under eighteen. Since I'm responsible for you, I'm punished if you do something wrong."

She studied him, interested now.

"Certain areas of the camp are classified, and you're not allowed to go anywhere where your code doesn't work."

"I didn't know my code wouldn't work until I tried it."

He blinked, surprised, it seemed, at her logic. "Oh. Well, your code only works in the places where I've previously shown you."

"Why doesn't it work over there?"

"Restrictions are for your protection."

"Seth is over there. Why is he locked up? Is he a prisoner?"

"Of course not. He came here voluntarily."

"Does that mean he can leave voluntarily?"

Her uncle paused, looked at her, then slowly began to cut his meat. She realized he was thinking of an answer.

"He is Dr. Wicker's patient. I don't know the details of his stay."

"So he's trapped by the witch? I thought you were the highest-ranking civilian here. Don't you know what she's up to?"

"The government leases parts of the facility to other groups and scientists, and they work with us, but we are not always privy to their research. There are thousands of highly classified projects being studied here. The less we know about the details of everyone else's work, the safer the security."

"So he's a prisoner."

"You're being absurd."

It hurt to be told that. She was being serious. She wanted answers. Instead, she felt like she was being put off. And it made her wonder if he was really on her side.

"In any case, you managed to get through. How did you know my code?"

That reminded her. She marched to the front door and pressed her code. It didn't work. That proved one thing. She was locked in at certain times. Her uncle watched and didn't say anything. She returned to the table and joined him for dinner, finally answering his question.

"I saw your code when you reset our system. It only worked on the first door, then I was trapped in the hallway and had to leave. I used the emergency exit since the guy in the lobby was kind of a jerk. Not much of an adventure. Boring, actually."

"I see."

She changed the subject. "Why does my code only work at certain times of the day?"

"For your safety, and because I can't babysit you twenty-four hours a day."

"I see." She repeated his words. He was as irritated with her as she was with him.

She didn't need a babysitter. However, knowing she wouldn't get anywhere while he was grumpy, she summoned her former self and changed the subject. "You don't really like this chicken, do you?" She wiggled it on her fork with a smile. "Plain, boiled chicken?

Disarmed, he smiled.

There. Better. For now. She couldn't let him know the direction her brain was going—not that her questions didn't make it obvious.

She watched as he slowly cut into the chicken then ate a bite. One thing he said tickled her brain. She waited for him to swallow and take a drink of water.

"What happens when I'm eighteen?"

His head lifted sharply. "Nothing." He blinked quickly.

Her skin tingled, alerted to his sudden panic.

"You said I couldn't sign a contract because I was under eighteen. So when I'm eighteen, I can sign contracts for myself?"

"No."

Instant rage shot through her. Liar! She could tell by how he thought about his answer too long. And the blinking. He blinked a lot when he lied.

Anger made energy whiz down her skin, this time causing his silverware to rattle. Her uncle's eyes darted toward the sound, worried. No...not just worried. Fearful. Was he afraid of her?

She froze the utensils in place. Control. Maintain control. She wanted to argue and shout, but she knew that stubborn expression. He would talk her into submission with one of his many explanations, and she would feel stupid and guilty for being ungrateful.

"Oh. I guess I was confused by what you said."

He nodded and smiled.

It hurt to do, but she smiled back, desperately trying to cover the feeling that her life was falling apart around her. Somehow she needed to get answers, and she couldn't trust anyone until she did.

She had a brother and sister who were alive. Where were they? How were they getting by? What if they needed her? Determination steeled her to learn the truth.

Morgan and Ben. She must find them.

Before it was too late.

CHAPTER FOURTEEN

Graeme waited a few days before confronting his dad about General Brody. Only a few news bloggers covered the story in detail, with one noting the deadly car accident was a bad first offense for a man who'd never had so much as a traffic ticket.

He wasn't exactly sure what he would say to his dad. There wasn't any evidence of a threat to his family. His dad appeared back to normal, and his mother seemed unconcerned about anything other than Morgan's grades. Since his mom was the former Governor of New York, she would know if there was a threat.

Still, he couldn't put it aside.

Sports played on the wall-sized TV across from the bar where his dad made a drink. He caught the bottled water his dad tossed him.

"What's on your mind?"

Just like his dad to lay it out there.

"You meet with General Brody secretly, and he dies three days later in a car accident. After never even having so much as a parking ticket. After serving in Iraq, Afghanistan, and probably surviving dozens of close calls."

"No one knows when their time will be." His dad took a swig of his scotch and soda, eyes on him. "A damn shame though."

"You visited his widow."

"That's what good people do. That's the kind of people we are."

"Glad you agree." Graeme drank some water. "I visited her, too."

His dad smiled like a male Mona Lisa. "She's a nice lady."

"Uh-huh." Graeme waited a moment. "She said her husband visited Holliwell just before his retirement."

His dad didn't exactly perk up, but there was a glint.

"Dad, come on. What's the connection to us? To Morgan and Ben? They do high-end weapons development and experimentation at Holliwell. Futuristic stuff. Scary stuff."

"Your mom would know better than I would. She has the government connections."

"Yeah, well, I worry about Morgan."

His dad's look hardened. "What are you saying?"

"Just that she has her moments. What if she's a target for experimentation? Or recruitment or something?"

"She's a fifteen-year-old girl obsessed with makeup, shopping, and the next great band. They'd have to be *really* desperate."

Graeme lifted his hands with a shrug. "She's got skills. That's all I'm saying."

His dad took a seat in a deep leather chair and lifted his glass for a slow drink before responding. "Has she been *using* these skills?"

Shoot. He didn't mean to get his sister in trouble. "No. But I know she practices stuff in her room. Mostly harmless parlor tricks. She's at an age where she might be tempted to use them publicly, show off maybe, but I think you and Mom have drilled it into her that it would be a bad idea. It doesn't mean someone in the house hasn't leaked info."

His dad nodded. "We'll have a talk with her and alert her security detail as well."

"Is that what Brody was telling you?"

"No." Quick and honest.

"Is it related to that?"

"Graeme, you don't need to be worried about this."

Graeme worried. "You avoided the answer."

"Brody was a guest at a function that had hundreds of politicians, businessmen, and their families. Running into someone in the men's room is fairly common."

"I *saw* him watching you. He followed you to the restroom."

His dad relaxed a little. "I'm known to give good stock tips." He finished his drink. "Come on. Your mom hates it when we're late for dinner."

Maybe he was overreacting, but his father was way too calm. "Okay."

His dad stood up. "It's nice that you're concerned about your sister." He put his arm around Graeme's shoulder and pulled him into his side briefly before slapping his shoulder. "Your mom said you were out earlier with a real estate agent. See anything you like?"

Graeme followed his dad's tight-lipped lead as they went to dinner. Despite his assurance that there was nothing to worry about, Graeme couldn't escape the niggling sensation.

There was something to worry about.

Jocelyn stretched, waiting for Sarge and Medina to arrive. It had been a week since she had tried to see Seth, a week since she discovered her brother and sister were alive, and a week of straining to pretend everything was normal.

She tried asking Liz questions, but everything came back to "you'll have to ask your uncle about that." When Jocelyn asked at what age she would no longer need to ask her uncle "about that," the response had been, "He'll always be there to help you."

It sounded like a death sentence.

She still loved her uncle, right? She didn't really know how much he knew about her circumstances. He might not know about Morgan and Ben, either. Maybe Wicker hadn't told anyone. Her stomach tensed.

She didn't really believe that. Uncle Laurence had been instrumental in saving her. According to the stories he and others had told, he'd watched her day and night until she recovered. He must have known what happened to her siblings…unless the government had kept that information from him?

Jocelyn stood at the sound of voices. Until she knew more, she'd follow Sergei's advice.

Trust no one.

Then Seth walked in.

"You're still here!" The excitement was obvious in her voice, but she didn't care. He smiled at the welcome and walked over to her, followed by Medina, Sarge, and General Martin.

"I'm told we'll be training together," Seth shared.

"I thought you were leaving."

"They wouldn't let me out. You're stuck with me."

"I don't mind."

"You might after they're done with us. According to Sarge, General Martin is here to *advance our capabilities*. It sounds ominous." Seth glanced over his shoulder. "But since it was that or certain death, I chose ominous. How have you been?"

Jocelyn shrugged. She didn't feel like pretending with Seth.

Seth lifted a brow.

"Overscheduled, overseen." She indicated the adults with a roll of her eyes. "By the overbearing."

"I feel your pain. Maybe we can make a break for it together."

Jocelyn smiled, knowing he spoke in jest, but liking the idea.

She said hello to the General, and grunted to Medina. With Medina here, it would be a grueling workout. It also meant they were training again for a field trip.

"Where are we going this time?" she asked him, as she always did.

"That's a need to know question. And you don't need to know," Medina answered as he always did, before turning his back on her and leading them to the rock wall.

She looked at the equipment, curious. It seemed they were going somewhere that might require climbing.

Three hours later, Jocelyn was dripping with sweat, every muscle in her body worked to a painful limit. Having Seth there to challenge her kept her going, but Medina was relentless. She'd already run thirty miles that morning, so pushing hard in training was unusual. After wall climbing, ropes training, and sprints, they finished with more upper body.

"Five more," Medina said.

Jocelyn dare not move her head. They were in push-up position, with Sarge balanced on them—one boot on Seth, one boot on her. Her arms felt like noodles, and if either of them lost rhythm, they risked two hundred and fifteen pounds crashing down on them. Jocelyn pushed up, watching the bend of Seth's elbow in the corner of her eye.

Five. Done. They held the "up" position, waiting for Sarge to get off.

General Martin joined them. "Twenty more," he said from the sideline.

Jocelyn felt an unsteady drop in Sarge's weight as Seth wavered. She tilted her head. Seth's arms trembled with effort.

"You heard the General," Medina barked.

They were both fatigued in their arms and chest. Her stomach growled loudly. "Use your core," she encouraged. "We can do it. Come on, Seth. Almost there." The temptation to use her energy was always there, but training was about physical development and stamina, so she never cheated. This might be an exception, but now, more than ever, she needed to be discreet about what she could do. She had a strong sense she was going to need every edge she could get in the future. Only, she didn't like seeing Seth forced to suffer with her.

Sarge adjusted his balance, his boot digging into the skin of her back.

"One," Medina began to count off the final twenty.

"You need...." Jocelyn said.

"Two."

"Lose weight," she finished.

"Three."

"No sh—," Seth added, his curse barely covered by the count.

"Four."

"Quiet," General Martin clipped, pacing in front of them.

"Five."

"Screw you," Seth said.

"Oh!" Jocelyn had never heard anyone talk back to an officer.

"Make that thirty, Sarge," the General said.

Ugh. And that's probably why. "Seriously?" she said.

"Six," Sarge counted.

"Seriously," the General repeated. "Or we can send Mr. Johnson back to 24C for the rest of the day."

Silence.

"Seven."

"Sorry," Seth gasped. She saw him turn his head to her in apology.

"Eight."

"Not your fault—."

"Nine."

"All the adults here are—." Jocelyn pushed up.

"Ten."

She sucked in a breath of air and released. "Assholes."

"Sunnie!" Sarge shouted.

Her body shook—from the effort to keep from laughing. She'd never sworn out loud. After the week she'd just had, it felt great. She saw Seth smile.

Jocelyn spotted the tip of the General's shiny black leather shoes under her nose. "Make it fifty, Sarge." She smiled. "You think that's funny, Cashus?"

Her body shook again. "Yes, sir!"

"Eleven," Sarge called out again.

"Almost there, Seth," she encouraged as she felt Sarge's balance adjust to their uneven tempo.

The General stayed squatted, observing her, moving his foot just in time to avoid her sweat dripping on it. "You're stubborn, Miss Cashus."

No one had ever told her that. She'd always been very amenable and obedient.

"That's good," he added surprising her before standing up. "It will make it harder to kill you."

She'd already technically died once when she was seven, and was slated to die in the very near future. She didn't think being stubborn would make a difference.

They finished the final push-up and lowered Sarge as they lay flattened on the floor. Neither of them moved until Seth rolled on his side and imitated the General's raspy voice. "It will make it harder to kill you." He rolled on his back and let out a sarcastic moan. "Outstanding."

Medina glanced down at them with his perpetually scowling face. "You have five minutes to shower. Clothes are in the locker. Meet me in the front of the building for pickup, or you won't get lunch. The General has a surprise for you."

Jocelyn dragged herself to her feet, too hungry and weary to care about her disheveled hair. She made eye contact with Medina. "That was fun. Thank you."

He slammed the cover of his e-pad closed and walked away.

Her stomach growled loudly. "Hungry," she moaned.

"Food in five minutes." Seth grasped a piece of her shirt and pulled her along. "Then our surprise. Should be *fun*," he said.

"I hate surprises."

CHAPTER FIFTEEN

Seth and Sunnie gorged at lunch, then were driven twenty-five minutes to the far western section of Camp Holliwell and a large lake surrounded by mountains and lush forest. Hanging out with Sunnie turned out to be way better than being poked and prodded by Wicker's team. Awaiting them were three super sleek speedboats.

"What. Are. *Those?*" His palms itched. Pure temptation for any self-respecting thief. Not normal speedboats. Twenty-two foot, sleek, reflecting, shallow water racing toys. "Very James Bond."

"Who's James Bond?" Sunnie asked.

"That." He pointed. "Cool."

"Oh." She stared at the dock, curious. "Have you done all the vehicle training already?"

"Vehicle training?"

"You know. Learning how to drive and operate various transportation devices."

He stared into her innocent eyes. "I don't think this is a transportation device."

"Of course it is. It's a boat."

"That's not what I meant. This is not for everyday transportation. This is spy material. Totally." He watched as one of the soldiers with them got into a boat and turned it on. The entire vehicle floated upward, seeming to barely touch the water. He nodded his head. "James Bond."

The General caught his eye and smiled, satisfied, his arms crossing over his chest.

"What kind of engine's in that?"

"Classified," General Martin said.

"Fuel-injected?"

"Classified," the General repeated.

"Horsepower?"

"And...classified," the General repeated. Some of the soldiers chuckled. "But," the General added, "you won't max it out."

Seth might have been annoyed, if not for the low-pitched hum that vibrated like a full G-chord across the lake. It had a pleasant buzz that got his attention. He looked out. Sunnie had already spotted it. She pointed.

"Look!"

Across the lake, the slim, narrow boat whizzed across, barely skimming the water...until something went wrong. The front twisted and the nose tipped down.

Sunnie gasped.

Seth expected disaster, waiting for the boat to flip over on itself—especially at the speed it flew.

It didn't.

It dove down, submerging in the water, and disappeared.

Less than a minute later it emerged, but if you didn't know it was there, you wouldn't have seen it. Then the cloaking device deactivated and the exterior material changed until it was visible again to the naked eye.

"No effing way." Simon adjusted his beanie. He was definitely going to find a way out and take one of these with him.

The vehicle hummed ever so silently to the dock.

"Wow!" Sunnie grinned. "That was cool! Was that James Bond, too?"

He shoved his hands in his pockets. "Totally."

"I like James Bond." She nodded like she now understood everything. It was cute.

The General stepped forward. "This week you two are going to learn how to drive the EmWAV 360. Water Assault Vehicle."

"What's the 'M' for?" Sunnie asked, her brows furrowing with thought.

"E-M. Electromagnetic," General Martin said. "But that's classified."

Seth nodded. Finally, something meaningful. Huh. Maybe the General wasn't a total jerk.

The General, Sarge, and Medina walked out onto the dock to greet the driver of the   EmWAV, leaving the two of them alone on land.

As if reading his mind, Sunnie turned to him. "It's good for students to know there's a reward for hard work. It makes them stay motivated and work harder. Sarge told me that. That's how they train soldiers. Only they punish soldiers a lot worse than us. At least that's what he says."

"In other words," Seth looked over at the General, "we're being manipulated."

She shrugged. "It will still be fun. I heard they were working on a new vehicle that utilized electromagnetic propulsion, but I didn't know they'd actually succeeded in creating a workable prototype. This is a really big reward." She gave him a warning look. "They're wooing us." She looked at Martin. "He's new. He thinks we can be wooed."

She was wary. He'd seen that expression a few times today. In fact, she'd kept to herself a lot today compared to the first time he'd met her. Vastly different from the wide-eyed, everyone-loves-me, innocent act. Or maybe this was the real deal?

Sarge waved for them to join him.

They walked to the metal dock together. "Did something happen?"

Her head whipped around to Seth in surprise. "What do you mean?"

Whoa. A little defensive. "Nothing. You're just different. Something's changed."

She stared at him before turning back to the boats. He thought she'd been about to say something, but instead, a barrier came down. She stopped and spun back to him. "Do *you* like being manipulated?"

He grinned. "Depends on whose doin' it."

She stared at him. No reaction.

He sighed. No surprise. She might seem different, but she was still innocent.

"Right. Anyway, maybe they'll let us race."

That earned a wide smile. "I'll slaughter you."

"Yeah, right. Do you even have a driver's license yet?"

Based on the flicker of confusion on her face, negative.

"What do you need to do to get one?"

"You need to be sixteen first."

"I am."

"Then just apply. After you learn to drive, that is."

"Are you always so, so—annoying?"

He laughed. "Guess so."

They walked over to where the team waited. Sunnie grabbed his arm and pulled him along until they were in front of Sarge. "Sarge, James here wants to race me in the EmWAVs."

"That's Bond, James Bond."

"Excuse me," she said to him before repeating to Sarge. "Bond, James Bond, wants to race."

"These aren't toys." Sarge didn't look up from his clipboard, but Seth could tell he was amused. It just wasn't Sarge-like to show emotion.

Sunnie leaned into him, her warm skin causing Seth's attention to waver. "What he means is, after you pass a training test and exam, maybe we'll look into it. Everything comes with a written and practical exam."

"Should've known. Too good to be true."

"Don't worry. We're definitely getting a ride and a tour of the capabilities. That's always on the first day."

"You do this a lot?"

"I don't have any kind of license, but I can drive a lot of vehicles—two that don't officially exist. Maybe this will be my third."

"Bragging isn't attractive in a chick."

"Jealousy isn't attractive in a…a *boy*."

"Ouch." He acted stung. "A *boy*? Really? That just hurts."

She laughed. It transformed her face and made him feel like he had just accomplished a lot more than two hundred and fifty push-ups with an ox on his back.

"Focus, children," the General called to them. "Suits, gloves, helmets, and boots are in the boathouse. You should be able to find your size. Gear up before boarding. We're taking you for a ride."

"Outstanding," Seth said. "Come on."

"You should worry a little, Seth. A helmet for a boat ride? And if my guess is correct, a fire-retardant jumpsuit."

"Even better. If you can't die, it's not fun."

She shook her head. "That's just stupid."

"We're all gonna die."

"Yeah. Some sooner than others."

The sigh that followed stopped him dead. "Whoa. Something did happen. Are you okay?"

She shrugged. "It's nothing. I just wish I could leave here and see the outside. Do something normal."

"Why don't you?"

They walked into the sleek, state-of-the-art boathouse and looked through the gear, starting with the loose black bodysuits.

Seth studied her, wondering how much she really knew about what was going on. "Have you ever tried just walking out?"

"Like, just leave the base?"

"Sure. There are gates everywhere. It's not like you're a prisoner, right? Or someone's science project." He tried to provoke her. "Just walk out the front gate. Tell them you're going for a jog."

She laughed, zipping up her black bodysuit over her clothes. "What?"

"I don't know," she said. "There's always someone with me making sure I'm okay. And I'm allergic to different things in the air, and I don't know...."

"Exactly. You don't know. And what you don't know can get you killed."

"Or the other way around."

Seth put on a pair of sturdy, steel-toed boots and tightened the thick laces. Sunnie was ready and had a helmet in her hand.

"When are you supposed to leave?" she asked.

"Sick of me already?" Seth gave her a wounded look. He wanted to talk, but wouldn't risk it in any structure that might have cameras or audio surveillance. They walked outside and he grabbed her bodysuit from behind, startling her. She turned around for an explanation.

He smiled big—for the General and others waiting about seventy feet away. "I'm going to fix your laces. Shut up and play along." He smiled larger. "They said once you trusted me and told me your secrets, I'd be released. The truth is, they aren't going to release me."

He bent down to redo her laces.

"Why tell me?" she asked.

"Because I figure, if they want me to spy on you, you're the only one here as screwed as I am."

He glanced up and winked. She gave him a silent stare of understanding.

Hell. Seems like she knew it. She really must be up shit creek.

"If you tell them I told you, I will be equally screwed, so now you have some power." He switched to the other boot. "And," he glanced up to make sure she could hear, "at some point, they will tell you *I* was spying on *you*, so that *you* trust *them* and not me. That's how it always works out in the movies. You'd know that if you were normal," he finished the boot and stood up, ending with a friendly whack on the shoulder, "and not a freak."

"I almost liked you for a minute."

"Okay, now smile" he coached. "And look excited about riding on these awesome assault vehicles."

They turned up the path to the docks. "What do they want to know about me?"

"They think you're hiding something."

"They already know I went to see you last week."

"Really?"

"I couldn't get in," she explained. "Are you really in cellblock 24C?"

"Yes, but they promised to move me to your part of town as soon as I come up with a juicy bit of information."

"Ha. You really are screwed." She whacked him back, hard on the shoulder.

"What? I thought we were friends?"

She ignored him, but smiled.

"They're going to start giving us twenty-minute breaks, so I can meet you at Starbucks and bond."

That made her happy. "It'll be fun! I like mango slushies, but I usually drink alone or Megan sits there and makes notes. Can you come tomorrow?"

"Maybe. We can lose Megan and go for a walk—away from the cameras and microphones."

"What do you mean?" She frowned anxiously.

"You know. We're tracked everywhere. Probably even the forest has microphones."

"Cameras. I don't think there's sound equipment."

"See."

"But that's to watch the running trail. For safety." New awareness crept into her voice, despite the company line she repeated.

"Right."

She swallowed hard.

"Here, take my hand," he said.

"Why?"

"Just do it," he said again, "with a smile."

She did. Her hand felt soft and incredibly warm. She definitely generated a lot of heat for a girl. He squeezed and she looked up at him, as if confused by the experience and still judging whether or not she liked it. Finally, she smiled back. A rush of satisfaction filled him. With any luck, she wouldn't out him.

"This is what friends do," he explained. "But—."

They were nearly to the General who raised a brow at their linked fingers.

"But?"

"But usually, you know, when they like each other."

"I do like you. I pretty much told you already. You're not going to keep asking, are you?"

"No, I mean, *like* each other." He tried to add the nuance so she would understand the difference between just friendship and attraction.

"So…you *like* me?" she repeated.

"Hell no," he teased. "I'm just trying to educate you."

She pulled her hand away, pretending to be offended.

"Let's just ride," she said in front of the General. "We'll see who needs to be educated, newbie. That's if you make it through without vomiting. I forgot to tell you. They always try to make you vomit the first time out." Then, as if regretting taking the fun out of the day, she added, "But I'm sure you'll be fine. It's only the regular humans who usually get sick."

Seth's stomach flipped nervously as he looked at two of the sleek watercraft humming quietly on the water, drivers waiting to help them board. Hell. The testing never ended. "Don't worry, freak. Bond, James Bond, doesn't throw up."

She smiled broadly at him and nodded before locking her boots into the bottom of the body-length passenger section. She was strapped in next to Medina before a metal cage came down around her.

Seth got into the other vehicle. Yeah. She liked him. Most girls did. But getting her to trust him would be another story.

CHAPTER SIXTEEN

The next day, she sat at Starbucks waiting for Seth. She knew she couldn't trust him, even if she wanted. Her uncle had him spying on her.

She checked her watch. There hadn't been any guarantee he would come today. Likely, he had no control over not being there, so it didn't make sense being angry with him. But she was. She was angry at everyone.

Time was too precious to waste. She got up. Seth wasn't going to make it.

Her next class was Advanced Physics and the professor was usually late. She'd told Megan she would met her at the study room.

She walked the other way instead.

Toward the main gate.

It wasn't that far, but at least a ten-minute drive. Behind the hospital was a row of vehicles and golf carts for use on the base. The keys were typically kept inside. She'd been allowed to drive them before. People were supposed to check them out, though.

She debated asking permission. It would be denied, since she had to go to class, so what was the point in asking?

Without thinking any further, she hopped into the front of a green Jeep and headed for the main entrance. Heart pounding, she stopped at the exit side of the main gate.

"License and security badge," the guard said.

She didn't think they'd check people leaving. She tapped her thin security bracelet to the reader. Jocelyn waited while the guard stood in front of the computer waiting for approval.

"One moment, miss." He picked up the phone and dialed a number, closing the window while he spoke.

Jocelyn looked at the gate. There was a wooden arm that went up and down, along with an automated metal wall that created an impossible barrier if not flattened to the ground. She'd watched it flatten when the car before her left.

The military guard stepped out of his door and came closer to the window. "I'm sorry, Miss Cashus. You're not authorized to leave."

"But I'm just going for a drive."

"Do you have a license?"

"No."

He lifted his hands, helpless. "The laws of the state require you to have a license in order to drive on public roads. On the base, we don't worry about you. But if you were in an accident with a civilian, it would be an issue. I'm sorry."

"Oh. I didn't know that. Sorry. I guess I'll need to get my license." She smiled at him. "Where do I go for that?"

The soldier looked uncomfortable. "Uh, well, the nearest offices are in Charlottesville."

"I suppose I have to drive there to get my license to drive?"

"Yes, miss. Or, in this case, have someone drive you."

"Okay. Thank you." Jocelyn reversed, trying not to squeal the tires with irritation. She parked the car in the nearest lot by the gate. Well, that was a legitimate reason to stop her from leaving, based on what Seth had said. You needed a license to drive. No conspiracy there.

The guard dealt with the next car. Jocelyn got out of the car and began to walk out the entrance instead. She took the paved path, past the guard gate and down the entry road, moving slowly into a jog. She had gained speed and distance before the guard called out to her.

She pretended not to hear.

In minutes, she was at a second gate. She realized this must be the actual main entrance. There were a number of friendly-looking buildings on both sides, with parking on the public side of the secured gate and parking on the military side. There was a car at the gate getting ready to enter. Jocelyn switched to the other side of the road to time her jog with the opening of the gate. Unfortunately, the gate didn't open. As she got closer, another guard walked out in front of the guard shack and waved her down. She debated ignoring him.

The main gate didn't budge, and there was no walking path between sides. This area was clearly designed to prevent humans from entering.

And leaving.

The guard put his hand on his firearm, his other one waving at her.

Great. What now? Jocelyn slowed down.

"Hey there, Miss Cashus."

"Hello." Everyone seemed to know her. How annoying. "Is there a problem?"

"Not that I know of," he said.

"Okay. I'm jogging. Do you mind if I pass? Doing a new path today. I have my badge." She displayed it. "I'll just be gone forty minutes. Twenty out, twenty back."

"I'm sorry, Miss Cashus. You aren't authorized to..." he paused, rethinking his words,   "exit this gate."

"Why?"

"I don't know, miss. I'm just enforcing the rules."

"That's a really weird rule, don't you think?" She smiled.

"Probably for your own safety. Just mountains and wild animals out there."

"Really?" She almost laughed, but smiled at him instead, good manners winning out. "How do the natives survive, I wonder?"

He smiled.

"Sorry, didn't mean to cause you a problem. I didn't know my personal freedom was limited to the military base." She hoped he understood the dig. There were people and buildings on either side of them. She looked at the person in the car. Another soldier checking in for duty. No one she knew. Eyeing the buildings off to the side, she got an idea.

She put a hand on her lower belly and switched feet. "Is there a restroom nearby?"

He smiled. "That first building. Better hurry. They're sending a car for you. I'm told your physics professor is waiting."

"Oh, yeah. Physics." She glanced ahead. "Tell them I'll be right out. Thanks!" She took off for the building, afraid to look back for fear of appearing guilty. When she opened the door to the building, she caught a glimpse of him walking back inside the guard booth.

Inside the building, she read signs that said Human Resources and Employee Relations. She'd never been in this building. A few people looked up from their work as she walked by, and she smiled or nodded at them. They did the same.

The offices were run by men and women in uniform, and some in civilian clothing. They chatted on the phone. A couple women hovered around a coffee station talking quietly about their plans for Spring Break. The difference here, unlike at the hospital, was their individual spaces were decorated with things. She stared, a little in awe at the pictures of family, exotic places around the world, funny little trinkets. She was tempted to take something to examine it. In the hospital and labs, she rarely saw any pictures or personal items. It was against the rules.

Jocelyn followed the signage to the ladies room. It was more of a locker room. She felt like pounding the wall in frustration. Was she really trapped? Or was this about school and not having a license? She leaned her head against a cool metal locker. Maybe she really was being childish.

But her brother and sister were *alive*.

That, she believed. Evil Wicker wouldn't have said that to Sergei if it weren't true. And she would never reach them or find them if she didn't get off this freaking base. She pounded a fist on the door of the locker, and it echoed in the room, the door opening partially. Alert, she checked the other lockers that didn't have pad locks to see if there was anything useful inside. Just when she was about to give up, she found an unlocked door with a green, short-sleeved olive Army shirt and camouflage cap. Mindless of the consequences, she put them on.

A women entered the space and used the toilet. She exited the locker room and turned right down the hall, walking with authority in the direction of the civilian entrance. The doors in this building, she discovered with a thrill, were meant to keep people out of the base, but not designed to keep you in.

This was outstanding!

Determining the entrance, she walked down an aisle with cubicles on the left and offices on the right. People went about their business. Her heart skipped a beat when an officer walked toward her in the hall. Energy flit across her skin.

A light flickered above them in the hall. They both glanced up.

Jocelyn took a slow, deep breath, willing her heart to slow down and willing the light to behave normally.

It did.

The officer nodded, satisfied, as if he had commanded the light to behave, and carried on.

Jocelyn swallowed and spun on her toe, pushing through the next door. She entered a small waiting room and realized, with shock, that the next door led outside. A severe-looking black man in a nice blue suit and yellow tie lifted his head from a magazine. She smiled at him. An academic, for sure.

"Good afternoon, sir."

"Ma'am."

Curious about what he was reading, she checked out the other magazines on the table. She'd never been allowed to read magazines. The injustice of that rule made her furious.

And curious.

She picked up one casually and kept walking. It said *People.* How bad could it be? There were pictures of lots of attractive people on the cover, but the biggest image was a pretty woman with a shiny metallic blouse and long, dangly earrings. Is that how people dressed on the outside?

She reached the final door, fighting to keep the smile off her face, anticipation bubbling up nearly uncontrollably as she turned the knob and pushed.

For a moment, her uncle's warnings hit her. Would her next breath kill her? Possibly send her into fits of choking?

Filled with fear, uncertainty, and defiance, she took a step forward and breathed deeply. If she died, make it a fast death.

She exhaled, still standing.

It was the second breath that convinced her the air on this side really was different.

It was free.

She laughed out loud, her skin absorbing the feel of the soft breeze. There was a hint of car exhaust and fresh rubber from a new vehicle. The large trash can was a cornucopia of strange scents—food and cigarettes and sugar. She wrinkled her nose. If this was pollution, she loved it.

Then caught herself. She needed to get out to the road as fast as possible. She didn't know where she was going. She just wanted to go. To see something new. To see if they would let her. Maybe she could find a town and someone who would help her find Morgan and Ben. She could learn the truth. Then she would have to go back. She needed her six o'clock meds, after all. There was only so much freedom she'd be allowed in one day.

Just as she relished her moment in the sun, a car approached. Even through the tinted windshield, she recognized Dr. Wicker. Gulping with horror, she dropped to her feet in front of the building. Realizing it looked weird, she fiddled with her shoelaces. She untied her right shoe and pretended to pull at the laces. Wicker's car stopped four feet away, trapping her between the door and the parking lot. She pulled her borrowed cap lower and slowly made a bow with her laces before switching feet, this time turning toward the curb as another woman exited the building. She heard Wicker say hi, and watched in the reflection of the glass door as the woman hopped into the SUV and they took off.

Jocelyn thought she might faint for the first time in her memory. She waited as long as possible before crossing to the row of cars nearest the road. She started to casually look inside a few vehicles to see if there were keys in the ignition, but it looked like people didn't do that on this side of the fence. That meant she was on foot. As another person left the building, she turned her back and ducked again, this time behind a black sedan.

Yikes. There seemed to be a lot of people coming and going.

She was going to get caught.

The stupidity of her actions began to sink in. Her uncle would kill her. Or at least punish her until she wished she were dead. She sunk into an even tighter ball, nearly under the sedan, her hands on her head wishing she could disappear.

The sound of tires crunching on gravel made her look up. A car turned down the aisle, coming right toward her. She couldn't get a break.

Jocelyn shivered despite the heat. This was it—capture and humiliation.

The car stopped next to her, and the sound of an electric window whirred open. Jocelyn put a hand over her face hoping it was no one she knew, dreading the inevitable. If only she'd been free a little longer, it would have been worth it.

"Hey," a female voice called. "Are you okay?"

No point in lying at this point. Turning her body slightly toward the voice, she shook her head negatively. The woman was silent.

"You're not trying to escape or anything are you?"

Caught.

Jocelyn looked at the woman. She didn't look very old. Maybe not much older than her. She had a bright red and white shirt, lots of cool shoulder-length braids, and brown-gold skin. As Jocelyn tried to decide what to do, the dark eyes became more worried. She had never seen the girl on the base before, but she might be a new recruit. Ultimately, Jocelyn decided trusting no one was really hard if you wanted to escape.

She slowly stood to her full height, twisting the rolled magazine with frustration and defiance. "I just wanted to see what was outside."

The girl stared at her silently a long moment before offering the magical words. "Need a ride?"

CHAPTER SEVENTEEN

Georgie's hands were clammy on the steering wheel. She'd seen the girl leave the office where her dad waited. They said it would be an hour-and-a-half, so she'd opted to study in the car while waiting. At least that's what she told them. Military people gave her the creeps. She didn't like the way they looked at her, all suspicious. Granted, she was equally suspicious, but driving past the curve where Brittany's Aunt Nancy died had raised goose bumps on her arms. She owed it to Brittany to at least check out people in the parking lot, right? Not that the visitors got much action.

Until *she* walked out.

Definitely suspicious, the way she covertly glanced about. And the laugh—not natural. Georgie did what any self-respecting seeker of knowledge would do.

She pulled the car around to check her out.

When she asked, "Need a ride?" she knew it went against everything her parents had drilled into her. She also knew there was something desperate, yet hopeful, in the other girl that she couldn't ignore. She'd been taught her entire life not to ignore, but to question. This, perhaps, was not how her father wanted her to question, but she had a feeling, somewhere in her family's honored history, her ancestors had seen this exact behavior—desperate, yet hopeful.

Vivid blue eyes widened, along with a tentative smile. "Yes, please. That would be outstanding." She ran and hopped into the passenger side holding a rolled up *People* magazine. "Thank you." She looked behind them as they drove out of the lot, bending over her shoes in her seat while they turned past the guard gate and the large, cheerful sign that said Camp Holliwell. The triangle icon with the logo—Science, Technology, Service—faded in the distance before she spoke to the girl.

She was still bent over her shoes.

"I think you can get up now."

Slowly, the girl sat up into the seat, picking up her magazine.

"Fasten your seatbelt," Georgie said.

Her passenger obeyed, quietly staring at Georgie. After another minute of silent staring, Georgie couldn't take it. "Stop staring. You're creeping me out. You have seen a black person before, haven't you?"

"What?"

"Nothing."

"My math tutor is African-American, and the biochemist, and many of the guards, and the food service lady, and my old nurse. There are lots of people from all over the world on the base. But I haven't met anyone from Qatar, or New Zealand, or Bhutan, or, well...from a lot of places."

Georgie glanced over at her briefly, then back at the road. "Uh-huh." She'd picked up a loony. "Where do you need to go?"

"Charlottesville, please. Can you take me there?" She glanced behind them.

Georgie looked into the rearview mirror. No one followed. They drove parallel to the base, and the girl continued to glance out nervously.

"I can take you to the rest stop twenty miles up the road. That's the nearest spot. I have to turn back after that and pick up my dad."

"Okay." The girl stared at her again. "Do you work on the base?"

Georgie laughed. She pointed to the nametag on her uniform.

"What's RCC?"

"The movie theater. Royal Crown Cinemas."

"You work in a movie theater?" the girl perked up, excited. "That must be so fun."

"Uh-huh."

"Is Georgie your name?"

"Uh-huh."

"It's a nice name. I really like your hair, too."

Georgie couldn't help smiling. "Thank you."

"I grabbed this magazine on the way out. Have you ever seen it before?"

"*People?*"

"Yes." She flipped through it. "It's all about different people. I've never heard of any of them before, but it looks interesting."

"That's Angelina Jolie on the cover."

"You know her?"

"Um..."

"Do you know these other people?" She opened to another page of celebrities.

"Uh, yeah. I mean, not personally. I know who they are."

"Oh."

Silence.

"Have you ever been to a Starbucks before?"

"Okay, now you're freaking me out."

"Sorry. I'm sorry. I just...."

"You don't get out often."

She nodded. "Exactly."

"Yeah." Brittany was totally not going to believe this. "So why are you trying to leave?"

The girl looked at her, then away, her response utterly dismal. "I know I have to go back. I just wanted to see if I was really allergic to the air outside the base." She opened the window and breathed deeply. "I feel fine." She laid her head on the window frame and closed her eyes, a light smile on her face.

Georgie let her have a moment. She probably needed it. But Georgie needed answers. Her dad wanted to work at Holliwell. What was he thinking?

"What's your name?"

"Oh, sorry. I'm Jocelyn. Jocelyn Albrecht. But everyone on the base calls me Sunnie, as in Sunday Cashus. Cashus for my uncle, who I realized recently is really not my uncle and might be hiding a lot of other things from me."

"Like?"

"Like my brother and sister are alive, and no one told me. Like I'm going to die, but not from cancer."

"Ohmigosh."

"Uh-huh," she mimicked Georgie's own response and breathed in another gulp of air out the window. "Like maybe I'm *not* allergic to the air."

"I don't think you are."

"Uh-huh!" She said it again in agreement.

"My dad wants to work at the base. Is it safe?" Thoughts of secret military experiments started setting off Georgie's freak-o-meter. "I thought there was crazy stuff going on there. I mean, I heard about stuff, but you know, you never know what's real, and it was so far-out, that really it was pretty crazy. But then Brittany's aunt died, and my cousin Al said stay away from Holliwell cause they're, like, trying to make super soldiers who will kill you, and now my dad is interviewing there. And you're like proof that it's a—a crazy place!" She looked over at the girl. "I mean, I don't know if you're crazy or anything. I didn't mean it that way." She just needed answers. "Do you know Nancy Watson? She was my friend's aunt. She worked at Holliwell."

Jocelyn tilted her head. "I knew a Nancy. One of my nurses was named Nancy. She took my daily measurements and was really nice. But none of the techs and nurses use last names, and no one is really allowed to talk about what they do. She was just Nancy."

"What did she look like?"

"Pretty. African-American with green eyes. Super short hair."

"Ohmigosh." Georgie's throat constricted painfully.

"You know her?" Jocelyn turned in her seat. "We know the same Nancy? Do you know where she transferred to? She didn't say goodbye. Actually, it kinda hurt my feelings," Jocelyn admitted before looking away.

Georgie nearly slammed on the breaks. Okay, this was too scary.

She pulled over into a turnout designed to allow traffic to pass, put the car in park, and pivoted in her seat, grabbing the girl's arm. Her skin shocked her with its warmth, and Georgie released her instantly.

With the crazy blue eyes staring at her, confused and expectant, she explained. "Nancy didn't transfer."

"What?" Jocelyn frowned.

Before Georgie could tell her the truth, loud sirens went off on the base, starting from the main gate and spreading out across the miles. The fence by the side of the road that separated them from the base had spinning lights on top of the posts that also began to flash and emit a blaring alarm.

Jocelyn mouthed a resigned, "Uh-oh."

Georgie couldn't hear a thing. She put the windows up, but it did a poor job of blocking out the sound.

"Jocelyn, listen to me. Look, I know you don't know me, but my friend's aunt was Nancy Watson. She used to work at Camp Holliwell. She died in car crash just over two weeks ago."

Jocelyn's face went white.

Then something really weird happened—stuff right out of paranormal horror films—everything in the car began to rattle. Items lifted off the dashboard in a frenzy of motion. The magnet that held her purse closed popped open, and small items began to float out.

Georgie stared, fear making the hair on her arms stand up.

Then it stopped, and everything fell to the floor.

Jocelyn breathed deeply. Like it hurt. Her eyes were watery…but not with regular tears.

Blue tears.

Just as suddenly, the sirens went off. It was silent in the car. Georgie was about to speak, but Jocelyn lifted her hand for silence, listening for something Georgie couldn't hear.

"They're coming for me. The helicopters will be here first, then a truck and Jeeps. You need to leave. Go to the place you were going to take me, and stay as long as you can before going back for your dad."

"Are you going to be okay? What will they do to you?"

"Don't worry about me. Just don't tell them we met or talked. I'm afraid for you. Please." She jumped out of the car, then quickly leaned back in, her blue nails distracting Georgie for a split second. My family is Morgan and Ben Albrecht. If I can't find them, maybe you can? Make sure they're safe?"

"I—I'll try."

"I don't know who to trust."

"You can trust me. We never met. But I work Thursday through Sunday at the RCC in Charlottesville. Everyone knows me there. If you need me…." *Right*, what could she do?

"Thank you, Georgie of the RCC," Jocelyn said. "I've never met anyone like you."

"Girlfriend, it's like you've never met anyone. But I won't hold it against you."

Jocelyn smiled widely. "Thanks." She looked at the sky as if counting the seconds. "The 'copters are about a minute out. You need to go."

Georgie didn't hear anything.

"Go!" she insisted, stepping away. "And don't stop!"

Jocelyn spun and took off the way they came. Georgie watched her disappear in the rearview mirror, partly in disbelief.

The girl was fast!

Shaking, she put the loose items back in her purse and tossed it on the floor before pulling onto the road.

"That did not just happen." She shook her head. "I don't know what just happened, but that did not just happen."

The loud vibration of a helicopter overhead nearly made her drive off the road again. Coincidence. Right? She'd get a coffee at the rest stop and something to eat. Yeah, that would make her feel better. If only that helicopter would go away. Trying not to panic, she kept driving. She got about half a mile when three army trucks came scrambling out a side gate entrance and zoomed up the road at her. She pulled over so they could pass.

They didn't pass.

She stared at the three trucks blocking the road and a lineup of green-uniformed men holding scary looking guns.

The hovering helicopter, as if seeing the men had her, took off. Surely that was not the case, though. She wasn't a threat.

She glanced toward her purse, thinking to call her dad, or at least record this with her phone. That's when she saw the *People* magazine with the address label for Camp Holliwell. Panicked, she grabbed her purse and put it over the magazine. When she looked up again, her heart stopped. The car was surrounded at gunpoint. She had to give the military credit— fast and efficient.

Trembling, Georgie clenched the wheel at ten o'clock and two o'clock. That's what you did when you got pulled over. She took a quick look at the crazy-eyed commandos.

But what did you do when this happened?

CHAPTER EIGHTEEN

Jocelyn ran back down the highway toward the base. She spotted two helicopters coming toward her and more trucks behind. Wow, really? This couldn't all be for her. One of the helicopters stayed overhead, while the second kept going. She had a bad feeling she'd just gotten Georgie of the RCC in a lot of trouble. She slowed to a walk, watching the military action unfold as she continued to the main entrance.

A voice from the open helicopter above called down with a megaphone. "Miss Cashus, please stay where you are."

Jocelyn stopped. She looked up to the men in the helicopter and waved.

"A truck will be here in a moment to transport you."

"I'm going there!" She pointed to herself, then the entrance, to indicate she could get there on her own and continued walking.

"Miss Cashus, please hold your position."

Jocelyn repeated the motion that she was returning.

"Please hold your position."

The more they said it, the more irritated she became. She lifted her hands up, open palmed. "Really?"

A car came from behind. She saw a soldier driving Georgie's blue car, while Georgie sat in the passenger seat gripping her purse. The car stopped at a safe distance. A big truck following it from behind stopped as well, both waiting for the action to be resolved.

"Is this necessary?" she yelled.

"Miss Cashus, please hold your position, or we will be forced to take action."

Jocelyn's mouth dropped. "You're going to shoot me?" She shouted loudly but doubted they could hear over the roar of the helicopter. Angry, she shook her head in disgust and began the walk back to the base again.

"Miss Cashus, please hold your position!"

She wished she knew some quality curses, but no doubt, it would get back to her uncle. She didn't think they would seriously shoot her, but when her super hearing caught a soldier asking if he should take the shot, she stopped, turned, and looked straight at him. His eyes met hers for a moment, and he wavered before retraining the gun at her. She shook her head again, this time making eye contact with him and the guy with the megaphone.

They didn't move. They really had lost their minds.

She turned her back on them and focused on the main gate, even more furious and unjustly harassed. That's when she heard the order.

"Take the shot."

Despite her disbelief, pure survival instinct made Jocelyn react. She pivoted and thrust her hands out protectively performing a deflecting tai chi maneuver. The fact that her brain worked faster than a physical object was all that saved her. Energy shot from her body and hands, radiating a field around her as she spun and seemingly guided the tranquilizer dart past her. It was nothing she knew for sure that she could do—until now. What she didn't know would happen is that the same energy would be strong enough to disrupt the helicopter. The sounds of panic reached her, and another shot was fired. She moved like lightning to avoid it, realizing too late that she had made herself a threat to them.

The helicopter finally balanced itself. Another cry got her attention, this time from Georgie. The men guarding her raised their weapons. She saw the driver shove Georgie's head down on the seat.

Moving her hands to a surrender pose, she stood there and waited.

No one moved.

She looked up at the helicopter into the eyes of the soldier. He took the shot.

The force of the tranquilizer surprised her. *Outstanding.* Isn't that how they took down animals? She yanked the needle out of her shoulder as a second one hit her thigh. Wow. She was going to be out for a while. Her vision blurred as knees hit the ground, and several soldiers surrounded her.

"Why are you doing this?" No one spoke to her. She felt really funny. She even smiled at them. "Does thiz mean I'm a prizonrrrr?"

She couldn't hear a response. Only silence and the whir of the helicopter receding with her consciousness.

One last thought remained.

Her uncle really *was* going to kill her.

Georgie heard her father before she saw him. "What do you mean you *have my daughter?*"

The door opened and Georgie rushed him, her arms squeezing around him tight. "Dad!"

Surprised, he pulled her close, then released her to get a look at her. "Are you okay? What happened?"

"I don't know." She already had a story figured out. She hadn't spoken since they took her, but now, with an escort and some military guy who seemed important standing with them listening, she played up the one thing the soldier had told her to calm her in the car. "They were having a military exercise, and I accidentally got in the way. I was headed back to the rest stop for a slushie and bam! Helicopters and trucks and green army men everywhere!"

Said out loud, it actually sounded funnier that it was.

"What?"

"Yeah. It was a little overwhelming, but apparently it's the norm around here. I just really wanted a cherry slushie." She wanted them to think she was an oblivious teenager. She put an arm around her dad's waist and leaned into him. Until she knew if there really was a Ben and Morgan Albrecht, the dumber she appeared the better.

Her father looked grim. "And what was today's exercise?"

The older officer stepped in. "Today, we simulated a capture of a civilian with mental illness. It's actually one of the better tests for a soldier in terms of learning how to deal with unstable characters."

Her father nodded, appeased.

"It was kinda cool, after I got over the freak out," Georgie confessed, thinking she'd totally gotten by.

The elder officer eyed her. "Did you see our target when you drove by?"

Georgie felt skin prickles behind her neck. The officer kept his unblinking eyes trained on her unnaturally. She wondered if there were cameras along the road. There must be. Her cousin Al said the Delta Force team knew you were coming when you were still miles away. It only made sense that they would watch the perimeter. Lying was not an option.

"Actually, I picked the woman up."

"You what?" her dad said, this time sounding furious.

"It's not like she was a hitchhiker, Dad. I saw she had a uniform on, so I knew she was from the base."

The boss man agreed. "That particular plant is exceptional. She always spins a good story."

"She does?" The question was out before Georgie could stop it. Was the girl a fake?

"Yes. What did she use today?" he asked.

Georgie swallowed, her heart beginning to pound faster. Was he trying to get information out of her? "I guess I missed out. She didn't talk at all, just looked at me, mostly."

He stood still. They all did. No way was she going to have a staring contest with him, either. She turned to her dad. "It was actually cool, Dad. Makes me feel better, knowing our military thinks of these things. I'm sorry if I messed anything up for you." She took his hand and squeezed hard. She'd lied well, and she only hoped her dad didn't screw this up. Though, she really *was* sorry about messing up his interview.

"I think we're done here." The boss man gave in. "Sergeant Lee does a full write-up of all our exercises for study and improvement, as well as to grade the team involved, so I'll leave him to get your report and let you be on your way. Mr.

Washington, can I interest you in a cup of coffee while they do that?"

Her dad looked uncertain about leaving her alone, and rightly so, but she shrugged to show him that it was okay.

Afterward, she'd wished he'd stayed. Another officer came and joined them while she gave her "report," which included everything she could remember about the subject. She was consistently vague about all of it, and told them the subject was a dark-haired, Hispanic woman, about twenty-five with gray eyes, or green eyes, or green-blue. "Sorry," she finally said. "I wasn't really paying attention 'cause the road is pretty curvy in spots, and I'm still a new driver, and my dad would kill me if I even dented the car—no matter *how* old it is."

They smiled and wrapped up. Apparently, things "checked out."

The drive from Holliwell felt like an eternity of winding roads, trees, and mountains. The views were gorgeous in spring, but she couldn't enjoy it.

She sat silently, pretending to read her history chapter. Her dad shot her a confused hairy eyeball, but she didn't engage. They'd taken the car from her. For all she knew, there could be an audio or GPS tracking bug on it now. Okay, maybe that was extreme, but so was shoving her face into the gear stick.

She couldn't wait to get to online and do the research to find out the truth. She only hoped Jocelyn wasn't in real trouble. She seemed young for her age, and younger than Georgie, for sure. Georgie sorted through the impressions from those short moments—innocence, excitement, hope, fear. It hadn't seemed faked. But maybe it was just a military exercise, like they'd said. That made more sense than a plot to keep a girl prisoner at a maximum security military base.

Right?

Only, that girl knew Brittany's dead Aunt Nancy, could hear vehicles well before they arrived, and when she wept—Georgie shivered at what it might mean—her tears were blue.

CHAPTER NINETEEN

Jocelyn heard voices the first time she roused. She tried to lift her hands, only to find them clamped down. Her eyes felt so heavy they were impossible to open. She had to rely on sound. The sound of her uncle's faraway voice did nothing to reassure her.

"Up the dosage. I want to keep her sedated."

"Yes, sir."

Jocelyn felt someone come near her. She tried to move her feet, but they were heavy and numb.

"For how long, Laurence?" a female voice asked.

Yes, for how long?

"Until we have a plan."

She slept again. Or whatever they call it when they drug you against your will. When she next woke, she was in bed. Her bed in the condo.

"Hey, sleepyhead."

Jocelyn used all her strength to turn to the voice. It was Liz.

"Some adventure you had. Your poor uncle has been worried out of his mind." She stood from her watchful position and leaned over, brushing hair off Jocelyn's forehead—as if to comfort her. Jocelyn didn't feel comforted.

"I'll go get him. He's been by your side all night, but I finally convinced him to take a nap."

"Okay." Jocelyn closed her eyes again. *That was a lie, right?* They were acting all concerned. After sending the military to arrest and shoot her down, they acted concerned?

She pulled the sheet up and curled into a ball. She really did feel tired. Then, the flashes of memory came back. The girl—

Georgie of the RCC. Did they get her? Did she say anything? And Nancy.

Jocelyn's skin came alive with a fizz of electricity. She sat up with a jolt. Nancy was dead. Was it an accident? What about all the other people she'd been told had transferred over the years? Had they been transferred, or retired, or something far worse? She rubbed her eyes fiercely, scared and angry and confused. Did Nancy die because of her? She couldn't find out without giving away Georgie. Her head spun with more unanswered questions, and more things that didn't add up.

Footsteps alerted her that Uncle Laurence was near. She opened her eyes. Uncle Laurence knelt in front of her and took her hand in his. "You're awake. What a relief. I'll order food. Are you hungry?"

Jocelyn thought a minute. "Starving."

He smiled. "Give me ten minutes. Why don't you take a shower? I'll invite Liz to join us."

He left the room, leaving Jocelyn staring at the door. *Okay. This is weird. He was being nice when she knew punishment awaited.*

Even more weird was trying to make her muscles move. She wobbled and swayed until she dragged herself into the shower. Ten minutes later, she gorged on chicken. Even the vegetables tasted good. She really *was* starving. That must be why she was so weak. *That and being harpooned by tranquilizers.*

She finished it all off with a cold glass of milk and waited for the explosion.

It didn't come.

They just kept smiling.

She'd have to wait them out. She smiled. More smiles back.

When they didn't respond, she gave in.

"Apparently, I need a driver's license to take a car on public roads. Can I get one? I'd like to visit one of the nearby towns." She took a very deliberate sip of milk and waited.

Her uncle's hand hit the table before he got control of himself.

Ha! Not the response he expected. If he thought she'd apologize, he was in for a long wait.

"Sunnie," Liz started.

"Yes?"

"I think we need to talk about what happened yesterday."

"Yesterday?" Holy moly! She'd been out for over a day.

"Yes."

"Okay. What do you want to talk about?"

The adults stared at her.

She laughed inside. Somewhere she'd gotten a bad attitude, and her uncle was about to go ballistic. Maybe he should rethink drugging her.

"Sunday," her uncle began. "The military on the base is for the protection of the country, not to save you."

"I agree. I don't need them to save me. In fact, I was walking back to the base of my own free will before they went all commando on me."

Liz released a small grin to Uncle Laurence. "It was pretty over the top."

"They were saving you from yourself."

Jocelyn didn't say anything, but let her disbelief show.

"You know your condition is sensitive."

She held back the scream of frustration. She'd already accepted—or at least blocked out—that she had only a handful of years left, so threatening her with death was not going to be very effective.

When she didn't answer, he insisted, "You do understand that, don't you?"

She shrugged. "Everyone dies sometime."

He tensed.

Liz intervened. "Sweetie, young people always think they're invincible. You're not. We've created a very safe atmosphere for you here."

"And I don't like that insolent attitude after all you've been given and all I've done for you."

Only her newly-learned self-control and distrust of adults helped her keep it together. That, and she didn't want another animal tranquilizer.

"Sorry, Uncle Laurence. I didn't mean it disrespectfully."

He relaxed a bit in his seat.

"But give me a little credit. The air isn't going to kill me faster than anything else."

"Perhaps not, but can you blame me for wanting to keep you around as long as possible? Any number of changes could affect your condition. That's why we monitor you so much. I know it's not fun, but I'm doing my best to keep you alive."

Jocelyn felt guilty. But she knew it was all a lie. Why, knowing the truth, did she feel guilty? How screwed up was that? Was Uncle Laurence sincere or psycho? He was the only one she had. If he was psycho and knew her family was alive, what *did* she have left?

She sighed, giving in. "Sorry. So what's my punishment? Three days in isolation with no food?"

Liz blinked surprised.

What? Like she didn't know that's what they did around here?

This time Uncle Laurence smiled for real. "You're not a child anymore. You'll need to apologize to the base commander, and General Martin didn't appreciate his training schedule being disrupted, but as long as you're healthy, it's okay."

No way. Huh. *Maybe she was wrong.*

"Oh, there is one other thing...."

Of course there is.

Her uncle spoke like it was an afterthought. "The team that brought you home said you deflected the first tranquilizers."

Jocelyn frowned, trying to remember. Yes, that statement was true. She'd surprised even herself with the power she'd emitted. It had scared her...especially when she realized she'd put others in danger. Maybe that had been the wind moving the helicopter and not her?

"I remember hearing them get ready to shoot and turned and moved quickly." She motioned with a couple tai chi deflection maneuvers to demonstrate.

"Oh," he said. "One of the soldiers thought there was a flash of something. Another said it made the helicopter nearly crash."

Great. No way was she going to let her uncle know she'd been practicing on her own. Especially now. It would mean a whole new series of tests. She had enough measurements taken daily, and they were nothing, if not thorough. That's the only reason she didn't tell the truth. That, and the instinct she'd had for a while—that she might need to use those powers someday to get out of here.

"Did the video cameras pick it up? Maybe if I saw it, I could tell you what I was thinking when it happened."

"No, we only have the description from eyewitnesses."

Good! "Oh. Sorry. I don't remember much else. It was noisy and traumatizing having all those guns pointed at me just because I went for a walk. Do you need a walking license as well as a driver's license?" It hadn't occurred to her, but there did seem to be a lot of rules.

"Of course not," Liz said.

"But there should be!" Uncle Laurence said.

It took Jocelyn a minute to realize he'd made a joke.

"Cool. Then can I get a driver's license so I can go on public roads?"

"Sunday!" her uncle said, exasperated.

"You said as long as I understand the risks it was okay. I understand the risks. I could die. I get it."

"Well, I'm not ready to let you die."

"So I'm stuck here in…Boresville? 'Til I do die?" This time her anger came out. She stood up, ready to leave the table.

"Sit down!" Uncle Laurence yelled. Now he was angry.

"No." She stalked to her room.

"You get back here. *Now!*"

She stopped at his tone and turned, waiting to see if he would offer an explanation or information. Anything to discredit what she was coming to believe.

He held out his hand palm down.

She looked at it, silent, her stomach suddenly queasy. He waited. She took a step backward, defying the forced affection.

"Sunday!" He breathed hard and said more patiently, "No matter if we disagree, we still love each other. We are still family."

Her uncle had a point—again. Jocelyn saw Liz watching them, curious. Slowly, Sunnie made herself go back to her uncle. She hated herself for it. She wanted to hit him. But she'd never been disrespectful in her life. So she did what she had to do. She walked back the interminable distance of the room, watching his self-satisfied smile twist with triumph. *That wasn't love was it? That was...smug.* The face that had ushered her through childhood seemed unrecognizable. Looking back, it hadn't been much of a relationship or much of a childhood...but it had been all she had, and all she thought she could hope for.

She took his hand and did the programmed action. She bent over and kissed it, letting it go as quickly as possible, struggling to form the words over the acid taste in her mouth. "I love you, Uncle Laurence."

It was the first time she'd done the act against her will. But she was also afraid of what would happen if she didn't do it. He always got the last word. He'd never let disobedience go unpunished.

"I love you, too."

Really? This was love? Torture, lies, domination, oppression? She hated love. She hated the word. She hated him. And she hated him for making her say and do things she didn't feel.

She didn't want anything to do with love. And she wasn't ever going to use the word again.

"Let me know when I can get my license. Goodnight, Liz." She slammed the door of her room and didn't open it the required amount. She wished she had a lock. From the other side she heard silence, then Liz's voice.

"Well. *That* went well."

Jocelyn bit her lip to keep from shouting back at them and the world, "*That* is just the beginning."

⸻

Laurence loaded a new magazine and cocked his gun with force before firing. Being patient with a bratty teen turned out to be a lot harder than he'd planned. He unloaded the weapon in the safety of the firing range, his marksmanship still perfect.

Truthfully, he never thought she'd turn on him. She'd always been perfectly well- behaved and adoring. She loved him! Plus, with all his psychological behavior training, she didn't have a choice.

He loaded another magazine. Maybe it was hormonal. According to Liz and the others, all teens turned on their parents or primary caregiver, usually before now. Maybe that's why he'd thought he was immune. He'd believed he would control her forever.

Laurence aimed at the shoulder of his target, careful to avoid the subclavian artery. There was no good place to be shot. The feedback machine at his station indicated survival time before bleeding out. He reset the target and continued. The only upside was that now Sunday was also angry at the military.

He needed the White House and the military to believe in him. That meant General Martin was his best ally, despite what Laurence wanted.

He also needed Sunday to trust him enough to share her new power, for there was no doubt in anyone's mind now that she was more powerful than they realized. If he could harness that, he'd be set for life.

He aimed again, careful to avoid the brachial plexus this time. Only Sunday didn't seem to trust him right now. He needed to find out why and fix that before it was too late.

Unfortunately, time was something he didn't have a lot of. He would need to adjust his methods. He released the remaining bullets.

Fortunately, he had plenty of methods yet to try.

CHAPTER TWENTY

Georgie's cousin Alastair was annoyed. Or worried. She couldn't tell exactly, but at the mention of Holliwell, he'd gotten even more upset. And he could do a hairy eyeball that would make her dad proud.

He stared at her like she'd lost her mind. Maybe she had. But after doing a little Internet research at her local library, she'd come across enough evidence to think the impossible might really be possible. If that girl really was Jocelyn Albrecht, everyone thought she was dead. Proving she was alive and needed their help would take an army—a different kind than the one hiding her at Holliwell.

"Geez, Georgie. Who'd 'ya think you are? Some black Nancy Drew?" He scowled more fiercely. "Your dad isn't serious, is he? I told you that place is trouble."

"I know! That's why I need you to…." She nodded to the vehicle in question, parked a block away. "I'm serious, Alastair. Just in case. It would put my mind at ease."

He shook his head several more times—but she realized he was shaking it at himself because he walked away to make a phone call. He came back, looking none too happy. "Okay. Richie said he'd take a look, but not at his place. Follow me, keep your radio on, and don't talk until he says so. And…." He gave her the double-hairy eyeball. "Whatever you do—don't say anything that's going to spook him. He's already freaked out, even though I told him you were just being dramatic. Got it?"

"Got it."

"Good. I don't want two girls on my hands."

"Thanks, Al."

"Yeah." Grumpy, he got into his shiny white truck. "Keep up."

Two hours later, on the lowest floor of the underground parking lot of the mall, a wide-eyed Richie rolled out from under her dad's car, camera in hand. He'd been taking pictures.

Richie had been a close friend of Al's at Holliwell, and legend had it he was a local child prodigy that burned out young. He was wiry in every way and didn't have an ounce of fat—more from not eating regularly than exercise, she guessed. The top of his close-cropped head just reached Al's shoulders, but he was taller than Georgie.

His smile had been friendly when they arrived. Now he looked at them and began shaking his head. She didn't know if it was out of misery, worry, fear, or if he was just annoyed that she'd taken precious time on his Saturday for a false alarm.

Al hopped off the edge of his truck bed. "Finally." He lobbed his empty soda can in the trash. "Let's see what evil lurks."

Yep. She felt really stupid now.

Richie walked over to her, then kept walking to the far side of the garage. He waved his hand for her to follow. He pulled a device out of his pocket, turned it on, and told her to hold it. He showed her the pictures in his digital camera. "First, you got a leaky oil pan and chewed-up air filter. No way to treat a little baby like this, and easy to fix."

"Sorry." Her response sounded lame even to her. "I'll tell my dad."

He looked at her, clearly doubtful that she would. "Uh-huh." He flipped through to a close-up. "Second," he said very slowly. "You are in a boatload of it, and you better get paddling really fast, sister."

Alastair stiffened. Georgie felt her heart rate speed up.

"This here," he held out the digital display to show her, "is a GPS tracking device, and it's currently bolted to the bottom of your car. High end. Probably used by the Pentagon or other well-funded military outfits."

"Oh sh—," Al said.

"Yeah." Richie nodded. "But not your worst problem."

Not your worst problem. Georgie's mouth felt like cotton. Her chest hurt.

Richie continued. "Thus, that handy little device Georgie is holding."

Georgie was in danger of dropping said device and took a deep breath, clutching the vibrating cylinder.

Richie adjusted her fingers. "Hold it like this. Don't block the transmission." He flicked to the next image. "This. Inside your car. Top of the line. If you don't know what to look for, you ain't gonna find it. Thin as a hair." He enlarged the photo. "Remote listening device. It can hear conversations from fifty feet away, easy. Least with the car doors open."

Al cursed, his expression grim. Georgie's body shook. She tried to remember her conversation with her dad coming back from Holliwell. She'd been pretty quiet, but when he asked if she was okay, she'd commented how nice everyone had been, and that the military exercises were really cool. Her dad had given her a strange look. Did he know? He'd been strangely quiet.

She nodded to Richie that she understood. "Can you…can you take them out?" The lightheaded feeling wasn't going away. She needed to get those things off the car.

"Georgie." Al shook her. "Georgie! You're hyperventilating. Slow down."

Richie shook his head. "Not a good idea."

"Wh-wh-why?"

"They, whoever *they* are—and I don't want to know—will know you found them, which means they'll know you were looking for them, which means they know you got somethin' to hide that *they* need to know. And that, little sister, is a boatload of no good that I want *no* part of."

Alastair intervened. "What are our options?"

"Sell the car. She can keep the scrambler. It takes AAA batteries. The GPS device might not survive a flooding. Hope for a big rain, then trash the underbelly of the car. You're a teenager. No one expects you to drive well."

"Thanks." Her sarcasm was lost on Richie. He went to put his stuff back in his tow truck. Alastair wasn't looking too happy, either. He slammed the truck bed door and went to the driver's seat. She stopped him. "Do you believe me now?"

"It doesn't matter. It's still none of your business, Georgie. People got bigger problems, and this is one you have no chance of fixin'."

"But, Al." Georgie squeezed the audio scrambler in her palm until it hurt, making sure she wasn't blocking the area Richie pointed out to her. "That girl is a prisoner at Holliwell! She was trying to escape. I'm sure of it."

"Then you can be sure it won't ever happen again," Alastair said, making clear the girl's fate had already been sealed. "She might be dead already."

Georgie's stomach lurched.

Richie froze mid-step and turned to them.

"*What?*" He walked over to Georgie and made sure the scrambler was still on. "What?" He grabbed Al's t-shirt even though Al was a foot taller and at least two feet broader than him. "What the—*Holliwell?* Brother, are you kiddin' me?"

Al remained calm.

"You know how I feel about that place. You know. And you drag me into this? *You know!*" Richie nearly shouted.

Al didn't move. He just waited. Georgie watched as Richie seemed to crumble before her. His eyes filled and his hands wrapped around his stomach protectively as he began to rock back and forth on his heels, self-comforting. It was like watching a man disappear before her eyes. "I gave them everything. I gave them my best work. And you know what they did to me and the others. Did you forget Bonnie already? I loved her, too, Al. But they tortured us. They tortured all of us, and they took my mind with them." He continued to rock, occasionally shuddering and squeezing his eyes at painful memories, muttering on and off, "They took my mind."

Georgie watched silently, not sure what to do. *Who was Bonnie?* Her cousin had blanched at her name.

Al gently guided Richie to the foot rail of his truck. "Sit."

Richie obeyed, while Al took the jack off her car and put Richie's stuff back in the tow truck. He walked Richie to his vehicle and closed the door. "You okay to drive?"

Richie nodded. He clicked the ignition, then turned and waved a finger at her.

"You seem like a nice girl. Just leave the country now. Change your name. Maybe change your look. Get some plastic surgery."

"Richie." Al put a hand on his shoulder. "Stop. I'll make sure she's okay. You just get home, okay? We took precautions. Nothing will be tracked to you."

Richie nodded again, rocking in his seat a little more.

"And, Richie," Al squeezed his friend's arm resting on the open window. "Your best work still lies ahead. They didn't get that."

Richie swallowed and acknowledged the encouragement.

When he left, Al spun on his heel and walked to his own truck. Georgie still held the transmitter protectively in front of her.

"Who's Bonnie?"

"Shut up."

"Okay, sensitive subject."

He kept walking.

"Al, wait."

"What?"

"We have to help her. Call the police or FBI, or somebody. They can't do this."

"They said it was a training exercise. Who's gonna believe you? You'll just make it worse for the girl. In turn, they will demolish you, bankrupt Uncle Henry and Aunt Jannie with IRS investigations, maybe even do something that damages their reputation. And that's if they decide to let you live. You said yourself, your friend's aunt died in a car accident. You think they can't make a hundred different types of accidents? You think other people—good people—haven't already tried to stop what's happening at Holliwell? Good men and women, Georgie. All smart. All dead. Trust me on this. I don't want to die. Neither does Richie, and neither should you. You have a nice family. They can take that from you. Don't think they can't."

"But if we don't stand up to them. If nobody tries, it will just get worse."

He shook his head. "It's too late. It goes too high. Believe me." His face turned bleak, a shadow of sadness overcoming him a moment before his jaw hardened with resolve. "It's no use."

Georgie just stared. She really didn't know what to do. Had Al tried to help before? He seemed to know a lot about it. "Is that why you were discharged?" She left out the less than honorable part. He hadn't spoken to anyone in the family for months after he left the Army. "Did you try to help one of those men? Or someone else?"

From his silence, she knew she was right. Al had been trying to help, and instead, he'd been framed. That had to be it. He'd never been into drugs. She'd never believed the charges...even with the damning evidence.

He gripped the steering wheel of the truck and changed the subject. "Where'd you do that research?" he asked.

"The library. I'm not stupid."

"Good. Don't ever go back there, okay?"

"Now you're being the dramatic one."

He glared at her.

Okay, moving on.

"Try to get your dad to sell the car."

"Okay."

"And stay out of trouble."

"*Okay!*"

"Look, just act normal, and they'll get bored and realize you're not a threat."

Georgie nodded. Then she asked the thing that had been bugging her for the last two years. "Al." She waited for him to look at her. "Did you really sell those drugs?"

He stared at her unflinching for a long moment. "Yeah. I did."

Her heart sank.

"I told you I wasn't one of the heroes."

It hurt to hear him say that. "I never believed it."

"I know."

"Why?" She had to understand.

He stared at the empty parking garage for a long moment before answering. "Seemed like a good idea at the time."

With that, he revved the engine and left.

Georgie stood there a long time after, the radio still going in the car. When her heart finally beat at a normal pace, she thought about Jocelyn's brother and sister. If the girl's story was true, her siblings were either being protected or being held hostage by one of the most powerful families in America. A family that may or may not be any more trustworthy than the government. And they, no doubt, came with a legion of lawyers. *Lawyers versus soldiers.* Ugh. Considering her options, she had about as much chance of recruiting the Rochester family as she did breaking into Holliwell.

She turned off the device, tossed it in her purse, and buckled her seat belt. A little adversity hadn't stopped anyone else in her family. She wouldn't let it stop her.

CHAPTER TWENTY-ONE

Within a week after her little "excursion" on the highway, Jocelyn's world seemed back on a predictable schedule.

She was in EmWAV training, using the time to better understand her surroundings and the boundaries of Camp Holliwell. Her next mission would use the EmWAVs on a river passage, so they had practiced on different waterways in the area.

"What's down there?" She indicated a long, narrow waterway between lakes.

"That connects to the public lakes, and farther on, to commercial and residential property."

"It's shallow on radar. Can the EmWAV handle that kind of terrain?" She studied the map, estimating a twenty-mile course before they reached the public sector. In the EmWAV, that might only take minutes.

"Yes, ma'am, this beauty handles shallow water no problem. Only problem is the gates."

"Gates?"

"A series of gates and locks set up to keep the public out, should we have any adventurous sorts." He pressed a button and gave her the aerial view. "And of course, there's the dam. A long fall if you get caught up in the current and sucked through the turbines to the other side. But I don't think you'd survive the turbines."

"Oh." That looked dangerous. "That's good. I was wondering how we protect against thieves and such out here."

"We've plenty of surveillance. Don't worry."

She banked sharply. Bummer.

"We have a good open space ahead. Do you want to try a topspin? Maybe a one-eighty?"

"Yes!" She repositioned the nose.

"Just take it up twenty notches. The momentum will eventually stand us up. Break, slide, turn—just like in the simulator."

"Got it." Jocelyn felt excitement as they shot up out of the water until she was in standing position in the EmWAV. The sensation of sliding was so thrilling, she nearly forgot to control the landing, and they hit a little hard on the water after the vehicle spun on its tail.

"Sorry." She looked at her trainer. He winced and nodded. "Have you tried the eject button yet?"

"Don't even joke, kid. A little slower, please."

"Okay. One more time?" She waited for her speed and lift points to line up. The vehicle stood, spun, and seemed to stop at the same time—a sensation she knew was deceptive, since landscape whizzed by. It was an important calculation when driving the EmWAVs manually—you didn't spin in place, you kept moving. If done right, it was fun—they literally danced across the water. If done wrong—it was potentially deadly. She hit the brakes, landing fairly easy on the water. Suddenly, her controls froze.

"I'll take it from here, Sunday."

She looked at her co-pilot. "But that was pretty good, wasn't it?"

"Yeah. Pretty good." He grinned. "Trying to put me out of a job?"

Jocelyn laughed. The only thing she wanted was options. Knowledge meant options.

The hatch opened on shore, and she was happy to get out and stretch.

She still had her helmet in hand when a Southern drawl called out, "Trying to show off for me?"

Seth!

Jocelyn spun and ran up the dock. He'd been out of sight for a week. She nearly ran into his arms, she'd been so worried about him. Instead, she stopped short to study him. No telling what the Wicked Dominator had done. She examined him for any noticeable damage. His eyes were clear, though wincing from the bright sunlight. There were no visible marks on his face or arms. He had the usual green fatigues and t-shirt on. She reached up and snatched his beanie, causing him to touch his head protectively.

"Still no hair," he said, taking the beanie back. "Just seven days of the worst migraines you could ever imagine."

"I never imagine pain. It's a waste of time." She wanted to ask him more. Like what caused the migraines? Did they do something? Did Dr. Wicker conduct some new experiment?

But she couldn't. Not in front of General Martin and the others. She just smiled and backed away. "You missed our Starbucks appointment."

"Sorry."

"Did they tell you what I did?"

He frowned. "No."

"Good. It was totally humiliating." She laughed. "I'll tell you when we're not surrounded."

She thought they would be training together the rest of the day until she caught sight of Megan in the Jeep, waiting. "Seth, suit up. Sunday, you're with Dr. Cashus."

Megan pulled the Jeep over. "Hurry. They have a ton of tests scheduled."

That sounded ominous. "Tests? What kind?" Medical or intellectual, they were all miserable.

"Physical," she answered.

Maybe that would be okay. They would give her food, for sure. She was starving and thirsty. She'd never be a pilot. Focusing in cramped quarters wore her out. Then she laughed out loud at herself. She wasn't ever going to be anything, let alone a pilot. She'd likely be dead before she hit twenty-one. Megan looked at her curiously, and she smiled in response.

"What about Seth?"

"You guys will be training together for the rest of the week. Don't worry."

She waved to Seth reluctantly and took off. At least physical tests were the easiest.

Her uncle sounded ready to kill her. He'd slipped up, speaking when she was in hearing distance. "We need to up the stress."

She'd been in the room for hours, battling Ping-Pong balls. Her skin stung from taking multiple hits for so long. Not true pain, but annoying stinging that made her skin itchy. Her uncle wanted her to control them with her powers, not ward them off with tai chi. He said he was trying to help her advance to the next level. She thought there might be something else to it.

Two hours became three. Three became four.

Still, her uncle refused to believe she couldn't stop an object at fast speeds. It was one thing to focus on still objects and move them. It took practice to measure and transmit the right amount of energy to counter a moving target, especially several of them. He believed she could do it. He was right. Had she not discovered her family was alive, she would have shared her skill with Uncle Laurence by now. Now she intended to hide every extra skill she had. It was her edge against scientists, soldiers, and surveillance.

Unfortunately, the helicopter thing had been a mistake.

They didn't believe her.

At the end of the session, her uncle entered the room and put a firm arm around her. "I know it's hard, Sunday. But you have to do better. Do you want to lose all this?"

"A pelting room? Yeah, I'll really miss *this*," she deadpanned, fighting hard to curb the disrespectful sarcasm, but with little success.

"You know what I mean. Our home. I'm trying to protect you, but if you don't display extraordinary improvement, we'll lose everything. I won't be able to get the medicine I need to keep you alive." He hugged her. "I can't bear the thought."

He hadn't hugged her before. Not like this.

She returned it tentatively, confused by his declaration as much as the hug. It made her feel like he cared. It also made her feel reassured that she wasn't alone. Real or not, she needed somebody on her side. But why the change?

That's when she heard the Russian accent in the observation room. "Lying bastard. This torture is only going to get worse."

"Very likely," Wicker said. "Should be interesting, at least."

Jocelyn tensed and pulled away from her uncle. Did Sergei know she could hear him? Was he trying to warn her?

Did she believe Sergei, or the concerned look on her uncle's face and the warm strength of his arms? He'd been the only one there for her the last nine years.

And he'd lied to her—about how much, she didn't know.

She took a breath and smiled up at her uncle, promising to do better. But all she could think about was the burning sensation left on her skin and Sergei's words. *This torture is only going to get worse.*

Georgie searched every social media sight for Morgan Albrechter aka Morgan Rochester, but it seemed like the girl had the one set of parents in America with a strict hold on their kids' online access. No cell phone listings, and the few sites she *was* on only accepted family or known friends. Even her high school blog at Resurrection Prep required a student ID to access.

Thus, Plan B—infiltrate the household staff. It had taken a serious amount of research to find the names of household help in the Rochester family home, but finally, her online sleuthing had scored a lead. A four-year-old society page column quoted both a head butler and housekeeper commenting on the July 4th celebrations. After a few days of stubborn determination, and sixty-eight precious dollars in change used at an antique, but anonymous, pay phone, she'd hit the jackpot with an employee's cellphone. Now she needed to get the house phone number so she could contact Morgan Albrecht.

"Hello, Mrs. Clarence? This is Mrs. Harrington from Trinity Church, downtown. How are you today?" Georgie's heart beat so fast she started to lose her breath.

"Fine." The voice sounded confused.

"I'm calling because Mrs. Rochester, that is, Mrs. Rachel Winslow Rochester, said you'd be interested in helping with our charity event."

"She did?"

"Yes, ma'am. You sound surprised, but she said so many nice things about you, I just know you'll be perfect."

"I'm not sure I have the time to volunteer—."

"I'm so sorry, this line really is crackly. Is this your cell phone per chance?"

"Yes—."

"That explains it. I have the same problem with my coverage. It's so annoying, isn't it?"

"Yes—."

"Are you by chance near a land line? I'll call you right back."

"Yes, but—."

"Perfect. What's the number, Mrs. Clarence?"

"Uh, it's 212...."

Georgie grinned triumphantly, writing the number down. "Wonderful! Now I'll call you right back. We need volunteers for tonight's event, and I can't wait to give you the details."

"Tonight?"

"Yes, ma'am. That's not a problem is it?"

"Well, yes. I'm working until ten, and usually I go right home. I'm sorry, I can't help you. I don't know what Mrs. Rochester was thinking."

"Oh, that's such a shame. She must have gotten your schedule confused."

"I guess so...." The woman sounded uncertain.

"Don't you worry about a thing. We have plenty of other volunteers who can help. I'm just grateful for your time and consideration. Your heart's in the right place. It was so nice to talk to you, Mrs. Clarence. You have a nice day, now."

"You, too. Thank you. Goodbye."

"Bye-bye."

Georgie took a deep breath and laughed against the phone. "Okay, the fake New York accent was pretty bad, but Nancy Drew, eat your heart out!" Georgie curled the phone number in her hand, and left the bus station triumphantly.

CHAPTER TWENTY-TWO

Jocelyn winced. Today she had been upgraded to a tennis ball pelting. It would have been comical, if they hadn't ratcheted up the force and made it so painful. No way could tai chi, karate, or judo stand up to a consistent barrage of increasingly faster tennis balls pelting her relentlessly. Her body felt swollen and her spirit crushed.

Her uncle had started slowly, but it made no difference. The number and speed of the tennis balls came at her until pain management was her primary focus.

"Clear your mind, Sunday, and use your power to block the balls."

She shouted back at her uncle. "I can't clear my mind while getting pummeled to death!" She hated him. "I can't do this. I don't understand why you're beating me."

"We're not beating you. We're teaching you. Try harder."

Seriously? *Teaching?* She looked at the ball pumps around the gym that had been modified and secured into the surrounding walls. Some were low enough to reach. She went to a lower one, caught a ball before it exited, and held it until the balls jammed up and the machine choked. She went to the next one, but they'd already turned off the lower machines. Instead, she scooped a bunch of tennis balls off the floor and aimed at the Plexiglas protecting her uncle. That's when the onslaught got worse. A tennis ball made contact with her cheek, high enough to stun her vision.

She threw another ball at the glass as hard as she could, creating a fierce rattling sound.

When a guard entered, she breathed a sigh of relief—only to be shot with a Taser. Her body writhed with electrical pulses as she fell to her knees. Anger and shock surged through her. Oh, she could focus, all right. She didn't want to be a puppet anymore, but her next action was pure self-defense. She focused her energy on where the Taser wire caught her chest and arm and sent energy back.

She felt no remorse when the guard's eyes went wide from the current that ricocheted at him. He dropped the device. This time *his* face showed surprise. The surge of power caused the Taser's electrodes to pop off her body with a crackling sound. The guard fell to the ground in the same moment, curling up like a baby. Well, as much as a six-foot-two-inch man could curl.

How do you like it, buddy?

Her own body still suffered as nerves and spasms racked her muscles. Two more guards came in to get their friend. She decided to lie there, since her body couldn't actually move anyway.

After they took the guard away and removed the Taser, her uncle came in. He knelt down and pulled her into his arms.

"How are you doing, kiddo?"

She grunted softly in response. She was exhausted. It was all she could manage.

"What you did with the Taser was very good. I'm proud of you."

He sounded insane. She forced a response from her body. "I just…want to make…you happy."

In truth, she believed only one thing now. Sergei was right.

The torture would get worse.

A quick pinch and sting proved her uncle had just injected her with a needle. She felt the effects instantly, as the edges of her vision blurred, then went black.

"Why?" she asked.

"For your own good, Sunday. You're making progress. I'm proud of you."

She closed her eyes in disbelief and disappointment, giving up and letting the drug take her to pain-free unconsciousness.

When she opened them again, she knew what came next would be anything but pain free.

She struggled violently against the bindings, terrified, only wanting to get out before it started. Her struggles were useless. She was in the same torture chamber, in the center of the room, this time with her wrists in thick steel cuffs and chained to opposite walls. Something came at her head, and she turned to avoid it. She didn't know how long she'd been out, but nothing had changed. Her eyes blinked, then blinked again. A tennis ball hit her left leg, over and over again. Then her face. She stood on her feet, and ducked as best she could with her arms stretched uncomfortably. Five more came at her chest, followed by ten at her back. She yanked on the chains desperately, furiously. Anger and hatred burned so powerfully in her body, she had an instant understanding of the power of rage.

"Seriously?" she shouted up to the room.

Megan responded. "Hi, Sunday. Everyone left for dinner. They told me to watch in case anything changed. I'm turning off the speaker now."

"Liar! I know they're with you. I know you're there, Laurence. You're a filthy, dirty liar. You are no longer my uncle!" Fury filled her. "You're sick! I hate you!"

The tennis balls picked up speed, randomly hitting her from all directions.

"I love you, Sunday," her uncle said over the microphone. "This is for your own good. You'll see. Once you have a breakthrough, you'll feel much better about this."

She swore. Then she swore again. Curse words she'd heard soldiers say when they thought she couldn't hear she yelled, pulling the chains bolted to the walls until her wrists bled and her bones felt like they might break.

She screamed. She called for help. She screamed some more. She vowed to scream for as long as they pelted her, in order to make them feel as bad as possible. But they were persistent. After an hour, her throat scratched raw and her body agonized, she let herself go limp, let her arms stretch painfully, and accepted the abuse. Years of meditating got her through what followed. She took her mind to a different place.

Three-hundred and seventy-one more hits were completed in silence. She kept her body as still as possible. A particularly steady stream on her left thigh was certain to leave her with a massive bruise. She swore to herself, in that silent hour, that she would *never* give her uncle the satisfaction of her screams again.

And she would never, ever, let him know how powerful she was, until she was safe.

Finally, a guard entered with her uncle. Her uncle came forward to where she was chained and put his hand out in front of her face. She didn't move. He put it under her eyes, waiting for her to bend her head. She turned her head away. He pushed the back of his hand on her mouth. He told her he loved her. "Maybe if you tried harder, we wouldn't have to do this again. You're bringing this on yourself, Sunday."

She didn't move, but turned her head again, trying to get away from his disgusting hand. She thought this might be the punishment for her walk outside the compound. She couldn't be sure. He might just be crazy.

"Sorry, Uncle Laurence." She wanted to be released. She'd say anything. They'd sent the big guard. The mean-looking one named Ruben. They must be afraid she'd hurt somebody. The guard took the thick cuffs off, and she fell to the ground. She thought she saw him blink in shock at the blotches of red and purple around her wrists before his expression went impassive again.

She moved gingerly to see how her body would react. The exposed skin on her arms appeared nearly purple in spots. She didn't dare look at the rest of her body—not that she could. Her left cheek and eye were swollen, limiting her vision. Everything hurt.

"You can go home for dinner now," her uncle said.

She didn't think she could stand, so she just said, "Okay." She was starving. Food would help her heal faster, but she couldn't move. She curled up on the cold, polished concrete, wondering if the stomach cramps were from the external pain of the tennis balls, or some new internal misery.

"Get up, Sunday."

"I think I'll just lay here for a minute. I *have* been on my feet all day."

"I don't want you to keep Liz waiting."

"She won't care."

"Don't talk back. She's waiting for you. If you miss your dinnertime, I'm not feeding you later."

"You're really grumpy today." She still didn't think she could move.

He kicked her in the thigh, the one already swollen and bruised, causing a jolt of surprise and renewed throbbing. She recoiled, but realized it was more from the shock of him physically striking her than the pain that radiated fire down her leg and up through her hip. She was naïve to be shocked by more abuse at this point. It was just that...this was the man who had raised her.

Whatever feeling for him that still remained in her heart died with the impact of his foot in her stomach.

She gagged and was nearly ill on his brown leather shoe, but instead curled up tighter. She thought she might end up sleeping here after all, foregoing any food. Likely her stomach wouldn't hold anything down anyway.

"Help her up," Laurence said.

The guard grabbed the scruff of her shirt and lifted her like a rag doll. She held onto his arm until her legs steadied and she could take a couple of steps. She focused on her feet, watching one foot appear in front of the other. It felt like a small miracle.

Her uncle led them out and waited for her to pass him in the hallway.

She stopped in front of him and Ruben stood guard next to her—as if to stop *her* from hurting anyone.

"Sorry about talking back just now, Uncle Laurence."

His face relaxed and he smiled.

She smiled back. "You know all those things I said in the torture room when I was angry?"

"Yes." He waited for her apology.

She nodded. "Just so you know, I meant every single one of them."

Her uncle's face contorted into a red blotch. That's when she saw it—a glimpse of someone she didn't yet know—or did she? He regained his composure.

Surprisingly, she thought she caught a hint of admiration from Ruben as he moved her along.

"I know you don't mean that, Sunday."

"Since you know everything, right?" she quipped. She really hated him. And the rage that coursed through her gave added strength—the strength to fight a little bit longer. "At least you admit it's a torture room."

"Thanks to your smart mouth, there will be plenty more of that, dear." He said it with perfect calm.

She smiled. "Cool. Not very creative, but I'm used to being bored by you." She enjoyed seeing that the extra dig made him blotchy again, and savored the moment as she turned down the hall and looked up at the stairway leading to the observation room. Dominique, Megan, and Sergei stared down at her.

She waved her hand. "That was fun."

Dominique merely smiled. Megan looked like she actually felt bad and glanced away, unable to meet her gaze. Sergei, behind them both, shook his head—either in disgust or to warn her. She took it as a warning for now and left the building.

The guard, Ruben, followed her all the way back, preventing her the chance to sit and recover a moment, but he did catch her when she stumbled once, so she gave him credit for being mildly useful.

She was about to enter her building at the end of Main Street when she caught the quiet sound of Russian words. She looked up at her burly escort to see if he'd heard them as well.

"If you can hear me, scratch your head."

She knew Sergei's voice and scratched her head while turning to enter her security code.

"Your family is alive. Remember that. Remember, you must survive to reach them."

Her heart leapt painfully, but she scratched her head again to signal she understood.

"If you have the power they say, you can't let them know. They will harvest your body for their own ends."

A shiver of fear shook her already fragile body. She bent to re-tie her shoelace. Ruben grunted impatiently and held open the door.

"Jocelyn, remember this, no matter what—keep your eyes on the prize, not the price. Nothing else here matters. Nothing and no one. Don't forget it. Escape is all there is."

She scratched her head again and stood up, entering the door being held for her. The soldier turned and left once she'd been secured. She called for the elevator. Maybe she had one person in her corner, but what did he know?

And how high a price was she going to have to pay for her freedom?

CHAPTER TWENTY-THREE

Georgie's heart fluttered faster than hummingbird wings. The voice that answered the phone sounded young. Could this be Benjamin Albrecht?

"Hi." She swallowed hard. "Is Morgan there?"

"Nope. She's at tennis practice."

"Oh."

"No. Wait, I think voice lessons, or maybe golf. I'm not sure," he decided. "It's something. Sorry. She's somewhere."

Georgie relaxed a moment. He sounded really normal. "No problem. Is this Ben?"

"Yes, who's this?" He sounded interested.

"Um, I'm a friend of your sister. I was just calling to help with something. I'll try her cellphone later." Georgie bluffed a little. "Wait, let me make sure I've got it. 2-1-2." She paused. "8-7—."

"Nope. It's—." He stopped. "I'd tell you, but I'm not supposed to give out our phone numbers. Want me to have her call you back?"

"No, I'll just call again. When do you think is a good time?"

"Probably never, but dinnertime she's usually around."

"Cool." Georgie didn't really want to hang up yet. She wondered if she could get some intel from the kid. "So how's school? Are you doing well?"

"Straight A's."

"That's awesome. I bet Morgan is jealous."

"She just doesn't like to study. You have to do the time."

Georgie laughed.

"That's what my dad says," he added.

"Yeah. Mine, too. Must be a dad thing." Georgie started to ask if he got along well with his parents when she heard a voice in the background asking Ben who he was talking to. Her palms started to sweat as she listened to Ben say a friend of Morgan's.

"Who?" The voice sounded suspicious.

"Uh, I don't know." Ben spoke into the phone. "What's your name?"

"Jenn," she answered, hoping that was a safe bet. "I go to Resurrection."

"Jenn, from Morgan's school."

"Really?" A male voice responded.

Ben spoke into the phone. "Sorry. I gotta go. My brother wants to talk to you."

A voice came on the line—deep, pleasant, and distinctly suspicious.

"What's the school motto?"

"What?"

"What's the school motto? You have two seconds before I track this line and have you arrested for harassment and trying to get information from an underage child."

"That's a little severe, don't you think? I was just calling for Morgan."

"The motto? One. Two—."

"In God We Trust!" Dumbest thing she could have said. "Wait, I'm just kidding!" She remembered a line from the website when researching. "With God, all things are possible."

She took a hard breath. There was silence on the other end.

"Close enough. Who is this, again?

"Jennifer. Listen, I don't have a lot of time, and I need to reach Morgan. It's really important."

"Uh-huh."

"Yes!"

"Keep talkin'. I'm listening."

Georgie didn't know what to say. "I'll just call back."

"From Virginia?"

"What?"

"That's right. I tracked you. None of Morgan's friends use phones for calling people. Text only. So what do you want?

Because I *will* track you and *hunt* you down if you try anything to hurt my family."

"Geez! I'm trying to help. This is about what happened to their—."

Georgie was so engrossed in getting through to the guy she nearly jumped out of her skin when a big, dark hand slammed down on the phone, cutting the connection.

The shock made her heart pound in her ears, and good thing, because it cut off the loud cursing from her cousin, Al.

How she missed a man as large and angry as Al sneaking up on her definitely humbled her about her spy skills. Especially on the heels of being phone tracked.

She didn't think it could get worse. Until the ancient payphone started to ring.

Al cursed, staring at the phone in what seemed half fear, half anger. "Georgie," he shook his head. "What have you done?"

Georgie reached to grab the phone.

Al yanked it from her hand and spoke into the mouthpiece.

"Listen, and don't speak. I don't care who you are or why you're calling. No one at this end wants trouble. If you want to live to see another day, lose this number and forget this call ever happened. It's not safe here for you or your family." Al slammed the phone and grabbed her forearm. She walked quickly so it wouldn't look like he was dragging her away—but he was dragging her away.

They got outside to his truck parked next to her dad's car, and he started to rifle around in her purse until he found the audio disruptor Richie had given her. Once on, he looked around casually and told her to smile and act normal.

She tried.

"So." He smiled broadly, his eyes squinting with fury. "What was that all about?"

"You don't want to know."

He took a breath and nodded.

"Is this thing still going on? Richie and I told you not to get involved."

"A person is being held captive, a hostage to the government. Can you stand there and not do anything?"

"I don't want to see you dead."

"Right. You know, you and my dad are so full of it. You're such *hypocrites*. It's all about our great black history, fighting slavery, standing up for what's right, and changing history, but when it comes to our turn, everyone—" she emphasized the next words "—*just turns away*." She took a breath to add, "So much for the great Washington family history."

To his credit, Al agreed. "Yeah. You're right about that. But with one twist. Neither I nor your dad think a teenage girl should be getting into the middle of a situation at a fully-armed military base, with no understanding of what she's up against, or who she's even helping."

Screw him for having a point. But the teenager thing was just wrong.

"Great-great-great grandmother Mary-Louise Chandler was fourteen when she led slaves across the border."

"She was always with family, most of them male. I know my history, too. You're not going to win this, Georgie. You don't know what you're doing."

"I know when someone needs help. I'm *going* to help. With your support, or not. And why were you following me anyway?" She added the last bit, suddenly outraged.

"To show you how easy it is!"

"Well, get a job!"

He pressed his lips tightly, almost making a fish face in frustration.

That last bit came out harsher than intended, since he was fresh out of jail, but he *did* need to get a job soon.

Al closed his eyes a moment and took a controlling breath. "Okay. So tell me who you were talking to just now? Someone powerful enough to track you in a minute, and someone suspicious enough to be prepared to do it. That either tells me they're bad and powerful, or they're rich and powerful. Which is it?"

This time Georgie made the fish face. "Maybe all of the above." She handed him the audio scrambler and dug into her purse for the keys.

"Perfect." He looked up to the sky as if praying for restraint. "Are you completely out of your mind?"

Georgie unlocked the car and threw her purse into the front seat before turning back to her cousin and retrieving the scrambler. "Alastair, listen to me. Ten years ago, there was an *accident*. Two world-renowned scientists died. Do you think it really was an accident? Their oldest daughter was declared dead, but is really being kept and maybe even *experimented on* by the government!" She got a little too passionate, so she dropped her voice. "And the two youngest are sent to live with…," she made air quotes, "*friends*."

"And these friends are?"

Georgie cracked her neck uncomfortably and mumbled, "The Rochesters."

"I'm sorry, who?"

She grimaced. "The Rochesters."

"Like?" His eyebrows came together. "The Rochesters of New York?"

She nodded. "Exactly."

"As in *Governor Winslow-Rochester*?"

She nodded again.

"As in the family that runs the largest privately-owned biotech company in the world?"

"Okay! I get it!"

"Uh-huh. You call them, and you don't think they're in on this? They may *know* she's alive. They own a pharmaceutical company, for crying out loud. Who do you think pays for these types of studies?"

"I don't know."

"Well, now you do. People like them." He looked her in the eye. "And now they know you know. And they know where you are, and they know to let the people at Holliwell know as well. So, what you might have just done is actually hurt your little friend even worse."

Georgie's throat closed tightly from stress. "Ohmigosh. What if that's true?"

"There's a good chance"—he took a breath—"it's true."

"Do *you* think it's true?"

"I don't know what to think other than we need to get you out of the country like Richie said." He smiled for the first time, lightening up briefly. "Any chance you'll get a scholarship to Oxford or something?"

Georgie shrugged silently in response.

"Come on. Just lay low, would you? And don't come back to this train station."

Georgie finally spoke. "Understood."

But in her family, *understanding* didn't mean agreement.

Graeme still hadn't let go of the phone. Finally, he placed it in the charger and turned to Benny. His little brother looked like he was expecting to be in trouble. In fact, his face was a little pale.

"Is everything okay?"

"Yeah." Graeme walked over to him and grabbed him under his arms, swinging him a bit before landing him on a sofa nearby. Stress was not good for Benny's condition. He checked his mini-exoskeleton to make sure the settings were comfortable for him. The new test was working well. He was going to try to match the other arm with the new material. He ruffled Benny's hair and kissed him on the forehead. It would be hard to watch his little brother deteriorate. Sergei Baratashvili had been their best hope for advancement. With him gone, and the formula unavailable, they were lifetimes away from a cure. Even with all the research A & R had done.

Graeme made up a story about the phone call. "Morgan left her Algebra homework on a lunch table at school, so Jenn just wanted to make sure she got it. No biggie."

"Oh." Ben looked relieved but slightly worried now about his sister. "Who's in Virginia?"

"What? Oh, not *in* Virginia. Virginia is a girl. She was, uh, at the lunch table, too." His explanation was rapidly deteriorating. "I don't think it was too important. How about some ice cream?"

"Yes!" Benny hopped up. "Wanna play my new Star Wars game?"

"Totally."

They headed for the kitchen while Benny chattered on about the new game. Graeme stayed focused and enjoyed his time with Benny, but forming his plan ultimately interfered with his scoring.

He couldn't stop thinking that Charlottesville, Virginia was only fifty-five miles northeast of Camp Holliwell.

The destination called to him.

CHAPTER TWENTY-FOUR

Seth smiled, surprisingly relaxed. It was Saturday afternoon, and Sunnie looked good for having survived over a week of stress testing. She was clearly happy to see him. He'd been aware of her growing caution around others, but with him, she seemed to breathe a sigh of relief. When the opportunity came along, she would even reach for his hand—to hold it for a few long seconds, squeeze, and let go. At first, he knew it had been because she thought he needed it. She worried about what they might be doing to him. Then he learned what they were doing to her, and realized he had it good.

"Stress testing still going on?"

She nodded. "I'm not recovering as quickly."

She sounded worried. On instinct, he pulled her close. She resisted, but not much. He wrapped his arms around her. Her body stilled, waiting. He held her tighter, and finally she gave in. Her body relaxed against his, and she released a heavy breath of air. Then another.

"Hugs are healing," he said.

Her body shook with laughter. She didn't believe him. He pulled back to study her smooth face and innocent blue eyes. He cared about her. That made her dangerous, for a number of reasons.

"Come on. It's Saturday. How about smoothies and a movie?"

"A movie?"

He grinned. No mistaking the excitement in her voice. "Yeah, they let me have my phone back—it's completely deactivated, but the music and videos can play on it. We have to share the headset." He pulled out the white ear buds. "But cozy is fun."

"I'm not complaining!"

"Let's go. They don't normally give us this much free time."

"Laurence said we would get some time every Saturday now. He said it's good for me to socialize." She leaned up to his ear. "By socialize, I think he meant spy."

"No doubt. I'm meant to work my charms on you."

"You are," she admitted. "Stop it, please."

"Don't be a wuss." He ruffled her hair. She had a forlorn expression, as if she expected him to abandon her. It made him feel guilty. He grabbed her hand and led her down Main Street to the Starbucks.

"What's the movie?" she asked.

"A classic. It's called The Shawshank Redemption. It was nominated for an Oscar."

"What's an Oscar?"

He stopped in his tracks, shook his head, then decided not to go into it. "It's an award they give to good movies." They kept walking.

"Oh. But it didn't win?"

"Robbed. Totally."

"Who robbed it?"

"I meant…."

"I know!" She laughed. "I'm starting to figure out you don't mean everything you say."

"But I do. It's just an expression."

"Okay." She pacified him. "What's the movie about?"

"It's a prison movie."

This time *she* stopped in her tracks. She looked around pointedly. "You said movies were for escapism. I don't think—."

"Yeah, yeah. But this one has a great escape. You'll love it. And a happy ending. Girls love happy endings."

"I guess 'cause they don't get them in real life."

"Wow, pity party today."

She smiled. "Sorry. I am really grateful. And this will be my first adult movie ever. The last movie I remember had a mermaid and talking crab." She shook her head. "That can't be right."

He laughed. Her pop culture knowledge was pathetic. "Ever seen Beauty and the Beast?"

She thought for a second. "I don't think so. What's it about?"

"Another prison movie. But you'll like it."

"I don't think so."

Seth laughed. "We'll see."

"Can't wait." She'd finally gotten sarcasm figured out. A second later, her expression changed. "Your nose is bleeding again."

He cursed and hurriedly pulled out the tissues he now kept on hand. They sat on a bench outside the shoe store, and he tilted his chin up, waiting.

"It's not normal, you know."

"I know."

"What do you think...."

He put a hand up to stop her speech. He didn't know if anyone could really hear them or not, but he didn't want *them* to know he suspected unauthorized medical procedures. He was pretending to be happy.

She waited in silence, but sat next to him, and held his free hand between both of hers. "Tell me about the movie."

An obvious attempt to distract him from his nose, but he appreciated it.

"This guy goes to prison for murder—."

"Did he do it?"

"You'll see. And it's about his life there and how he gets out."

"Oh."

"And the friend who's in there with him, who knows nothing about the outside world."

"Oh?"

From the corner of his eye, he saw her sit up, interest perked. He tested his nose and put his chin down. "There." They got up, and he tossed the tissues in a trash can.

"What about the friend, does she get out?"

"He."

"Oh."

"It's an all-guy prison. That's how most prisons are. Single sex."

"Oh." She thought about it. "So does the friend get out?"

"Not right away, but eventually. Come on. I don't want to ruin it. Let's get our smoothies first." They were nearly at Starbucks.

"Is your nose okay?"

"Yeah. Thanks for holding my hand. That was sweet."

She smiled at the compliment, and he kissed her impulsively on the forehead, surprising them both. But what the hell. It was beautiful out, he had a spunky, gorgeous girl by his side, they walked down a pristine street on their first official "date"—in any other circumstance, it would be ideal.

In any other circumstance, he would have thought his life had turned out a lot better than anyone expected, himself included.

He clutched the small media device in his fist like a weapon. In any other circumstance, he wouldn't have met Sunnie. And he wouldn't be trying to escape from her and everything she represented.

Laurence Cashus leaned across the table wanting to reach through the telepresence conference technology and strangle the Secretary of Information. A few members of his team sat quietly with him while the SOI gave them the bad news.

"Dr. Cashus, your service to your country and to this project is not in question. It's simply that your methods are not achieving the results we'd hoped. We've discussed this."

"The plan was to re-evaluate in May." It was only March. Laurence couldn't believe this conversation was happening. He already knew from the SOI's set expression that the decision had been made. Somehow, their leadership had been poisoned against him.

No one noted that all their success in the last nine to ten years was based on Laurence's years of study and documentation. None of them would have made the leaps they had without Sunday and her blood samples. *He* had saved her life—not them. How dare they try to take her from him?

"It will traumatize her if you move her."

"We are not suggesting she be moved, only…." The Secretary of Information leaned in, his eyes expressionless. "We think she needs a different type of training that she is not getting under your care. Think of it as a mentorship."

"What do you mean?"

"Regardless of whether she can usefully control energy in the way that you believe—."

"Biotransmit energy."

"Exactly. Regardless of that, her other talents are of immense value to the government. Her next assignment is perfect for her. If she does well, it's good for everyone. You included. And she will need everyone's support."

"But if she fails or is killed in the process, we lose everything."

The Secretary leaned in. "This is worth the risk. Sergei Baratashvili was working on a nanotech solution that could be implanted in the early stages of child development. We believe there are several subjects in his hometown who have benefited from this work. If successful, the Russians, and any of their allies with the right funding, would have access to a generation of H-plus citizens and soldiers who may or may not be friendly to us. We want the coding process in our hands, and all the research destroyed."

"What do you want Sunday to do that a SEAL team can't?" Laurence asked.

"She can enter where we can't. She speaks the language. A little more time spent with Sergei, and she'll perfect the dialect. More importantly—she's young. She can pass for one of the test subjects. This is not their first generation of H-pluses, Dr. Cashus. This is their third. She's our in."

Laurence froze. Sergei had advanced the technology this far, and now Dominique had him helping her? Damn it. If only he'd been able to salvage Illeana's research, he'd be so much further along and not in this position. *Damn Sunday.* No one had yet been able to create an H-plus who could control energy. That power was hers alone. If she would just use it to the magnitude he believed she was capable of, and not just to play with Ping-Pong balls, his work would not be in vain. With that power to study, they would never risk sending her into the field. She'd become a permanent living prototype, and he'd be set for life. Or at least until long after hers ended.

"I understand what you're saying, gentlemen." Laurence took a breath before starting negotiations. "All I ask is that I have through May to prove she is more valuable as a test subject than as a weapon."

"One moment." The line went mute and the White House emblem displayed on the screen as the party in Washington discussed the issue. He felt sure everyone in the room with him held their breath. Finally, they were back.

"We think three weeks is sufficient time to get new results."

"That's ridiculous," he said tersely.

"That's what you have, Dr. Cashus. Take it or leave it."

He stood his ground, but braced himself. "It's a ridiculously short amount of time, but the team here will do everything possible to show you her value as a scientific asset."

"We wish you luck. Thank you all for your hard work, and we will reconvene in three weeks, or sooner, should you have any success. Goodbye."

"Goodbye," Laurence echoed. He sat silently, filled with emotion. He didn't feel worried or upset. Rage burned inside him at the injustice. After all he had done, they were going to cut him out, all because Sunday wouldn't obey.

He would *make* her obey if he had to beat the life out of her. How *dare* she betray him after all he had done for her. He would get her back in line. She needed to understand that she had *nothing* unless he chose to give it to her. He was everything. She would learn that and bend to kiss his hand in obedience and gratitude. He wouldn't settle for anything less.

Georgie and Brittany met Lena at a back table in the corner of the school library. There were stacks of books set up strategically to block the view of the table from other students.

Lena leaned into Brittany and Georgie, who turned on her voice scrambler for extra security.

"I have news." She slid an envelope across the table. "My FBI contact wasn't able to break into the Holliwell servers without triggering alerts, but she was able to explain more about the DNA reports." Lena nodded for Brittany to open the envelope.

Inside was the report they had given her, printed, but with highlights on certain elements.

"This is a report on the same person, but a before-and-after analysis of their genes."

Georgie looked closely. "They're very different."

"Yes. And a lot of genes have been changed. At least that's what I was told. This is beyond what is currently practiced. Some scientists can turn genes on or off in the body. They can even do things with unique combinations that are essentially played in a certain order—imagine that the genes are like notes, but that you can program a song into those genes that would allow people to do things they couldn't do before."

"Things no one could do before?" Georgie asked.

Lena bobbed her head. "Exactly."

Brittany frowned. "I don't understand. How is that bad?"

"Well, it's not necessarily bad, but it's powerful. Some of these combinations," she pointed to the first two highlighted ones, "can give a regular person super-hearing and super-vision." She pointed to a cluster on the report. "These are believed to give people extra strength, endurance, and longevity. At least in theory."

"Super-strength?" Georgie suggested.

"Potentially," Lena said. "Scientists can program DNA to get rid of...." Lena pulled out a piece of paper with her notes on it. "*Senescent* cells. These kind don't divide, and as they get old, they hurt neighboring cells and it contributes to aging. But this DNA is programmed to purge those cells."

"So people live longer and healthier. Huh." Brittany approved. "That doesn't sound so bad."

"Maybe," Lena said, remaining objective.

Georgie had other ideas. "They could be trying to make super soldiers or super people."

"*Trying* being the keyword." She bent closer to them and pointed out the information at the end of the file. "Gender, ethnicity, DOB, that is, date of birth, and…." She touched the last note. "TOD."

Brittany scowled. "Time of Death?"

Lena nodded. "This subject wasn't very old. Seventeen. I looked at the others, and they all ranged from eight to nineteen when they died."

"So they were all likely treated when they were underage," Brittany deduced. "Did their parents agree to this?"

"I don't know," Lena said.

"Do you think they were involuntary subjects?"

"Don't know that, either. But maybe your aunt was trying to help them. Or stop others from continuing what they were doing."

Brittany nodded. It seemed to make sense to her.

"There's one other little bombshell here."

Georgie sat up straight. She wondered if it had anything to do with Jocelyn. She hadn't told them anything about the girl yet.

"Well, the person who analyzed this said it was highly-advanced work, and that basically the exact same transformation in DNA was being applied to all the subjects. Which means there's a single donor DNA they're using as the template."

Brittany leaped to a conclusion that Lena seemed to share. "Ohmigosh! Do you think it's alien DNA?"

Lena shrugged. "Maybe. It would make sense. There's nothing like this out there currently."

The two started in on their alien theories, while Georgie wondered how much she should say about the girl who could run fast, control objects, and had blue tears. At one point in her life, she'd been a regular human. She definitely wasn't now, but was Jocelyn another experiment…or the donor?

Georgie knew she needed to come clean with Lena and Brit, but she feared revealing too much of Jocelyn's identity might, as Al had said, make things worse for Jocelyn and possibly put the other girls in danger—maybe even Jocelyn's real family.

Still, she had to tell them something. She would leave out last names and the family information she'd found.

"Hey." She waited for them to pause their excited hypothesizing and took a deep breath, adjusting the audio scrambler between them. "There's something I need to tell you."

CHAPTER TWENTY-FIVE

Another week passed. Jocelyn and her uncle came to an impasse on their nightly ritual. She refused to touch him or speak to him. He, in turn, began taking away her dinners, mango smoothies, pillows, etc. Every day she refused to obey him, he took something else away. There wasn't much left in her room. Her mattress had gone missing a few days ago—all that remained where the bed had been was a folded blanket. She'd almost told him he was pathetic, but instead, she'd started laughing. She'd even walked out of the room, holding her sides from laughter—and partial hunger—and told him he was looking desperate. He was. But he was also exercising his power over her, and it was substantial.

It wasn't easy fighting his dominance. She just felt she had to do it to keep some part of her spirit intact. Even at her weakest, it made her feel more powerful.

She left her building on Saturday to meet Seth at Starbucks, only to find Megan waiting in the Jeep outside her building.

"Hey, Sunnie, hop in. Seth and your uncle are out at the landing. He said something about a hike and a picnic."

Jocelyn paused on the front step. That didn't sound right. Even if it was a new approach, it was not her uncle's style.

"Are we training this afternoon? I thought I had three hours off."

"You do. I think your uncle just wants quality time."

That *definitely* didn't sound right.

Her uncle was all love and encouragement in front of people, but when he spoke to her privately, it was to blame her for destroying his work and causing everyone to lose their jobs.

Or he would "instruct" her on her lack of character and bad decision-making—all done out of *love*, of course.

Jocelyn looked at Megan, trying to figure out the truth. She wanted to take it all at face value. She wanted to believe Megan was just helping. But Megan had watched silently from the lab during those days of stress testing and did nothing when it became torture.

Megan put her hands on the wheel and looked away, waiting. Looking away was always bad.

"I think I'll skip the hike."

Megan sighed, frustrated. "Sunnie, just get in. I'm only the messenger. And Seth *is* out there waiting."

Jocelyn knew she'd have to go. At least she'd have Seth as company. Not how she wanted to spend her afternoon, but she shouldn't have counted on anything. That lesson was a hard one to keep learning. Reluctantly, she climbed into the Jeep and Megan whirled the vehicle around, taking off. It was a twenty-minute drive through the paved, tree-lined road, then a mile up a steep, dirt road to the landing.

The landing was basically a clearing at the end of one of the running paths with a small lookout area. This end of the camp was mountainous and covered with lush, beautiful forest with views of the lake where they did their EmWAV training. It was a nice place for a picnic and a hike.

They parked near her uncle's SUV and another car she recognized as Dominique's.

More wary than ever, she got out. An instant later, the hair on her arms sparked to attention.

She heard him from the hundred or so feet that separated the dirt parking lot from the landing. It was the sound of someone struggling, his mouth covered.

She ran before thinking, her only thought for Seth.

Jocelyn spotted him in seconds, two soldiers propping him on his feet, his hands chained behind his back, his feet likewise chained. He didn't have his beanie on, and his bare scalp made him seem especially vulnerable. There was a fresh cut on the side of his cheek, red and slightly swollen. He hadn't come willingly.

Furious, she ran to him, intending to rip the chains free with her bare hands.

A gunshot sounded, and something whizzed in front of her feet.

She froze, stunned and terrified that someone actually shot at her. When she saw her Uncle Laurence holding the Glock 9 millimeter, her horror was complete.

"Uncle Laurence?"

Confusion flooded her mind—but only for an instant. She started to sort information. She heard Sergei's voice, somewhere else in the forest, whispering. Trying to warn her. *Prize, not price.* His voice acted as a reminder, encouragement, support—and it scared her even more.

What kind of test was this now?

She felt the hot sensation of energy emanate from her blood, her nerves, and her skin. She couldn't control it. She was too afraid. The dirt at her feet sifted and whirled. She breathed slowly and moved forward to hide the unfocused energy building around her, but leaves ruffled mysteriously around her with each step.

She kept her eyes on her uncle, all the while trying to get closer to Seth.

"Stop there, Sunday," her uncle said. He spoke with the calm, assured voice of someone who knew where all the land mines were on the battlefield.

Her throat clenched. "What's going on?"

"I'm going to shoot Seth. I wanted you to watch."

She sucked in air. Her chest hurt from the fierceness of her pounding heart. The leaves on the trees fluttered and swayed all around her. The two soldiers holding Seth stepped away with worried expressions. Were they part of this? Or possible allies?

"Please, Uncle Laurence. Please, I'll do whatever you want. I'm right here." She could hear the tremble in her voice and took a calming breath, recalling her negotiation studies from last year. She needed to keep her voice relaxed and conversational. She needed to get him talking. "Explain this to me. What do you want? What do you want me to do?"

"Very good, Sunday." He smiled at her. "Things will go much better when you start obeying me."

"Yes, Uncle Laurence. You're right. You're always right. I'm sorry if I haven't been as understanding lately. I'm just tired, I guess, but I'll try harder. Let's go home. We can have lunch or an early dinner. Maybe Liz will join us." Uncle Laurence's smile grew so she kept talking. "It will be q-quality family time."

It wasn't working. She knew it. She kept trying anyway. He'd set this up with deliberation. As soon as that thought sunk in, she spotted the first video camera, planted in the V of some branches above his head. She spotted another trained on her.

She took a deep breath. *What is going on?* She wished she could ask, but she feared she already knew.

Her uncle raised the gun to Seth. There was no way she could reach Seth before a bullet, or reach her uncle before he shot Seth. No way to protect him without revealing herself. But what power would that give her uncle over her? What would they do to her? Would they really dissect her? She felt an edge of darkness and lightheadedness fill her until she realized there was no way the Wicked Dominatrix would let anyone touch her best experiment. She focused her hearing beyond what she could see. Whispers in the trees gave her a clue. Dominique watched somewhere with Sergei. She enjoyed taunting Jocelyn, but she wouldn't kill Seth, right? It didn't make sense. They were scientists who worked with assets. Seth was a valuable asset. *Right?*

Oh, God. The truth was she didn't know. She didn't know anything.

Her uncle lifted the gun and she saw the green laser focus on the center of Seth's chest.

"Please! Uncle Laurence! Please don't."

"Stop me, Sunday. You have the power to stop me. Do it."

"I don't know what you mean." Fear and frustration came out. "I can't. Please, don't do this. It's a mistake."

She looked at Seth. His mouth was covered in duct tape, but his eyes met hers in what she thought might be panic and disbelief. He remained unusually still as he turned back to her uncle, one chained foot inching backward, as if preparing for the worst. She didn't know how strong he was. Could he move fast enough, jump high enough, or do anything to stop the incoming attack?

"You'll have plenty of time, Sunday. On the count of three. Use your energy. I'm aiming for his heart, Sunday. If you're not going to save him, you better say goodbye. One…two…."

Jocelyn didn't know what to do. Conflicting arguments, instincts, and feelings collided. She had to make a choice.

Her uncle met her eyes before focusing again. "Three."

She recognized her scream from a distant part of her brain as she held her energy and covered her ears. It didn't help. The gunshot exploded.

Birds screeched from the surrounding trees.

She chose nothing.

The bullet hit Seth with a thud, and he flew backward, nearly knocking his head on a tree root. He moved slightly, eyes blinking, as he turned his pained expression on her.

"No!" Everyone stared at her. Her uncle looked more furious than ever. She swayed in shock and stumbled toward Seth. Another bullet hit the ground and whizzed past her feet, warning her to stop. Only a couple yards separated them. Something wasn't right. An intense pulse of relief swept through her when she solved the puzzle. They'd put a bulletproof vest on him. They didn't mean to murder him. It was a test, another test. Intense relief made her legs week. She took a breath, struggling to keep her bearing.

A warning shot made her jump back. Her uncle had his gun trained on her.

She checked on Seth. "Are you okay?"

Seth turned his head and she saw his expression—anger and hurt. She hadn't saved him. She'd risked his life for the sake of her own. She saw it in his face. Betrayal.

Still on his back, he turned his head away at the same time two soldiers came to help him to his feet. She closed her eyes. She needed to pull herself together. She listened. There were no clues from Sergei, but she heard Wicker's snide comment to Sergei. *Well, that didn't work.* The soldiers scuffled a bit, lifting Seth and awaiting directions. It grew unnaturally quiet. She opened her eyes, nearly calm. Megan had absconded to the car, ready to hop in or hide behind it should the need arise. Perhaps she didn't trust her uncle as much now and didn't want to become the next target. Jocelyn didn't blame her.

Her uncle possessed a deadly calm. "I don't believe you, Sunday. You didn't even try. That means you're hiding something from me." He took a step further, speaking with resignation. "I can do this forever, you know. Test you with any number of unimaginable things. Please don't make me."

"I was scared. I couldn't think. I froze," she said vehemently.

"You were willing to let your friend be killed."

"You mean murdered? You've lost your mind. You shot him. Are you insane?"

"Insane enough to try it again." He lifted and aimed the gun at her.

She heard a shocked grunt from Seth and knew panic showed in her eyes. She looked for help. Even the two soldiers had expressions of concern and confusion. They gave each other looks as if to ask what was going on.

"This is your last chance, Sunday. You need to save yourself. You don't understand what will happen if you continue to fail. This is going to hurt if you fail. I'm an excellent shot, but try not to move. I don't want to hit your heart accidentally."

One of the soldiers pulled his gun. The other followed suit, albeit nervously. "Dr. Cashus, that's enough. Stand down."

"Uncle." She saw the green laser sight touch her left shoulder and pleaded.

"Sir! Put down your weapon."

"Don't order me, you twit. Do you know who I am? I'm your enemies' worst enemy. I'm the interrogator they send in for the really tough cases. I'm the one who put mind control on the map for the U.S. government." He glared at the two men. "I've created more scientific assets for Uncle Sam than your combined ages. I'm untouchable." His face twisted into an unexpected smile, and a hint of sympathy struck his tone. "I understand my methods seem unorthodox, but I know this girl. I know what she can do. She's not human."

"I am human!" Sunnie shouted. She saw the uncertain looks on the soldiers. "Please."

"Don't worry." Cashus glared at Sunnie. "One bullet isn't going to kill her."

The soldier held his position. "All the same—."

He didn't finish his sentence.

The loud release of a bullet captured Jocelyn's complete attention and focused her life in an instant.

CHAPTER TWENTY-SIX

She heard the muffled protest from Seth, a shocked gasp from Megan by the car, a curse from one of the soldiers. In the distance, a rush of footsteps along with Sergei's panting breaths of concern.

The benefit of super vision, super speed, and super strength was that she could watch a speeding bullet almost in slow motion. At least with this one she could. Perhaps because it would kill her? She knew a bullet could kill her despite all her skills. This one was aimed to set her back for a while—and no military field trips right away.

She could have stopped the bullet—just as she could have stopped the one that hit Seth.

She didn't.

She thought about her sister and brother, somewhere out in the world. Perhaps they were being held captive just as she was. She had to reach them. Which meant she had to get out of here and away from Cashus as soon as possible. She accepted that now. She embraced it. And she stood perfectly still as the knowledge burned through her skin and came to a dead stop, once fully embedded.

She'd been fighting and rebelling and questioning everyone, including herself. But no longer. From now on, she played her own game.

The pain didn't register in the first second. It was the second and third seconds before the fiery heat of the injury reached her brain and wreaked havoc with her heart. The adrenaline rush was dizzying. She touched the entry wound, pressing to stop the blood from escaping, the warm rush of liquid on her hand surreal. Energy pulsed around hot lead, holding it still. She hadn't stopped the bullet, but she stopped it from doing too much damage. At least she hoped.

Seth struggled violently. The men had trouble holding him back. She met his eyes and mouthed her apology as her legs buckled. Maybe he wasn't completely angry with her for not saving him.

Her knees hit the ground hard as Sergei burst through the trees with Wicker on his heels. Russian curses flew from his lips as he ran to her assistance. Megan came out from hiding and hurried over with a first aid kit. That's when another bullet sounded sharp in the forest.

"Everyone get away. She brought this on herself."

Her uncle walked over and kicked Megan aside with his foot. She scurried back.

"Dr. Baratashvili, please step away from my niece."

"She needs help. This was not part of your test."

"We'll leave the first aid kit. She's trained. Let's make sure her expensive and extensive studies have not been wasted."

Jocelyn stared into Sergei's concerned face, wanting him to stay. She was scared, and despite her training, her body was in shock.

"You must stop the bleeding," Sergei warned her. "You have less than fifteen minutes, or you will bleed out. Do not let your suffering be for nothing."

"The sooner we leave, the sooner she can help herself," her uncle said.

"Sergei, let's go. We can't help here," Dr. Wicker said. To Laurence she said, "You owe me big for this."

Wicker ordered the soldiers to take Seth back to his cellblock for examination. "We'll see her at the hospital soon. Don't worry, she can make it."

Jocelyn glanced at Wicker, surprised at the woman's confidence. Wicker met her look with an affirming nod. It was strangely reassuring. Did they believe she could handle this? She could. She really believed she could handle anything at this point, but that was no reason to shoot her.

Her uncle pulled Sergei away, and the others scrambled to their cars. Jocelyn wanted to believe they all left because they believed her uncle—she would pass this test. Her brain and body were too busy processing pain.

The sound of cars proceeding down the road faded, and she remained on her knees staring at the first aid kit. The only good news was she was right-handed. She opened the first aid pack and sorted through it to find QuikClot sponges and combat gauze. She prepped them to put on, then dealt with her shirt.

Getting her shirt off was torture, but she willed herself through it, careful to ignore the large and quickly growing blood stains. She wanted the bullet out. *Now.*

She wrapped one layer of gauze over her shoulder and under her arm to prep a sling.

Taking the sponges, she lied down and put her legs up on the nearest tree's root system to get elevation. She needed blood in her brain before she passed out.

Jocelyn put her palm over the entry wound, under the gauze, and focused. Years of practice helped her tune her sense of space and objects. The bullet was easy to find, since it didn't belong. Extracting it was more difficult. Her energy and flow were severely disrupted.

She took a slow breath and tried to pull the lead into her palm. If the pain was any indication, it moved, but not outward.

She needed more energy. She focused on the energy emanating from nature and made her body receptive. Energy swirled and spun and moved. It was an abundant resource. She willed it into her body, felt the first tingle on every exposed inch of skin, and breathed again with determination until that energy wrapped her in a cocoon of warmth. She placed her hand over the wound again.

This time, the bullet seared a path outward, into her palm. She exhaled and dropped the offending object on the ground.

Grateful no one was around to hear her cry of agony and pathetic whimpers, she peeled up the gauze, already stuck to the congealing blood, and pressed the sponges firmly into the entry wound.

She didn't move for several moments. It was all she could handle. She sucked in air through her teeth fighting the hot pinprick of tears. Justice and revenge vied for her energy. It kept the tears at bay.

She thought of Morgan and Ben, of escaping, and of finding out the truth. Finally, with a slow deep breath, she rolled to her good side, and pushed herself up to her knees. She wrapped the wound some more, added an Ace bandage, and attached her arm to her body in a makeshift sling. The hemorrhaging had stopped, and she carefully stood, surprised her brain was fairly balanced despite two wobbly legs.

She was exhausted but had to think. *Keep fighting, even if it means fighting myself.*

She sucked in a shallow but determined breath, and finding nothing else of use in the first aid kit, kicked it aside as she stumbled forward.

The hospital was twenty minutes by Jeep, and fifteen minutes if she'd been able to run at top speed. Her uncle would be waiting for her there with proper medical attention.

The lake was closer. There were Special Forces there that reported directly to General Martin, and it seemed as good a time as any to make an alliance with the General. Certainly, no one on the science team was sane.

Of course, she'd need to reach the General in one piece.

She stumbled down to the edge of the clearing and looked for a way down. There was a narrow path below that cut along the edge of the mountain to the lake where they practiced maneuvers. She estimated the path was about ten feet below her—an easy hop…if she was healthy.

She forged through the trees to get lower on the tree line and found a spot where she could climb down the sheer edge to the path. She lost her footing, tripped, and screamed in agony when she landed on her bad shoulder before nearly rolling off the narrow edge. Gasping, heart racing, the edges of her vision turning black, she experienced a strong sense of her own mortality. She needed to pull it together. On her knees, she reach for a rock jutted slightly from the mountainside and pulled herself up. She hoped she'd stopped the bleeding in time, and that she'd stay conscious long enough to get real help.

The lake seemed far away. Freedom even farther.

And the memory of her family drifted away like a distant dream.

Seth bounced in the back of a Jeep moving erratically down the hill. One of the soldiers ripped the silver duct tape from his mouth, and Seth let out a loud curse of pain followed by a stream of additional curses and demands.

"Get this freakin' vest off me. I can't breathe. I think my ribs are broken!"

"Take it easy. I got it." The soldier next to him looked pale and glanced at his partner in the rearview mirror. "I didn't sign up for this, Olsen."

Olsen glanced in the rearview mirror. "No kidding. But there are no reassignments, so take it easy."

"Take it easy?" The soldier next to him shook his head. "This is seriously messed up. I'm going to unchain you," he said to Seth.

Seth took a breath. "Thanks." He lifted his feet. "These, too."

The soldier complied.

"She'll die if we don't go back," Seth said.

"We're not going back," Olsen said from the front.

Seth looked at the soldier next to him. "She's just a kid. Do you want her death on your conscience? Do you know how sweet she is? She's never hurt a fly, and her uncle shot her because she couldn't pass one of his bizarro *tests*. She's up there alone and confused and bleeding to death."

The soldiers didn't answer.

"Look, you don't need to help, just slow down. You can say you were trying to give me first aid for my ribs, but I was pumped up on adrenaline and worry, and went crazy and disappeared into the woods. Just give me a minute head start. Please."

No luck.

Seth debated the vertical drop off the side of the dirt road. Not a great spot to jump, but the guys seemed torn, and he'd closed harder deals than this. "You saw it in her eyes. She's the innocent here. We're supposed to protect people like her."

He was so involved in his plea, he missed that the Jeep was slowing. Olsen gave him a nod in the rearview mirror as they neared a turnoff in the road. No one spoke.

Surprised, but grateful, there was some humanity left on earth, he jumped out of the car and didn't look back.

He couldn't believe they'd helped. Maybe there were people on this base who cared. What were the odds?

His heart pounded, and his ribs throbbed as he raced up the dirt path, grateful for the drugs that gave him super-speed and extra strength.

He reached the clearing within a couple of minutes—only to find it empty.

Panic struck. The first aid kit was torn apart and covered in blood. *Not good. Please don't be passed out somewhere, Sunnie.* He looked for signs. She hadn't taken the car path, so there had to be other exits. He ran to where Sergei and Dominique had viewed the shooting. Woods surrounded the small area. He returned to the clearing and looked again. There was a narrow hiking path that led out to the edge of the mountain. He ran down it, pushing brush away until he came to the edge and froze. The lake lay below, placid and still, reflecting the mountains around. He could just make out the dock where they did their EmWAV training. She must have gone this way, but why? Was she making a run for it?

Bad idea. *You'll be dead before you reach the perimeter of this place, Sunnie. Now where are you?* He scanned the panorama for movement. His instinct paid off. Something stirred in the brush. A moment later, he saw Sunnie stumbling down a steep section of switchbacks. He took off after her.

Seth called out to Sunnie the instant he caught up to her. She didn't respond. She just walked quickly, single-mindedly down the path—her white bra covered in blood, shoulder bandaged, and staring at the trail as if looking for tripwires. He shouted her name louder, and finally, she jolted around in shock. He took in her one-armed bandage wrap, pale face, and tangled hair. A smear of blood covered her cheek.

"Seth?" She blinked, confused, as if she wasn't sure of her own vision. "What are you doing here?"

"I thought you might need help." He stepped closer to her, cautious not to make her nervous. She had a deer in the headlights expression, and one false step on the path could send her over the side of the switchback.

"They're killing me."

"I see that." He took another step and slowly reached out for her. "The bleeding stopped?"

"I used the QuikClot."

"Never heard of it."

"Stops bleeding fast."

"Glad to hear that. You had me worried."

She smiled weakly. "I'm sorry he shot you. I hate him." Her voice was more a whisper. She was losing energy fast. "I think I went into shock. Now I can't get out of it. Trying to breathe. Stay calm."

"That's good," he encouraged, terrified for her. "You're going to be fine. No reason to be worried."

She nodded and turned back to the path with a stumbling walk.

"Why are you going this way?"

"General Martin's men will help me."

He followed, ready to catch her at any moment.

"I have a plan," she continued.

"Does it include falling off this over-crop?"

"No." She gasped for breath. "The pain isn't so bad anymore. I can make it to the bottom."

She was right, and she did. She was indomitable.

Eventually, the path evened out. They were about a half-mile from the docks where there would be a guard shack and a vehicle to take her to the hospital. Finally, she stopped and leaned her good side into his shoulder. "I think you should carry me now."

"I think so, too."

He lifted her easily, and she wrapped her right arm around his neck, emitting only the softest cries at the pain his arm caused being braced under her back. He couldn't stand that he'd added to her pain, but he was damn grateful to get her off her feet.

"That better?" He waited for her to adjust. Her head went down and her eyes closed. "Wow, you really trust me."

Her lips cracked the slightest amount. He took off at a fast walk, clutching her tightly to prevent movement that would cause injury.

They didn't need to go far before a soldier spotted them and ran up. He radioed for his partner to bring the Jeep, his face registering panic when he recognized Sunnie.

Sunnie, for her part, wouldn't let the soldier leave. She told him how cold she was, and the guard let Seth bring her inside the larger guardhouse at the EmWAV dock. A quick look told Seth this was where they had the override controls to the EmWAVs. Sunnie seemed to take that in as well before the soldier came back with a blanket and first aid kit.

"Please, get General Martin. Dr. Laurence shot me. He's trying to kill me. Please, you can't take me back to him."

The terror on her face was enough to make Seth want to kill Laurence. He thought the soldier would, too. No guy could resist a girl with big, blue eyes fighting for her life and begging for protection.

"Please," her hoarse voice began to die out. "General Martin is the only one I trust. He's the only one who can help me."

Then she closed her eyes.

Seth panicked and yelled for the guy to hurry.

Geez, Sunnie. Don't give up on me now.

CHAPTER TWENTY-SEVEN

Jocelyn didn't want to overplay her injury, but she *had* been shot. And she was in shock. She knew that. As much as she fought to stay calm, the shivers and nausea were still right on the edge, and she hated that nothing she tried helped it.

She listened while the two soldiers fussed around her, making sure she and Seth were safe in the Jeep. Seth still held her, and she found she didn't mind being in his lap with his arm around her. It was comforting and helped to keep the chills at bay more than the blanket tucked over her.

Finally, she let her eyes flutter open to assess the surroundings. The soldier in the passenger side of the Jeep turned to keep an eye on her.

"We reached General Martin. He's going to meet us at the hospital."

"No!" she cried. "Please don't take me back. He'll kill me. Dr. Cashus is insane. He'll kill me. Please!"

"Don't worry," he assured her quickly. There's a military wing, and another escort is on the way. No one will take you without General Martin's okay."

She swallowed and nodded as feebly as she could before resting her head against Seth's beating heart.

This might actually work.

They were at the hospital in no time, and she clung to Seth until the doctors brought her into surgery, her eyes wide with what she hoped looked like worry, but taking in every detail of her environment. General Martin arrived just before they took her to the operating room. He comforted her and told her not to worry about anything, but that's what you said to people while they were being rolled into surgery.

She grabbed his hand from the stretcher while Seth walked with them. "Seth saved me."

The General nodded, a frown of worry on his face, but he acknowledged Seth.

"Please, can he stay until I wake up? I don't want to be alone."

The General nodded again. "I'll keep an eye on him until all this is sorted out."

"Thank you." She breathed a sigh of relief. "I knew I could trust you."

An anesthesiologist fiddling with her IV got her attention. "Start counting backward from ten, Sunnie."

She ignored him, one more thought taking precedence. "Make sure they fix me good, General. So I can still be a soldier." She closed her eyes. "I don't want my life wasted."

Jocelyn remembered waking up several times in the following twenty-four hours, and Seth was always there. There was a second bed in her room, and he passed out on it. At one point, she watched him sleep. He tossed and frowned a lot in his sleep, and she wondered at the bad dreams that seemed to torture him. She also wondered if he had tried to escape yet.

A nurse came in and gave her more drugs, and she slept soundly until voices woke her.

The sun was shining.

Seth sat in a chair next to her bed, a remote in his hand as he flipped channels on the TV. She tried to turn and look at the television. Her uncle hadn't let her watch much TV.

"Five hundred channels and nothing on," Seth said, not turning his head, but aware that she was awake.

"They let you stay." That was a small triumph.

"Yeah," Seth said. "I think the General wants to make sure you trust him." Seth turned and looked at her. She could tell he wanted to say more, but was wary.

"Have you heard from the mad scientists?" she asked.

He smiled. "Oh, yeah." Seth's glance indicated the soldiers outside their door. "They got some action last night when Uncle Laurence demanded to see you. Dominique isn't too happy, either. I'll have to go back to her soon. The General is conducting an investigation. That means you and I get a military vacation."

He sat back in the chair and put his feet up on the side table, still flipping through channels. "Well played, my friend."

Jocelyn bit back the smirk, hoping he wasn't going to tell on her. Finally, he turned his head and really looked at her. "I was scared, Sunnie. I don't ever want to feel that way again."

"I'm sorry."

He shrugged. "It's good to know you can take care of yourself. I'm not always going to be around, you know." He said it like a joke, but she caught the undertone. "The doctors said your shoulder will be good as new. Maybe even better. You heal fast. Some kind of miracle that the bullet stopped before it hit bone."

This time she heard the question in the statement, but made no comment.

He shrugged. "Just means it won't be a long military vacation."

"Thank you for helping me. And staying with me."

"Sure." He scooted his chair over and leaned into her ear. "I checked for cameras and audio devices. I think the room is clean. But better safe than sorry."

Which meant don't say anything you'll regret.

"Come closer," she said.

He did, and she held out her palm.

"Draw pictures for me."

He frowned, confused. She stared at him intently, trying to convey what she meant.

"Show me around this place."

Awareness dawned. "Ah."

Seth gave her the grand tour until General Martin joined them.

"Seth, Sunday. How are you today?"

"Good," she said.

He nodded, his lips pressed as he looked at Seth.

Seth sighed, understanding. "Time to go back?"

"My men will take you."

She grabbed Seth's hand, squeezing.

"Don't worry, you two will see each other soon enough."

They nodded, and Seth left quietly. Jocelyn adjusted herself on her good shoulder so she could face the General. He took a seat near her side and leaned forward, ready to have a serious conversation.

"You had us worried, soldier."

She smiled. "Sorry. I wasn't expecting an attack at home. You didn't train me for that."

He nodded. "Do you want to continue training? Military training?"

"Yes!" She shifted in the bed, with just a hint of concern. "I want to. Is my shoulder going to be a problem?"

"No, no. Doc says it will be fine. New methods and all that. But you've been here a long time with Dr. Cashus. The science team would miss you."

She didn't know how to respond exactly, so she nodded in agreement. "But I think I'm good at the military stuff. And I'm getting better. I think I could be useful." He remained silent. She added, "I just think everyone should have a purpose and be good at something. If you take it away…there's nothing left for me to do."

"Dr. Cashus says you're rebellious and stubborn. That Seth has been a bad influence on you. That your judgment is impaired."

Her eyes opened wide.

He smiled. "I know. *That* from the man who shot you point blank."

"I'm not rebellious. I have done every single thing they've asked me to do for nearly ten years. And my uncle *shoots* me? Do you know he's been chaining me and torturing me for weeks? I go to bed every night covered in bruises. He said he had a lot more things he can do to me, too. Please don't make me go back. He's going to kill me. Yes, I have opinions, but he treats me like I'm still ten. I need to know what the world is like. I can't be a super spy then get shot in the field because someone asks me who Oscar is."

"Who's Oscar?"

"I don't know," she pointed out. "Some guy who gives out awards!"

He laughed.

She had him. She lay back on the mattress, tired. "I'm not allergic to air. He told me I was allergic to the pollution outside the camp, but I'm not. I think it would be fine if I went into town. He lied to me. That's why I'm mad at him...and the torture, of course. Then there's the shooting." She smiled weakly. "That came after. All I think now is that he's willing to kill to prove something."

She closed her eyes trying to figure out how she really did feel about her uncle. Maybe as a kid she had loved him because there was no one else. He had saved her life at one point. He had even liked her at one point...right? Because the other possibility, that she'd always been just an experiment, hurt too much to believe. Had she been completely unlovable?

They'd never done anything social other than dinner, and that was more a report of her day. Any holiday, she spent alone with facilitators to make sure she did her exercises. He'd never actually gotten her anything. At first, she thought it was because she hadn't been good, but later, he'd explained he didn't believe in gifts. There were no memories of her childhood with him where Santa Claus existed or birthdays were celebrated. That left one conclusion. The soldiers had been right. She was a lab rat. She felt stupid and embarrassed about it now. And *angry*.

Would they joke when she finally died? Would they put "lab rat" on her grave, or just demolish the evidence of her ever existing? Or worse, would they keep her body in the freezer and bring it out to display to other scientists and government officials?

She put a hand on her stomach, ill at the thought. She had never been a kid or a niece to Uncle Laurence. That knowledge burned her insides worse than the gunshot had.

A warm hand gently touched her good shoulder and gave a light squeeze. She opened her eyes as the General stood up.

"I don't know much about raising kids, but I can make you a good soldier and prepare you for the future with skills you can use. What you do with them is up to you."

"I'd like that."

"Unfortunately, there's no eliminating the science part."

Her hope plummeted.

"But Dr. Cashus no longer has the final word when it comes to you. I have some control over that. If you succeed on this next mission, things will be different around here. That's for sure."

She understood. "I'm in, General."

He left, but instead of resting, her mind and body felt in turmoil. She planned the next step of her escape. Eyes on the prize, not the price. Sergei had it right.

But she fought something else now, too—an intense thirst. And with every ache of her recovery, the thirst grew.

She held her good arm up and channeled her energy. It had taken time and practice to understand how to awaken her body with control, but once she had, the force of her power had surprised her. She'd kept a large degree of her skill to herself, instinctively knowing it would scare people. Now she was glad. Her uncle and others suspected—there was no doubt of that. But she would never give them the opportunity to use her again.

A stream of energy ruffled her blanket and caused her hair to lift gently. She knew she could create a strong force around her, but only recently had she found a reason for practicing directional skills.

She cocked her finger like a gun and aimed.

The chair on the other side of the room didn't move. She put her hand down and snuggled back under the blanket.

On the cushion of the chair's back, a hole approximately a half-inch in diameter remained. She was never going back to her uncle, no matter what anyone said.

A slight smile tugged at her lips. She closed her eyes.

Patience and sacrifice were what mattered now. In the end, she'd surprise them all. She might even get her revenge.

CHAPTER TWENTY-EIGHT

Sergei sighed with relief when he finally saw Jocelyn for himself a week later in her daily measurement room. General Martin had shaved down the people on the science team who had access to her, but she still had a core team of doctors and technicians for her measurements and medications. Dominique had the upper hand over the narcissistic madman Cashus, at least for the moment, and she'd assigned Sergei to study Jocelyn's cellular makeup.

He was an expert in regenerative cell therapy, and there was something naturally embedded in Jocelyn's DNA that allowed her to self-heal at an unusual pace. It was not perfect. She still seemed to scar, but where her blood flowed freely, she achieved amazing results.

That might account for her quick recovery. Holliwell also had the top surgeons in nearly every field. She'd been cleaned up by the best, most advanced methods. And miraculously, according to the reports, the bullet hadn't penetrated very far. *Interesting* as well as miraculous.

Jocelyn interrupted his thoughts, greeting him at the door with a genuine smile.

"You are doing okay?" he asked.

She nodded. "I was surprised when they told me you were going to be my doctor."

"So it seems." He invited her in and had her stand while he put sensors on her hands and skull and down her spine, explaining that he would be taking measurements while she read.

He handed her a book.

She perked up, more interested. "What are we reading?"

"A novel. Crime and Punishment."

She flopped into a chair. "Is this a new type of torture? Uncle Laurence can just tell me how he's going to punish me for my crimes. He doesn't have to draw it out."

Sergei patted her shoulder. "I picked it myself. You'll like it."

She looked doubtful. "What's it about?"

"A man who thinks that he has the right to kill other people for a greater good." He handed her the book.

"Sounds familiar. Does he die in the end?"

"No."

"Not interested." She picked up the book and opened the cover anyway. "I prefer happy endings."

"He goes to prison, though."

"Outstanding. Another prison story. Is the whole world in jail?"

"Just start reading," Sergei commanded with amused tolerance, checking his computer read out.

She began to read the novel in Russian. Every once in a while, Sergei would correct her pronunciation and make her repeat a word. At the end of thirty minutes, he gave her a piece of paper and told her to write down the words he'd corrected her on in the order that they reviewed them. Slowly, she started to make the list.

"Okay. I'm done," she said.

He looked at her column while she continued to stare at it, as if trying to grasp something important.

"Excellent. Now quietly read through the list of words to see if you have missed anything. Include any duplicates." He typed on the computer. "I'll finish saving this session."

She read through them again, and suddenly the equipment on his counter began to vibrate. She understood. Her eyes blazed bright with fury. She took a breath of control and handed him the paper.

There was a camera in the room. They both knew where it was.

Sergei put the paper down next to his report notes glancing at the Russian words. It was the English translation he wanted her to remember. *I saw your records. Uncle knows your brother and sister live. The science team wants you back. Uncle's methods were extreme, but calculated. He still has support. Might get you back in time.*

"Very good." With his back to the camera, he picked up the paper, studied it, wrote in his notebook, and added, "Practice your vowels. Your accent is not half bad, eh?"

Then slowly he tore the paper in half, again and again until he had a stack of small squares. "That will be all for today." Covertly, he placed the squares of paper in his mouth, swallowed some water, and waved goodbye.

Graeme took off his light jacket and slammed the car door. It was early spring, but there was still a chill in the air. The classic Porsche had died just inside Charlottesville—totally unfair timing, especially when he was there to make sure his family really was safe.

He put on his augmented sunglasses. "Temperature." The temperature eased into his field of vision from the side of the glasses. *58 Fahrenheit, 86% humidity.*

His glasses had been specifically designed for gaming in a real-world environment, but he'd made some last minute modifications before the trip, updating the image capture and recognition software to enable a faster flow of stats with a link to his smartphone.

He checked into the game temporarily. There were still three enemy players alive, and he was barely within the game boundaries. Any farther south or west, and he would have to forfeit his life.

Switching back to his present situation, Graeme touched the side of his glasses capturing the image of the man in the tow truck. He read the instant download. Richie Dubois. Owner of AAA Auto Repair. Age 23, Army vet, served four-and-a-half years. Administrative discharge. *Hmmm. Wonder what that was for?*

The man walking toward him was the closest expert on Porsches in the area and had excellent reviews. A little bit quirky, according to a few customers, but absolutely brilliant with cars and anything mechanical. Graeme could put up with quirky.

Richie Dubois gave him an assessing look before popping the hood and inspecting the classic car. "Nice. Gonna be a pleasure to work on this." He laughed, "Expensive, but a pleasure."

"Yeah, I'm more concerned about how long it will take."

"We'll get it back to the shop and find out. Just a matter of getting parts. Heh, heh, heh."

"Why doesn't that sound promising?"

"A '65 Porsche 911. Heh, heh, heh."

"Yeah." *Not promising.*

"Just like Christmas." Richie closed the rear hood and pet the cobalt blue car gently. "Don't worry, baby. You're in the right hands now."

Graeme wasn't so sure of that. He read his viewer, checking for any additional information on Mr. Dubois. Other than the outstanding reviews for his auto work, it was surprisingly sparse. No family, no home address, no phone number, other than the business, and no hits on social media, not even to market his business.

Richie chained the underbelly of the Porsche and gently wheeled it onto the truck. He was friendly and chatty to the car, petting and comforting it. He even offered Graeme an easy smile. Graeme took his seat in the cab of the truck. This would slow his investigation down, but there was a reason for everything.

"Where do people hang out here?"

Richie glanced at him. It was a look of suspicion, as if something just occurred to him. "What are you in town for?"

"A girl." Graeme didn't miss a beat answering him.

Richie relaxed again. "Downtown is nice. Little shops, restaurants, movie theater. All the amenities."

"Cool. Thanks. I held a reservation at Brandy's Bed and Breakfast as back up. You know it?"

"Sure. Pricey for what you get." He glanced over again, staring at Graeme's sunglasses. "But looks like you can afford it."

Graeme shrugged. "I just launched a game that's doing well. Do you game?"

"Only on my phone."

"You can download it. It's called Zombie Master."

"What?" Richie turned, excited.

"Have you played it?"

Richie lifted his brow in an act of supremacy. "I *finished* it, man. What are you doing wasting your time chasing a girl when you should be working on Zombie Master 2?"

Graeme laughed. It felt good to have people enjoy his stuff.

"I didn't think anyone would make it to Level 13 so quickly."

"It was a bitch. Those damn leeches almost had me greened out. I wasn't going down for some bloodsucking parasites."

They talked about gaming all the way to Richie's shop. Graeme called for a rental car to pick him up there, and once the Porsche was safe in the garage, he grabbed one of Richie's cards and headed out. He had an appointment at the train station he knew better than to be late.

It had been a major task to find someone who could get him access to the security video. He'd originally planned on filing stalking charges and getting a subpoena, but that would have made his investigation public and potentially expose the mysterious caller before he could reach her. Instead he called the train station, chatted up one of the surveillance technicians, and made a deal.

"You said you have forty-eight cameras, inside and out?"

"Yep." Miss Willie, the well-coiffed, elderly technician at the train station had already prepped the dates and times for him. "We usually cover the phones 'cuz that's where the juicy deals go down."

"No doubt," Graeme grinned. "Did you pull the footage outside the station as well?"

"Yep." Miss Willie pulled up an additional angle. "You can see them exit here, then go off screen. She's parked in the lot. He looks kind of angry, but I can't tell if it's aggressive or protective. Could be her pimp or her brother. You know what I'm saying?"

"Yeah."

"But this...." She grinned sideways at Graeme, like a gloating new granny. "*This* is the money shot."

Graeme felt his blood tingle with triumph as he watched the girl back out of the parking space and execute a perfect three-point turn. "Gotcha."

Miss Willie froze the frame. "I'm betting you can run a license check on that baby. Am I right?" Miss Willie lifted a heavily ringed hand to high-five him.

"Definitely the money shot. Thanks, Miss Willie. Can you capture all four angles for me from ten minutes before arrival to ten minutes after?"

"Already done. Just need to copy it to your drive."

He handed her his drive with five hundred cash. "That will help with the bar tab on your cruise."

"At least half of it," she teased.

The footage was black and white, low resolution, and without audio, so it was hard to guess at the relationship between the two people. But it did narrow down his search to a young African-American girl with braids, about 5'4, cute figure. He didn't get more than a profile view of the face. He was hoping to freeze-frame her surreptitious sideways glance and see what he could do. The man, also African-American, a foot taller, looked like a fighter, maybe military. Not someone you wanted to meet in an alley—but not a bum. He was sure of that. The guy dressed like he thought something of himself, or like he had just interviewed for a job.

Graeme was steps closer to figuring out another piece of this mystery and couldn't wait to study these new clues. The copying finished, and with a kiss on Miss Willie's check, he left to start putting the pieces together.

There was no way Jocelyn was going back to her uncle. Never. Not going to happen. She had a plan and she had focus.

Her uncle no longer visited her for dinner. Instead, Liz had taken his place as her immediate guardian and temporarily stayed in the penthouse condo with her. Jocelyn still had to deal with her uncle for some tests, but they were back to testing with small objects. No stress testing. Despite her anger at him, she tried to improve the relationship with her uncle. She finally understood the expression Sarge used to joke about. Keep your friends close and your enemies closer. Her uncle must have understood that as well, because he made an effort to be nice in public.

He was good at it, too—which made life all the more painful and confusing. At least when he was mean, it was honest and she knew what she was dealing with. Now, she constantly walked on eggshells, waiting for the next blowup, snide comment, or complaint about her ingratitude.

She had a lot more time with Sergei, and that was always her favorite part of the day. One day he even told her a little about his wife and family.

She'd advanced quite a bit in understanding his messages. They were different every time, but he always passed on information he thought she might care to know or need to know.

In return for the better treatment, she was an ideal student once again. She wasn't rebellious, or disrespectful, or difficult. She excelled at everything, and only hinted to the General that maybe they could catch a movie in town sometime.

That sometime finally came.

Seth wasn't allowed to join them, she guessed because guarding one freak was hard enough. Still, she was ecstatic. She couldn't hold back her grins, and she didn't need to, since the General knew she'd been dying for a little freedom.

She also wasn't under the delusion that this was anything other than a test.

They wanted to see if she would make a run for it.

The General and a very impersonal female soldier, Private Jensen, took her into Charlottesville late Saturday morning. They'd picked a movie that was playing at the RCC. Her excitement peaked when she wondered if Georgie still worked there. She hoped she did. Otherwise, her escape plan was going to take a lot longer than she wanted.

Jocelyn wore her usual green army sweats and some half-worn running shoes. She didn't have much in the way of t-shirts other than army issue, so she picked a white one. Liz

loaned her a white zip-up hoodie in case she got cool in the
theater, which wasn't likely since she was generally warm, but
she appreciated the gesture.

It didn't take more than a short drive into town to realize she
didn't dress like anyone else, or at least not like other girls. Not
much she could do about that. She didn't have any money to
buy anything.

Mostly, Jocelyn was just in awe that she was leaving camp
and going into town. It was nothing short of a miracle. She
didn't stop thanking General Martin, and it was sincere. She
was out in the world. And it was beautiful.

Laurence was a jerk. All those years he kept her under lock
and key…. She blocked it out, wanting to enjoy the moment.
"It's really pretty, isn't it?" she enthused to the General. The
camp's Main Street must have been modeled after this town,
but this was bigger and better.

"It's charming," he said.

She nodded. "Yes, I feel very charmed. I like all the little
brick buildings and shops." She took in the colorful awnings
and patio dining on the streets where cars weren't allowed.
Couples and families with strollers were sitting outside
enjoying late breakfasts. She listened in on some of their
conversations fascinated by the relationships, the mundane, and
especially, how the parents treated the smallest children with
complete adoration. It triggered her longing to be part of a real
family.

"Maybe we can eat outdoors afterward?"

The General smiled. "We'll see how the time is."

Private Jensen checked her watch. "Are you allowed to eat
that kind of food?"

Jocelyn frowned. "I think so." Was the food different?
"Someone must serve boiled chicken or grilled steak with
boring vegetables."

General Martin laughed. "I think we can do better than
that."

"Do a lot of the soldiers and scientific staff live here?"

"Some," General Martin answered. "Most stay on base since
it's cheaper."

She wanted to ask dozens more questions but just took it all in, making mental notes of shops that might be useful, the types of cars that were in the street, and what regular girls looked like. At the very least, she needed some jeans and t-shirts that didn't look like she borrowed them from a guy.

A short time later, popcorn in hand and the movie starting, she forgot all about clothes and escaping. She didn't even care what the film was about. The lights went down and then there were a bunch of really short movies called previews before the main event. Just before it started, she turned to the General excitedly. "This is outstanding! Isn't it?"

He stared a moment in the light of the screen, taken off guard, then agreed. She heard Jensen laugh at her. If the woman couldn't appreciate a day out at the movies, that was her problem. *This* was *outstanding.*

She'd seen movies as a child but couldn't remember this experience of being in the theater—the lights going dark, then an explosion of light and sound and beauty. What a great place to work. For almost two hours, she forgot completely about her life of captivity and that she was going to die in a few years. It was a nice break from reality even if the movie was a cartoon about talking planes and cars trying to find self-fulfillment.

It was over too soon, and they were walking back into the lobby area when Jocelyn spotted her.

Georgie of the RCC.

Jocelyn nearly stumbled and apologized to Private Jensen before mentioning she needed to use the restroom. Before Jensen could tell her where to go, Jocelyn walked over to where Georgie served behind the snack bar with a couple other employees. She asked for the restrooms and tried to make a signal to Georgie, but to no avail. The boy nearest pointed her the right way.

Jensen followed her into the restroom, right up to the stall. "You're not coming in, are you?"

"Do you know how to wipe yourself?"

"Can you wait outside? It's embarrassing."

"I have to go myself," she said. "Don't dawdle."

"I'll tell that to my bladder," Jocelyn said.

"Shouldn't have drunk all that lemonade." She got into the stall next to her, and Jocelyn dawdled as long as possible, scoping out the public stall for places one could hide secret messages. Her escort finished and said to meet her outside the door.

Jocelyn breathed a moment of relief. She listened carefully to hear the private out in the hall tell the General that she got embarrassed easily. That gave her a few minutes. She washed her hands as a group of girls and women crowded the restroom, no doubt due to the end of another movie.

"There are a lot of military peeps here today, huh?"

Jocelyn looked up into the mirror. She breathed a sigh of relief, hope, and fear all at once as she met the eyes of Georgie of the RCC. She glanced around for other military personnel, but it seemed safe. She smiled back and said, "Yeah."

Jocelyn pulled out the message she'd stuck under the tongue of her shoe, and when it seemed safe, placed it casually on the counter with her hoodie for Georgie to read. Georgie washed her hands while reading, then looked up in the mirror, staring at her wide-eyed and speechless. Jocelyn's throat tightened. Not the reaction she'd hoped for, but what could she expect? She was a stranger and a freak from a military base.

Quickly, she tore the small message in half three times and shoved the paper in her mouth before anyone could notice. It stuck in her throat. Sergei made it look so easy. She cupped her hands under the faucet for a little water to make the paper go down—along with her plan, it seemed.

Private Jensen came back to check on her.

"Sorry," Jocelyn choked. "I dawdled. Everything is so different. I can't help it."

Private Jensen took her arm wordlessly and led her out.

"Wait, miss!"

Jocelyn looked back. Georgie had Liz's hoodie.

"You forgot this."

"Thank you."

Georgie stared at her, her face anxious. Then something miraculous happened. She nodded her head. "Happy to help." She nodded again to make her answer clear. Then she made a face at the private behind her back. "Ya'll come back soon."

Jocelyn smiled and said they would, her step suddenly lighter and her heart expanding.

The plan forming in her head just might work.

CHAPTER TWENTY-NINE

Graeme sat outside the men's room in the Royal Crown Cinema, clicking his phone app while aiming his camera glasses at various theater goers. A week of tracking Henrietta Georgina Washington had finally paid off. There was definitely a link between the movie clerk and Holliwell. The movie theater was crawling with plainclothes army types.

He took as many pictures as possible so he could identify them later, then exited. A car pulled up to the corner by the theater entrance. The driver, in military uniform, got out of the black SUV and waved to someone exiting. He turned abruptly to look, surprising the person behind him who bumped into his chest.

She grabbed him instinctively, and his hands whipped out to catch her. A rush of pleasant heat and energy jolted through the center of his palms and seemed to fan out through his body. She froze a second in confusion, long enough for him to register curious, brilliantly blue eyes and feel the strength of slender muscles under ultra-soft skin.

"Sorry," she said, automatically.

He blinked, still holding her. "I'm not." It was a programmed response. He was a guy. What was a guy to do but flirt?

She blinked in surprise, her cheeks turning a light shade of pink as she smiled up at him, a little embarrassed, but thankfully interested enough to meet his gaze.

Wow. He couldn't stop looking. She was close enough for him to catch a faint scent of lemon soap mixed with buttered popcorn. Suddenly, it was the most comforting and exotic smell in the world.

A man with her immediately reached for Graeme's arm and pulled him away, breaking their contact. He apologized instantly to the girl and the older man taking her away.

"No harm," the man returned. "Excuse us."

A tough-looking woman stepped to the other side of the girl, grabbed her arm, and directed her to the car. "This way. Let's go."

The blue-eyed girl's smile instantly changed to an expression he could only think of as bland pleasantness. It was a mask. He'd seen his mother use it at times in the office, or on the campaign trail when she was tired or needed to be patient with someone and endure her work just a little longer. He wondered how long this girl had been enduring. He wanted to follow her and find out.

He heard the conversation as she stepped off the curb into the SUV. He'd already photographed the plates—they were military.

"Are we going to eat?"

"Not today," the older man said. "Sorry, we'll get you fed when we're back."

She nodded silently and seemed to pull her arm away from the female guardian. The woman held on, so she yanked it defiantly and said something to her that he couldn't make out. Probably that she could walk by herself.

Just before she ducked to get in, she glanced back. He lifted a hand in farewell. Their eyes linked before the guardian lady pushed her head down through the door like a cop managed a criminal.

As if on cue, nearly all the cars on the street pulled away after the vehicle. If he wasn't mistaken, that was a security detail. Who was she? What was that heat that shot through him? Was that his body reacting to her? Wow. If that's what chemistry was, no wonder people fell in love at first sight. She had the smile of a heartbreaker. He caught himself fantasizing and stopped. She was probably a General's daughter. *Never get involved with a General's daughter.* His brother Rex had drilled that into him—after he'd gotten involved with a

General's daughter. Rex was dedicated to upholding the law and breaking the rules. It was one of the few things that made him lovable.

His phone rang, and Richie updated him on Nellie. His Porsche now had a name. Parts were installed and running fine, and did he want Richie to do a little customization to make her really hum? Graeme listened to the suggestions. Richie was no ordinary mechanic.

"Wow. You can do that?" Graeme asked.

"Yup. Got all the parts."

"Can you add a location scrambler that acts like an invisibility cloak, night-vision driving, and heat-guided missiles?"

There was a pause on the other side of the line. "The location scrambler will cost you. Missiles come standard."

Graeme laughed. "I don't really need the missiles."

"You say that now. But when that girl breaks your heart, you might wish you had them."

Graeme stared at the phone. Was he serious? With Richie, he'd quickly learned the dude had access to tech that could do serious damage.

"It's not legal, of course," Richie said. "But I can hide one-inchers underneath the sunroof. Just make sure the sunroof is open when you launch. Otherwise, it will rip off the entire hood. Uh, and it'll be bad for your hearing, too, obviously."

"Obviously." Graeme briefly considered mini-missiles launching from his classic Porsche. "Let's just go with the night-vision for now."

"Cool. I knew you'd be a good customer," Richie said. "I can have it ready in a few days. You're gonna love it."

"Cool," Graeme echoed. Richie had already hung up. He shook his head. It was nice having his Porsche upgraded, but maybe he was getting a little carried away. Naw. Missiles would have been too much. This was okay.

He turned his thoughts back to the girl. He'd probably been overthinking it. She was just a normal kid. Too young for him. Army brat, for sure. But those eyes...yeah, those eyes could break your heart. But missiles were still overkill.

He scrolled through his images from the last two hours, disappointed when he realized he hadn't gotten a single picture of her.

Georgie's heart didn't stop palpitating her entire shift. She wanted to tell Al what had happened, but her cousin would probably have her locked up. She debated filling in Brittany, but she owed it to her friend. They were in this together. And Georgie was going to need help.

On the way home, she stopped in a nearly-empty grocery store parking lot and ran over a few white parking space stops. Eventually, the GPS tracking device attached to the undercarriage of her dad's car fell off. She ran over it and left it there. Now the only thing she had to worry about was the listening device—but at least she had a special tool to solve that.

At home, she visited her dad in his study. He was up late typing away at his computer, glasses perched on his nose, the light from a reading lamp making him look more stern than usual. Behind him on the wall was a blown-up photo of the Harlem Hellfighters. Beneath, in a beautifully-encased temperature and humidity-controlled box, sat a picture of her great-grandfather with his medal, the Croix de Guerre. It was the highest military honor awarded by the French government, given to her great-granddaddy Henry during World War II. He'd been eighteen.

She stared at it over her dad's head.

Looking up at her, he took off his glasses. "Everything okay, honey?"

Something in her face must have given her away. She wanted to confide in him. She needed his advice and encouragement in a way she never did before. But she also knew he would protect her first. So how could she help the girl and still tell the truth?

Sighing, Georgie perused the shelves of history books, her hand stopping when she came to the section on the Underground Railroad. Greedy slave owners were a lot different from a highly-militarized government. How would her ancestors have dealt with this situation?

Her dad closed his book and put it aside. "Anxious about college acceptances?"

She shook her head. "No. I'm excited."

"Boy trouble?"

Georgie smiled. "No. You scare off all the boys, remember?"

"I'm just testing them. A good one wouldn't scare off."

"I'm worried about a friend." She saw his knowing look. "And before you start thinking the friend is me, it's not. She's in a totally different situation."

"Um-hmm." He waited.

"I think she needs help. And I want to help her."

"What's her situation?"

"Umm. It's complicated. Really strict parents. I think she's being abused. But I'm not sure by whom exactly."

"How do you know this?"

"I know she wants to run away. It must be bad if she's planning to do that." She waited for his response. He didn't give one. Instead, he lowered his glasses and started typing.

She waited while the printer spit out a sheet of paper.

"Give her that. It's the number for Child Protective Services. They can get her out of her current situation. If she's under eighteen, she can also ask the court to emancipate her. I don't know the details of that, but she can find out."

Georgie took the paper and sat in the chair across from him. "Thanks, Dad." She stared at it. "What if her parents come after her? I'm afraid there might be some kind of violence."

"Don't get involved in that, sweetheart."

They were the last words she thought she'd ever hear from her dad. Granted, he was being protective, but it still sounded wrong.

"If there's any kind of bad behavior going on, I don't want you anywhere near her house. Give her that information or have her talk with a school counselor. People who specialize in this are what's needed."

She nodded. It wasn't what she really wanted to hear. For once, she wanted him to repeat the heroic feats of their ancestors, remind her there must be individuals in every generation who stand up and stand out, no matter the cost.

"Running away doesn't help, baby. And a young girl on her own will become an even worse victim. If you want to help her, help her to make the hard decisions."

Georgie's throat tightened a little. She didn't think Child Protective Services would have any jurisdiction at Holliwell.

"Okay. Thanks, Dad. I should get to bed." She didn't want to be around him. He couldn't help her, and she didn't want him to know it. She didn't want him to feel bad about it.

But how could she explain this certainty that the girl with the blue tears was in danger? And if she was who she said she was, how could Georgie explain that everyone thought she was dead, no one was looking for her, and no one wanted her to be found?

Something wasn't right, and Georgie had a chance to help fix it. She had to at least try. She might fail miserably. And that might have worse consequences than she could imagine. But could she turn her head away and pretend not to see? Could she spend the rest of her life wondering what had become of that strange girl? Could she, for her own safety, decide not to help?

That wasn't how she'd been raised. In the end, her father couldn't deny that.

She kissed him goodnight and put the paper in her backpack, hugging it to her chest, recalling the beseeching look on the girl's face and the carefully printed words: *I'm going to escape soon. Will you help me? If so, same place—two weeks—hopefully.*

Georgie needed to make some plans and get some resources lined up.

Two weeks was not a lot of time to plan an escape from Holliwell. Whatever Jocelyn Albrecht had in mind, it had better be good.

CHAPTER THIRTY

Jocelyn passed her Charlottesville test. She hadn't made a run for it, though it crossed her mind a few times. There'd been back-up in the theater, and for all she knew, some of the employees were military plants.

They stopped at a store on the way back for supplies, and the General bought her a hoodie of her own. She picked black. It was the most useful color. She also asked for a pink t-shirt with orange and yellow flowers on it. It served to throw General Martin off the trail. She liked the t-shirt, of course, but there was no room in her plans for being a regular girl. She had limited resources and couldn't waste them.

Still, she wished she had been wearing it today when she ran into that guy with the green eyes. Her body got warm just thinking of him. He'd looked at her as if he *saw* her—which she knew was stupid, because of course he saw her. *It was just different.* Everyone studied and measured her. Even Seth looked at her in an assessing way.

Then, she'd caught his gaze before getting into the car and decided she didn't like that he saw her, because she realized maybe others could see that she was faking it, too.

How could he tell?

It must have been her imagination.

Her uncle had warned her that girls get to an age where they project their emotions and desires on boys, and the boys are just thinking about sports and boobs. That's probably what his look was about. She looked down at her breasts, contemplating. Not much to think about there. She always had a sports bra on. Compared to the other girls and women she'd seen in the movie theater, she was virtually flat chested. Maybe he'd been stunned by how flat she was. Or he'd been thinking about sports, and that's why they had bumped into each other. Yes, that was more likely. He hadn't looked down at her chest at all. She shook the mental conversation off. *What was wrong with her?*

Likely he thought she was a soldier.

She closed her eyes and told herself not to think about the dark hair that fell over his forehead, or the gentle strength he'd used as he caught her.

Who knows, he might even be a plant that Uncle Laurence sent to town to test her. He was so worried about Seth, that wouldn't surprise her. In any case, she wouldn't think about those green eyes, or how she'd been able to hear his heart beat faster when he caught her, and feel the quickening of his pulse through the connection of his hands on her. She could sense those things with everyone. There was nothing different about it with him, except that he was a stranger she would never see again, and he reminded her that she couldn't be too careful when it came to masking her emotions.

The next few days were uneventful. She continued to live in the condo, and Liz had dinner and conversation with her every night. Uncle Laurence joined them once, under Liz's supervision, and Jocelyn did her best to be civil.

While General Martin continued to train her for the next field trip, she began planning her own exit strategy.

She studied where supplies were, where keys were kept, how long it would take to get in, get out, and where the security cameras were planted.

Other than her meds, Jocelyn felt she could survive with limited clothing. Food would be the biggest issue without any money to pay for it, but she could work. And water was available everywhere. What else could she need?

She stretched at the edge of the forest track waiting for Seth. They were doing a marathon run this morning.

He was another challenge. She couldn't leave Seth behind.

She walked to him eagerly as he got out of the Jeep, stopping short before a hug could take place.

Megan and Sarge warmed them up and sent them on their way, tracking them in the Jeep. Jocelyn was surprised Dominique wasn't there, but it seemed she'd begun to trust Uncle Laurence's team, and they were working together moderately well—which was probably not a good sign for Jocelyn and Seth.

Seth was fast, but it took time to build up the heart muscles for long distances. That's how she knew he hadn't been a freak as long as she had. Certain body tissues and functions hadn't caught up yet.

Seth chatted the entire time. She wasn't used to talking while running. It was her private time to enjoy the outdoors and think.

He chatted. About everything.

When he brought up food, she begged him to stop. He talked about food that was fantastical. It couldn't be real.

"I don't believe you."

"It's true. I've been there a hundred times."

"But you never got the free dinner?"

"No. I came close once. I could do it now."

"Easily," she agreed.

"You?"

"Uh-huh. Seventy-two ounce steak with corn, cranberries, mashed potatoes, and all the bread they can cook in less than one hour?" She hopped over a fallen tree branch. "Easy."

"It's a bet."

She laughed. The idea of the two of them at a roadside restaurant in Texas eating giant steaks seemed beyond impossible. "And you get it free?" She laughed again. "You're lying."

"I'm not. Most normal people can't eat that much. You're going to have a really big food bill if you ever get out of here. You might want to get a job at a restaurant like that. All the Texas steak you can eat for free."

He had a point there.

"We'll make it our Mexico. Promise to meet me there."

"Our Mexico?"

"Yeah, like Andy and Red." He huffed after completing a series of artificial hurdles in the path.

"Oh! The prison movie." She smiled. "I liked that ending."

"You, me, and two seventy-two ounce steaks. That will be our happy ending."

She kept running. That would be a dream, all right.

"Promise?"

"What?" she asked.

"Promise that you'll meet me there."

"Okay." They were running through a straight section in the path, thick with blossoming trees. She jumped high now and then to touch the leaves and feel the nourishing energy directly on her skin.

Seth huffed to keep up. "Even if I don't get out, promise me you'll go when you get out."

"Not if you're not there. It would be too sad."

"No it won't. Free steak. Plus, you get to see the great state of Texas. It's a small thing to ask, but I guess if our friendship means so little...."

"Okay, okay." She laughed.

"Promise me."

"I promise."

"As soon as you get outta here."

She jumped one last time, reluctant to admit the possibility. "I might never get out of here."

"Keep working it. You will."

She didn't say anything. She sort of had a plan, but it wasn't fully worked out. She just knew it would require patience. The patience of Andy Dufresne.

Eyes on the prize, not the price.

Seth stopped chatting for a while. She could tell he was losing energy. She adjusted to a slower speed. "Gonna make it?"

"Yeah."

"Ten more miles. Easy though."

"I got it."

"I know."

They passed a final checkpoint of visual surveillance. "They're going to move me soon."

Jocelyn literally skid to a stop. "What?"

Seth kept going. "Catch up."

When she didn't, he turned and finally stopped.

She ran to him and grabbed his forearms in hers, holding him in front of her. "What do you mean? How? When?" Her blood seemed to sting throughout her body—the dirt shifted around them, followed by a quick burst of panic that fluttered the trees and sent birds flying away.

Seth watched the birds fly away. "Not sure. I overhead a tech say they were moving me to a facility in Colorado."

"Colorado!" It may as well have been the moon. The distance was, well, *far*. "It can't happen."

"It won't."

"Good." She breathed hopefully, then remembered there was no hope. "Okay, wait. What do you mean?"

"Let's run."

He didn't need to explain. They were acting suspicious.

"What I mean," he continued, "is that I'm getting off before they get me there."

"How?"

"Don't worry about that, just know it. And take care of yourself. No one's going to rescue you."

"I know."

"Okay, then stick to the plan. Seventy-two ounce steaks."

"Oh, Seth." Jocelyn stopped running again, this time feeling sick.

He came over to her and pushed her back forcefully. "Don't be a wimp."

He wanted to toughen her up. She understood that, but it didn't matter. "I can't do this alone." A deep sense of isolation sucked the energy from her. She hadn't realized how much she depended on him emotionally. Having him there, even when she couldn't see him, was like having someone in her corner. He gave her the courage to take the risks she'd never taken before. She'd lost her family, then her uncle showed his true colors, then the security she'd felt on the base—no matter how false it had been—was gone. This was too soon. She couldn't lose another person.

She threw herself into his arms and hugged him tight, knowing in her heart she couldn't be the problem that held him back. "If you have the chance, I want you to be free." She lifted her head, feeling her eyes burn a little. "I was just being selfish."

"You are the least selfish person I've ever met." He cupped her cheeks gently and kissed her forehead so softly it felt like a breeze on her skin. "You need to be *more* selfish. You need to think only of yourself. If you have even a window on this mission they are planning for you...." He looked directly into her eyes and spoke with quiet force. "*Take it.*"

His lips pressed against hers. She didn't know what to do. The force was not unpleasant, then he relented, pulled back, and tenderly explored her lips. He lifted his head before she could respond or engage. And, well, she didn't really know what to do anyway.

"I've never done that before."

"I can tell." He stepped back.

She stepped forward.

"Wait." She grabbed the front of his t-shirt and pulled. "Can we do it again?"

He answered with action.

Nice. She sighed, relaxing for a split second before remembering the guy with the green eyes. She blocked that vision and focused back on Seth, trying to understand how she felt—how *this* felt. His fingers grazed down her neck. *Very nice.*

The honking of the Jeep interrupted them. Megan shouted over a megaphone. "Move along. We're waiting." Jocelyn didn't know how they could tell where they were, but Megan seemed to have the general direction through the trees. Very annoying. From the look on Seth's face, he must have felt the same.

"Come on," he said. "Race you." He slapped her butt and ran off. She chased after him but let him win. Besides, the view was nice from behind. And it might not be for long.

CHAPTER THIRTY-ONE

Two weeks passed, and though it had taken some finagling of General Martin, she was able to get him to approve another movie trip. They both knew that soon their mission training would be all-encompassing, and she played up the few opportunities there might be prior.

He didn't join her on the next trip, so she was stuck with Private Jensen and another Sergeant accompanying her to the first show of the day. The theater attendance was light, with mostly parents and little kids. This time, she saw Georgie right away, prepping the snack bar. She went for popcorn and overheard Georgie asking a co-worker to cover her while she ran to the restroom.

Jocelyn handed off her popcorn to Private Jensen telling her she needed to use the restroom and ran to join Georgie. Jensen wasn't happy about it. No doubt the woman would be on her heels.

Jocelyn pretended to look underneath the stalls for an empty one while hunting for the red sneakers Georgie wore. She stepped into the stall next to her and waved a hand underneath. Her hand was grabbed, and a few pages of paper were pressed into it with a pen.

Jocelyn unfolded the papers. The first page had a picture of some people. She realized it was a copy of a paper—*The New York Times*. It took her a moment to realize the people in the story were Jocelyn and her parents. Her pulse quickened, and her heart pounded unnaturally. She stared at her photo for a long moment—she was six, almost seven. The picture was her first grade photo. She had an open, happy grin, one front tooth missing. She looked at her parents. The photos looked like work portraits. They wore lab coats. She remembered the lab coats. She liked to wear her mom's white coat and pretend she was a scientist. Sometimes they wore them together when they were baking. Their deaths were caused by a home laboratory accident.

Jocelyn stared, mesmerized. Their eyes looked directly at her. Her mother was dark-haired, dark-eyed, and golden-skinned. Her father the opposite—so pale, even his eyebrows were blond. But his eyes made her breath catch.

Sharp blue eyes.

Her eyes.

She wanted to press the photos to her heart, but knew there wasn't much time. She read the next bit of story. The survivors, Morgan and Benjamin Albrecht, were currently staying with friends of the family. Jocelyn looked at the next page. Two more photos. School photos. She swallowed hard, her eyes welling up. The photos were from this year. Morgan at fifteen and Ben ten years old. They looked bright and happy, despite the plaid school uniforms.

She turned to the third page. It had a typed paragraph from Georgie.

Morgan and Benjamin Albrecht were adopted by Mr. Ford Rochester and his wife, then New York State Governor Rachel Winslow-Rochester. They are one of the wealthiest families in America. Ford Rochester is CEO and Chairman of the Board of A & R Technologies. The A is for Albrecht, which the company kept in honor of two of the three founding partners—Dr. Illeana Marques Albrecht and Dr. Grayson Albrecht, who died in an accident that, according to reports, still has some mystery surrounding it. No one knows what caused it, if it really was an accident, or if it was deliberate. One thing we do know is that the people who benefited the most are the Rochesters. The bio-technology the Albrechts developed was the foundation for 75% of the products and 90% of the profits that A & R grossed in the last fifteen years. Don't know if the Rochesters are good or bad, but they seem to have taken good care of Ben and Morgan. The security around the family is very tight, and it would be hard to reach them, even if one was in

New York City where they live and go to school. That's the summary of what I found so far.

What do you need?

When do you need it?

Jocelyn finished reading Georgie's note, amazed and less certain of things than ever before. She looked at her parents and siblings, trying desperately to remember more. They were like strangers. It made her feel even more lost. She was barely able to recognize her own face from childhood. But still, she couldn't stop staring at the portrait of the brown-haired girl with the wide, toothless smile. She appeared so open and happy. Like she'd been loved and was confident because of it. Jocelyn felt her chest constrict at a memory that flickered on the remotest edges of her mind—sitting on her mother's lap and playing the strings of an instrument, her hands guiding her, the comfort and warmth of her mother's voice, calm and reassuring.

A voice from the washing area called to her, coming closer.

"Sunnie?" It was Private Jensen. "Where are you?" She sounded concerned.

"I'm here. There was a line." Jocelyn scribbled on the paper quickly—*Transportation. Midnight. West side of the Dam Bridge. Date TBD. Maybe four weeks. Standby.*

Private Jensen stood outside the stall, her boots visible underneath the door. Jocelyn was afraid to fold the papers and make noise.

"Just a minute."

Jocelyn heard a banging sound and a frustrated sigh from Georgie. She stared to her right, panicked the girl would give her away.

"Hey, can someone pass me some toilet paper?" Georgie said loudly.

Brilliant! Georgie was brilliant. Jocelyn pulled a roll of paper from her metal holder. "I have an extra roll sitting here. Once second." She flushed, used the sound to shove the papers in the center of the roll, and handed it underneath the stall. She stuck the pen under the back of the seat and left the stall, bumping into a suspicious Jensen outside.

Jensen grabbed her arm. "Wait." She stepped into the stall and looked around, taking a quick glance behind the door, practically dragging Jocelyn with her—which was very awkward. "Let me see your pockets."

"What?" She really *was* suspicious. Jocelyn's heart beat a little too fast. Reluctantly, she pulled out her pockets.

Jensen eyed her pulled-out pockets, debating something. "Just want to make sure you're not vandalizing property or anything like that."

Jocelyn pulled her arm away, insulted. "I wouldn't vandalize. It's disrespectful and against the law." She shook her head and went to the sinks. "Come on. I don't want to miss the previews."

Georgie still hadn't left her stall, and Jocelyn wanted to exit before she did. They found their seats, but not before she spotted a soldier in the dark talking to two other men who quickly took seats near the exits. It was a good lesson to learn that the General didn't fully trust her, and there were always extra eyes on her.

The previews began, and the movie was another animated feature. This one about a princess trapped in a tower—another prison movie. It could have been about anything. She stared and smiled, and laughed when the audience laughed. She didn't see more than a few frames of the movie. All she could see were faces of her family staring at her, happy and content. Even her parents looked happy before they died. At least that was good. But what about this Rochester family? Who were they? Did they have something to do with her parents' deaths? Were her brother and sister really happy, or were they also planning an escape? Or maybe they were like she had been— clueless, innocent, eager-to-please, afraid to lose what they had left, and mostly…happy.

Jocelyn couldn't blame them. Might as well be happy while you could, even if it wasn't real.

Graeme knew he was being tracked. It didn't help. He should have expected it. Prepared for it. While he had been tracking Georgie, someone had been tracking him.

Definitely not good timing. He'd finally gotten a break. Georgie had done research on Ben and Morgan. He'd tracked her searches at a branch library in the next town. She was being careful not to use her own computer, so for whatever reason, she didn't want to leave traces. Nothing she'd done was illegal, so there was nothing he could really do at this point.

He considered approaching her and just asking what she wanted, but he wasn't the only one who was watching Georgie. The big guy from the train station videos checked in on her a lot. Alastair Washington—her cousin. Definitely not a dude he wanted to take on alone despite his own 6'1" height. Interestingly, Alastair had been at Holliwell for a time before his discharge. It was one more connection.

Graeme ducked into the coffee shop across from the theater and took a spot by the window, donning his Augmented Reality glasses. Slowly, he scanned the seating areas outside. He ran the facial recognition software from his phone and tried to identify anyone who didn't belong. His first search eliminated any civilian residents from Charlottesville. That erased 85%. When he added Virginia that erased all but three targets.

Not good.

Three of them.

Across the street. Two females chatting. A guy leaning against a tree texting...right by his rental car.

Not a coincidence.

He dialed Richie. "Hey. It's Graeme. I need your help. Is Nellie in driving condition?"

"Yep."

"Great. Bring her around the Coffee Cottage. Pull up so the passenger side faces the entrance. I'm in a little bit of a bind. Hurry, but don't draw any attention."

Richie sounded concerned and said he'd be there ASAP.

Three minutes later, Graeme watched as his classic Porsche passed the coffee shop, screeched across the road in a one-eighty spin, leaving skid marks and terrifying bystanders before pulling up three feet from him. The passenger side door shot open. After a moment of shock, he ran to safety.

Richie sat at the wheel, grinning from ear to ear. "Didn't see that comin', did ya?"

"I said don't draw attention!"

"You said hurry."

"Yeah, but...." Graeme laughed. It was hard to be mad at Richie. He was sincerely sweet and wacky at the same time. "Just go straight and make the next left."

Richie made a fast, hard left. Graeme's eyes bulged as the car cornered like it was on rails, hugging the ground. "Wow."

"Riiiight?" Richie bobbed his head, dragging out the acknowledgement. "I fine-tuned that a little bit for you."

"Awesome," Graeme agreed. "Another left down that alley. Stop just past the movie theater. But quietly. I need the element of surprise."

Richie brought the vehicle to a purring stop. Nellie sounded good. Richie put down the window and winked at him. "Should we wait here?"

"Yeah. This might take about ten to fifteen minutes. Don't go anywhere." Graeme moved stealthily to the other end of the building and peeked around the corner. The two girls and the guy were at a table talking to each other. Probably reevaluating now that their cover was blown. But how could he get three at once?

He went back around the alley. Richie was grooving to some music, relaxing in the driver's seat of the Porsche, and didn't even notice him. Graeme laughed to himself again. The dude needed a hobby.

He went through the back entrance of the café. It was a casual place run by college students. He pulled an apron off one of the doors, donned it, grabbed a used serving tray a waiter put down on the counter, took two waters that were lined up for the servers in advance, and headed to the front.

Graeme didn't say a word when he reached them. His left hand dumped the tray on the girl to the left. She jumped up and knocked her chair back in surprise. He touched the earpiece of his glasses and stunned the guy in his left lens, turned and got the girl next to him when she looked up. With his left hand, he pulled his phone to stun the last victim fussing over her lap of ice water. It was over before any of them could make a sound.

Then they cursed.

M.I.T. had just been taken down.

The final assassinations added up across his lenses, and his phone fired up with messages.

"I can't believe you *did* that," the girl with the wet lap shouted. "That was so *dirty*."

The other guy shrugged. "It was three on one." Dirty was fair play.

"I hate you, Rochester," the other girl said. Daphne was the name on her assassination report. "You're such a bastard."

Graeme thought about that. "Actually, I'm not." He saw the cars pull up just like last time. He sat down with the three M.I.T. assassins and waited. It was the girl again. The movie must be over. Dang it, he was going to miss her now.

"Look, I'll cover your lunch or brunch here and take you to dinner before you leave." He saw people begin to exit the movie theater. "But there's a girl who's going to exit the theater in a minute with a bunch of bodyguards, and I need a picture of her." He looked to the girls. "Can you walk that way and get one?"

"What does she look like?"

"Dark hair in a ponytail, black hoodie." He'd seen them enter earlier. "There." She walked out, but her head was down today, either thoughtful or distracted. The same woman was with her, a hand on her arm, a different man behind them.

Daphne jumped up and shouted, waving to the crowd. "Hey, girlfriend!"

Everyone turned and looked at her—including his mystery girl. Daphne waved, as if waving to someone behind them, and the girl turned and looked the other way, curious, all the while being led to the car. As before, the older woman tucked her head in and followed, while the soldier went to the other side of the car and got in. The sedan took off and the other cars followed. But one car pulled up to where they sat and stopped to check them out.

Graeme kept his head down and turned away from their gaze, while Daphne yelled to a random girl down the street staring at her. "Sorry! Thought you were someone else." She sat down, apologizing to the surrounding customers. "My bad. Sorry."

The sedan pulled away, and Graeme was careful not to look for others that might be lingering.

"I think I got it," Daphne said.

Graeme could have kissed her.

"But it's gonna cost you."

"Of course," he said.

Minutes later he was tapping Richie on the shoulder. "I'll drive."

"Cool. I'll take you through the mods. But the night-vision..."—he went around the passenger side and got in—"can only be appreciated at night."

"Of course," Graeme found himself saying again.

"There's more I can do, you know. Bulletproof glass, remote access—in case you're car jacked. If you have your phone, you can stop the car. Even control it."

"Really?"

"Yep. And check this out."

Graeme watched as the spot that used to hold the ashtray opened to display white tablets. "What are those?"

Richie spoke clearly. "Porsche mints. For before you pick up your date." Richie popped one in his mouth and held another up for Graeme. "See, shaped like a Porsche. These are the '65."

Graeme took one from the dish and popped it into his mouth. "Nice touch." They fist bumped.

"Mints are on the house."

"Thanks, man. I probably don't need the bulletproof glass."

"How about the remote access?"

"I'm gonna need the car back, Richie."

"Wait." Richie reached behind the driver's side and eagerly pulled out a compact contraption. He placed it above him to demonstrate where it would go. "How about the missile launcher?"

Graeme nearly crashed into a tree. "I thought we agreed no missile launcher?" He stared at the foot-long, slender missile in Richie's hand, back at the road, then back at Richie.

"Pretty badass though, right?" Richie encouraged, hopeful.

Graeme grinned back helplessly. "It is badass." He shook his head. "But I'm gonna need the car back, Richie."

Richie wilted in the seat, hugging his missile launcher like a little kid whose precious toy had just been insulted. He seemed to shrink in size.

It was silent in the car. Graeme took another look at Richie. The guy seemed to come alive when working on stuff. "I'm going to be around a little longer. How long does it take to install the bulletproof glass?"

Richie perked up. "I can do it in a day."

Graeme wavered then gave in. "Sure, let's do it. Let me know when it's in, okay?"

"Already ordered." Richie smiled.

Graeme nodded. Sometimes people just needed something to look forward to. He tapped his phone at a red light and looked at the picture of the mysterious girl. He'd been hoping to see her again.

"Is that her?" Richie asked, curious.

"Uh…." Graeme didn't want to lie. "It's complicated."

Richie lifted his hands. "*That's* why you need bulletproof glass."

CHAPTER THIRTY-TWO

On their final official EmWAV lesson, Jocelyn and Seth faced an obstacle course. They still had their assistant drivers on board to make sure they didn't get too crazy, but the instructors weren't allowed to help. First one through the paces won. Medina rode with Jocelyn.

Jocelyn had no intention of winning. She had another test she wanted to run.

As far as she could tell, the lake zone was the farthest area west on Holliwell. It bordered a National Park, but the area between Holliwell and the public had layers of security to deter any curious visitors. The forest was thick, and the fastest connection was one narrow waterway with a collection of gates to prevent recreational vehicles from entering. She needed to find a way to maneuver around them—or over them. She'd figured out enough from the EmWAV manual, and from talking to other trained drivers, to know the vehicles were capable of a hop. The questions she needed to answer were how quickly could they hop, within what distance, and how many times before it turned disastrous.

She hit the start button in her EmWAV and felt the light thrum of the power interact with her own energy. The communications board had streaming video of the team at headquarters and Seth in the other EmWAV.

A collection of topography maps with water depths, objects, and landmasses were projected in 3D in front of her, and she could switch views as needed. She and Seth had never used the weapons options in the EmWAV, and she hoped they were never used on her. According to the manual, the missiles "hunt their prey with speed and precision."

She took a breath as headquarters gave them the countdown.

Seth's voice entered her cockpit as clear as if he was next to her. "I'm going to crush you, rookie."

She smiled, glad he still had some competitive juices left, even if it was all bravado. "We'll see, 006."

"That's—."

She took off with a leap ahead of him. "Exactly."

They raced across the water, and she made the first dive before banking quickly to start the underwater slalom, her grip easy on the two directional joysticks. Next were three surface leaps through circular targets. She emerged too late on the first one, hit it, and it exploded around her, throwing off her trajectory and requiring her to adjust her speed in order to make the second target. It was enough time for Seth to catch up on the matching course.

They had a little breather, but then her radar and maps suddenly went off. She flipped on the satellite visual instantly and zoomed in on her location while alerting HQ. "My maps are down."

"Mine, too," Seth's voice echoed.

"We are aware," General Martin said over the com. "You'll need to finish without them."

"Seth, use your satellite tracking," she said.

"Got it. Thanks."

The new challenge had given her an edge, only because she had responded faster. They were about to finish the final challenge. This was where they had the option to improvise. Based on Seth's acceleration, he was planning on jumping all three water fences at once. No way would he make it, but he didn't have any errors yet, and that would give him a timing edge, even hitting the last one.

Jocelyn was fully submerged and slowed down to half her current speed while directing her EmWAV upward. It wasn't a 90 degree spike, but it sure felt like it. Medina balked in surprise as she powered it up just before surfacing, ignoring his curse.

She hopped the first gate no problem.

The next one was harder. She had done the calculations ahead of time, but adjusting the controls manually required practice she didn't have. She released the power, then boosted it again when the tail of the EmWAV touched water. They submerged about eight feet in standing position, then shot up again over the next gate. She succeeded, but overshot it, putting her too close to the final gate. When she adjusted for distance, it was still too late. She cut the gate in half, and in the process, threw off the trajectory of the EmWAV midflight.

They flipped mid-air, over and over, across the water nearly to the other side of the lake. Medina's curses filled the cockpit, but her instincts for recovery were right on.

"I got it!" she told him, not wanting him to take the controls. She reverse-thrusted and had them back on a path to the dock. Seth pulled in ahead of her.

Jocelyn crawled out of her cockpit, a little wobbly.

Seth rushed forward. "Dude! What was that?"

Medina took off his helmet and shook his head. "I didn't teach her that."

"I thought it might be a possible solution to the challenge. I guess my math was off."

"Or," Seth said, "you actually thought *you* were 007 and not me. I think we cleared that up." He patted her on the head. "Good try, though."

The General looked at her, curious. "What made you think you could make it?"

"I knew you couldn't jump all three at once with the power and distance available, so I thought this was a challenge to find another solution."

"Hmm. Actually, it's designed to force you to miss at some point to see your ability to recover. Nothing ever goes perfectly in the field. You have to improvise. I guess overall it wasn't bad, but you were close to crashing a twelve-million-dollar prototype vehicle, so I think we'll keep Medina in the driver's seat."

Jocelyn nodded. "Sorry, sir."

He turned away shaking his head, but not before she saw him begin to smile.

She'd lost the race, but in her mind, she was reviewing everything necessary to get it right next time. She'd need to redo the calculations and visualize the maneuvers until it was beyond instinct, but she was certain she'd just found a possible way out.

The President dismissed his advisors, except Jerry. His Secretary of Information was his top advisor and henchman. If Jerry worried, he worried.

But there was nothing to worry about. His latest appearances on morning and evening talk show circuits had boosted his presidential likeability ratings. If Jerry secured a few more Congressmen, he could pass his tax package, print more money, and send checks to Russia and Egypt. Keeping the peace was expensive.

"What is it, Jerry? You've been scowling and texting and not paying attention for the last hour."

"I didn't know your social schedule required my attention."

"Don't be snippy."

"I'm not. I just don't care who you golf with."

"You should. They might be trying to take your job."

"You can't fire me. I know too much, Mr. President."

"Wow, you *are* having a bad day." He took a seat on the sofa across from Jerry and leaned forward, elbows on knees, hands folded. It was the position that usually let people know he was concerned and attentive. His body language coach would be pleased. "Lay it on me. What do you need?"

"There's been more snooping around Project Sunday."

"And?"

"And a lot of hits on the Albrechts in New York, Virginia, and—," he looked pointedly at the President, "D.C."

The President sat back against the cushions. "Who in D.C.?"

"An assistant at the FBI. We already took care of it. She only reached the frontline files. And she's about to be fired for conduct ill-becoming an agent. We found some opportunities in her taxes. Easy stuff. But we can't have the I.R.S. detouring everyone."

"So?"

"So, it may not end there. We tracked at least one inquiry to Ford Rochester. He might keep trying to get information."

"I'd be more worried about his wife. But Ford? Let him know we can make any and all future FDA approvals very difficult."

"That's not how he operates."

"That's how they all operate." The President smirked. "Look, he's got a private plane, he helicopter skis, there are plenty of options if he doesn't get the message. I'm sure someone in his house looks at porn. Make it public. That's why we fund in-home monitoring. In the meantime, track anyone in their family who poses a threat to our National Security."

"Already done, sir."

"How is the mission training going?"

"Excellent. No cause for worry there."

The President nodded. "So, in theory, once we have the Intel from Baratashvili, we won't need to continue our studies of Project Sunday."

"In theory, yes."

The President nodded again and eyed Jerry. The solution was obvious. "Everyone already thinks she's dead, so if she doesn't survive the mission, that wraps up all the loose ends, right?"

"In theory."

"Okay then."

"Okay…what?" Jerry asked, clearly knowing.

"Okay, handle it."

"You want me to kill her?"

"Geez, Jerry, I didn't say that. Don't be so crass!" the President bristled. Never had they referred to cleanup in such terms. It was an unspoken rule. The President was the one person who kept his hands clean—and he did that by not knowing the details. "Just handle any threats to our National Security. I don't want to lose a reelection over this. The Rochesters are a problem, but they'll stop if they believe she's dead. Make sure the records show an identifiable culprit for everything—someone in the FBI, CIA, or State Department.

Just keep the White House clean. That's your job. I'm going out on the road again to meet with my people."

Jerry took a breath to hold back his irritation. "You should take your wife. Her ratings are high, and she'll give you an extra pop."

"You're not helping my mood, Jerry."

"You need to be careful. I won't always be able to clean up after you."

The President stood up and slapped him on the shoulder with a wink. "Of course you will, Jerry. Because you're the one who goes down right before me."

CHAPTER THIRTY-THREE

Seth rolled his shoulders back and stretched. He was getting stronger. There was no mistaking it. His hearing had sharpened, his sense of smell was uncanny, his vision something an eagle would envy. His muscles were growing. Not bulging or freaky, but bigger. And he could feel the energy building inside him. He wanted to tear something apart. Maybe rip Dominique's head from her body...after he ripped off Cashus's. He couldn't decide who was worse—a controlling, power-hungry, psycho bitch, or an evil, manipulative, self-obsessed narcissist. There was no denying both were brilliant in their own right. But they were also completely vile. He'd grown up fast and knew how to read people. He'd seen it all. These two were not the only bad people in the world, they just happened to have resources that could turn them into super-villains of epic proportions.

He didn't plan on sticking around to see their work firsthand.

Dominique didn't know that he'd gained a heightened ability to hear and see. In fact, she was confused, or at least disappointed, by his very slight decline in speed and strength. He'd heard her put it down to the inability of his body to adapt. They were scheduling another dose.

Granted, whatever they gave him was murderously painful, but if his high school science panned out, it would make him even stronger—an outcome worth sacrificing for. He only hoped they did it before they transported him. A little boost wouldn't hurt.

The door buzzed and Nurse Betsy entered. She wasn't hot, but she wasn't ugly, and definitely young enough to like flirting with him. He'd taken her hand yesterday, and she hadn't pulled away. His science might be high school level, but he had a Master's degree in Women. This one was his to take.

He was on his feet instantly, invading her space and circling as she laid his meds on a table.

She smiled directly at him, warning, "There are cameras on us."

"Everywhere?"

She grinned, pressed the measurements device to his arm for vitals, and began to chart.

"No blood today?" he asked. Usually they took a vial.

"Nope."

"Must mean they don't like the results anymore."

"Or you're doing well." She handed him the paper cup of pills.

He swallowed them in one take with a gulp of the water. "I doubt it." She gathered her things and got up. He followed on her heels and put his hands above her shoulders against the door, trapping her. "Can they see here, too?"

"Yes." Her eyes darted left to the corner indicating a safe spot. She turned and ducked, escaping him.

He smiled and followed her to the safe zone. His arm snaked around her waist, quickly pulling her to him until her breasts smashed against his chest. She held her medical supplies in one hand and used the other to brace herself on his chest. He could hear her heart beating rapidly. Even her scent changed. Fascinating. Her lips parted slightly. Oh, yeah. No need for super skills to know she wanted him. He leaned down and kissed her cheek, the side of her neck, then gave her a full-mouthed dose of Texas.

She devoured him.

Nothing like the sweet-tasting Sunnie. Sunnie, whose kisses were fresh and soft as she explored the experience with openness and curiosity. Kisses that were exactly like her.

This woman was ravenous—like all the people here. They all wanted a part of him.

He nearly shoved her away with distaste. Instead, he let out a breath near her ear. "Are you going to Colorado with me? I'd hate to leave you behind."

She pulled back. "I put in for the transfer."

He kissed her cheek again. "And?"

"I leave same time as you. Next week."

"Outstanding." He grabbed her butt and squeezed hard. "You better run before they check the cameras. I'll catch you later."

"Promise?" she teased.

He winked. "Texans don't lie."

She laughed. The door slid open just enough for him to see the armed guard outside. Then it closed, the metal locks clicking in place, echoing inside the wall.

He wiped his mouth with his hand and leaned back into the corner. They would be moving him next week. His heart pounded, part excitement and part panic. Once he was off camp, he'd make his move. He just needed to let Sunnie know before it happened.

The field trip planning with General Martin moved to full gear.

Jocelyn sat with Medina in the War Room as they went through photos and aerial views of the site. The fine hairs on Jocelyn's body lifted and she rubbed her arms, trying to smooth the internal tension. The site was an underground military campus and hospital outside the small village of Oni, off the River Rioni.

In Georgia.

Where Sergei was from.

That couldn't be a coincidence.

She listened while the General explained.

According to General Martin, ever since the invasion in Ukraine, the Russians had adopted a more stealthy method of infiltrating the surrounding nations. In Georgia, they now had control of the land and airspace beyond the Caucasus Mountains and deep inside the border. The target area was home to a small army, but west of that was relatively safe and patrolled by Georgian and NATO partners. She was introduced to the unit that would be responsible for dropping them in and picking them up. Since they were using the EmWAV to get in and out, she was curious how that would work. Unfortunately, that wasn't part of her "need to know" just yet.

The objective was to enter the hospital as a patient coming in for an initial exam, get the intel required from the lower floors, and blow the complex—without destroying the village directly above ground.

The General must have seen the concern on her face. "They built it like this deliberately to mask their work and use innocent people as their shield. Don't let their choices affect your mission."

"Yes, sir." She kept her head down, staring at the aerial photos of the tiny village. Finally, she raised her hand and waited for the General to call on her. "What is it that they're doing there?"

"Biological weapons. That's all we've been told. And that the threat is real."

She nodded. It didn't help her growing confusion.

"Cashus, how are the languages coming?"

"Fine, sir." Sergei always spoke to her in his dialect. Had they told him to? Did he know about her field trip? Which side was he on?

"Cashus, Sergei Baratashvili has been leading a group of scientists for more than two decades to create the ultimate biological weapons. He's worked with the Russians to make his weapons available to terrorist organizations around the world."

She didn't believe it. It couldn't be.

"Believe it." He must have read her mind. "Now others are continuing this work. It must be stopped."

Jocelyn put a hand on the desk to steady herself. This couldn't be right. Please don't let this be true. Everyone turned and stared at her, waiting. Was this a test? Everything was a test, right? This one was about loyalty, and to whom. She straightened. "I understand. Now that I have this information, I'll pay more attention and see if I can learn anything useful."

The General nodded, and two more officers took the floor to walk them through the details of the field trip.

It was all she could do to concentrate. Other than Seth, Sergei had been her one friend, and the only person at Holliwell who actually gave her useful information. Now she had to wonder if he'd been manipulating her all along. Maybe he was the one doing the real spying on her, and she'd been too blind to see it. She was so eager for a friend, she couldn't see the real enemies all around her. She didn't know whom to trust. She especially didn't trust her own judgment right now.

Jocelyn circled the target on the map. If Sergei was innocent, as he claimed, she was about to rain terror down on the village he grew up in, and the one place he fondly spoke of as home.

It would be better if she just believed General Martin. He seemed to believe what he said. They couldn't both be right, could they? She had to pick. Only, she was uncertain. Lack of certainty was a sure way to be killed in battle—another Sarge-ism. She had been trained so that her reactions would be instinctive. If she went into the field trip doubting Sergei's guilt, she would become distracted. Distraction equaled death.

Her stomach churned during her afternoon testing with Sergei. She knew she was unusually reserved. He asked about her progress with the book, and they discussed it briefly.

"I got you a bookmark in the little bookstore on Main Street. It has a calendar on it, so it serves two purposes."

Jocelyn took the bookmark and looked at it. Some of the numbers on the two sides had dates that were smudged. It was not discernible at first. Maybe not even to the average eye.

She nodded that she understood, thanked him, and slid it into the book, unbending the corner page where she had stopped reading.

"I leave for my field trip in a couple days."

His head nodded very gently. "You will see where I grew up."

Her head shot up. "You know?"

He shrugged. "Soldiers talk. People listen."

"Do you know what the mission is?"

"I can guess."

She doubted he knew they were going to blow the place to pieces.

"Did the Russians make you do things you didn't want to do?"

"As much as you Americans have. But there are governments that are worse."

She scowled. "Did you test on kids, too?"

"*I* don't have a morgue filled with the bodies of children and colleagues." He tapped the bookmark.

She paused. He'd given her the code to the morgue? What was down there? Did she want to know?

"You are not a killer. Don't let them make you one."

"I don't have a choice."

"You always have a choice."

Megan peeked in the open door to see if everything was okay.

"I'm done," Sergei said.

"But—."

"Enough." He cut Jocelyn off. "There is truth if one has the will to find it."

Jocelyn clutched the book to her stomach. She desperately wanted to know the truth—about everything. She just wasn't sure she had the will to go to the morgue and find it.

Seth was allowed to see Sunnie one last time before his transfer—fifteen minutes in their compacted schedules to walk to Starbucks for a smoothie. He took it.

"When do you leave on the field trip?" he asked.

"Tomorrow."

"Nervous?"

"No." She smiled robotically. "I'm trained and prepared to do the job. Just need to trust my commanding officer. Piece of cake."

"Are you trained to say that, too?"

"Yep."

He scowled. "Outstanding."

She shrugged helplessly and guided them away from the overly-monitored coffee shop. They made their way down the spotless street, slushies in hand. There were very few people about. Those who took a break from their work generally went to Starbucks.

Sunnie sipped her slushie and spoke with her lips around the straw, making her words mostly unintelligible unless he was right next to her. "I'll find you and get you out."

He put his lips around his own straw. "Don't."

She slurped, meeting his eyes. "Yes."

"No." He eyed her angrily. He took his mouth off the straw. "Don't get all emo on me. That's the last thing I need."

She blinked, hurt. "I'm not emo."

"See?"

"What is that anyway?"

"*Emo*tional. Don't get emotional. Think about steak, potatoes, corn on the cob, hot biscuits...got it? I don't need your help."

"But—."

He threw his half-finished slushie into the trash with more force than he'd meant. "Don't ruin our last moments together." He wanted to shake her. Instead, he caught himself. People were likely watching, and women responded better to charm. He took a breath getting his darker side under control. Gently, he grazed her upper arm with his fingers then slid them down to her hand, pulling her close and leaning his forehead onto hers.

"Save yourself, okay?" He touched her lips lightly and felt the chill from the frozen slushie as he whispered against the softness. Her lips responded with the lightest of kisses, and he pulled back. "Don't give up. And don't let them change you." He pressed his cheek to hers, to whisper in her ear. "You're the most outstanding girl I ever met."

She squeezed his hand tightly and whispered back, "You'll always be my favorite Bond, James Bond."

His body shook. If felt strange to laugh. It felt good to laugh. And it made the feelings raging inside him all the more powerful and conflicted. He could fall for her. Maybe he already had. But there was no room for that. When she came back, he would be gone.

His hand roamed back up her arm, then shoulder until his fingers threaded themselves through her dark, silky hair. She tilted her chin to look at him and smiled gently. Damn, she was so sweet and naive. She had no idea how she would be used, what they would have her do—and what they would do to her.

The thought of it filled him with rage.

As if reading his mind, she gently stroked his chest, to give comfort. "Don't worry. I can take care of myself."

"I wish you didn't have to."

She shrugged. "We have to play the hand that's been dealt. That's what Sarge says."

"Probably not a good thing that your whole life philosophy has been shaped by your army captor."

"He's not so bad."

"Did my kisses make you stupid?"

Sunnie laughed unexpectedly. "No. But we have to enjoy the time we have." She took his hand and led them down the road toward where the street met forest. Did she want to get away from monitoring devices?

Megan called from down the street. "Sunnie! Don't wander off."

"Okay!" Sunnie waved back to acknowledge the instruction but kept walking, tossing her slushie cup in the trash on the way.

She stopped a safe distance from Main Street and turned to him, her voice soft. "I'll miss you, Bond, James Bond."

"I'll miss you too, freak." He leaned forward, and she wrapped her arms around him in a tight hug. Her head tucked perfectly under his chin, and a silky thread of hair caught by the breeze tickled him. He caught it and stroked the dark wisp back through her hair, releasing a deep sigh in sync with her. He wondered, for an instant, if they would have been friends in other circumstances—if he could have become the kind of person she would *choose* as a friend, rather than this. A last resort. If he was a better person, he'd find a way to get her out of this place. But she was the prototype. He was one of a hundred experiments. They would keep her alive as long as possible. They would also guard her with a level of security impossible to breach. He had a chance. She didn't.

As if sensing his turmoil, she leaned back in his arms to look at him. "What is it?"

"Sunnie, just remember everything you've learned."

She nodded.

"And stay alive."

She nodded again.

"Most important, and I mean this—if you have a chance, take it. Don't let your emotions hold you back from an opportunity to be free. Do you understand? You need to be ruthless. *Ruthless*," he emphasized.

She nodded solemnly, her gaze full of sadness and concern, blue eyes sparkling more brightly than usual. He took advantage of the emotion. This would be his only opportunity, and hell, he was an opportunist. He could be honest about that, if nothing else.

That, and he wanted her.

He tightened his hold, met her eyes, and slowly bent until her lashes fluttered down, her face tilted farther back, and his lips touched hers.

Softness and warmth were the first sensations. Freshness and purity struck him next. After that, instinct kicked in. He gave and he took. His fingers wove through her thick hair, catching it in his fist. He wanted to make an imprint on her. He wanted to matter.

Then he felt something else.

Heat.

It surrounded him. A warmth radiating from her hands— from her entire body. It melted into him, comforting and soothing, even in the sunshine. He lifted his head, confused. She smiled at him, waiting to see his reaction.

"Do you like that?"

He laughed. "Your kisses or your heating pad maneuver?"

She considered quickly. "Both."

"Yeah, I definitely liked both." He leaned down again. "But the kissing more." Which was why he decided to do more of it. She moved her arms from around his back and wrapped them around his neck. A yell interrupted them.

"Sunnie," Megan called out. "Wrap it up!"

Sunnie sighed.

Seth dipped her backward for a final kiss, just like in the old movies. He grinned when she gasped from losing balance and held him tighter. *Yeah, that was the plan.*

Delight caught her by surprise. She laughed. It was the sound that made him most happy. What was a future without it?

He planted a final kiss on her. "Remember everything I told you. And seventy-two ounce steaks. It's something to live for." He pecked her nose and swooshed her upright.

They walked back toward Main Street and spotted Megan and his guard waiting. Sunnie examined him thoughtfully, then reached for the top of his head, pulling off his beanie. He felt naked without it, the sun striking the pale skin of his scalp.

"Can I have your beanie?"

He thought about it.

"As a remembrance," she added.

"Sure."

"Thanks." She smiled and put it on. "How's it look?"

He adjusted it and approved. "Cute."

"Okay." She took his hand. "It's time."

"I know."

"I'm glad I met you," she said.

"Me, too."

"We'll meet again. I'm sure of it."

"Definitely." He squeezed her hand. With any luck, he would be free, so meeting again would never happen. But he needed to stay strong and give her hope. Maybe some day that hope would rub off on him.

Laurence waited for Seth to join them in the conference room. The lanky teen entered, grabbed some licorice from the side counter, and fell into a chair, throwing a leg over the arm. He bit off three vines at once, smiling at them.

Wicker had a little less patience than Laurence did. "So?" she asked.

Seth didn't hesitate. "She can generate heat."

"Heat?" Cashus repeated.

"Yeah. Heat. She warmed me with her hands and body." The bald-headed wonder took a big bite and chewed some more.

Laurence's mind spun in several directions at one. *Of course.* It was possible, but how did she learn to do that? Had she been experimenting with her powers? He thought of the energy experts in the Chemistry complex and could barely hold back his delight. They would kill to study how Sunday did that. If they could replicate it...what would that mean for energy and sustainability?

Laurence turned the ideas around in his head. "Wait, what did it feel like?" he asked.

Seth shrugged. "Just warmth. Nothing earthshattering."

"From her hands, or everywhere?"

"I felt it in the front of my body and around back where her hands were. She gave me a hug." His cheeks turned a little pink, and he rubbed his scalp self-consciously.

"Thank you. This is very helpful." Laurence could barely repress his smirk. "Dominique, well worth whatever reward you have in store."

Wicker nodded to the kid. "You'll find the accommodations in Colorado much more pleasant. And I'll make sure Betsy gets to escort you."

Laurence rose to go, but she stopped him. "Would you like to talk further, Dr. Cashus?"

Hah. She wanted to know what he had in mind. "No, no. I should leave you. You have preparations to make. Safe journeys to you both. I know the new facility will be a tremendous help to your work."

"I don't leave for another month," Wicker reminded him.

"Of course. Excuse me."

Cashus couldn't wait to get out of there. His plan was taking shape, and he wanted to outline it while the ideas were fresh. This was sure to put him back on top as the base's lead science officer. Especially if he was able to pull all the disciplines together.

"Thanks, Dominique. That was very helpful."

Dominique looked less and less happy the more he smiled. Finally, he had the upper hand. He had learned to manage his public relations image better since Dominique had inserted herself in his life. She played the helpful, concerned card very well. He could do the same. He could be helpful to every scientist at the camp and still control the research *and* Sunday.

He'd have the best of both worlds.

CHAPTER THIRTY-FOUR

Only the stars provided light when Medina and Jocelyn entered the EmWAV and their carrier lowered them to the Rioni River to start the long journey through enemy territory.

Once at their destination, Medina used the remote auto lock to cloak and submerge the vehicle by the river's edge, then led the way with confidence. Chilly air whipped against her cheeks as they took off into the darkness across an open valley while Caucasus mountain range loomed behind them like a great shadow.

Even with her excellent vision, it was hard to detect things in the distance, so she was surprised when Medina led them straight to a road she hadn't noticed. He wasn't the chatty type, which left only the sound of the whistling wind sweeping through the mountains and trees, broken by the steady crunch of their footsteps on gravel and the occasional huff of Medina's breath.

The road eventually parted, and instead of continuing toward the lights, Medina detoured upward, and they came upon a used, but surprisingly modern, SUV parked among the trees. Medina went to the front of the car, reached under it, and pulled out a magnetic box. It contained the key.

"That's convenient."

He grunted and pulled out a bundle of clothes for her. She loosely braided her hair and changed quickly into the local outfit, carefully latching the plastic hooks of the sweater and counting the buttons on the coat. Everything seemed in order.

"Check," she said, letting him know this step was complete. "Why didn't we just drive in from down below?"

"We're not the only government monitoring the site. The Russians have infiltrated most of the region. They're guarding the hospital grounds."

"I didn't know about the car." With all the training they'd done, she'd only learned her part of the mission. The hairs on her arms spiked in warning. *What else didn't she know?*

He loaded their gear into the back of the SUV. "Everything's on a need-to-know basis."

"Anything else I need to know?"

Medina closed the trunk and turned to her. "I'll let you know."

She nodded. "Right."

They hopped in the SUV and took off. Jocelyn checked out Medina's appearance while he drove. He'd acquired a distinctly more European look. He would be roaming the town as a photographer. Supposedly, this was a great location for adventure photography—waterfalls, caves, natural springs. It gave Medina a reason to be up at sunrise, collecting data, and carrying lots of gear.

As if sensing her thoughts, Medina added to their earlier conversation. "Training is very precise. It's better for each person to know their part perfectly than try to judge everyone else's job. It keeps focus and forces each member of the team to trust in all the others. Everyone trusts that you will do your part, and you have to trust them equally. We are all pieces of the bigger puzzle."

She nodded, understanding. "Thank you."

"Don't thank me. Do your job."

They drove another thirty minutes until they reached the village. Medina parked and put on his communication set. He tested the equipment. Satisfied, he motioned to her, and she held her hair back while he affixed a miniature device against the curve of cartilage in her left earlobe.

"Test. Test."

"Copy. Copy," she replied. She gave Medina a big smile. He really needed to relax.

"Your cover is a terminally ill patient. You're not supposed to look happy."

Jocelyn swallowed hard, deflating. It was a little too close to home.

"Stay focused."

"I am," she answered.

"Nervous?"

"Not yet. We haven't done anything. And we practiced enough times. Piece o' cake, remember?"

"Yeah. Piece o' cake." He grunted again. "Surefire way to jinx another field trip."

"I didn't know you were superstitious."

"I didn't know you were so damned chatty. You're up for this, right?" He sounded doubtful.

"Yes."

"Don't be a rookie."

"Don't be a jerk," she shot back.

Medina grunted with approval then proceeded to ignore her. "Patient Imeda ready," he said to basecamp.

That was her. Imeda.

He handed her a wrinkled form—her doctor's referral, her "in" to the first floor of the medical facility. Getting to the lower floors was up to her.

Medina dropped her off at a little stone house on the edge of town just as the sun rose, then drove off, presumably to capture some sunrise photos. The owner was her "auntie," who had lived in the town many years now and was known about the village. She stood a stout five feet tall and wore no makeup. Gray strands wove into dark hair. She nodded brusquely to Jocelyn, bringing her inside.

The cottage had worn hardwood floors and smelled of a wood burning fireplace and fresh herbal bread. Her auntie fed her a breakfast of oatmeal, warm bread, and juice, then gave her a blanket to sit with by the fire. Jocelyn's appointment was not until 08:30. She wanted to chat the woman up and learn more about the town, but had been told not to talk with other contacts. Listening devices were common, and as of now, she was on stage.

At first, it was strange being in a place where no one was allowed to talk to you, until she realized it was no different from Camp Holliwell—just fewer fences.

Jocelyn took the short time to enjoy being in a new place. This place was earthy and grounded. In other circumstances it would be peaceful and relaxing, but her hearing detected her hostess in the other room reporting to basecamp. So far, there had been no direct communication on her earpiece, except when they tested it. She was on a different frequency, only her super hearing revealed things she didn't "need to know."

She pulled her knees up to her chest and hugged them. She had no doubt there were dozens of Holliwell spies throughout the town, tracking her, waiting for her to enter the hospital this morning. If she tried to abandon the field trip, there were only two ways out of the village—by road and by river. Both paths were highly monitored, according to their intelligence.

She looked out the window toward the mountains. The view was green and majestic in the morning light. She understood why Sergei spoke longingly of his homeland. The area was bucolic, the rare medieval buildings charming, and the mountain ranges inspiring. In the distance, she could hear the Rioni River. She wondered if she would walk by someone in Sergei's family today in the village, or in the course of her field trip. She closed her eyes and blocked that out. She must not become sympathetic or emotional. She had a job to do. She repeated that over and over in her head, going through the steps she had practiced. This mission was merely another important step in acquiring General Martin's trust and getting more freedoms.

The moment came when her auntie walked her upriver to the hospital compound. The building looked like the shell of a Jewish temple. When she entered, it was completely modern. Surprised, she looked around at the mix of glossy wood and steel. Everyone spoke Russian, though a few people switched back and forth between Georgian and Russian. Her auntie spoke to her in Georgian.

The first thing they encountered was security. A few people were ahead of them. Her auntie checked her in with the security host and they entered the line, taking off their outer coats, shoes, and phones, and putting them through an x-ray machine while they were scanned separately. Their items passed. They took their stuff and went through another door to the official lobby area of the hospital. Here there was no evidence that they were in an ancient temple.

The lobby had shiny, golden wood floors and a steel-covered wraparound desk. There were flowers on a table in front of two waiting chairs, a sofa, and modern art on the walls. It felt warm and welcoming. Her auntie explained again that her niece had an appointment. Jocelyn pulled out the referral paper and gave it to one of the kind-faced women at the desk. The woman noted the doctor and appointment time, and handed her auntie a clipboard with some papers to fill out. When done, they waited to be called.

A security guard came out from a door behind the check-in desk, and Jocelyn was called to join him. She once again did a security check, spreading her legs, sticking out her arms for scanning. The scanner beeped, and Jocelyn took off her coat. He scanned her again, then the coat, determined the buttons were the cause for the beeping and handed back her coat.

Her auntie acted unsure, not wanting to leave her. It was part of the act. Jocelyn held up her mobile phone and reassured her that she would call as soon as she was done, but the appointment could last two to three hours, and she didn't want her to wait. Her auntie pet and kissed her, finally leaving after a strong hug that made her think the woman was younger than she looked. Either way, it was the most attention Jocelyn could recall getting in her entire life. The Georgians really were family oriented, it seemed.

A smiling woman with a white smock took her to an elevator, and that's when Jocelyn discovered there were four floors below the entrance. The entire underground had been built out toward the river. *Interesting.*

The woman took Jocelyn down one floor and led her to a room not unlike the ones where she had her daily measurements. The only difference was that the nurse, Ketevan, according to her nametag, was nice. She had shoulder length light brown hair, brown eyes, and a strong straight nose. Jocelyn stared at her, curious, wondering why she looked so familiar. She caught Jocelyn's curious gaze and smiled back, chatting about the weather while taking her vitals.

She pressed her hand to Jocelyn's forehead, surprised by her temperature, and immediately touched a meter to her skin, noting her vitals. Soon the woman noticed her nails. Jocelyn curled them into her fists, uncomfortable and nervous. Her freakiness was meant to get her admitted to the hospital. All she needed to do was act sick.

She hugged her stomach nervously. Ketevan took one of her arms and pulled it gently toward her, uncurling the fist. She inspected Jocelyn's nails, curiously, her brows furrowing a little before she smiled in a way meant to comfort.

"Don't worry, Imeda. You are in a safe place. We have helped many kids just like you."

She wondered if they were really like her. "With blue nails?"

The nurse paused, as if wondering if she needed to be delicate. "I think blue is very pretty and a popular nail color these days, right?" She made a note in her file, then sat down in a chair across from her. "We have had patients come here much worse than you. Your vitals are strong, so we can figure the rest out, yes? There is always hope. You must never give up. Promise?"

Jocelyn nodded, but her throat felt tight with emotion.

Ketevan was kind and sincere and really wanted to help. It only succeeded in making Jocelyn feel guilty for not really being sick—at least not in the way Ketevan expected. Did all spies feel like this?

"How long have your nails been like this?"

"Since the accident at the factory." Jocelyn revealed her cover story. "My job was checking pipes. It was very easy, but one day there was a leak, and we were evacuated. I didn't get out soon enough. I woke up in the hospital. That's all I remember." She took a heavy breath. "Now I'm tired all the time."

Nurse Ketevan pulled out a vial and syringe. "I'm going to take some blood, okay? Very standard."

Jocelyn nodded. She'd been told this was likely, but since the building would be blown up, her blood samples wouldn't matter.

Ketevan efficiently took the samples, then made a call letting Dr. Baba's office know she was bringing down Imeda St. Petre. Ketevan smiled at her. Jocelyn forced a smile back and listened carefully. It would be an hour. Long enough for her to wander about.

"Imeda, would you like to go to our Recreation Hall while you wait for Dr. Baba? He is still in surgery, and it might be awhile. The other patients will be having breakfast and usually go there afterward. You can talk with someone your age, yes?"

Others her age? Super soldiers started young, it seemed.

More curious than ever, Jocelyn nodded and was escorted down a long hall. Nurse Ketevan gave her a publicity-style tour of the facility, very proud of it. It included exercise areas, healing natural springs in the gardens, a small movie theater, and indoor recreation space. When they reached the Recreation Hall, Jocelyn could not have been more surprised. The space had high ceilings and stone walls that led out toward a giant stone deck jutting from the side of the mountain and over the river. The only thing separating the hall from the deck was eighteen-foot- tall windows. The view lured her, and she walked straight outside gasping at the spectacular scenery.

They weren't under the town, they were in the mountain. That couldn't be right. How was the intel wrong? Or was this just a wing of the facility that hadn't been recorded. And why would anyone want to destroy something so beautiful?

She walked back in, looking about, absorbing the dozen or so teens and children reading books, competing at video games, and basically...playing. They didn't look like super soldiers.

"What's wrong with them?"

"Nothing, now," Ketevan answered confidently. "But they are in recovery and physical therapy to get their strength back. Several had chemical poisoning that caused muscle atrophy and required intensive treatment. That is why the hospital was founded. But since we have treated a number of diseases with similar symptoms, I am confident we will discover what is needed to help you."

This Dr. Baba must be a miracle worker. "What kind of doctor is Dr. Baba?" She'd not been given intel on anyone who worked here, just that there was a large team of scientists and doctors doing experimental work. Perhaps this intel would help General Martin.

"Dr. Baratashvili is a geneticist and surgeon."

"Who?" Jocelyn's stomach lurched.

"You know Dr. Baba is his nickname, right? The kids use it. Easier than Baratashvili. And it makes him more approachable. He and my father founded the hospital." She smiled warmly. "We are family here in many ways."

Jocelyn swallowed hard against growing uneasiness, "Your father?"

Ketevan turned back toward the entrance of the large room and pointed to something on the wall—an oversized portrait.

Jocelyn stared in shock. She knew the face well.

It was Sergei.

CHAPTER THIRTY-FIVE

Laurence reviewed his initial list of research participants and grant applications with a certain amount of glee. The opportunity to use Sunday as a true scientific platform was invaluable, and within 24 hours of putting out the offer to the Holliwell science community, he'd received a number of inquiries and proposals.

So far, he counted thirty-one viable opportunities while Sunday was still alive. There were even more for when she died. Everyone wanted to study her system, DNA, organ structure, brain. He puffed his chest with immense self-satisfaction. He would be the supervising doctor on every team. That was part of the agreement—but each team had research that could be valued in hundreds of millions, and the outcome…priceless and awarding-winning to start. It made his fingers tingle in anticipation.

Soon he would review the grants with the Secretary of Information. Finally, he would prove his case to make Sunday purely a scientific asset. *And he would have full control.*

"Dr. Cashus?" His secretary knocked on the door. "Dr. Wicker is here to see you. She said it's urgent."

Dominique didn't wait for his permission to enter. "Laurence, it's life-threateningly urgent." She turned to the other woman. "Get out." His secretary made haste to shut the door firmly.

"Is your precious Seth in danger?"

"He's out like a corpse on transport to Denver." She checked her watch. "Probably in the MedVan right now. It's

Sunday I'm talking about. I was just in my weekly conference with the SOI."

Laurence's attention caught. He didn't have a weekly call with the Secretary of Information. Dammit. He'd be glad when Dominique and her team moved to the new Colorado facility.

"Yes?" he asked.

"Don't be defensive. This is about her as an asset to science, not you and me. I pitched him a project, and I gleaned from our discussion that she might not be coming back from her current assignment."

Laurence sat up straight. "What do you mean?" His mind raced. Sunday was only meant to be gone three days. This was the second day. The third was transport home. If something was going to happen, or already had....

"I'll be getting the science intel from this mission. And I have Baratashvili on top of that. He's thought to be years ahead of where we are with Sunday. Once we have that intel, the SOI said we don't need Sunday, and there are complications around her history. Or at least that was my interpretation. I persisted, and he finally said Project Sunday was being terminated. I took that to mean more than the project funding. I think they want to wipe out all evidence of her. Despite our differences, we can't let that happen. The value to science is immeasurable, and at the very least, we need to preserve her body for further study. The Memory team is still in the telepresence room with the Secretary. That gives us some time, but we have to hurry."

Laurence was already grabbing his tablet with the collection of Project Sunday grants. "I got it. Let's go."

Seth listened to action around him. He was finally fully awake from the last shot and had no intention of receiving another.

A guard yelled from the front of the MedVan. "Betsy, come on out and join us. He's going to be out until we arrive." They were halfway up the mountainous climb in Colorado and not far from the final destination. There wasn't much time.

Betsy buttoned her shirt. "It's almost time for another shot."

Her backup nurse called out. "I'll take care of it." The doorknob jostled. "Hey, it's locked. You okay?"

Another voice joined the nurse outside the door. A guard. He tried the door as well.

"Yes, one second." Betsy straightened her clothes and hurried to unlock the door. The guard pushed his way into the patient section of the MedVan. "I need to give him the last dose."

Seth lay strapped to a gurney. The guard shoved Seth's shoulder a bit. When nothing happened, the guard grabbed Seth's nose and shook his head. No reaction. "I'd say he's out."

The guard joked at Seth's expense. Betsy laughed uncomfortably.

"We've got twenty miles left." The guard reassured, "The hard part is over. We just dump him in a bed when we arrive."

The other nurse stood in the doorway. "We should still give the last dose."

Betsy prepped the syringe. "I've got it," she told her. "I want to watch and make sure his vitals stay normal. Besides, it gets crowded in here."

The other nurse went back to her seat. *One disaster averted.*

The guard stayed. "Come out and have a break."

Betsy hemmed. "Let me finish, and I'll get my stuff together."

"Need help?" Did the guy have a thing for Betsy? He stood by the gurney chatting like an expert. "Know what they do in hospitals to make sure a patient isn't faking?"

Betsy panicked. "Please don't."

"Just kidding," the guard defended.

"Well, the way you manhandled him was inappropriate," Betsy said.

"Got a thing for him?" Suspicion sounded in the guard's voice. "You're taking mighty long to inject him."

"Now you're going to judge how I do my job? I think you should leave," Betsy said.

"Actually, I think I should stay and make sure you do this."

Betsy swabbed Seth's arm. Next came the needle. *Not in his plan.*

It never connected. Seth's eyes shot open, surprising the guard.

The man cursed.

Seth reached across his body and grabbed the syringe, swinging back to land it below the guard's throat in one movement that brought him to a sitting position, facing the guard. Two beefy hands gripped Seth's right wrist as he pressed the needle in place, holding while his left injected.

The guard swung wildly, and he countered with a tight uppercut that sent the guard against the MedVan's wall, shaking the entire vehicle with his power.

He grabbed the guard's holstered gun, and when the connecting door swung open, shot at the second guard headed toward him. The bullet missed and went straight through the front windshield, surprising everyone, including the driver who swerved, throwing them all off balance. Betsy screamed.

They were on a curvy mountain road with oncoming traffic. The guard yelled for him to freeze. Seth unloaded the gun at the second guard. Fire and thunder filled the vehicle with chaos until the second guard stopped shooting.

Betsy stumbled in shock on the other side of the gurney. She was shot in the arm during the crossfire. She'd been entertaining him while the last bit of medication wore off. Her face had been flushed minutes earlier when she'd been laying on top of him. Now she looked pale, realizing her mistake. Her hand fumbled, reaching desperately for a new syringe.

Seth yelled for the driver to pull over.

The driver was slumped over the wheel. *Oh, shit.*

To his left, the backup nurse stared in shock, holding onto the lunch table, not knowing what to do.

The vehicle swerved.

Seth maneuvered to get out the door when the vehicle swerved sharply again, this time hitting something. He flew forward, facing the wide front window. He saw what was coming because what he saw was nothing. No road, no mountain, no other vehicle—just air, with a magnificent view of the Rocky Mountains in the distance.

He turned and struggled to reach the back of the vehicle and the double doors to freedom.

The vehicle tipped, the gurney slid, Betsy screamed, and he knew his last moments had not been well played as the MedVan hung for a precarious moment before flipping off the narrow road.

Jocelyn froze in shock as her memory clicked. She knew Ketevan's face from her mission in Paris. She'd been distracted by a mother and crying girl. Ketevan was the mother. *Sergei was Ketevan's father?*

She mentally cursed, trying to sort through what she knew.

Her stomach twisted in pain. She definitely felt nauseous. For real.

Sergei had been kidnapped, he said. Recently. Had that been the goal of her last field trip? She'd been on a "need-to-know basis" there, too, and she didn't know anything for sure.

What had they really been doing? Why were they *really* at Sergei's hospital? Was she on the wrong side? *The bad side?*

Ketevan saw her discomfort and put an arm around her, leading her to a table. She introduced "Imeda" to a boy and girl her age before promising to come back for her in an hour.

Jocelyn recovered as best she could and chatted to them softly, echoing their local dialect and asking about their health. The girl smiled when Jocelyn asked if she was much stronger now.

The boy nodded, encouraging her. "Go ahead, Ana. Show her what you can do."

Jocelyn's interest perked. Maybe they had freak talents? The idea of more kids like her was appealing.

"Well." Ana lifted her arm up and down. "Before, I could not do this. Or this," she flexed her fingers in a fist, picked some dice off a game board, and tossed them.

The boy patted her on the shoulder. "She is much more fun to play with now. I'm not constantly picking up after her." He used his arm to playfully imitate her previously stiff, erratic motions. Ana slapped him on the shoulder, laughing.

"I was not like that."

Jocelyn smiled again, but it was a frozen one. Heat made her skin prickle, and she felt the hairs of her arm flare in warning. She rubbed herself quickly, trying to dispel the panic. Not freaks. Just kids.

This was not right.

The explosives would kill everyone in the building—these two included. Ana's super strength was that she could use her arm. That didn't seem all that dangerous. These were not the super soldiers she'd been led to believe were a danger to humanity. Perhaps the soldiers were in a different building in the compound?

Jocelyn chatted a little more and asked when they would be going home. She learned about their parents and families. They were not orphans. They were looking forward to going home and doing normal things.

They were nothing like Jocelyn.

Jocelyn was the super soldier. Jocelyn was the one who was a danger to them. Her eyes burned with fear and self-disgust. She was the killer.

Her face must have indicated how ill she felt, since Ana asked if she was okay.

She definitely was not, but said it was not so bad. She just needed fresh air and maybe a nurse.

She'd thought playing up her illness would be the hardest part. It wasn't.

There were several nurses nearby, but none seemed to think it out of place that she turned and ducked into a nearby elevator. This elevator was different than the one at the entrance. It was helpfully tagged—Cafeteria, Dormitory, Hospital, Lab, and a fifth floor below ground that was unmarked—perhaps maintenance?

She pressed the button to the Lab and computer server room.

The doors opened, and she breathed a sigh of relief. The spatial area was exactly as replicated in their training. She only needed to plant four explosives in the four key pillars of the structure. She expected the cameras and had a device that interrupted their electrical connection. She pointed at the camera hidden in the one-way glass of a small unit from the ceiling. Her sight and hearing made this part of the mission particularly easy.

She ripped off the first hook on her sweater and peeled off the top layer. She molded the putty and pressed it into the wall in the first corner.

She took a breath. The first explosive.

Three more to go.

Just obey. Follow orders. Eyes on the prize, not the price. Sergei had told her himself. This was payment if she wanted to stay in the military wing and have any hope for freedom. *Orders required trust. Don't break the command.*

A voice on the Comm questioned her. "Status?"

"Proceeding."

"Copy."

She temporarily disrupted each camera, which strategically allowed her to pass through the halls unnoticed and made her way around the large floor of the building, planting her portion of the off-white, malleable explosives in the corners. Her last location led her to the server room as planned. She touched the middle button of her coat to the locking mechanism on the door and waited.

Nothing happened.

"I'm here," she spoke so Headquarters could hear her.

The decoder answered. "One second. It's a little different."

She waited, trying not to tense up about being out in the open. The cameras triggered maintenance if they froze longer than twenty-nine seconds. She looked to the nearest one and counted the seconds on her watch.

Her heartbeat thudded loudly in her ears. Five seconds left…four, three—.

"Okay, tap the button."

She did, releasing the camera. The door clicked, and she slipped inside the cold chamber filled with computers.

"In."

Her software specialist spoke calmly over the communication device. "Tell me what you see."

There had been no rehearsal replica for this space. "Four long rows of tall metal shelves filled with computer equipment and a lot of blinking lights. Walking down the first aisle." She continued her monologue. "At the end of this aisle, the computers are different. They are encased in the shelves. All the others have open access.

"That's it. It will have two other systems just like it nearby. Duplicates."

Jocelyn noted the other two. "Copy that."

"Connect to the one that indicates it's the master system."

Jocelyn pulled off the metal covers guarding the three systems and looked at the labels typed in official Georgian. "Um, okay. They are labeled: Rustaveli, Tabidze, Gamsakhurdia."

Silence on the other side.

A female voice answered. "Those are literary heroes. Rustaveli is the oldest, use that one."

"Copy." Jocelyn snatched the bottom button of her coat firmly and yanked it free. She pulled off the covering and inserted the USB in the side of the master server. "In."

"Copy," answered the software specialist. "One moment."

They would be cracking the firewall now. She waited, impatient. Everything was perfectly timed. Would this be as easy as planned?

"Downloading."

"How long?" Jocelyn asked.

"Fifteen to download. Ten to verify."

That was shorter than she'd expected. Fifteen minutes shorter. That was a lot to be off schedule. She needed to get out quickly. Only she couldn't. Not yet.

"HQ?"

"Copy. Is there a problem?"

"There are no super soldiers here. Only children."

"Imeda. Stay on mission."

"Yes, sir. But there might be value in saving the hospital. The children don't have any powers. They are weak."

"Copy."

Nothing else.

"I'm on my way to rendezvous point. Over." She hated them. Pure and simple. Okay, maybe she didn't know the details of the mission. Maybe this was a test, and they weren't going to kill everyone. Maybe she was on the wrong team. For all those reasons, she hated them. She didn't know who was bad and who was good.

Eyes on the prize, not the price. She muttered the words angrily to herself.

She left discreetly and easily made it to the elevator. It stopped on the patient level. A nurse joined her.

She closed her eyes trying not to listen to the noise in the Recreation Hall. *Eyes on the prize.*

The elevator door was nearly closed.

She stuck her foot out.

She had to do something. She turned back to the Recreation Hall. It was filled with about sixty young patients. They were dressed similar to her, crowded in a circle and laughing at something. Definitely not the behavior of super soldiers. Again, she got a cramp of worry in her stomach, but her curiosity got the best of her. She walked to the circle of kids. Someone smiled at her and let her in to see. In the center was a little boy, about ten, doing magic tricks with a deck of cards.

The building would blow in twenty-two minutes. She felt faint.

"Imeda?"

She turned to see Ketevan with a man.

"Dr. Baba can see you now."

CHAPTER THIRTY-SIX

Dr. Baba's office was very friendly and pretty standard in layout—a big desk and two chairs in front of it for guests. The walls had a combination of medical certificates and awards, along with what seemed to be photos of patients, colleagues, and family. One picture specifically worried her—a photo of Sergei with Ketevan and Dr. Baba in a small frame on the corner of his desk near the lamp.

Jocelyn sat in turmoil. Nineteen minutes to evacuate.

Dr. Baba sat behind his desk. "Imeda, we did a quick run on your blood and found it quite unusual." He looked at her records, then put the folder down to look at her. "The test was not consistent with radiation poisoning."

Yep, that cover didn't work. "I suppose that's good?" She needed to get out of the building and clear of the explosion in eighteen minutes.

"Maybe. But until we can diagnose your illness, I'm not sure we can help you."

Jocelyn slouched in the chair. "You mean you haven't seen anyone with my problem before."

"Well, that's not exactly true."

She shifted, curious.

"Your chemistry is reflective of a process we tried many years ago, without success. Has anyone else treated you, or given you medication?"

She shook her head.

"I don't understand, really. I'd like to keep you here for a few days and run some tests. We can contact your aunt."

"I'd prefer to stay with my aunt and just come here for tests."

"Of course. I just thought you might like to be around the other kids. The village is sparse for entertainment."

"No, thank you."

He nodded again. "We can do several today."

She nodded agreement, her stomach clenching. Finally, she grabbed the photo.

"Does he still work here?" She pointed to Sergei.

He blinked with surprise. "My uncle?" He came around to her side of the desk, took the picture, and set it back down on the desk. "He died."

Jocelyn stared in silence. *What? They thought he was dead.* What should she do?

"Are you all right, Imeda?"

"I need to see my auntie. She needs to know about the tests."

"Of course."

She felt dizzy. *Someone tell me what to do? If there is a God, tell me what to do.*

Jocelyn heard the voice in her communicator. "Fifteen minutes." She needed to get out. Now. Fast.

She had no choice.

Not following orders was treason.

You let them shoot Seth. That was the price. She risked Seth to someday get to Morgan and Ben. To have her own freedom. To save her own family. This was one more step.

But innocent people would die.

She shook her head negatively, fighting the internal debate. "Imeda?"

She held a finger to her lips, getting his confused attention. She took a breath, and with no going back, ripped the small receiver out of her ear. His confusion turned to shock. She put her finger to her lips again as he jumped out of his chair, outraged, worried, concerned.

She was about to do for Sergei what no one had done for her. She had to.

"Sometimes I feel a little dizzy," she noted for Headquarters. She pushed him aside, looking for paper. He understood and handed her a pen.

"I'll get you some water."

"Thank you."

She wrote quickly in Georgian. *Sergei is alive. Camp Holliwell, Virginia, U.S.A. You have less than twelve minutes to get everyone evacuated before the building explodes.*

Jocelyn held up the paper for him to read. He looked at her as if he didn't know what to believe. She took the paper, ripped it into squares, and swallowed.

Dr. Baba watched and turned pale. "My God."

Then he lunged at her like he wanted to kill her.

⸺

It took them a few minutes to get from Laurence's office to the telepresence conference room in cellblock 24, but Laurence and Dominique made record time. Laurence wasted no time in addressing the matter.

"Secretary Ramstein." Laurence Cashus barged in and faced the secretary on the other side of the table from his office in the White House. "I have an urgent request regarding Project Sunday."

The memory team nodded, pre-prepped for the intrusion, and quietly moved aside.

"You can have the floor, Dr. Cashus. We are wrapping."

"Sir, in only the last few days, I have gathered over fifty grant requests from scientific teams all over camp who have a project or academic study that would benefit from using Project Sunday. She is currently on her mission with General Martin, but I'm requesting her full transfer back to the science team. The estimates of these studies alone are in the hundreds of millions, and none could be done without Project Sunday. We recently discovered she has the ability to generate heat— real energy. Nothing in any previous studies has captured that. The usefulness of this capability alone would be remarkable.

The energy team submitted ten of the requests. Imagine the ability to give a soldier a pill to survive extreme temperatures. Or if something in her makeup can show us a design for clean energy?

Laurence pressed the limits, but he was desperate.

The SOI looked more annoyed than anything else.

"My office is sending the grant requests to you now. Please have a look. The possibilities are endless. And the price to keep her alive is quite small compared to the value of her as a test platform for all these studies. With all our teams finally working together, collaborating on this, I feel confident the results will be beyond your imagination."

The SOI looked at his tablet. "I received your mail. I'll get back to you." He leaned forward on the desk and pressed a button.

The entire screen wiped clean with just a blue background and the emblem for the President of the United States of America.

Laurence froze in shock. Was that it? Silence in the room. Everyone looked at him. His life's work hung in the balance.

"I'll wait here," he told the others. They nodded and slowly gathered their laptops and bags. Dominique stayed.

"You have over fifty teams?"

He nodded.

She sat down. "Impressive."

"The potential is."

She pulled out her phone. "Give me the numbers."

"What?"

"Let's get all the project leaders in here. And have them call his office as well. It's harder to turn down fifty people. Strength in numbers. That's how I do it. Who's first?"

Laurence scrolled to the list, willing to try anything. "Dr. Philomena Screetch." Laurence read the number. Dominique dialed.

It was the last thing he'd have expected—an unholy alliance with his fiercest competitor—but there were some things worth fighting for. In this case, both their life's work, and the future they could secure together for themselves and the evolution of humanity.

Dr. Baba leaped at Jocelyn with youth and fury. Instinct controlled her reaction. She flicked her hand up and sent him into the wall. She didn't have a lot of time for hand-to-hand combat.

She pressed her finger over the miniature receiver and applied heat. It softened in her hand, and she crushed the tiny electronics with a paperweight of Mt. Shkhara on his desk.

Baba was on the floor looking dazed and trying to get back on his feet.

"There's no time."

"Who are you?"

"Someone who knows your uncle."

"Why should I believe you?"

"We have ten minutes before you and everyone here are blown to pieces and float down the river. You should decide quickly. I've risked everything to tell you this, and I have to get back before they realize what's happened." She was already out the door and running for the elevator.

She was at the end of the hall when an alarm went off and flashing lights began in the hallways. She took that as his decision.

She circled the corner for the exit and met a rush of worried-looking teens and kids coming from the Recreation Hall. A confused nurse called for them to hurry.

Jocelyn searched out the stairs. It was only one flight up to the main floor and exits.

"This way!"

The nurse nodded relief, and the group hurried into the stairwell. Jocelyn saw the nurse go back to the Hall and yelled for her. That's when she saw four patients, two in wheelchairs and two with standing walkers.

Her heart pounded. She checked her watch. They wouldn't make it.

She ran after the nurse and they doubled the kids into 2 wheelchairs and pushed as fast as possible. Jocelyn stopped at the elevators. The nurse told them it was shut down in emergencies. They had only the stairs.

She told the nurse to carry the youngest, and put the child on the nurse's back. There were two other smallish children and an older girl.

"Take my brother," the older girl urged. "Please."

"No! Natty, not without you," the boy in the wheelchair said.

Jocelyn did the best she could. "All of us are going." To the boy, "Put him on my back." To the two larger kids, "Can you make it if I help you?"

They nodded, frightened but unwavering.

Jocelyn put one arm around each back and under their arms. She gripped them tightly, while the boy clung to her throat nearly choking her. Getting to the stairs was easier than getting up. Her mental clock ticked. Now was not the time to be meek. She lifted the patients with each arm and moved quickly up the stairs, partially dragging the oldest girl. She could hear the sounds outside as she turned the corner of the landing. Almost there. The emergency exit led them outside.

Two male hospital workers ran to them, one taking the boy off her back, the other scooped up the older girl while Jocelyn helped the last child. She noted armed soldiers directing everyone across the field, away from the hospital.

Jocelyn checked her watch. "Run!"

Thirty seconds. They needed to be far enough from the epicenter, or their insides would be reduced to mush. They ran.

To her surprise, she saw Medina helping patients. He found her and grabbed the last boy. They dashed across the field, past the hospital entrance and toward the forest. Other guards were helping.

They were all too close.

She felt, rather than heard, the first explosion deep underground. She tracked its instantaneous movement as excruciating vibrations threatened to release in her next breath.

They weren't going to make it.

Jocelyn felt the fear around her. It might be her last day, and she would be taking a hundred innocent people with her. In the seconds remaining, she became acutely aware of the world around her. The day was cold, but the sky was a crisp blue. The valley enclosing them created a powerful source for nature to flourish. This was the world outside Camp Holliwell—one filled with beauty and possibility. One she would be destroying. Only minutes before, these children had been laughing, innocent to the schemes of men and scientists and governments. She could feel everything in her midst as she sucked in deeply, absorbing the energy, letting it thicken around her.

Her skin charged electrically, becoming an engine. She breathed in transformable energy through every cell of her being.

With her eyes on the many in front of her, she focused, her arms spread out like an eagle reaching its wings to protect.

Fear and determination fueled the vibrant force that burst through her being just as the chain of explosions caught up to them.

CHAPTER THIRTY-SEVEN

If Jocelyn was lucky, no one would ever know what happened next.

Bodies flew across the ground. Children were lifted across the grassy valley to safety, some landing in a heap, but all able to get up again.

Jocelyn stumbled to her knees, heaving.

After the explosions ended, the land over the hospital collapsed inward, and portions of land and structure near the edge of the mountain fell to the depths below.

Her hand touched the earth. Her vision closed into darkness a moment before clearing. Tremors rocked the area, not unlike the ones shaking her body. Desperately, she sucked in air. She had to get up. *Get up!*

She swallowed hard, her saliva tasting like metal. The hand touching the earth felt bracing, and she realized there was energy yet that she could use. She stumbled to her feet, slowly moving past victims, her ears picking up every sound and her mind registering their grateful praises for angelic intervention.

She was no angel.

Jocelyn breathed in cooling air. Energy surged again through her body. She vibrated with it. And she kept moving.

Her walk became a jog as she searched out Medina. She'd thrust him forcefully forward into the safe zone. Still holding a child, he'd landed on the ground and rolled. They were ahead of her near the road. She ran to him. People lay strewn on the ground around her looking stunned and in shock. She reached Medina and dragged him to his feet. They kept going. She saw the SUV up ahead.

Gunfire made her turn in time to see Medina fall.

He pulled his firearm and shot from his prone position, making contact and causing the shooter to back away, but alerting at least a dozen soldiers. Clearly, they were suspect now. *Outstanding.*

Medina scrambled to his feet, limping, and tossed her the keys. "This way! You drive." She went to help him, but he flicked his elbow up and out at her defiantly. "I'm fine. Move it!"

He jumped in the back of the SUV, loaded his gun, and kicked out the back window with his good leg, swearing up a storm.

"HQ. We've got a problem. Heading to extraction zone."

Jocelyn strained to hear inside his Comm. She wanted to make sure she'd not been exposed.

"Copy. Re-coordinate to Delta location. Team is near."

"Copy."

The voice continued. "New orders for extraction. Terminate Imeda on arrival."

Jocelyn swerved then straightened out. *Terminate Imeda?* She glanced in the rearview mirror and met Medina's eyes. He looked surprised and suddenly wary of her. Like he didn't know who she was. She heard the cock of his pistol.

She didn't need to turn to know it was on her.

"Everything okay?" she asked.

"Just drive. You're going to veer right at the fork."

"Got it."

He couldn't kill her while she was driving, right? That would be dangerous.

"What happened to you?" Medina asked.

"What do you mean?"

"Your eyes. Were you infected by something?"

Jocelyn didn't know what he was talking about. She pulled the rearview mirror for a quick look and nearly crashed.

"Eyes on the road!"

"Got it."

She had trouble breathing. The whites of her eyes were laced with blue. Not normal. No wonder he was freaking.

"I'm good. Just stay calm." *Don't shoot me.*

She felt queasy. Who wouldn't be if they looked in the mirror and their eyes looked like this? There was more. She felt weak, getting weaker by the moment. "Do we have food?"

She turned her head, not liking the direction of the gun. "Can you point that somewhere else?"

"What's going on?"

"We accomplished our goals. Now we're going to the extraction point. They got the download, right?"

"Yes."

The bombs were placed correctly and went off on cue, right?"

"Yes."

"So all is good." The tension in her body denied it.

"Maybe."

She focused on the road. "You should wrap your leg. You're losing blood."

He kept his gun on her.

"How far to the fork?"

"About five miles."

"Long enough for you to bleed out. Where's the first aid kit?"

"I got it."

"You gonna use it?"

"Yeah." He grunted. "Right at the fork," he reminded her. The gun went down.

They drove in silence while he worked on his leg.

"I don't feel well. Do we have any food here?"

"Glove compartment."

She reached for it, getting a little frantic. Her hands shook. Her body cried out for nourishment. It was a new feeling—one she didn't like.

There were a handful of locally-made nut bars. She ripped one open, then another, devouring both. After another minute or so, she felt the effect. Her body stabilized. She breathed with relief, checking her eyes again. The blue within was fading, but underneath her eyes, she had the blue smudges of someone who was…not normal.

They reached the fork in the road, and she made a sharp right toward the river.

Medina spoke to HQ. "Nearly at extraction. Confirm final orders. Over."

Their eyes met in the mirror, as they both heard the order again.

"Terminate Imeda."

Laurence waited anxiously in the telepresence room. There were ten more scientists assembled with him and Dominique when the blue screen flashed back to reveal the Secretary of Information.

The SOI put his tablet down in front of him. "You've surprised me, Dr. Cashus. I hadn't taken you as a visionary before."

It was a backhanded compliment, but Laurence felt instant pride—followed by hope and relief.

"We," he lifted a hand to the others assembled, "and many others, believe we have the opportunity to change history and humanity for the better. And this knowledge, with the capabilities that come with it, should remain in the hands of our government. We believe in ten to twenty years, many of the proposals we are suggesting will be viable in other centers of science, but we clearly have an opportunity to get there first, to lead, and to stay ahead—and, well, you can, of course, imagine the military possibilities."

The Secretary smiled. "You present a compelling argument. I congratulate you on that. However, the order for termination has already been given."

Jocelyn parked by the river and jumped from the car, all in a single move. Getting shot again was not an option.

Medina jumped out of the vehicle just as quickly, but it cost him with his injured leg. He was conflicted. She could see it in his face. She moved around the car, backing away. "Please, Medina. It must be a mistake." His gun pointed at her.

"HQ, we're at the extraction."

"Wav-1 is standing by."

She backed up toward the river, hoping to spot the EmWAV.

"Did you tip them off?"

"I did my part of the mission. Getting the intel and planting the explosives. Helping those kids just came up. No one said we weren't supposed to help kids, right? They wanted the information and the facility destroyed. We did that. We obeyed orders. And your orders were to get me in and get me out. We were successful. I don't know why anyone wants me dead. But if you really are going to kill me, Medina, then just tell me one thing. Are we the good guys or the bad guys? I really want to know. Because in Paris, I thought we were good, but that team kidnapped Sergei, right? That's what we were there for, right?"

His furious eyes told her it was the truth.

"How is that good?"

No answer.

"Just now, we were going to kill hundreds of innocent kids. Right? *Answer me*. I don't care what the answer is, but for once, just once before I die, I want to know the truth! I want someone to tell me the *truth*."

Medina snarled. "Just shut up!" He cursed loudly. "You're always talking."

"No one talks to me," she said softly. "But if they want me dead, they might want you dead, too."

He must have suspected that as well, because he didn't disagree. "Then we're screwed. The forests around here are swarming with Russians. We won't make it fifteen minutes before we're caught and interrogated. And you do not want to be interrogated by the Russians. Trust me." He swore again, trying to think it through.

There was nowhere to run, no cover to be found. Her energy was low. Whatever she had done during the explosion, she thought she might be able to do again, if only her body would obey her. If only Medina would stop yelling. If only she could make sense of the world.

Finally, Medina relented. He holstered his gun. "Let's stick to the original plan."

He was breaking the rules—for her. He disobeyed the line of command. It was everything he believed in. She breathed with relief. She could forgive him for being stressed out and putting a gun to her head.

Jocelyn kept an eye on him while getting the gear from the SUV. Not wanting to risk being left behind, she repelled down the vertical bank to the river first. She was nearly at the EmWAV when he called out.

"Don't try to leave without me, Cashus."

"I'm not." She pulled the gear free, wrapped it, and shoved it in the storage section of the water vehicle. She helped him when he reached the bottom and took care of the equipment. Helmets on, they closed the EmWav cockpit, hit the cloaking, and submerged as the first shots rang out.

"Great. They know where we are." Medina flipped on the engine. "I'll drive, you shoot."

"Got it." She aimed a missile at the truck tracking them along the river. "You want me to kill them?"

"*Seriously?*" he shouted in frustration.

"I've never killed anyone!"

He cursed even more colorfully than before. "I should have killed you. Drive. I got this."

Jocelyn scrambled to take the controls, navigating in and out of shallow waters to deeper parts of the river. She heard the sound of a beeping alert that got closer and faster, indicating a target. "Is that you?"

"No. They've got a missile locked on us."

"Shoot it down."

"I'm trying!"

She watched the missile get closer on the radar. The timing impact showed on her screen in milliseconds. She wasn't going to wait for Medina to stop it. She thrust straight up, zipped out of the water, bounced, then thrust again as the missile entered the water beneath them, exploding rock and debris, sending shock waves of heat radiating around them. She glided the vehicle across the surface and re-entered the water.

"What the hell was that maneuver?" he asked.

She answered, still tense and alert. "Bond, James Bond."

"No shit." Medina grinned. "Who knew you'd be useful."

"I won't let it go to my head. Are you going to take care of this next one?"

Medina launched before the enemy could. She saw the target neutralized on her screen. "Don't let it bother you too much. They just tried to kill you."

"Well, we did just blow up a hospital—with a bunch of little kids in it."

"Stop talking now."

She complied and focused on maneuvering the EmWAV through the river. "We have two helicopters approaching."

"Stay cool. Our extraction craft is five miles away. They can't detect us if we stay low."

"They could estimate our location by the change in the motion of the water, if they had the right equipment."

"They don't."

As he said it, something exploded directly to her left, throwing the vehicle sideways.

"Stay on course."

Teeth gritted, she struggled with the controls, pulling the EmWAV back on track and as low to the river's bottom as possible. "You were saying?"

Medina ignored her. "HQ, we have two copters on our six. Assistance needed."

"We have them in sight. Continue your course. Friendly airspace is near. Rendezvous in six minutes."

Another missile hit right in front of them. It sent them flying upward with force. They smashed back on the river, exposed. Jocelyn took note of their position, making sure the cloaking device was still activated. It didn't hide them perfectly, but it would give her a few seconds. She flipped the vehicle and dropped them down as quickly as possible.

The two helicopters backed away. Medina took the controls. "You're not trained for this part."

"What part?"

The extraction aircraft lowered to the river. Medina emerged and gave them a countdown.

Jocelyn watched the video of the aircraft in front of them. The rear entry door lowered, while Medina lined up the marks on his display.

"We're not flying into that aircraft, are we?"

"Brace yourself," Medina answered.

The EmWAV surged up and forward. She thought they would take the aircraft down with them, but trip wires caught the bottom of Wav-1, braking them hard and fast.

Finally frozen in place, she took a breath and turned to Medina. Utterly serious he said, "Now *that*, rookie, was Bond, James Bond."

She nodded. "Are you going to let them kill me now?"

He scowled, mood ruined, and reached for the gun at his side, flicking the safety off. "We'll see."

The doors to the EmWAV opened.

"Cashus!"

A Lieutenant pulled her out of the vehicle, and Medina lifted his gun. She wasn't clear if it was to shoot her or the officer.

"Thank, God. The orders were rescinded. The enemy got through the Comm device somehow."

"So…you don't want me to kill her?" Medina asked, his gun trained on her.

"No."

Medina lowered his gun but kept it in hand. Jocelyn took a seat next to him. His gun had been on her, but his eyes were on the lieutenant. It gave him away. He was going to shoot the officer, not her. She was sure of it. As much a pain as he was, he was the only one she trusted right now.

She didn't believe the enemy had sabotaged them. She was meant to be left behind, and nothing could erase the uneasy feeling that she'd been expendable, or that someone wanted to get rid of her. Was General Martin or Sarge in on it?

She might never know, but the fact that they had changed their mind scared her even more.

Death might be better than what awaited her back at Holliwell.

CHAPTER THIRTY-EIGHT

The science teams were celebrating their success at winning the Secretary of Information's support and recovering Project Sunday when Dr. Wicker received the unfortunate news.

A photo of the twisted MedVan had been texted to her from officials in Colorado. The words following: *No survivors.*

No additional information was forthcoming, but there would be a full investigation.

Laurence felt deeply sorry for the inconvenience this would cause. The loss of Seth was a wasted asset, and hiring more guards, nurses, and technicians was an arduous process in order to ensure people kept the confidentiality required of Holliwell. But it was remarkable how death could bring people together, and considering her recent assistance and advocacy, everyone present endeavored to bolster Dominique's spirits and offer support. Laurence included his, with the offer of Sunday's blood samples so she could continue her experimentation.

He assured her that she would find another successful "Seth" sooner than she expected.

General Martin met Jocelyn and Medina in the landing space at the edge of Holliwell.

She and Medina were taken for yet another debrief. It made Jocelyn a little nervous. Were they trying to get her to crack? Did they want to find anomalies in their stories?

At no time did Jocelyn admit to warning Dr. Baba of the danger. She stuck with her story that the alarms went off, and no one knew why. The nurses were confused, she told them. They thought it might be a chemical release or fire danger. She wondered aloud if the computer breach was what actually set off the security systems.

As she told her story for the third time under videotaped scrutiny, she knew there was a chance that Dr. Baba had already told someone, perhaps a local spy, and given her away.

General Martin tapped his stylus on the e-pad, thinking about his questions, occasionally making a check mark before going back to the tapping. It played havoc with her already-frayed nerves and ears that were still sensitive to sound from the explosions.

It took stubborn patience and willpower to sit through the process. Those who knew her knew she liked to chat and be around people. This was work. Hours of questions, sometimes the same ones. She waited silently between each question giving minimal input. At the end of the interview, just before they were about to turn off the camera, she had a question for them.

"General Martin, one last thing."

He looked at her like he already knew the topic.

She shook her head. "I did my job. Why did you give the order to kill me?"

His tapping stopped. His lips pressed as if he might apologize, but he didn't. "It wasn't my order."

Her fingertips tingled. *Not an enemy intercepting their communication then?* "You gave it to the team. Who gave it to you?" she asked tersely.

"It came from above. We all follow orders, Cashus. You know that. We have to trust our commanders, or nothing works. We don't always have the bigger picture. And sometimes...well...sometimes, those orders are just a test."

The tapping began again as he observed her reactions.

The heat from her fingertips spread up her arms. She wanted to use some of the curses she'd recently learned from Medina. What was the truth?

"Why did the orders change?"

He didn't answer.

One of her fingers raised off the table with focused intent. The stylus shot from his hand and flew against the wall. Tapping over. She heard the heartbeats of the General and the two soldiers speed up. She didn't care.

"Why did the orders change?" she repeated.

"You can thank your uncle for that."

Thank my uncle for anything? That will be the day.

"He convinced Washington you're valuable."

Her body tensed. Valuable sounded like a prison sentence. "Who is Washington?"

He smiled. It infuriated her more than the tapping.

"It doesn't matter. People higher than me. They've decided you shouldn't be doing field trips anymore."

She sat up straight, in shock. "What? *Why?*"

"You're too valuable," General Martin said. He made a note on his digital notebook with his finger.

"That *is* my value. I want to work with the team and do more." Panic filled her. The military wing was her only way out. That was her plan for escape.

"Your uncle made the case for your value to science, Cashus. Don't worry. I'm sure it's an easier life." He stood up, patently dismissing her.

"It's not!" She looked at the soldiers in the room, the one still videotaping. The General motioned for him to cut off. "No. You know what my uncle is capable of. He's going to kill me. He'll experiment on me until I die, then he'll cut me up for science shows."

She saw sympathy in the eyes of two of the soldiers, even a sense of wanting to do something. People couldn't think this was okay. She must appeal to their humanity. "Maybe you could help me find my family outside Holliwell. I might have grandparents who are still alive. Or aunts and uncles. I could live with them instead. Please, don't send me back to Dr. Cashus. He's insane. Please."

The door opened, and her uncle entered.

"Sunnie, this obsession of yours must end."

Jocelyn stood so quickly, the chair behind her fell backward. Her uncle's voice came across calm and assured. It terrified her. He was in charge again. A soldier came behind her, reaching for her arms. She yanked free but was backed into a corner of the small room.

She focused on Martin and the faces that were sympathetic. "Please don't let him take me. Let me go free. Let me leave this place." She saw her uncle pull the tranquilizer shot from the pocket of his white coat. "Please, this is not fair."

Like hell you're going to use that on me.

She focused on the syringe, and it flew from her uncle's hand. One of the soldiers pulled his weapon.

Her uncle's lips curled with pleasure. "This is why you are dangerous, Sunnie."

"I'm not. I'm good. I *help* people."

"You can't obey. Therefore, how can you be good?" He spoke the words with a condescending smile.

And confidence.

The confidence scared her the most. The space was concrete. There was little energy for her to draw on, but she had a lot inside her. Enough to knock them out. Then they would know more. They would know she was powerful.

She heard the voices of others outside the room alerted and assembling.

General Martin took a step closer and held out his hand to her. "It's going to be okay, Sunnie."

He never used her first name.

She shook her head. "Are you one of the evil ones, General Martin? Was I wrong about you?" Could it be possible that everyone was evil? "I'm innocent. He is not my uncle."

"Sunnie!" Dr. Cashus spoke. "See, this is the delusional part."

"General, my name is Jocelyn Albrecht." She didn't want to lose her identity again, or the precious little memory of where she came from. "I am still alive."

"*Silence!* You're delusional."

The sound of her real name made Cashus's face turn purple and distorted. She said it again, shouting it at him. "I'm Jocelyn Albrecht! My parents were Dr. Illeana Albrecht and Dr. Grayson Albrecht. I remember my parents. *You,*" she pointed to Cashus, "are not my uncle. You are a lying, evil, manipulative dictator." She spit on him to show her disgust. "You make me sick."

He wiped his cheek in shock, then exploded toward her, veins bulging around his eyes and across his forehead.

This time she used her fists. The swift hook and uppercut sent him stumbling backward. The raw feeling on her knuckles had an immensely satisfying sting. Cashus looked about to pass out as another soldier flew into the room and shot her with a tranquilizer. She ripped it from her stomach, agonized.

"I am Jocelyn Albrecht. My parents...I am Jocelyn Albrecht. My...." She stumbled, then fell to her knees. Someone must have turned the camera on again. As her vision grew gray and fuzzy around the edges, she stared at the blinking light, desperate to hold onto consciousness. To hope. To hold onto herself.

Darkness enclosed quickly. "I am Jocelyn Albrecht." Head spinning, she clenched her cramping stomach. Hopelessness and futility were a heavy weight bearing down on her, crushing her chest, making it harder to breathe.

She willed the truth from her body. "I am...."

CHAPTER THIRTY-NINE

Graeme studied the pictures on the walls around him in the small warehouse office. His Charlottesville surveillance had turned into an interesting project of sorts, and he'd rented his only little space to park and set up shop. The place was sparse, but he didn't need much—just answers.

He had names and bios on everyone except one. "Who are you?" He'd been looking at her face for a long time. It was a good face—sensitive, beautiful, with kindhearted, curious, unusual blue eyes. A little cagey, but he liked her.

His exhaustive research determined she was not the daughter of some General. Certainly not General Martin's. He tapped his fingers. Absolutely no face recognition. With all the girls her age posting selfies, it seemed completely impossible that he didn't have a dozen plus hits of her in the bathroom doing poses in front of a camera.

The mystery of it only intrigued him further. "Who are you?"

He didn't think she had a connection to his family, but she did live at Holliwell, so she might know stuff.

His cellphone rang. Rex. He smiled. He missed his brothers. Benny face-timed every day, and they discussed his lightsaber, sports, games, life—sometimes they just laughed over a video on YouTube. Rex was harder to reach—in a lot of ways.

"Hey, bro!"

"Hey, little bro. How are you?"

"Good. Just hanging out, working on a project."

"Yeah? What kind?"

Graeme hadn't been home in almost a month. His family wasn't used to that unless he was at college.

"Just finishing up my thesis project, doing research, thinking about my next steps, you know. How about you?" He tried to change the subject.

"You going to be home soon? Mom is worried."

"I talk to her every other day. She's not worried."

"Okay, well, she misses you and wants to make sure you're not involved with a girl and making bad decisions."

Graeme laughed. "Well, I'm not involved with a girl."

"You should really leave the bad decisions to me, Graeme."

"I'll be home soon."

"Cool. So I don't have to worry."

The buzzer of the warehouse rang. Graeme listened, surprised. No one knew he was here except Richie. And Richie wasn't coming by today. Graeme got up from his chair and walked out of the one room office. The buzzer rang again and again, more persistent.

Rex continued chatting on the phone. "I'm bummed you're not here. Wanted to grab a beer and some chicken wings and kick back."

Graeme went to the security buzzer that allowed entrance to the warehouse. On the black and white monitor next to the buzzer was his brother. "What the...." Graeme laughed.

Rex grinned up at the camera and lifted a bag with a hot wings label and a six pack of beer. "Here to break in your new digs."

Graeme let him in, looking down from the second floor office loft as Rex entered. "I can't believe you're here." He was happy to see Rex, but his brother would want details.

Rex observed the sparse warehouse, folding table, and chairs. "Uh-huh." He put the food and drinks down. "I can't believe you're here, either. They have some nice hotels in town, you know."

"I like the space."

Rex opened a beer and stared at him. "So?"

"Let me shut things down upstairs."

Rex was up the stairs and on his heels. "Is this where the magic happens?"

"It's just my computer, nothing cool."

"I came all this way. At least give me the grand tour." He handed Graeme a cold beer.

Graeme cracked the drink open, accepting the inevitable. There was no keeping his brother out of the office. At least Graeme had folded the blankets on the cot today.

Rex noted the generic rental parked inside the warehouse. "Where's the Porsche?"

"Getting some modifications."

"I won't ask."

"Better that way." Graeme opened the door to his office. It was filled with folding tables, computers, and surveillance equipment.

"Oh, shit." His brother turned to him. "You're a terrorist."

Graeme laughed.

Rex guessed again. "Serial killer."

"Shut up, you ass." Still, he needed an answer for his brother. "I'm figuring out the value of certain networked software solutions."

"You are so full of it. You're spying." His brother looked around. "Who are you spying on? Is it a girl? That's stalking, you know. Not healthy. Not healthy at all. No girl is worth it." Rex stopped and leaned in to get a better look at the mysterious blue-eyed girl. "Well, maybe this one. Who's this?" Rex nodded to himself. "*She's* hot."

"She's a person, not an object."

"Yeah. Thank you, Governor Mom."

Graeme laughed at the old reference to their mom. "I actually don't know who she is. Not part of my project. I just saw her and thought she was cute, so I got a picture."

"Uh-huh." Rex took a drink of beer and studied him silently, disbelief on his face.

Graeme took a swig of beer as well. "The wings smell good."

"Changing the subject. Always effective." Rex allowed himself to be led out of the office.

"I'll be home soon. I'm not really getting anywhere. I'm starting to think my hypothesis is totally wrong."

"The one about an evil government plot to destroy our family?"

Graeme blinked. His brother joked, but that wasn't far off.

"There are a lot of military types in your photos," Rex noted. "I totally don't get the movie theater and coffee shop thing, but I know my people."

Graeme shrugged. "I suppose this area has a lot of military in general. My tracking is about the movement of traffic and gathering samples from various cities around the country to see if there's a new model for how to do marketing." *And...lies, lies. Smile.*

Rex nodded and slapped him hard on the back. "Whatever you say—stalker."

Rex was a West Point graduate and served for four years while getting a Master's degree in Chemical Engineering. He was finishing his MBA at Harvard and was poised to someday take over the reins of A & R Technologies or follow their mom's footsteps into politics. Based on his playboy status of late, Graeme didn't think politics was his focus, but he still wasn't going to get one over on his brother.

"Anyway, it's a good test for my imaging software."

"I'm sure."

"But the challenge is, what if someone is not on the Internet?" Graeme split open the wings bag and dug in. The smell reminded him he was hungry. He dipped one into some Ranch dressing, ate it in two bites, then tried one with barbeque sauce. He took another long drink, relaxing a little.

"Everyone is online unless they're dead, and even then, they are." Rex opened the sweet mustard and double dipped.

"Okay, let's assume they're alive."

"Have you run a filter as a missing person?"

"Yes. Nothing. Not missing."

"Okay, have you tried that?" Rex gulped some beer. "Wow, those are spicy."

"Tried what?"

"Not missing. How they look now is not on the Internet."

"Oh...I could try an age regression match." Graeme talked through the idea.

Rex nodded. "Or they're dead."

"Not dead. Trust me."

"Well, you could ask her what her name is."

Graeme took another chicken wing. "It's complicated."

"Those are the worst kind. Can't tell Mom that."

"Did she send you?"

"Yes. She has all the cars on tracking devices, you know."

"I asked Wheeler to take mine out." Wheeler maintained all the family vehicles.

Rex laughed. "Of course you did. But he doesn't work for you."

"Fine. I'll find it and take it out myself."

"Then she'll really worry. You want a permanent security detail?"

"Hell."

"Anyway, once I had your city, I logged into your bank account, got your deposit info made out to a property manager, called their office and said I was your brother, in town and lost. They gave me directions. The people are so helpful here."

"You logged into my bank account?"

"You really need to change your password."

"Well, just tell Mom I came to see about a girl. Make up the rest. Like she's a computer science major at University of Virginia. Or neuroscience. That's even better." Graeme thought it through. "Tell her I just needed time away to have a clear vision of what I want to do next. I might not want to make games the rest of my life. So now is the time to explore options."

Rex opened two more beers and handed him one. "Okay, okay. I got you covered. Don't worry. Just don't miss your own graduation."

"Does Dad know I'm here, too? In Charlottesville?"

"No." Rex wiped the mustard dish clean with a wing. "After I spoke with Wheeler, we agreed not to out you yet. I told Mom and Dad you were in Chicago but moving around a lot testing your final thesis project. It sounded way better than Charlottesville. Plus, I figured you were hiding something, so I covered your ass just in case."

"Thanks. I don't really want them to know I'm here."

"You didn't wreck the Porsche, did you?"

"No."

"And no one's pregnant?"

"No!" Graeme laughed.

"Good. Learn from my mistakes." Rex finished his beer. "So everything really is fine, right? 'Cause I can stay in town if you need backup or a wingman."

"You suck at being a wingman."

Rex grinned. "I know. I can't help goin' for the girl. Sue me." He stood up. "Speaking of which, I have a date."

"Here? Tonight?"

"I met her at the hotel. Want me to see if she has a friend?"

Graeme laughed. "No thanks. Enjoy." He grabbed the food bag. "But I'm keeping the rest of the wings."

"I'll pick you up for breakfast tomorrow before I leave." Rex pulled him into a bear hug and slapped him on the back three times. "Seriously, though, I can stay as long as you need."

"It's cool. I'll be home soon anyway."

"All right."

His brother didn't look satisfied, but he also respected Graeme's space. Graeme had never given the family anything to worry about, and despite his amateur spy network, that wasn't likely to change.

After his brother left, Graeme phoned Richie.

"Hey, can you look for a tracking device on my car? Probably in the frame behind the rearview mirror. My mom's a little neurotic about some things."

Richie grunted. "Your mom, huh?"

"She was the Governor of New York. It made her paranoid about the government, ironically."

"They're all out to control us. I would listen to her."

"Yeah, well. She likes to know where her children are at all times."

"That," Richie said, "is a mom thing. My momma was the same. Let me check while you're on the phone."

Graeme waited. A few minutes later, Richie spoke. "Yeah, this is pretty basic commercial tracking, but useful. If you want, I can program it so it tracks from your computer instead of the administrator."

"That's cool. Can you use my phone instead of the computer?"

"No reason why not."

"Make it so."

"You got it, boss," Richie responded cheerfully.

Graeme went back to his surveillance work and flipped on the monitors. He listened in on the movie theater for a while. Georgie and Brittany were working tonight. He always got better insight when those two were together. It explained the link to Holliwell, at least partially. If his hypothesis was right, there was a connection between Brittany's aunt and General Brody. They had found out something that had gotten them mysteriously killed, but he had no idea what—except for the possible connection to Morgan and Ben.

After listening for a time, it seemed like a normal night at the movie house.

Graeme switched back to his mystery girl. He thought for a while, then started typing. Following Rex's advice, he took off the 'missing' filter, and wrote two searches with an age regression program set at five and ten years ago. It was a long shot, but maybe something would get a hit.

He reviewed the photo Daphne had taken of the girl. She looked surprised, curious, and concerned, but her posture conveyed defensiveness and distrust. He zoomed in and cropped the face creating a portrait-sized image, still fascinated by her blue eyes, even after staring at them for so long. He may not figure out the Holliwell mystery, but he was going to figure her out.

He finished the program, gave her a final look, and pressed enter.

CHAPTER FORTY

Jocelyn awoke drowsy and disoriented. She had no idea where she was, what had happened, or how she got here. Her instinct told her not to speak. She couldn't if she wanted to. Her mouth felt like cotton. It reminded her of post-anesthesia symptoms. She must have been sick or operated on. It was normal to not remember when you regained consciousness after surgery. She knew that. *How did she know that?*

A nurse saw her movements and came over to offer water from a straw. She tried to reach for the cup, but her arms and wrists were strapped to the bed with thick metal collars. Panic started in her chest. She moved her feet and felt a similar sensation.

"Shhh," the nurse said. She touched one of Jocelyn's hands at the metal cuffs. "These are just for your protection."

Jocelyn closed her eyes and breathed slowly for control. Her nose hurt, and there was something in it. She looked down at her hands and saw multiple I.V. ports on each one. She'd definitely been under for something. She tried to assess if all her body parts were still attached. It seemed so. Her stomach and organs also seemed fine. She breathed through her mouth this time.

Remaining silent, she tentatively smiled at the nurse and drank thirstily from the straw. The nurse pulled it away before she could get very much, then left, presumably to alert her uncle or another doctor.

Jocelyn closed her eyes. The activity made her head hurt. Just as quickly, she opened them. Someone else was in the room—had been there the whole time.

She turned her head a little and saw him gently close his book and walk over to the bed. He was lean and spry, not too tall, and in his late sixties. He leaned over her and spoke barely above a whisper, directly into her ear, his Georgian accent familiar. His stroked a cool hand over her forehead as if to comfort her. His words were not comforting.

"The Energy team has implanted nanotransmitters that will measure the activity in your brain when you do certain tasks. Tiny microbots, smaller than a cell, were injected up your nose and into your brain. They are designed to test for an eight-week period, and by the end of the eighth week will dissolve and be absorbed into your body tissue. However, over the next few days, they will stimulate your brain cells. This work is to see if we can activate different portions of the brain. The challenge is that, due to some brain swelling during the operation, there is a very slight, but possible, chance you will have lost some of your recent memory. You might not even know who I am. It would be very fortunate if *that* were the case. Blink twice if you understand."

Jocelyn looked into brown eyes lined with wrinkles and blinked twice.

"It is also possible that after the swelling goes down, your memory will be stronger due to some minor side effects. Regardless," he continued, "—your uncle saved your life after your last field trip so that you could be used as a scientific platform for multi-disciplinary study and experimentation."

Jocelyn's heartbeat quickened. The monitors in the room started beeping louder and faster.

His hand grasped her arm with a firm warning. "Control your breathing. It is not safe for you to panic. There is a camera on you even now. Your uncle will be here soon, and I am to be moved now that I have served my purpose."

Jocelyn blinked twice and slowly breathed in through her hypersensitive nose.

"As part of the energy test, Cashus has given you another dose of the original serum that infected you and killed your parents. This is the same concoction you've received every two to three years since you came under his guardianship. It will make you sick and weak for a short while, and he will tell you it's medicine for your cancer. You will recover quickly and possibly gain in strength. I think he only does this to keep you afraid and dependent on him, yes?"

She tried to answer, but her cottonmouth had returned. She closed her eyes, emotionally exhausted.

"I have been modifying this serum for Dr. Wicker. She is using it on several subjects. The first few were not successful, but I have hopes we will go through less test subjects soon. I am sorry for my role in this. It was a negotiation."

He paused a moment and squeezed her hand gently. This time it was to comfort. "New tests will continue on you every three months. Several dozen science teams on camp have agreed to a quarterly division of time in which they can share your body."

Her eyes flashed open in horror. Fury was a very close second to the terror burning inside. She felt her skin heat dramatically and again heard machines begin to beep in response. She wanted to cry out from the injustice and torment, and cry tears from the frustration and hopelessness. It hurt to inhale, but she did it again, forcing her body to be calm.

The man continued, regardless of her obvious distress. "This will continue for the next several years, until you die. At that point, the research teams will continue to study every part of your anatomy and keep you entombed in their morgue with all of their other failed experiments. You can go see for yourself. You remember the passcode?"

She blinked twice.

"You are not a person anymore. Those who would help you will be hunted down and killed if they are caught. It would be fortunate, perhaps, if you don't remember me or anyone else from the last few months. Close your eyes and remember the carefree, loving girl that you once were. Perhaps she can help you where no one else can. Do you *understand* everything that I am saying?"

He was trying to give her another chance, a new start. She blinked twice, confirming.

The man moved his chair closer to her bed and began to softly read aloud from his book. Jocelyn closed her eyes and did as he suggested. She tried to remember.

Georgie couldn't get rid of the feeling that Jocelyn was in trouble. Brittany didn't help. She said she'd had the same feeling just before she learned about her aunt.

As soon as she had a fifteen-minute break at the theater, Georgie bugged a co-worker to use his computer. Quickly, she scanned the Internet for any more Holliwell-related accidents. Brittany's aunt came up, and farther down, an accident in Colorado was linked. Two of the deceased had been longtime residents of Charlottesville. She quickly read further. The MedVan was carrying a patient. *Ohmigosh.* Her heart raced as she wondered if it was Jocelyn. She pounded the scroll key, searching frantically. *Give me a name. Give me a name. Did you escape? Jocelyn, did you escape?* A hundred thoughts rushed her at once until she read the name of the patient being transported—Seth Johnson.

Georgie printed the article, folded it up, and put it in her pocket. She would save it, just in case. How many young patients were there at Holliwell? Did they know each other?

She was still wondering about the fate of Jocelyn when she got home. Her father awaited her in the living room, sitting in his oversized leather chair, glasses perched on his nose, reading a new history book.

"Hi, Dad. Goodnight, Dad." Georgie's feet were tired, she smelled like popcorn, another person was dead, and Jocelyn was missing. She didn't really want a long conversation tonight.

"Everything okay?"

"Yes, just tired."

"Come over and sit down. I haven't had your company lately."

She stared at him, her mind saying *seriously*, while her heart still wanted to be young enough to snuggle close and have him solve the world's problems.

She dropped her backpack and sat on the sofa, facing the wall-sized, hand-quilted blanket her grandmother had made for her parents' wedding. It contained patches of material from nearly every member of the family from the previous three generations, including a piece of great-granddaddy's army uniform and Mary-Louise Chandler Washington's wedding dress. Despite the mash-up of colors and materials, it was really beautiful and had the effect it always did—it made her remember history and appreciate the possibilities. Slowly, she relaxed into the leather sofa, let her head drop back, and closed her eyes with a sigh.

Her hand slipped into the lower pocket of her uniform and fiddled with the article she still had there. Seth Johnson was young. So was Jocelyn. What was going on at Holliwell?

"Hard day?"

Georgie smiled. There were no hard days in their house. "Every day above ground is a good day. Every challenge an opportunity to learn and grow. Every ray of sunshine a blessing from the Almighty. There are no hard days like the days past, only days of wasted hours,"—her throat tightened unexpectedly—"and regret."

She had meant the recitation of her father's repetitious lecture on life to be lighthearted, but she wondered if she had failed utterly to help another human in need. Her eyes burned and she kept her head tilted up to get control. She did *not* want to cry in front of her dad and have to explain something he would probably think was stupid.

He didn't speak, but she heard him put the book down on the coffee table. "Sounds like it was a hard day."

She laughed. And sniffed.

"Whatever happened with your friend who was in trouble?"

Her eyes flooded. Dead giveaway. Of all the things he could ask her, how did he manage to be spot on?

She shook her head, struggling to speak. "I don't know. I haven't seen her."

"She's not in school?"

"Homeschooled."

"She might be on vacation."

Georgie nodded agreeably.

"Can you call her?"

"No. She doesn't have a phone. They keep pretty strict control over her."

"It's not illegal." Her father leaned forward, hands clasped between his knees.

She nodded again.

"Not helping?" he asked.

She saw his smile and gave one back. "No."

"Sorry, love."

She sighed and sat up. "I just feel like I didn't do enough, or should have done something else."

He nodded this time.

"What if she gives up? I mean, how do people live with constant oppression? How do you breathe? How do you keep going and still be a good person?"

"People have. For hundreds of years. In every country in every time, oppression and slavery live on. We're lucky, but that doesn't mean everyone is. Even in our country, children are abused. Others are smuggled in to become all types of slaves. People are kidnapped when they travel. There is evil in the world."

Georgie sucked her breath in. "Geez, Dad! *Really.* Not helping."

"But I was going to add," he smiled, "that people also overcome. They hold on. They find in the darkness the glimmers of hope they need to believe in themselves and in others, and in the possibility for a different life—a better life. The human spirit struggles, and out of the magnificent struggle can also come unspeakable beauty...true honor...unexpected glory."

The weight in Georgie's chest lifted and released. Her body felt lighter again.

She tilted her head and smiled at her dad.

He held up his hands for her response. "Not bad, eh?"

She grinned wider. "You have your moments."

He got up and opened his arms to hug her. She stood and let him wrap her up in the safety of his love, and squeezed tight.

"Just never forget, daughter. You are *my* beauty, honor, and glory. For me, *you* are more precious than all the world can offer."

"I love you, too, Dad." She squeezed him again as the light went on behind them. Her mom walked down the stairs.

"I'm craving pancakes. You two hungry?"

"I could eat pancakes," Georgie said.

"I'll cook you ladies pancakes," her dad said.

"*You're* gonna cook us pancakes?" Georgie's mom went into the kitchen and pulled up a stool to the kitchen bar. "Well, this is a treat. Georgie, get the camera out. I want a picture of your dad cooking pancakes. No one's gonna believe it."

Her dad took on an offended look. "Woman, these are gonna be the best pancakes you ever had!"

"Well, they'll be the first ones I didn't make myself."

The two continued to tease each other, and Georgie enjoyed their banter and hanging out. It had been awhile since they'd done something like this. She loved her family. Even when her parents were tough, they were always solid and loving and fun. Now might be a good time to tell them she'd been accepted to three universities in New York.

Her dad flipped a pancake. *Naw.* It was rare to see her dad so carefree. She'd wait to see if she got any scholarships. There was no point bringing it up otherwise. The good news was that if there were people like her parents in the world, there was hope. Even for someone like Jocelyn.

She had to believe that.

CHAPTER FORTY-ONE

Laurence arrived the minute he heard Sunday was awake. According to the reports, she was very amenable. He took a breath before opening the door to her room, prepared for battle.

Sunday smiled when he entered, trying to sit up. She'd been asking for him. Relief covered her face as he approached.

He felt an equal amount of relief, but remained cautious.

"Uncle Laurence!" She smiled. Her hand reached out—as far as it could with the metal cuff.

Sergei Baratashvili closed his book and stood at the foot of the bed. "She's been a model patient."

Laurence went to the clasp at her right wrist and undid the metal cuff. "Sorry about this. We were concerned you would move too much in surgery and recovery."

"It's okay."

He undid the upper right arm as well, but none of the others.

"I'm just glad you're here. I was scared. I didn't know anyone. And no one told me what happened. Am I sick? Did I have a relapse?" Fear showed in her eyes.

Laurence continued to hold her hand and study her. He glanced at Sergei, who gave a slight shake of his head. What did she remember? Was this a benefit due to temporary swelling? If only he could have a redo. He'd manage her much better.

"Yes. You did, in fact, have a relapse. You've been given a dose of chemical therapy for extra insurance. You should begin to feel stronger in a couple days. In fact, you might be strong enough to come home tomorrow."

She closed her eyes, her body relaxing. "Thank you." She squeezed his hand before releasing it. "I knew it would all be okay once you got here." She opened her eyes and smiled with gratitude.

"I'll leave you two to catch up," Sergei said. "Nice to meet you, Sunday."

"Thank you for reading to me," she said. He left and she frowned. "Who was that?"

"Sergei?"

She grinned. "His name is Sergei?" She grinned more broadly.

"Yes, why?"

"I don't know. Don't you think it's funny everyone from Russia is named Sergei?"

He shared the joke. "Yes, it is odd." Her body shook with laughter and she winced.

"You might have some headaches, but they will go away. Let me know if it gets too bad, and we'll give you something, okay?"

She nodded.

"What's the last thing you remember?"

She stared at him, a confused expression on her face. "I'm not sure. I think—." She closed her eyes and opened again. "I think just asking you if I could have a mango slushie."

"It's all going to be okay. You might have a little memory loss, but nothing to worry about. Everything will be just like it used to be, Sunday, but even better."

She nodded again. He could see that she wanted to believe him and felt a renewed sense of power and confidence. "The nurses will help you get up after I leave, and we'll see how that goes. If you're up for it, you can come home tomorrow. Okay?"

"Okay." She smiled and he moved to go. "Wait!" It was an urgent whisper.

"What is it?"

She clasped his hand and pulled it to her lips. She pressed a long kiss on top, then held it to her cheek before releasing him. "I love you, Uncle Laurence. Thank you for taking care of me."

He nodded approval. "I love you, too, Sunday."

Laurence left the hospital room with hope. This altered state might last forever, or it might last a few months. Either way, he would take advantage of it.

Jocelyn shook as she stared at herself in the bathroom mirror. The hair on her pillow had been a warning, but nothing had prepared her for this. Her face was blue-white, her eyebrows had wiped off with soap when she'd washed her face. For some reason, her eyelashes were holding on. She shouldn't expect that for much longer. She used the hospital comb on her hair, but it only pulled it out more. She tried to fight off the trembling, to fight off the tears, to breathe, and be calm. She dropped the comb in the trash, holding onto the sink to get control. It didn't work. It was hopeless. Her arms had thinned out in just the two days she'd been here, and her entire being felt hollow and beaten.

"Everything all right, Sunday?" the nurse asked from the other side of the door. "Are you okay, or was that soup too much?"

Just then her stomach decided the soup was too much. She fell to her knees and vomited. The soup came up in multiple colors of blue. Blue poison, she thought. Her body heaved and choked even after there was nothing left. She flushed, grabbed blindly for toilet paper to wipe her mouth, blow her nose, and flushed again. She wiped the bluish tears from her eyes. The nurse came in and gave her a damp washcloth for her face. Wordless, she helped Sunday to her feet and handed her a toothbrush and toothpaste.

Jocelyn bent on her elbow over the sink to brush.

"When you're done with that, I can shave your head," the nurse offered. "It's going to come out anyway, so that will avoid the mess."

"Thanks," she mumbled. *Wouldn't want to make a mess.*

Jocelyn rinsed and stood straight again. She gazed at her reflection and saw what looked like an anemic blue alien. Her eyes were blueshot instead of bloodshot. The skin around her eyes was significantly blue. Her fingernails seemed the same, but with her pallor, they looked even more blue than normal.

But she wasn't normal. She certainly didn't feel normal. Not anymore.

Oh, God. What had they done to her?

Her thinning frame shuddered with roiling emotion. Her chest hurt trying to hold everything in, and her throat felt so tight it was hard to inhale. But she forced herself. She forced herself to look and examine. Finally, she put her face in her hands, defeated and surrendering to the fear.

Who she was didn't matter anymore. The only question that raced in circles through her mind was *what am I?*

Sergei stood with his bag packed, amazed.

They were letting him go.

Would Jocelyn show up in time? She was back on a schedule. He checked the time. 9:30. She might not make it to say goodbye. Or she didn't want to. Dr. Cashus said she hadn't felt the need, but he would talk to her.

The Russian government had traded for him. Who knew what the deal was? He wasn't sure how they knew he was even alive, let alone where he was. There must have been some high-end political or scientific assets at play. Or information. Despite worldwide tapping, knowledge could still be kept hidden. Apparently, he'd been worth whatever price they had agreed on. And now he would owe the Russians—again.

Freedom meant he would see his family—if they were still alive. He'd come to accept that there was a possibility they were dead. He'd heard about Jocelyn's "field trip" from Dominique. She'd let him know that his value was much lower now, and he needed to watch himself. In other words, she was in control.

It was no secret that the U.S. government wanted the biotechnology he invented, not the patients and not the practitioners. Jocelyn, her parents, his children, himself—they were all either competition or collateral damage. The current administration would do anything to make sure the U.S. was the country with this power for as long as possible.

Human enhancement was the arms race of this generation.

He and Jocelyn were just in the middle of it.

Now he would be leaving.

He doubted he would ever see her again. She'd shown no recognition or acknowledgement of their prior friendship. Friendship was perhaps too strong a word. They were prisoners together. A shared camaraderie was a more realistic view. At one time, he had been friends with her mother, even a trusted mentor. Again, a long time ago.

Or perhaps she had *understood his advice the day after her surgery in the hospital?*

He looked and suddenly she was there, ambling down the street with as much energy as one could expect after your brain had been injected with nanobots on and your body destroyed by chemicals. But she had bounced back. Four days after waking, and she seemed about eighty percent better. At least her color was more normal. She had a black beanie on her head.

"Hello," she said hesitantly, looking none too sure what to expect from him. She eyed the three soldiers escorting him on the flight to Geneva. They were his regulars. Ruben still looked terrifying and towered over them, all bulk and intimidation. "Uh, hi guys," she acknowledged them, and they grunted back.

"I'm glad you had time to come by," Sergei said.

She lifted a book. "Yeah. I, uh, saw your name in this and thought I should return it. I don't think I finished it. Or maybe I did and will remember later? My uncle said it might be awhile before all of my memory comes back, but I'm guessing a lot of the recent stuff is gone. There's a price for everything."

"Yes." *Was she trying to tell him something?*

"So, I'm sorry I don't remember you, and thank you for…whatever you did. Oh, and for reading to me while I was in the hospital. That was thoughtful." She handed him the book and smiled. Then waited. She looked at Megan, as if to see if she could leave yet, then added hurriedly, "It was nice to know you. Hope you have a pleasant flight."

Sergei smiled. The poor kid was out of niceties. "Thank you."

"I should go now. I have classes and therapy and stuff."

"Of course. Thank you for stopping by."

"Sure. Bye." To the soldiers, "Bye."

Ruben took his arm and pulled out the handcuffs. "Ready to go?"

Sergei stuffed the book in his suitcase. "It's not as if I'm unwilling to leave. Is this necessary?"

"Standard stuff. For old time's sake. We'll miss you, too, old man."

"Thanks. I can now leave this place without any regrets." He let the sarcasm drip.

Jocelyn walked away, Megan by her side. "Goodbye, my friend. Good luck." Sergei spoke in Russian. He waited to see if she heard. If she did, she made no indication of it.

This really was goodbye. He should feel a lot happier than he did.

Jocelyn woke with a start, her heart racing, her body covered in moisture. She wiped the sweat from her brow and took a breath. Just a bad dream. She pushed it away as she pushed out of bed. It was past midnight.

She was in the kitchen when she heard the door to her uncle's room open, and he came out in his pajamas and robe.

"Are you okay, Sunday?"

"Yes. Just restless dreams, but I'm okay. I wanted some water. Is it okay if I eat an orange?"

He came up and examined her face, as if doing so would give any indication why she couldn't sleep. "Sure. How is your stomach doing?"

"Better." She took the largest orange and began to peel it. The fruit smelled like citrus heaven—cold, sweet, and juicy. She forced herself to eat it very slowly without slurping—for her stomach and to make sure she didn't upset her uncle by eating too fast. "Do you want me to make you some tea?"

"I'll get it. You sit down."

He didn't need to ask twice. They sat quietly for a while. She rubbed her smooth head between eating orange slices.

"The headaches will get better soon."

"I know. I feel like I'll get little bits of memory back, too."

"You do?" He sounded worried.

"Maybe. I keep thinking I went to a movie theater. Did you take me to a movie? I keep seeing myself sitting in a theater watching cartoons."

He smiled. "Yes, you went a couple times. Would you like to go again?"

"Really?" The excitement was real. "Yes! When?"

"We could arrange something for this weekend."

"Really? That would be so incredible. It will be something to look forward to. Thank you so much, Uncle Laurence. I can't believe it. I'm so excited." She jumped up and kissed his hand thankfully, hopping around with barely-contained excitement. She could tell he was satisfied with himself.

"I will be the perfect student this week, I promise."

"Of course."

"Okay, I better get to sleep. Thank you again, Uncle Laurence."

"I love you, Sunday."

She took his hand again, kissed the top, and repeated the words back to him. Then she went back to her room, laid flat on her back, and folded her hands over her chest. She closed her eyes with a satisfied smile.

That had been much easier than expected.

CHAPTER FORTY-TWO

Georgie was in the middle of a cleaning check of the theaters when Brittany texted her "Code Blue" from the ticket booth.

Her heart thumped double time as she ran to the lockers and grabbed the information she'd been saving for Jocelyn. She spotted the girl walking with an older man and woman toward theater two. Georgie casually walked toward them hoping Jocelyn would see her before she needed to turn into the restroom. She did.

She heard Jocelyn behind her, telling the couple she should make a stop before the movie started.

The ladies' room was fairly empty. There was music pumped in, so it wasn't completely quiet. A mom with her child was in one of the handicapped stalls. A couple of tween girls entered and started putting on lip-gloss and taking selfies, turning their heads for just the right angle.

Jocelyn walked in hesitantly, another woman with her. Georgie fixed her hair in the mirror, checking them out. This woman was a little older—not the usual military escort, though there were plenty outside hanging out for the early show.

"Liz, do you need to go?"

"No, I'll just wash up and wait for you."

"Okay, I'll be just a second." Jocelyn smiled and headed for a stall.

Geez, she looks bad.

Her color was off...like a lot. *And what happened.... Ohmigosh, no eyebrows?* She looked at the black beanie creeping up Jocelyn's scalp as she entered a stall. *No hair. What happened to you, Jocelyn?*

Jocelyn entered a stall, and Georgie took the adjacent one. In seconds, a hand reached under with a small piece of paper. Georgie quickly opened it. It was covered in writing. Date, time, location, warning, and more. Her heart nearly exploded. She handed her article under the stall, and Jocelyn grabbed it. She'd written a question on it. *Did you know him?*

A pained gasp sounded, and the metal separating them flexed as if Jocelyn had put her hand against it for restraint. She heard another sharp intake as the girl fought to breathe.

She knew him.

Georgie cursed, sorry now for sharing the news.

An exhale came out partially as a whimper, followed by another shuddering inhale. Georgie did the only thing she could do. She reached for her hand under the stall.

"Take it."

A trembling, pale hand clasped hers tightly and held, while shudders seemed to rack her body.

"I got you," Georgie whispered. "I got you." She held on, trying to send strength and comfort to the other side, as another harsh breath of sorrow escaped Jocelyn's control and heat rushed up Georgie's arm. She clasped her strange friend's hand tighter.

Finally the shaking stopped. The woman called out to her from the sink area. "Are you ready?" A toilet flushed, then another. Jocelyn let go. Georgie heard the crinkle of paper and flush of the toilet. Jocelyn walked out to the waiting companion.

Georgie stayed where she was.

The image of the pale hand with the blue nails wrapped in her healthy grasp seared her mind and pierced her heart. Jocelyn had held onto her so desperately it made Georgie want to weep, but not as much as the sound of Jocelyn's heart-wrenching gasps for control, and the realization that the girl was not allowed to mourn anything that she lost—or in this case, any*one*.

Georgie wiped her eyes and blew her nose.

She took the note out of her pocket again and read the carefully-printed directions. It wasn't likely she'd see Jocelyn before the night in question.

Only six days away.

She was going to need a whole lot of help.

Graeme rushed inside the theater lobby. Something was up. He'd been wrapping up his makeshift office when he heard Georgie confer with Brittany that Code Blue needed their help—Saturday night. It didn't sound like a fashion mission, either. Cars, disguises, alibis? What was going down? And who or what was Code Blue?

He was so intent on figuring out what had just happened, he didn't see the people coming out of the theater. Granted, they turned a corner right into him.

He knocked someone flat on her butt before he realized it was his mystery girl. The man with her gave a vocal, "Hey!" Graeme apologized immediately and profusely.

He reached a hand to her before the man could. She didn't look well. He almost didn't recognize her.

She accepted his hand, and her grip was warm and strong as he pulled her to her feet. She stared at him, and he thought maybe she recognized him from before.

"Hi, I'm Graeme."

"I'm—."

"Sunnie, let's go. Are you okay?"

"I'm fine, Uncle Laurence."

The tall man turned toward him. "You need to watch yourself, boy."

"Yes, sir," he responded automatically, his eyes still on the girl. Had she been sick? Cancer? Hell. No wonder she kept to herself. Everyone around her was pretty protective, too.

Fierce blue eyes stared at him, as if wanting to communicate something. He felt a tug and realized he still held her hand. He freed it reluctantly and heard a low acknowledgement.

"Hi, Graeme." She stared at him, curious, but guarded, and maybe a little sad. She pulled her beanie lower over her ears, and pulled the edges of her hoodie around her stomach.

"I'm really sorry," he said.

"It's okay." As if feeling sorry for him she added, "I'm tougher than I look."

The older woman put a hand at her elbow to guide her away.

"Wait!" he called out, and she turned halfway back to him. "Do you live around here? Maybe we could go out some time."

The older woman spoke. "She's not allowed to date. And you're much too old for her. Excuse us."

He grinned at being dressed down for his age.

The girl appeared equally bemused by the older woman's reaction but allowed herself to be led away. She turned and waved a moment later, a hint of rebellion on her face. "Bye, Graeme."

The older man took her other arm and quickly ushered her out of the theater—to a waiting car, no doubt.

He stared after them. Huh. When he looked toward the snack bar, Georgie watched him with an expression of distrust.

Code Blue?

Was his mystery girl Code Blue?

If Sunnie was Code Blue, what was going down Saturday night? And would she have a massive military escort in tow? And if so, what was the connection between her and General Brody or Brittany's Aunt Nancy?

Getting through the weekend appearing cheerful had been exhausting for Jocelyn when all she could think about was Seth. She needed to focus on her escape. Only, she couldn't leave without knowing if he was down there, in the morgue. She wouldn't believe Seth was dead until she saw his body.

She had a short, free interval between measurements and a Starbucks stop. No one would look for her for at least twenty minutes.

Everyone at the hospital had been so solicitous, it had been annoying. It also made moving around difficult, but she'd been

able to take the stairs unnoticed and went to the basement. The
door was locked.

She turned the door harder, broke the lock, and peeked out
of the stairwell.

There was a camera in the hall between the elevator and the
doors to the morgue.

Carefully, she focused on the camera until the whir of the
camera stopped. She hurried to the door, pressing the code
Sergei had given her. It still worked.

The scent struck her before she stepped inside. No antiseptic
or airproof enclosure could cover the odor of formaldehyde.
She put a hand over her nose to stop the assault as she
adjusted—this was not the kind of scenario where you wanted
super smelling abilities.

She entered as the heavy doors closed behind her with an
ominous click. What she beheld was much more than she
expected.

Row upon row of deep metal drawers—walls of them.

There were no cameras in here that she could detect. She
walked slowly into the middle aisle. Four drawers high and one
hundred and fifty bodies long, if her count was correct. The
room was enormous, she guessed the size of the entire first
floor of the hospital, which was two blocks of Main Street.

She had fifteen minutes to find Seth, and she didn't know
where to start.

Then, absolute clarity struck, making her dizzy.

This was where she would be one day if she didn't escape.

With a deep breath, she read the end of each aisle. There
were notations of projects and lead scientists. With some quick
sleuthing, she discovered that half of the morgue was still
empty. She focused on where the bodies seemed to be,
hurrying down the aisle to check for a familiar name.

She found one.

Dr. Dominique Wicker. Project Sunday, Phase Two. What
did that mean? And who or what was Phase One?

She turned down the aisle, dread filling her. Wicker hadn't
been joking about dissection. She seemed to keep all of her
specimens, and there were several of them.

There was a touchscreen video display on each of the file drawers, and Jocelyn hurriedly scanned them, going down the row, reading the names in an attempt to find Seth. Her hands began to tremble with shock while her stomach twisted and soured. Some were kids younger than her. She checked the termination dates and thought she might be getting closer. MacKenzie Lee, Ken Wrightman, Riley Stevens, Maia Stein, Samantha Goodman.

She stopped, and her whole body shuddered as she read the screen. *Seth Johnson.*

"No, no, no." She rocked and spoke to herself in denial, her head getting light as the edges of her vision closed in. She needed to stand and be strong for Seth. She tried to read the information on the electronic file, but only one button stood out.

Eject.

She pressed it.

The smooth whir of electronics sounded before the drawer unlocked and popped open. She pulled it back, looked inside, and swallowed hard. "Ohmi—."

Her heart thudded, her pulse stuck in her throat.

Before she could recover, she heard a sound from the entrance. Someone else was coming in.

She stared at the empty drawer they had assigned to Seth, and without thinking, jumped inside and closed it, careful not to lock herself in.

She listened to people chatting about a sports game as they transported a body. Minutes later, they were gone.

She crawled out of the cold, dark drawer shaking uncontrollably. The icy feeling of death felt permanently absorbed through her skin. She wanted to scream and run.

Instead she went searching.

She found Project Sunday, Phase One. Dr. Laurence Cashus. He didn't have as many bodies as Wicker. She followed the path and came to a wall. She pressed some of the touchscreens and found the most recent was over a year ago— Bonnie Hill. The dates continued to go back...by years.

Dread increased, Jocelyn kept going...until the end...nearly ten years back. That's where she found them. Dr. Illeana

Marques Albrecht and Dr. Grayson Albrecht. There was another drawer above them. She pressed the screen. Jocelyn Esperanza Albrecht. Expected termination, three years, eleven months, and ten days. There was a countdown on hers. Did they have her time of death down to a science, or did they have an agreement with the government to terminate her?

She looked at her date of birth and realized it had been her birthday two weeks ago. Didn't even know it. She was seventeen. No one had said a word. Based on the timer, she was scheduled to terminate at twenty-one years old exactly.

She stared at the drawers with her parents' names, touching the door as if it would connect her to them.

Were they in here?

With trembling hand, she pressed the eject button. It opened.

There was a body inside, but it was covered with a dark green bag. She reached in and touched. It was a head. Her mother's skull? Her precious mother, so beautiful and talented and loving. She was gone forever yet trapped in this prison. Fury filled her.

She yanked her hand back and heard her own whimper. It seemed like it came from another person—as if her body had disconnected from reality because the horror, shock, and loss was too much.

Who would do this? For ten years, they had kept her mother's body preserved in some godforsaken state. And her father as well?

Tremors racked her body so hard, she thought she would faint. She touched the front of the drawer, and it slammed shut from the unintended force of fear surging through her skin. She had to get away. They were going to kill her. She believed it now. She wished with all her strength that she could carry her mother and father out with her. She couldn't.

She did the only thing her brain could process after witnessing this holocaust. She ran.

Her fear energized around her, and she slammed out of the exit and up the stairwell. No one was around the first floor. She forced herself to walk down the hall to the exit. A nurse walked by and said hello. Jocelyn responded politely, her smile tighter than a mask.

Sunlight beckoned her from a window. Doors were just ahead. She thrust her hand out, releasing power before she touched the doors. They flew open hard and wide from the unrestrained force pulsing through her.

Then there was silence.

The clean, quaint Main Street was the same. A couple of people were in line inside Starbucks. Someone read a book at an outside table. People entered the bakery next door. She heard the sound of camp Jeeps driving by, likely heading toward a training session.

She reached a bench by the curb under a tree, fell to her knees on the grass, then proceeded to vomit violently into the gutter, one hand clutching the bench for support against the anger and horror expelling from her being.

Someone called out, but she couldn't respond. Megan found her minutes later, asking what happened. She had to document everything, after all.

"My head hurt," she gasped. "I rested, but I got sick."

"It's all right," Megan said. "Let's get you some water." She helped her to a sitting position on the bench. "Keep your head down. I'll be right back."

"Okay."

"Don't worry. It's going to be okay," she said as she ran off.

"Okay."

It was not okay. Nothing was okay. Nothing about this would *ever* be okay.

Her parents were dead. Dead and being used as science projects. Her eyes burned more as she heaved again, partially crying, the pain as acute as if they had just died. Seth was dead. *But where was he?* And she was going to die as well. Trapped here, kept here, frozen. Just one more scientific number. Escape was impossible.

Her plan seemed impossible. Seth had told her not to let them change her. But they had. In more ways than Seth could ever imagine.

She pulled the beanie off her head, her body hot from the vomiting. She clutched the wool material, wishing it was Seth she held. Wishing they could do this together. She couldn't do it alone. She was too afraid. She didn't understand why any of this was happening, or what even waited outside the walls of Holliwell. She pressed the beanie against her eyes to absorb the tears.

Megan arrived with water. Jocelyn drank and nodded that she was a little better.

She had to pull herself together.

She'd made a promise. She would do whatever it took to escape. The price was a lot higher than she realized, but she would make the sacrifice. There was nothing to lose. She would be ruthless. She'd have to be. Seth was right about that. With fury driving her, ruthless would be easy. If she had to sacrifice others on the way, she would. Her family had been sacrificed. She wouldn't care about anyone else.

Her prize was freedom—at any price.

CHAPTER FORTY-THREE

Graeme stared at the results on his computer screen, not sure what to make of them.

The couple with Sunnie at the movies was a psychologist, Elizabeth Horten, and a neuropsychiatrist, Laurence Cashus. The man was noted for being a specialist in mind control and manipulation. He'd been a government consultant for three years and an employee for fifteen. Creepy.

Graeme cross-referenced them with his family, and a picture came up—Cashus with Morgan and Ben's mom at an awards dinner. They knew each other. Had they dated? Been rivals? Old friends? Graeme hunted...they attended the same University post grad, but Cashus was two years ahead. How did Cashus fit in with this mystery?

And if he was connected to the Albrechts, who was the girl? She called him uncle. Graeme searched again. Cashus was an only child, divorced, two kids, both in high school in Maryland. Huh. Maybe she was Elizabeth Horten's kid? No resemblance, but you never know. He researched Liz. One divorce. No kids.

He tapped his fingers, thinking of all the nefarious possibilities. His age regression attempts on Sunnie had come up with over five thousand hits. He'd given up halfway through. Now he took those results and narrowed them down by adding "Dr. Laurence Cashus" to the search criteria.

One page came up. The hit was on Cashus's name for a quote on the tragedy that took the lives of the Albrechts ten years ago. "It's a tragedy that could have been prevented. Private labs have no place in society. There is no way to regulate safety, and this is an example of what can happen. It's fortunate that more lives were not lost."

"A real compassionate guy," Graeme muttered.

He scrolled through the article looking at the pictures. He remembered the ones they had used over and over—PR photos of the Albrechts, Morgan, Ben, and one of little Jocelyn from her first grade pictures. Grayson Albrecht had brilliant blue eyes. The article was in black and white. He couldn't remember Jocelyn that well. Morgan had hazel-green eyes, and Ben had big brown eyes. He looked at the regression photo for ten years prior, then scrolled back up to the picture of seven-year-old Jocelyn. They'd buried her with her parents, but he couldn't help staring at the pictures, comparing.

He started a new search when an alert from the coffee shop got his attention. He flipped the audio feeds on and listened as police disrupted the students and confiscated computers. Shouting and chaos ensued. He turned on the movie theater feed, and the same was happening there. Either they had tracked *him*, or someone he was tracking. With no time to waste, he pulled the feeds and erased all the records.

Next, he shut down his system and started throwing everything in his suitcase.

He ripped the pictures off the wall, folded up the one of Sunnie to save, and put the rest in the sink where he lit a match. It was only a matter of time before they realized he had routed his searches through multiple Wi-Fi channels. He loaded the trunk of the rental car and threw in the computers, monitors, and extras. With a final check, he rolled out of the warehouse, locked it, and drove away. He didn't look back as sirens sounded behind him. They were close. He turned into a nearby neighborhood, parked the car in a driveway, and ducked down on the floor as cars raced toward the warehouse down the street.

He rang his mom's old security expert for advice—legal advice—and left a message.

He had definitely stumbled onto something. But what? He didn't have any earth shattering info. Granted, with the new laws, Homeland Security and the Office of Information were allowed to freely investigate and confiscate anything and anyone they suspected of terrorist activities. They'd been watching Internet searches for a while. Apparently, he had looked up something the government felt was sensitive.

He only hoped he hadn't blown the cover off whatever Georgie and Brittany had planned for their Code Blue. He had a feeling they didn't know what they'd gotten into. He just knew there was a rendezvous point Saturday night, west of the dam. He planned on being there to find out what was going on, and if needed, he would help.

Whatever they had stumbled onto, it was over their heads and not for public consumption.

That's why he had to go.

Georgie had preparations to make. She wished she could have one more planning session with Jocelyn, but did the best she could. She would pick up Jocelyn on the north side of the bridge and bring her to the small town of Vesuvius, where she planned to have a car Jocelyn could drive until she was somewhere safe. *Easy.*

What was not easy was that her curfew was midnight, and teenagers out at one o'clock in the morning were always suspect by the police. Midnight Saturday to early Easter Sunday was good timing for an escape if you weren't under twenty-one.

That being the case, she would tell her parents she was staying the night at Brit's. It was the night of Spring Fling, so her parents would likely be okay with it so long as she got home in time for Sunday morning church.

In advance of the event, she and Brittany dressed up in their Spring Fling outfits and took pictures and selfies at Brit's house and at the late night coffee shop. She'd use these to text her mom and post to Instagram that night. Her dad always tracked her posts.

She just needed to get Al on board. She couldn't drive anyone else's car. Her dad's had been bugged and was likely listed with some secret government agency, Brittany's mom's car might have been bugged, and they were using Lena's car in

Vesuvius—Al was the only one left that she could trust, and he was going to be difficult to persuade.

She pulled up to his building with Brittany and Lena, strategizing. Al was outside washing his truck in the outdoor parking area of his apartment. He didn't have a shirt on. Brittany and Lena appreciated that. From their sighs and stares, a little too much. "Okay, guys, he's my cousin, and he's too old for you."

"In four years, he'll be the perfect age," Brittany said.

Lena just leaned between the two front seats of the car to watch. She was too shy to talk to him, but not to look at him. She sighed again. "He is *all* that."

"Right." Definitely not letting them out of the car. "You two stay here. He's very private and doesn't like teenagers in general. It's one of his rules."

"That's a dumb rule," Lena said.

"I know. He has it just to irritate us."

"It's a cover," Brit said. "Tough on the outside, tenderhearted on the inside."

"Uh, yeah." Georgie hoped there was something of the old Al left, but there hadn't been many signs of it since his release. He hadn't even stopped by to see her parents. Her dad was mad, but not *that* mad.

She got out and approached him. "Hey."

"Hey." He turned off the water and started drying his truck. She followed him around to the side.

"So...."

"So...," he repeated.

"So, I...."

He kept drying. Nothing to do but just spit it out.

"I wanted to see if I could borrow your truck Saturday night."

"No."

"I'll have it back, safe and sound, before you even wake up."

"No."

"It's important."

"Important?" He paused from drying and pretended to consider her request. "No."

"You don't have to be a jerk."

"Do you only come by when you want something?"

"I've never wanted anything. I called you three times to see if you wanted to have coffee or lunch, or meet me after work. Do you think you saying 'No' every time makes me feel good? And you haven't even come by the house to see my mom and dad."

"Wasn't invited."

"Well, you probably would have said 'No' anyway."

"Probably."

"See!" Georgie felt long, pent up anger toward him swell. "You were like my brother. What happened? Tell me what happened. 'Cause I don't believe a person can change that much in just a few years. You were a good guy. I know you still are. Somewhere in there." She poked him hard on his arm with her finger. Then did it again because she was so pissed her eyes started to burn. "I thought we were going to fight for justice together?"

"You thought wrong."

She could tell he said it just to irritate her.

He picked up some glass spray and worked on the windows.

"Fine, I'll have to save the world without you."

"Okay, Nancy. You Bess and George go do that."

"The fact that you know all their names just proves I'm right. Either that, or you're a nine-year mystery nerd under that skin."

"Hey!" Alastair stood to his full 6'3" and looked down his nose at her.

She could literally hear Brit and Lena squeal with pleasure.

"Don't come down on me because I'm reader. I read them to you." He shook his head, humor returning, and waved to the girls. "What's so important?"

"A rescue mission."

"Dog rescue?"

"No. Can I borrow your truck or not?"

"No. I already told you."

"Well, why not?"

"'Cuz it's mine."

"I'll be careful."

"I don't care."

"I'm going to do this with or without your help."

"Good. Either pick up a towel and dry, or get your friends out of here. They're disturbing my peace."

Georgie walked over to her friends. "Just another minute. I think I'm getting through to him. But just, like, put up the windows and stop drooling. It's freaking him out."

"Okay," Brittany said. "But can I get a picture with him afterward?"

Georgie shook her head with disgust and mouthed 'No' before walking away.

She grabbed a towel and started drying.

"You're back," Al said.

"So here's the thing. Brittany's aunt worked at Holliwell and she died mysteriously, and we think her mom's car and house might be bugged. We know my dad's car is bugged. I damaged the tracking system, but it's still not safe until I trade it in for a new car. My friend at the movie theater, whose computer I used, just got raided as part of the downtown Homeland Security hunt. We don't think anything is safe related to him, and Lena's car is our getaway car. We just need a ride to the rendezvous point. We'll drop off the package at Lena's car then bring the truck back here. You'll never know it's gone."

Al froze, then spun, grabbed her upper arms fierce enough to bruise, and shouted in her face. "What the holy frick are you talking about?"

Trying not to feel threatened, she answered, equally fierce. "I'm on a mission. We're taking down the evil empire, Al. It's time, and someone's gotta do it. I'm not afraid."

He paled. "What's this package?"

She took the glass cleaner from him and sprayed the side view mirror. "The girl I was telling you about. The one at Holliwell. She's going to escape. She needs a ride."

Silence.

Good. That shut him up. She turned finally after the silence stretched too long. Uh-oh. Uber pale. Not a good sign. She grabbed his arm. "You should sit."

She helped him to the ground and pushed his head between his knees.

He lifted his head. "She just needs a ride?"

She pushed his head down again. "Yeah. That's why I need the truck. Do you understand now?"

"You can't break anyone out of Holliwell."

"I'm not. She's getting out on her own. I'm merely the transportation to the next town—more or less."

"Everyone on the base will be after her. And after you." He lifted his head. "Are you insane?"

"Well, if they don't know she's gone...."

"They'll know. You'll be harboring a fugitive."

"I'll be careful."

"She might be dangerous."

"She's not. She's sick. They've done something to her. I can tell. And another kid from there died, too. He was only nineteen, Al. They're doing something awful to kids there. It's not right. She just wants to find her family and make sure they're safe. If we don't help, who will? What if she gets out, but is stranded? They'll catch her for sure. Maybe she won't make it—fine. But I have to be there just in case. I can't turn my back and pretend it's all okay." She pulled his head up and looked him in the eyes. "Whatever's going on—it's *not* okay." She shoved his head down again.

Al put his hands on his head resting...or thinking. She couldn't really tell, but he was definitely stressed out. She held a finger up to her friends to indicate she needed another minute.

Finally, he lifted his head. He reached out and took one of her hands.

"Georgie. If they catch you, they *will* destroy you." He took a controlled breath. "And everyone you love."

"I was afraid of that." She took a knee in front of him and grabbed his other hand, holding tight. She was scared. No lie. "Will you let me take the truck?"

"One condition." He squeezed her hands, stood tall, and pulled her to her feet. "I drive."

CHAPTER FORTY-FOUR

Al coasted into Richie's garage and hopped out of the Prius. Music filled the air, cars lined up outside for repairs, and Richie stood with his back to him, wiggling his hips with his head inside the engine of a Porsche.

He hadn't seen Richie this happy in years. It wasn't normal.

Not wanting to startle him, Al walked to the side of the car and waited. Something inside the car got his attention.

Richie looked up. "Hey, bro, 'sup?"

Al reached into the passenger seat of the Porsche and lifted the apparatus for viewing. "Is this a rocket launcher?"

Richie's expression changed to one of a kid getting caught with his hand in the cookie jar. He took the weapon and put it back. "A mini-launcher. Double shooter. I was just uh…checking it out for a client."

"Uh-huh."

"Whatta ya think of her?" He referred to the Porsche.

"Piece of art."

"Right?" Richie's question was rhetorical.

Al studied the vehicle. Richie must have made some modifications. He tapped the glass. "Bulletproof?"

"Uh-huh," Richie echoed him. "Tracking system. Tight suspension. All the goodies."

"Nice."

"She's my new baby."

"Yours?"

"Client. Awesome client. Appreciates the little things."

"Like rocket launchers?"

"I was just testing that out."

"Right." That's what worried him. "Well, it's good to see you humming around the shop again."

Richie bobbed his head with a grin. "What's that piece over there? A step down?"

"I've picked up a little side work. It's a donation to a church in Vesuvius. I just need someone to drop it off."

"Why not drive it there."

"I'd need a ride back." He pulled out a couple hundred. "The woman who donated it wanted to make sure it got there with no wear and tear."

Richie took the money. "When's it due?"

"Saturday. They'll pick it up Sunday after services."

"Okay."

"But it needs to be there, Richie."

"I got it."

He handed him the key in a magnetic box with the address. "Put this above the front tire, driver's side."

Richie pocketed the key and paper.

"Don't get distracted. I know what happens when you've got a project."

Richie pulled out his phone and entered the task on the calendar. "There. With a twenty-four hour alert and a three hour alert. Okay?"

"Thanks." Al paused before leaving. Richie hummed away. He always did love the more interesting challenges. A Porsche was a good change up from the usual Hondas and Toyotas he got. He was too talented to be a garage mechanic, but it was easier on his mental state, post Holliwell. "It's good to see you doing well."

"Yeah." Richie nodded. He closed the hood of the Porsche, wiped the front with a rag he kept in his back pocket, then gave Al a fist bump. "You too, man. You need a ride?"

"Naw. My cousin's picking me up."

Georgie arrived on cue in his truck and scooted over to the passenger's side. She gave Richie a wave.

He waved back, a little wary. "She staying out of trouble?"

"As much as a teenager can."

Richie bobbed his head again. "All right, man. Say no to drugs."

"I always do." Al and Richie laughed. That was the irony—for both of them. But they were moving on, little by little.

Al just had one thing to do before he could completely move on. With any luck, no one would be killed this time.

Jocelyn wrapped up her books and notes for the weekend. Megan had her schedule worked out, and Jocelyn had been cheerful enough about it, happy to be back at nearly full strength. Actually, she thought she might be better than full strength, but she was easing the team into it. She knew she had charmed the Energy Team this week. They were nice, and a lot more fun than Laurence's usual group.

People were leaving the base early on Friday for Easter weekend. By four o'clock, the base felt mostly empty. For some it was a three-day weekend. For others, the beginning of Spring Break with their families.

She was surprised when her uncle requested she come to see him at the hospital. Megan escorted her to a small conference room where Wicker and her uncle stood waiting. They asked her to have a seat. A shiver of trepidation shot up Jocelyn's spine.

Did they suspect her plan?

She fought back panic, doing her best to present a curious, innocent face. It didn't feel like it was working. Nervous, she asked, "Is everything okay?"

"Sunday, we wanted to see if you could help us with something."

She sat up. Great. Not in trouble. "Of course! What is it?"

"Dr. Wicker's team had an accident a couple weeks ago."

"Oh, I'm so sorry." Sweat started to bead on her back. Was this Seth's team?

"One of Dr. Wicker's patient's died in the accident."

Jocelyn thanked Georgie a million times in her head for preparing her for this moment. She glanced at Wicker sympathetically. "I'm so sorry."

Wicker nodded, but her look was dark and assessing. Jocelyn turned her attention to her uncle.

"You might remember him," her uncle said.

"Maybe." She didn't sound certain, but that was deliberate.

Her uncle put down a picture of Seth. She looked at it. He had hair. She barely recognized him, so it was easy to shake her head blankly. Her uncle put down a more recent picture of him hairless.

"Hmm," she frowned, remembering. "I think I know him."

"You two were friends of a sort."

"Oh." Not much to add to that.

Wicker spoke. "Did you know he was seeing a nurse here?"

A whisk of shock and offense went through Jocelyn's blood. "No."

"Apparently, it was quite hot and heavy," Wicker explained.

"Maybe the nurse could help you," Jocelyn suggested.

Wicker folded her arms and spoke harshly. "She's dead, too."

She gave her uncle a look that suggested she didn't know what she was supposed to do with all this information. She didn't trust Wicker, and Wicker clearly didn't trust her. But she did remember Seth was supposed to spy on her. He told her. And he told her they would use this against him at some point. She wondered if this was that point. She folded her hands together tightly under the conference table, grateful they couldn't see them.

Her uncle shared next. "Seth is the one who told us you could transmit heat."

Jocelyn tilted her head. "Doesn't everyone?" He'd betrayed her. She hadn't thought about that possibility. He had warned her, but as their relationship grew, she forgot. Or maybe she'd hoped she'd meant enough to him that he wouldn't. Sergei had been right. Trust no one. Thankfully, she hadn't told Seth about her family. He'd betrayed her, but he used information as a bartering tool. It was all he had in this prison. She hoped he received something good in exchange.

"Um. Yes, but this was more than normal."

She frowned. "Why can't I remember that?" She turned to Megan, ignoring the fact that they had essentially tested her to see her reaction to Seth spying on her. "Megan, have we practiced that?"

Megan shook her head. "No. This is the first I've heard about it. I'll figure out some meditation exercises."

"Maybe we could work on it this weekend," Jocelyn said eagerly.

Her uncle interrupted them. "In any case, we have another picture to show you. I was hoping it might trigger something. It's from the scene of the crash."

Jocelyn lifted her brows, shook her head negatively, and put a hand up in defense. "It's not dead bodies, is it? I really don't want to see dead bodies, whether I remember the people or not. It's just gross. Sorry, no disrespect."

Megan's lips twitched a little in humor.

Her uncle put the picture down. "No dead bodies." The picture showed a crashed MedVan at the bottom of a ravine. It looked like a long way down.

All Jocelyn's humor and bravado left her body, the energy completely leaving her.

Silence.

It wasn't the vehicle that left Jocelyn stunned. It was the symbol on the side of the vehicle, visible to the photographer from where it had been shot from above.

She swallowed. Her eyes burned a little, betraying her, so she carefully inhaled.

"That was a bad crash." She waited for them to ask what they wanted. All the while, she studied the picture, schooling her face into a blank but somber expression.

Her uncle broke the silence. "We were hoping you might know what the symbol is on the side of the Medical Van."

"The symbol?"

Her uncle pointed to the marks burned or scratched into the vehicle by an unknown force.

"Those aren't normal?"

"No. Does it trigger any memory for you? Something Seth might have said?"

She shook her head. "Why?"

Dr. Wicker stepped closer. "We thought someone might have wanted to hurt Seth. Someone from his past. Any clue might help us get justice for him and the others."

Jocelyn turned the picture around a few times, trying to recall something. "I don't know. ZL? Is it someone's initials maybe?" She grasped at straws. "I don't really remember him. I just sort of have a vague feeling. It's weird. I'm sorry I can't be more helpful."

"No problem," her uncle said. "If you remember something, let me know."

Wicker took the photos, her eyes still on Jocelyn.

Jocelyn nodded to both and followed Megan out.

She heard Wicker from down the hall. "She's hiding something. I don't trust her."

"She still has brain swelling, Dominique. Let's give it a little time. For now, I like that she's at least more manageable."

That's right, Uncle Laurence. I'm manageable. It makes your life a lot easier, I'm sure. Jocelyn smiled up at Megan as they exited the hospital. "I'm ready for a quiet weekend."

"Me, too," Megan said.

"Oh, and it's cool I do that heat thing. We'll have to figure that out. We can surprise Uncle Laurence next week."

"Sounds like a plan."

Inside, Jocelyn's heart exploded with hope. She lifted her face to the sunshine, letting the energy all around nourish and feed her. She wasn't going to be here next week. The photo was just the shot in the arm she needed.

Seth was alive, and he'd left her a message. She wanted to laugh out loud with joy. She had somewhere to go and someone waiting for her. She could do this. She *would* do this.

CHAPTER FORTY-FIVE

My name is Jocelyn Esperanza Albrecht.

Jocelyn wrote out the rest of the message. *I am the eldest daughter of Illeana Marques and Grayson Albrecht. My parents were longevity scientists. The irony is that, due to their breakthrough, I now have a life expectancy of twenty-one. I just turned seventeen. That leaves about four years. Three good ones...if I'm successful tonight.*

She finally stopped and ripped up the paper systematically before eating. There could be no evidence that would give anyone a head start on catching her.

She swallowed hard, forcing the paper down.

It was beautiful out. Clear. How many times had she looked out and admired the view, grateful to the scientists at Holliwell who had kept her alive—only to discover it was for their own experiments.

She walked through her plans again, visualizing. Just like on her field trips, planning was everything.

Movement on the street below distracted her. Soldiers escorted someone to the civilian side of the hospital. Her uncle was working late...they weren't going to him, were they?

The captive's elbow shot up and out. Her heart beat faster, and energy whizzed down the skin of her arms.

Medina.

Oh, no. Medina, I hope you aren't in trouble. Please don't give me away. All those weeks of holding back her power, and she made one mistake on their field trip. She'd given in to compassion. If anyone discovered the phenomenon that saved everyone had been her, she'd be hunted forever.

Don't give me away, Medina. Please. I'm so close.

Sergei stood speechless, relieved to be holding his daughter and nephew. His life's work had been destroyed and nearly everyone who was a part of it.

That had been her mission. Jocelyn. She'd done it well.

Perhaps that was the only reason Wicker had agreed to his release. Or perhaps it had not been her choice. He didn't care. It didn't matter.

The Russians had gotten them the best rooms in Moscow, but it was only when they were free of surveillance that his nephew told him more.

She stole their technology and records, planted explosives, then of all things, tried to save everyone.

What had General Martin told her? Had some compassion survived her brainwashing and training? She'd been able to think and act for herself. That one act had been a big one. It would come back to haunt her, for sure. Her uncle and the General must suspect even now. That's why they'd kept her sedated.

He was torn, but he couldn't blame her. She was trapped as he had been. He knew the compromises one made to survive. There was nothing lost that he couldn't rebuild, but it would have been different had Ketevan been hurt.

They returned to the hotel, and Sergei went to the small bag of items he'd kept from Holliwell. The book was still on top. He flipped through it, looking for a new message, anything she might have communicated. Nothing.

He checked the front inside cover again. Then the back. He almost missed it, the writing was so light. Three words printed carefully. She must have written it right before she returned it.

Price = friendship + ID

Identity. She'd given up their friendship and her identity. That was the price she must pay. As he had done in his own past, she must now decide the price she was willing to pay.

This was everyone's struggle—only hers was more dangerous. If she was willing to risk her very being, she was willing to risk anything.

He needed to decide if he would tell anyone.

He stared a long time at the message.

Uncertain, he closed the book and put it away.

"Thanks for staying over, Liz. This is going to be fun tonight." Jocelyn cleaned off the table and prepped tea and popcorn like a good hostess.

Liz smiled agreeably. "I'm looking forward to it. Which one do you want to start with?" She held up three DVDs.

Jocelyn went to the living room and studied the backs of them. "Hmm. Princess trapped in a tower by a woman claiming to be her mom. Princess trapped in a dungeon by a beast. Or princess trapped in eternal sleep by a wicked queen. Yep, all prison movies. Let's go with princess in the tower."

Liz laughed. "You put it in. I'll make your cocoa."

"Okay." Jocelyn smiled and obediently inserted the movie while Liz prepped their drinks.

She took her cocoa and pretended to sip...the same way she pretended to take her evening meds, but had spit them out. She didn't want to risk being put to sleep. Tonight, Liz was going to be the one sleeping. Liz put the popcorn into a bowl.

They watched the movie, and Liz asked how she was feeling.

"Great. Not tired at all."

"How was your cocoa?"

"I don't really like cocoa. I just drink it to be polite. Since we're such good friends now, I thought I should tell you."

Liz smiled. "I had a feeling. Your uncle likes the idea still. He wants to keep you young."

"And under his control."

"That's every parent," Liz said, missing the tension in Jocelyn's voice.

"Huh." She lifted the cocoa. "You try it."

"No, thank you."

"Come on, Liz. Just one sip." Jocelyn cajoled. "It's not like it will make you pass out or anything."

Liz blinked.

"Yes. I know you've been giving me this for years to make me sleep more at night. Do the medications I take during my afternoon measurements have a sleep aid, too?"

"Uh, yes, I believe so. You have very high energy, so your uncle makes sure you get enough sleep."

"He's always so thoughtful." Jocelyn slowly finished the last few pieces of popcorn. "I guess we're going to be up all night tonight."

"What?"

Jocelyn smiled. "I didn't take that little cup of pills tonight." She lifted her fingers to her lips. "Shh. Don't tell anyone." Jocelyn went to the sink, not missing Liz reaching for her purse. Casually, she rinsed the cup out then reached under the cabinet into a pot. She pulled out the syringe and put it on the counter before spinning and stunning Liz with a left uppercut. Liz deserved it for getting the Taser out. She grabbed the offending wrist until the weapon fell to the kitchen floor, then she turned Liz around, pressing her twisted arm up her back until the older woman whimpered.

"Don't hurt me, Sunnie. This isn't you. They'll torture you for this."

Jocelyn felt heat flare up her arms in anger. She shoved Liz's face into the granite so she couldn't speak, and put her mouth a mere hair from Liz's ear. "Torture me, Liz? What do you call the past ten years? The manipulation, the lies, the so-called stress testing, the operations, the killing of innocent kids like me? What do you call that? I call it evil. *You* are evil."

Liz mumbled against the stone. "I wasn't part of that."

"You did nothing to stop it, and you gained from it. Your new grant? Was that to study me?"

Silence.

"Right. So let's just settle on the fact that you're evil, just as evil as Cashus and Wicker and just as selfish. I only hope you live long enough to be punished for what you've done."

She grabbed the syringe and jabbed Liz's arm, releasing the fluid in one quick moment.

Liz screamed into the granite, and Jocelyn laughed really loud to cover it, just in case the audio sensors in her room picked up anything.

She helped Liz to the sofa, laid her down, and pulled a blanket over her, adjusting the pillow while Liz's eyes slowly began to flutter closed.

"You really were a terrible friend, Liz. You have a lot to think about. Maybe you should talk to someone about your behavior. Get a little clarity."

She grabbed the Taser and searched Liz's bag to find a phone, thirty-three dollars in cash, her security badge, and a set of keys—presumably to her car. She opened the closet near the door and pulled out her black beanie and hoodie, phone still in hand. She'd seen Liz's phone password earlier when she'd tapped in the master code for the condo. Not very smart, but it made things a lot easier. She unlocked the phone and selected the email function. Her fingers trembled as she typed in the address Georgie had found. Quickly she typed her message.

Jocelyn Albrecht is alive. I'm treating her at Camp Holliwell, VA. They call her Sunday Cashus. Please help.

Jocelyn pressed send on her very first email.

Then she found the master password.

No one would suspect anything if their door opened. They would assume it was Liz leaving for the night.

Once in the hallways, Jocelyn focused on the lights, igniting each until it exploded and her path was dark. She bypassed the elevators and scampered down the ten flights, exiting the only home she'd known for the last nine years with just her clothes, thirty-three dollars, and hopefully, a security badge that would get her to the next step.

* * *

Richie parked the car in the dark lot of the little church. He checked his watch, then flipped the magnetic key holder in his hand with satisfaction before sticking it up under the tire. Right on time. Okay, so he'd forgotten about it. But then he remembered, and he got the car here on Saturday with an hour to spare. He looked up at the full moon, took a deep breath, and released it. He'd done good. This was good. Life was good. For the first time in a long while, he felt safe—and optimistic.

He hopped back in the tow truck, turned on some tunes, and began the trek back to Charlottesville. At least the roads would be empty.

Georgie and Brittany took pictures at the dance with their other friends, texted them to their parents, and said how beautiful the decorations were. Lena found them on cue. She wore a short black dress with black leggings, black sensible boots, and carried a black leather jacket for warmth. The days had warmed up, but the nighttime air was cool. She took one look at Brittany's white dress and frowned.

"What kind of material is this?" Lena fingered the fabric. "It's so soft and delicate."

"It's a new textile formulated from…" Brittany hesitated, "milk."

"Milk?"

"Yeah, funny, right? Milk ain't so bad. I designed the dress to showcase it. Actually, it's sour milk, but you can't tell from the smell." She lifted a wispy sleeve for Lena to sniff.

Lena suppressed a smile but complied. "Smells fine. It's very unique."

"Of course," Brittany stated. "Did you come with a date?"

"I came with the Chess Team."

"Of course you did. Bless your heart." Brittany shook her head at Georgie.

"Don't worry. They have me covered. I'm not missing this. Especially not after I let you borrow my car. So—."

"Okay, okay. Sheesh." Brittany's car was in the parking lot. She and Georgie grabbed their tennis shoes and jackets, then went to the curb. Fortunately, Brittany had a dark jacket to put over her very white dress.

Alastair pulled up and they all climbed in. He looked at the two other girls, then at Georgie. "Seriously? Charlie's Angels?"

"Who are they?" Lena asked.

"And the albino?"

"See!" Brittany whacked Georgie in the shoulder. "Even he thinks so."

"I'm not—."

"That's what I keep saying," Brittany said to Al, squeezing next to him in the front seat while Georgie took the window and Lena crawled into the narrow back seat of the cab.

"I'm Swedish. And I'm wearing black as a disguise, since it's nighttime. You don't wear white on a secret mission."

This time they all looked at her. Her skin was a beacon in the night, making her arms and head stand out like light bulbs.

Brittany shook her head and circled a finger around those parts. "Still target practice."

"Not helping," Georgie said. "Let's just go. Anyway, diversity is what makes a team successful."

"Then we're in a boatload of trouble," Al said, putting the truck in drive. "Because we're all nuts."

CHAPTER FORTY-SIX

Jocelyn couldn't get far without her meds. That's one thing she knew. An orderly she hadn't seen before walked into the hospital ahead of her and gave her a look. She smiled and said hi. He said hi back. She didn't know any nighttime staff. That was a plus. She used Liz's access code to enter the hallway of exam rooms where she went everyday for measurements.

At the pharmaceutical room, she entered the code Sergei had given her and filled what she hoped was a six-month supply.

The pill containers fit into the small bag that she tucked inside her hoodie. She turned off the lights and walked toward the patient ward.

"Sunnie?" Megan called her name.

She turned. Nothing worked better than a guilt-free smile. "Hi, Megan!"

"What are you doing here?"

"I'm having a movie night with Liz."

"I know."

"Oh. Then why did you ask?"

"I meant, why aren't you with Liz?"

"She had a bad headache so she called over here for some pills, and I came to pick them up. I'm headed back now. Do you want to come over? We're watching Sleeping Beauty next."

"Ah, no, thank you." Megan still seemed uncertain.

"What are you doing over here?" Jocelyn asked.

"Working out."

"Where?" Jocelyn started walking toward where Megan had come from, and Megan hurried to catch up. They were near the tennis-pelting torture room. She kept walking. "Is this a gym?"

"Sort of."

"It seems familiar. What do they play here?"

"Uh, tennis and other sports."

"I hope you're good at tennis."

"Why's that?"

Megan didn't see it coming. Jocelyn gave her two punches to the face—one that broke her nose and a hook that knocked her sideways onto her knees. A strong kick to her temple knocked Megan out.

Jocelyn kicked open the door and carried Megan inside, trying not to get blood spurting from Megan's nose on her clothes. While she lay on the floor, Jocelyn pulled the restraints from the wall. In no time, Megan's arms were secured. Jocelyn turned and left the room. The stairs to the control room were to her left.

Hmm. Very tempting.

Jocelyn hurried up. She flipped the light on in the room and saw Megan below, beginning to rouse.

"Hello, Megan," she said deeply into the microphone. "I hope you're comfortable. There are a lot of buttons here. I wonder what they do?"

She started pressing buttons, and tennis balls popped out toward Megan. She had to aim them better to hit Megan, but it eventually worked, even on the lowest speed. The balls lobbed toward her, one hitting her head and comically bouncing off. It was annoying, no doubt, but not hurtful—unless humiliation was hurtful.

Megan screamed at her and called her a list of names, which were muted by the thick glass partition. Jocelyn debated upping the speed, but didn't. "Megan, don't tempt me, please. You watched them torture me—for days. Would you like to feel what those tennis balls felt like? Do you want a sample?"

She waited.

Finally, Megan shook her head.

"Megan, just so we're clear, I will never forgive you for your part in my torture and my captivity. And I will never forget. Should you ever meet me on the street, turn and walk away, because I might not be as kind as I am tonight. I'm turning off the lights and sound now. Someone will likely find you in the morning. In the meantime, you can practice using your mind to deflect tennis balls."

"You'll never get away. They'll make it worse for you, Sunnie. Let me out now, and I'll help you."

"Megan, you have not proven yourself trustworthy." Jocelyn took on her uncle's condescending tone. "I'm very disappointed in you."

With that, she turned out the lights, cut the audio feed from the auditorium, and locked the doors on her way out.

A part of her thought it was wrong, but she needed to keep Megan tied up for now. The part of her that didn't think it was wrong thought this was a small, but appropriate, punishment for the devil's babysitter.

She took Megan's duffle bag with her. There were keys to Megan's camp Jeep parked outside. That might be better than using Liz's...but there was one more thing she needed to check on.

She ran down the hall to her uncle's patient ward.

Graeme was pretty sure the smart thing would be to turn around and head home. Whatever Georgie and friends had planned, Code Blue was probably more like a post dance party or rendezvous spot.

"I'm an idiot." He parked the newly-enhanced Porsche in the lot of a diner just south of the dam. It was the only place around for miles. Maybe he would grab a bite and call this the end. He texted his brother. *You awake?*

A minute later, a selfie arrived of Rex inside some club with a girl on either side of him kissing his cheeks.

He laughed. A text followed.

U Ok?

Yeah, he texted. *Coming home.*

Good. We miss you.

She found Medina strapped down in one of the few secured patient rooms. There was duct tape over his mouth. Inquisition style.

She tried Liz's code on the door and was surprised when it opened.

The bed was adjustable, so she put it into sitting position while he stared at her not making a peep—his dark eyes intense and angry. He didn't look particularly well, but he hadn't been beaten that she could tell.

"Hello, Medina."

He didn't respond. If anything, his gaze became darker and more furious.

"Don't be mad at me." She ripped the duct tape off his mouth as quickly as possible.

He cursed. She freed one hand, and he rubbed his mouth and the tender skin around it. "What the hell are you doing here?"

"I saw them take you."

"And?"

"I thought—."

"What? That I needed you to rescue me? What are you, an idiot?"

She flinched.

"Don't you know what you are?"

She didn't understand the question. Actually, she was afraid to understand the question.

"You're a lab rat. A human that nobody cares about or knows exists, that they can experiment on at will—physically, psychologically, medically—you name it. And when you cease to serve their needs, you will be a liability and marked for termination. What the flying"—he let out a stream of some choice, livid curses—"are you doing wandering around trying to rescue people?"

Her eyes burned. A sick, gnawing sensation cramped her stomach. She slammed the duct tape back on his face, part in anger, part in fear.

"I'm leaving."

He ripped the used tape off his mouth. "Good."

"Forever."

"'Bout time."

She was nearly out the door. She turned back. Despite his words, she saw fear in his eyes. She couldn't leave him. "Why do you hate me?"

"I don't. You're a damn freakin' idiot."

"Stop calling me that," she whispered furiously.

"I hate myself. I hate living with myself knowing what I know and never helping you." He unlocked the other arm with his freed one. "It didn't seem like a smart move."

She swallowed hard. Her throat tightened with understanding. "It wasn't a smart move," she said. "It's still not."

"No shit."

"Do you want me to tie you back up?"

"No. How did you get in?"

"Liz's security band."

"Give it to me. When they realize you're gone, all hell will break loose. What else did you take?"

"Phone and car keys."

"Perfect. They can track you with the phone, so don't ever steal one."

"Oh." That could have been dangerous. "Did you tell them about me?"

"Nothing they didn't already suspect. I didn't see what happened on the last field trip, so even with truth serum, I could neither confirm nor deny what saved all those people." He stood up and cracked the knuckles on his fists and loosened his shoulders as if readying for a fight. "What direction are you headed?"

"West."

"I'll go south toward the airstrip. All the main gates are on lockdown."

"I'm not going out a gate."

He nodded. "Just don't get caught. No matter what." He grabbed her arm and squeezed hard, emphasizing. "The things they've done to you are *nothing*. Do you understand?"

She nodded.

"Don't let them catch you, Sunnie."

Fear shivered down her spine, but she shook it off. "Thanks, Medina. Never knew you cared."

A hint of humor touched his lips. "I don't. Now get lost, kid. *Really* lost."

"I think I have to go to the bathroom."

Georgie turned to Lena in the back seat of the truck, her mouth dropping. "There's no bathroom where we're going. We're on a secret mission to save someone's life."

"Sure, but aren't we early? We could stop."

"I kinda have to go, too," Brittany said.

"Why didn't you go at the dance?"

"I didn't have to then," Brit said. "And I was too nervous. We've been driving an hour. Now I have to go."

"Me too," Lena said.

"There's a diner just before the dam," Al said. "About fifteen minutes away. Can you hold it until then?"

Georgie stared at her cousin. He was the last one she expected to be amenable. He smiled at her. "When you gotta go...."

Brittany and Lena agreed.

"You're thinking of The Dam Diner, right?" Lena asked. "I go there all the time after hiking. Good pie."

"Here we go," Brittany said.

Georgie ignored them. She clutched the backpack on her lap and glanced at Al again, suspicious. His mood had definitely changed since they left the dance. She was the one with the plan, right?

If so, why did it feel like nothing was about to go according to plan?

Jocelyn took Megan's Jeep across camp. She kept the lights off and drove carefully. There wouldn't be any guards until the EmWAV guardhouse. She pulled into the trees shortly before arriving and pulled out her next syringe on approach. She knew how to be quiet. She just needed to get the soldier outside, and she could unlock a vehicle. She checked the time. It was nearly 23:30. She waited, listening carefully. A very light breeze shifted the trees. She heard the soldier clear his throat. He swayed back and forth on his feet, impatient. Finally, the check-in call came.

She listened while he reported back the all clear. Then he stepped out of the shack and lit a cigarette.

Perfect.

She walked up to him, and by the time he heard the noise, the syringe was in his neck. She laid him down comfortably inside the small building and brought up the EmWAV interface on the computer, unlocking Wav-1. Next, she put her hand on the power deck and sent a surge of energy sparking the electronics.

Her heartbeat raced. Nearly home free.

She ran to the boathouse, grabbed a helmet, and was about to lock into Wav-1 when someone called out.

"Hey! What are you doing?"

She saw two people stand up in the far corner of the boathouse—a male with no shirt on and a female scrambling for shoes.

"Nighttime surveillance practice." It came out of her mouth like she was a natural born liar. "What are *you* doing?"

The question stalled them long enough for her to lock her feet into position and close the overhead hatch. She wished it would close faster. He walked over, clearly planning to question her further. She lowered the face shield on the helmet, effectively disguising herself. He banged on the hood of the EmWAV, but she ignored him, instead giving a cheerful thumbs up sign.

Crud. This might be bad.

She hoped her path and calculations were correct—otherwise, this field trip was going to turn sour fast.

The floor opened up, and Jocelyn submerged under the boathouse, then jettisoned through the water, across the lake. She just had to make it up the river, over the gates, and into the public side before she reached the dam. She could make it. She *would* make it.

Her radar screen was clear.

And then it wasn't.

The Communication board blasted into the cockpit. "Wav-1, come in. Wav-1, please report."

She stared at the Comm, panicking.

Then a blip sounded on her radar. How was that possible? She'd deactivated the local security board. The couple must have sounded the alarm. Not good.

She stared at the blip on the map getting closer.

Wav-6 was after her.

CHAPTER FORTY-SEVEN

Jocelyn raced the vehicle across the lake, toward the river. In the more narrow sections she had to slow down, but it wasn't long before she saw the gates coming into view on her maps. She prepared mentally to make the multiple jumps.

That's when her radar beeped frantically.

Wav-6 had a missile locked on her.

Would they destroy a twelve-million-dollar vehicle? She brought the EmWAV to the surface, preparing for the gate jump.

"Wav-1, this is General Martin."

Her heart skipped a beat. She mentally said a list of Medina-approved curses, squeezing her controls with fear.

"Surrender the vehicle now, and you will live. I have the authority to destroy you and the vehicle should you cross into civilian territory. I repeat, surrender now."

She considered answering in another language to throw them off, but worried about her voice being recognized. They already knew she was female, right? Granted, she looked masculine with the beanie and hoodie, so she couldn't blame the Wav-6 pilot for the mistake. What would they do when they learned *she* was in the EmWAV?

The beep continued. It locked on her, awaiting Martin's command. The gates were just a minute away. She couldn't jump too soon, or she wouldn't clear the third and fourth gates.

Her warning radar beeped into full alert. Three, two…she would have to jump early.

She tilted up preparing for the surge, cleared the first gate, then the second.

It was the third gate she wasn't going to make....

At the alarms, Dominique rushed to the hospital to check on Medina, her phone ringing for Cashus at the same time. "Laurence?"

He sounded instantly awake. "Dominique? What's going on?"

"There's some kind of alert on camp. I'm in the hospital now." She arrived at Medina's room. Technicians and guards surrounded it. "Medina got out."

"How?" he asked, concerned.

"I don't know, but I called Liz to check on Sunday, and there was no answer. Is she accounted for yet?"

Silence on the line.

"Maybe he helped her? Or she helped him?"

"It's impossible. It has to be." Concern turned to panic.

"I'll send security to check," she answered. "You better get here."

She ended the call and pulled out her gun as she checked the tech rooms. It was possible Medina was still on the premises. Had Medina gotten out alone? Had a nurse helped? She left the medical side and crossed the hallway into the training areas. There was a muffled noise coming from somewhere. She listened another moment, then ran when she recognized the sound, finding the lights, and bursting open the doors to the gym.

"Help!"

Megan struggled in her chains, her face covered in blood from her nose on down. A tennis ball bounced gently at Megan, and she twisted to avoid it. Dominique knew instantly who had done this.

"Megan. What happened?"

"Sunnie. She's loose. She locked me in here. She's angry. She said she would never forgive me for my part in torturing her and keeping her captive."

Dominique nodded, calculating. "You never did anything to help her. Seems like a just punishment. I'm surprised she didn't turn the tennis balls on harder. I would have."

Megan's eyes widened. "You're one to talk. Just let me out, please."

"How long ago was she here?"

"I don't know. At least twenty minutes. Maybe thirty."

Dominique turned and headed back toward the exit. She turned off the lights.

"Wait! Let me out! Let me out!"

Three gunshots rang out.

Then it was silent, other than the gentle lobbing of tennis balls bouncing in the dark, occasionally thumping with a dead stop on their mark.

The girls jumped out of the truck with relief. Georgie held the door while her cousin Al just looked ahead with a smile on his face, arm relaxed over the seat.

"Don't worry," Brittany said. "We're twenty minutes early."

"We'll be right back. The Dam Bridge is right ahead," Lena added. "That's what it's called, I mean. The Dam Bridge."

"I know," Georgie told her. "And that's The Dam Diner, so move it, would you?" Her nerve endings were about shot between the three of them.

"You should go, too, Cuz," Al said. "It might be a long wait."

Her eyes scrunched. She jumped back in the cab. "You're not getting rid of me."

"Suit yourself." He turned off the engine. "How about getting me a soda?"

"How about I don't trust you right now. What's up with this good mood?"

"I can't help it if I find your friends entertaining."

"Uh-huh."

"She might not even show up, you know."

"I know. But we have to be there just in case." Georgie checked the supplies in her backpack for the umpteenth time.

"No one escapes Holliwell."

"She's not no one."

"That'll make it even harder," he warned.

Georgie thought about that and realized he was right. She sighed. "Whoever she really is and whatever she really is—she's a person, and it's not right."

"Nobody cares."

"I care!"

"One person is not enough."

"Can you go back to being quiet?"

"Sure." He started the engine again. "Last chance to get a damn drink at The Dam Diner."

She put on her seatbelt. Brittany and Lena were going to be pissed. "Let's go."

Al put the truck into gear, and they headed back to the road. The bridge was still a few minutes away.

The missile destroyed the first three gates, with the fourth exploding around Jocelyn before she could jump it. The sound and vibrations cut straight through her core, making her pulse ragged. She grasped the safety cage as the EmWAV shot into the air from the turbulence, hit the edge of the riverbank, and flipped multiple times before it crashed back into the water with a jolt.

Her stomach hurt from the turmoil, not to mention her head, even with the helmet on. Jocelyn squinted at the control panel, trying her best to refocus. She took several slow breaths, quickly assessing the vehicle and her body.

The engine had survived, but the rumble was more like a wounded purr. She pressed the acceleration instinctively without knowing which way was up. The vehicle was designed to survive more than this little obstacle. She scanned her fingers over the options and adjusted the direction just in time to prevent herself from driving into the riverbank.

Grateful the machine still responded, she jettisoned into high gear. She was nearly at the dam. She could see it on her screen.

Jocelyn could also see and hear another alarm as Wav-6 locked in a second missile.

She pushed the EmWAV to its limit. Just a little farther....

Dominique went with the guard, Ruben, to General Martin's command center.

Martin took one look at her, then another at the oversized soldier.

"It appears that Medina and Project Sunday have escaped," she informed him. I've alerted Dr. Cashus. He's on his way. The guards reported in on my way here. Sunnie drugged Dr. Liz Horten, but that's not all."

Martin scowled. "Go ahead."

"It appears she is exacting some kind of revenge, General. Megan was found in the training room, tennis balls launching at her. She's been shot dead."

The General's face froze in disbelief.

Her escort, Ruben, blanched. "Sir," he interrupted.

The General held up a hand. "We'll investigate. For now, we have to assume the worst, and that she's armed and dangerous."

Dominique repressed a satisfied smile. "We do want her alive, General. She's of immense value to science."

"I understand, Dr. Wicker. My first priority is to protect civilians and other soldiers, as well as any technology she might expose. You'll understand if science is not my top priority."

"Of course. She is trained to kill, after all. Now that we know her true disposition, that's something the science team can manage should you capture her."

He turned away, frowning, likely with the knowledge that the military had trained her, and little Sunnie had fooled them all.

"Track all devices that Dr. Horten, Megan, and Medina have assigned to them, including vehicles. We need to know which one is in the EmWAV and who's helping whom. Let's get the drone patrol out to the Dam Bridge, ASAP. Lock down every exit until both Project Sunday and Medina are secured. And get a roadblock strategy in place."

"Yes, sir!" His Lieutenant exited hurriedly.

Dominique took a seat in the back of the room. This was going to be an interesting night. She looked forward to locking little Sunnie back down on a gurney. A number of brain explorations and studies flitted through her mind as she fantasized about the possibilities.

The big man, Ruben, prepared to leave. She nodded politely as he walked by. His clear gray eyes met hers—icy and assessing. She shivered unexpectedly. Soldiers could switch on killer instincts in a blink. Little Miss Cashus better watch out.

A voice came over the Comm. "Sir, I have a lock on Wav-1."

Another soldier at the command center turned to him. "We activated her tracker. It's Sunday Cashus."

"Hold. I repeat. Hold," General Martin said. "Sunnie? If you can hear me, answer. We have a missile locked on you. We will not hesitate to kill you should you cross the civilian threshold."

Dominique relaxed back and waited. They would have Sunday under control soon enough. She was certain of it.

Jocelyn stared at the Comm.

"Sunnie, we are locked on you. Surrender. I promise it will go better."

They had her. Fear and anger surged through her as she listened to the beeping of the missile alarm. Frustrated, she connected to HQ one last time. "You broke the trust, General."

"Sunnie, listen to me—."

Jocelyn turned off the Communication device. She watched Wav-6 get closer on the mapping system. She could see the dam ahead.

The alarm quickened as Wav-6 launched the missile.

She accelerated full throttle, straight for the wall, and clicked on the autopilot. "Eyes on the prize," she snarled. She snapped the emergency suit around her body and pulled the eject lever with all her might.

Graeme sighed and answered his phone. He was sitting in the Porsche on the side of the road, in the dark, looking out over the bridge like a dork, waiting for something to happen. He zipped up his light jacket and opened the sunroof. At least it was a nice night.

"Hey, nerd. Everything okay?" Rex's face came up on his phone, but was muffled by the sound of music in the background.

"Yeah. Sort of. Just sitting here thinking."

"I hope you haven't been listening to sappy music."

Graeme hastily muted the love song currently playing. *Busted.*

His brother lifted a brow and shook his head. "Talk radio. Best thing to listen to if you're getting over a girl. No music. You still in Charlottesville?"

Graeme looked around at the forest, mountains, and the large dam in front of him. "Not exactly. About an hour away from there. I had one last lead to follow. I'll be heading home tomorrow. Back to regular life."

"Regular life is very good."

"I know."

"Let it go, Graeme. I see it on your face. Whatever it is, it's not good. Let it go. It's not real. This is real, up here." Two girls with drinks in hand, heavy makeup, and tiny, sexy clubbing dresses came into view over Rex's shoulder. He grinned then motioned them away.

"You're at a club, half-buzzed, with women who look a little less than real and are throwing themselves at you because they think you're heir to a four-billion-dollar fortune."

"Are you saying I'm not good-looking?" His brother didn't miss a beat.

"I just needed to understand what was going on and what it meant."

"Not everything means something. Nor does it have to. Thus, the joy of clubbing."

"You hate it, admit it."

"Never!" Rex shouted, baiting him. "Anyway, I have to get back."

Graeme heard some girls telling him to invite his friend to join them. His brother must have walked away from the crowd as his voice became clearer.

"Call me when you're on your way tomorrow. Talk radio only. Don't make me worry about you."

"Okay. Got it." Graeme smiled. The night sky was perfect. He looked at the stars through the sunroof. "Thanks for the pep—."

The night sky lit up thunderously in front of him. "What the...."

Something exploded in mid-air. Torn pieces of what it had been shot outward in a spray of shrapnel. And the parts...they were flying right toward him.

"Oh sh—," he yelped in shock, dropping the phone as he dove below the windshield for cover. He heard a loud crash just in front of him, warning him of impact, then a huge piece of metal bounced right over the car. He sat up to see the wreckage roll into the side of the road behind him. He turned back to the dam to see another explosion as other parts hit the dam.

His ears throbbed and hurt from the reverberations. He was barely aware of his brother's voice coming from somewhere off in the distance. "What the hell just flew over your car? I saw something over the sunroof. Graeme? *Graeme?*"

Certain he was somewhat safe, Graeme's mind began to spin and assess what might have happened. Then a body flew hard onto the pavement in the middle of the bridge, feet touching before rolling with speed from the hard landing. A third explosion sent waves of energy outward. The parachute flew backward, dragging and lifting the person to the side of the bridge.

Graeme gassed it across the bridge. He didn't remember stopping his car. He just felt himself running. There were giant turbines under the bridge, flushing water from the reservoir down to the river on the other side.

This person was about to be sucked in alive.

Lena and Brittany exited the bathroom.

Some guy who looked maybe college age called out to them. "Hey! It's Salt-N-Pepa!"

"Real original," Brittany said, her look scathing. "Milk, you need a drink?"

"Yes. And a coconut cream pie to go," she told the server. The lady at the counter wrapped it up while they waited. "You know, you can see the dam from this side. It's pretty awesome with the waterfalls."

"The viewing deck is open out back," the waitress pointed.

"Maybe later, when we're done." Brittany tapped her fingers on the counter and checked her watch. Finally, the lady handed over a whole boxed pie to Lena, and they headed back to the parking lot. Brittany looked around. "All right. Where'd they go?"

A heavy sound echoed in the distance, and light appeared above the trees.

"What was that?" Lena asked.

They stared paralyzed until the light disappeared.

Brittany instantly began running toward the direction of the explosion, worried about Georgie. Lena was right behind her.

"You don't think this girl is really real, do you? She's really trying to escape?" Lena ran with pie and drink in hand. "I mean, I thought it would be cool." She ran past Brittany, her voice getting more excited. "But I also thought you two were just crazy or pulling my leg or something."

"They totally left without us." Brittany huffed up to the turnoff. "It's almost another mile to the Dam Bridge." She looked at Lena, furious.

"You had to go, too. Don't blame me."

"Let's go. They might actually need us. Not that Diet Coke and cream pie make for great weapons." She huffed down the side of the road. There weren't any cars around, but it wasn't the safest thing to be doing. She checked her phone and looked at the text from Georgie. *Stay there. We'll be back.* "Be back, my ass! Unbelievable. Leaving me at a strange place in the middle of the night." Brittany was going to kill them. Plus, she didn't want to miss any action. "It's not right. What kind of friend does that?"

When there was no answer from Lena, she turned around. No one was there.

"Milk?" A shiver ran up her arms. The night suddenly felt shrouded in danger. "*Milk!*"

Once ejected, Jocelyn shot up into the sky. The missile hit Wav-1 just below, while she blindly created a defense field for protection, deflecting the spray of metal shooting up from below. Her parachute opened and pulled abruptly. A stray piece of shrapnel shot through the material, cutting it and causing her to lose control mid-flight.

Pieces of the EmWAV hit the wall of the dam, and another explosion sounded as the engine blew up, light and fire sending a rush of hot air that pushed her sideways. She could see the bridge. Every muscle in her body pulled on the chute to direct herself to the narrow landing spot. Anywhere would do, just not where Wav-6 hovered on the water below. She heard a sound and saw the cockpit of the Wav-6 open in the water below as her body rushed toward the cement. The pilot was about to shoot something.

Her feet touched ground, then another explosion caught her parachute and sent it backward, pulling her with it. Her body dragged, then hit hard against the wall of the highway bridge. She tried to grab at something, anything, as she was yanked upward. With a free hand, she desperately reached to unlock the harness from her body. She got one side loose but was tangled in the cords. Her helmet banged against the wall as wind surged, and the chute flapped uncontrollably, half of it caught on the bridge lighting structure. She tried to separate the straps and free herself.

The other half of the parachute got caught by a force below the bridge and sucked downward, pulling her up and over the side.

She panicked.

Her hands flailed for anything to hold onto. She heard the thunder of water rushing, the turning of giant engines, and her own heartbeat accelerating in terror as the material caught on the lighting structure began to rip.

The force from below pulled, and with a jolt, the overhead lighting cracked free and tumbled down with deadly intent as she dropped.

A cry of terror escaped as deafening turbines threatened to devour everything in their way.

CHAPTER FORTY-EIGHT

The truck swerved around the final curve before the Dam Bridge. Georgie and Al saw the dark sky light and spark with something that definitely was not weekend fireworks.

Al pulled the truck to the side of the road as parts of a vehicle exploded and slammed into the wall of the dam.

"Ohmigosh. Al, what if that was her? *Ohmigosh!*" Georgie jumped from the truck for a better view. Her stomach plummeted so fast she thought she might be sick. Jocelyn was dead for sure.

Al was right behind her. He grabbed her arm. "Look!"

"Where?" She looked. Finally, she saw the parachute and the figure in the air, moving fast toward the bridge before crashing hard on the ground. "Let's go!"

They ran back to the truck, and Al gassed it.

Graeme caught a piece of parachute line just before it disappeared over the edge. The weight at the end nearly pulled him over as well. He wrapped the short piece of heavy cord around his forearm and wrist, bracing his body with his other arm wrapped under the rail so he could lean over and assess the situation. His body strained as he spotted the struggling figure.

Down below, there was a water vehicle of some kind. He stared a moment as the hood closed and the driver jumped back inside. An instant later it disappeared.

"What the...." He blinked, confused, not sure what he saw. What was real was the struggling person below him.

He looked along the dam wall and eventually spotted what he needed—a metal safety ladder built into the dam. They were put at intermittent locations. He wasn't sure he could get this person to the nearest one, but he had to try.

He moved about a foot before a ripping sound warned him. Half of the chute was stuck to the decorative arch now broken and hanging precariously over him. Once loose, the pull of the man's weight would be even worse. And if the material got sucked into the turbines...he didn't want to think about it. His arm was already burning with the strain.

He yelled to the person below. The helmet-covered head looked up. He pointed. "Ladder!"

The next instant, he regretted that suggestion. Okay, so it was the only choice, but the guy was now swinging and trying to run along the wall to the ladder, using Graeme's arm as the fulcrum. He got closer each time. On the third, with a desperate push off the wall at the end, the guy launched himself at the metal inserts and grabbed, nearly pulling Graeme over the wall with him.

Graeme unwound the cords from his arm and tied them on the rail. The other half of the torn parachute seemed to be the problem. It was already being sucked into a turbine and pulling the victim with it. The guy hugged the metal rails of the ladder, struggling desperately.

"Take off the chute!"

The person shook their head negatively.

"Take off the chute!"

Graeme ran to his trunk and found a military knife his brother had given him for utilitarian purposes. He looked over the side, his stomach plummeting. He was going to have to climb down and cut the person free. Not good. Not good at all.

He attached the knife to his belt and climbed over. It was going to be a tight fit for two people on the metal steps. The lower he got, the stronger the wind became. A piece of shrapnel that had caught on the bridge loosened, fell, and flew by, nearly knocking him off. His right arm and grip were already shaky from holding the line a minute before. He paused a moment, debating, then pushed on.

He got nearly even with the parachutist. The guy was slender and not dressed very military, other than the black hoodie and crash helmet. He shouted, "I'm cutting it off."

"I need the under pack."

Ah, a human voice. Young. He looked and realized the parachute lines had caught on a small pack under the person's hoodie. The wind, or just the ejection process, had shoved the hoodie up and created a tangled mess. But if this person was willing to risk their life for the pack...not good. He hoped it wasn't a nuclear bomb or something. This could be a spy the military was stopping. Maybe he shouldn't be helping.

He nodded that he understood. He could see the thin pack and cut the cords and straps around it as the person clung to the metal rungs. The parachutist tried to unlatch the pack—an impossible task with one hand. Together, they freed it from his shoulders. Once loose, it caught more air and whipped his companion backward and nearly pulled him off the rungs as the lighting structure fell, cracked, and sparked all around them. Graeme's heart leapt as a piece of metal fell in close proximity, banging against the cement near his back as it fell to the water with a splash a hundred feet below.

He grabbed and held an arm around the smaller guy until he was secure. The chute, pack, and wildly-flapping cords, now free, floated downward before switching directions and getting sucked into the turbine.

Graeme didn't wait. He climbed back up to the bridge first. It was quite likely this person had done something illegal, and he wasn't going to have a stranger kill him after risking his life.

Once safe, he pulled the guy over the side of the bridge and slid to the ground against the wall with exhaustion, holding his knife protectively to his stomach. The guy crumpled next to him. He thought he heard copters in the distance, but decided it was just the rush of water below and the pounding of his heart thrumming in his ears.

His companion carefully took off his helmet, put it in his lap, and straightened his beanie.

"Thank you for helping me."

He turned at the sound of a female voice. *He* was a *she*.

And not any she. *His* she.

"Are you serious?" He studied her. She looked pale under the bridge lights. But who wouldn't be after what she'd just gone through. Her eyes were even more brilliantly blue than he remembered. "Sunnie?"

Surprise filled her expression. Then she leapt for his knife.

He grabbed her hand defensively with his free one. She put one over his and squeezed, gently but firm. "Trust me...Graeme."

At the sound of his name, he smiled with bemusement and let her take the knife as three big ass, metal-cladded drones lifted in formation before them, rising over the side of the bridge.

Al braked hard.

"Ohmigosh." She'd never seen a drone before. "Is that a...."

"Drone? *Yes!*" Al hit reverse as a drone split off from the formation of three and flew at them, driving them backward. It was about twenty feet long with a thirty-foot wingspan— impressive and intimidating.

Al screeched to a stop at the crossroads and lifted his hands off the wheel, one of them reaching around Georgie's shoulders protectively. "Hey, man! We're just driving home. We can go another way. The long way is fine."

A voice sounded from the floating machine. "Stand down. We have a military training exercise in session. This road is closed for the rest of the night."

Al and Georgie nodded. "We'll just turn around...." Al made a spinning motion with his finger to communicate his words.

The drone stood guard over them. Al put the truck in gear but watched the action down the road. There was movement by the Porsche. Bodies on the ground. A drone went down. Then another. Whatever was going on, someone up there had skills.

It didn't take long before the drone blocking them turned and raced back down the bridge to the Porsche.

Al lifted both hands and made a totally different gesture with his fingers.

Graeme heard a megaphone voice command them.

"Drop your—."

The girl let loose with the knife. He was barely able to make out the movement of her arm it was so fast. The knife hit the camera on target, cut through the core of the drone, and lodged somewhere that caused it to spin uncontrollably. The second drone shot a line of bullets toward them. He jumped to pull Sunnie down, rolling them toward the Porsche for cover. He stopped on top of the girl, his body protecting hers. It didn't mean the force of many bullets couldn't go right through him to kill her, if that's what the person on the other end of the drone wanted to do, but he still tried to shelter her. His body told him one thing very clearly. *Definitely a girl.*

He lifted his head to see if she was okay. She had to be pretty damn special or completely dangerous for anyone to want to kill her.

Maybe both.

She looked back at him. Her face had been ravaged by chemistry. He had assumed chemotherapy, but under the current circumstances, he suspected it might be something more exotic. Her eyebrows were gone. The edge of the beanie drifted up to reveal her scalp where he once recalled her beautiful, dark hair. He lifted up on an elbow to adjust the beanie on one side. Their eyes met. He sensed fear and fury.

Then she stared past him.

"There's one right above us, isn't there?"

She lifted her hand, and he felt a surge of energy that made him lightheaded, followed by a loud pop.

"Not anymore."

She rolled, flipping him over, until she was on her feet. A spinning drone crashed against the wall of the dam, but there weren't any weapons in her hand. Giant turbines crunched loudly. Her eyes glittered brightly as she offered him a hand up. He took it, heat enveloping him at the connection. She released him and pulled off her hoodie and backpack.

"What's in the bag?"

"Nothing bad. Just stuff I need to survive."

"Lipstick, toothbrush, bug spray?"

She stared at him, curious. "Why are you here?"

He waved a hand to the Porsche. "I think I'm your ride."

"Did Georgie of the RCC send you?"

He laughed and nodded. "Something like that."

"I'll drive," she said.

"Not after that crash. What was that, by the way?"

"A twelve-million-dollar top secret prototype vehicle," she said nonchalantly, inspecting the car before putting her stuff inside.

"Yeah." He took the wheel. "I'm definitely driving."

The third drone had been on the south side of the bridge warning oncoming traffic. He bet the owner of the truck was freaking out about now. He put the car in gear. Unfortunately, said drone was now racing toward them.

"We better hurry," she said.

Vibrations shook the car as bullets sprayed the Porsche.

She ducked, then looked around, surprised by the bulletproof glass. Her foot hit something, and she pulled up the portable missile launcher. "You *are* prepared." She examined the weapon. "Is this a NRC-14 missile launcher?"

"Uhh...." He didn't exactly know what Richie had hooked him up with. "Yeah?"

"Perfect." She got on her knees. "Put down the sunroof and turn off your lights. I'll take care of this last one."

Graeme glanced over as she quickly snapped the two missiles in place with the familiarity other girls snapped the cap back on their lipstick. He grinned and killed the lights. *Hot.*

The night vision activated on the windshield. Whoa, Nellie. "I owe you one, Richie."

She stood until she was outside the open sunroof. The drone operator recognized the threat and made an evasive maneuver. She anticipated it and hit, but only enough to unbalance the machine. The second shot was clean. It blew to smithereens.

She ducked back into the car. "Do you have any more missiles?"

"Actually, no." *Didn't know I had those.*

She nodded and stared out the window. "It's not safe for you now. They know it's me, and there will be more."

"More drones?"

She shook her head dismally. "More *everything.*"

A phone slid from under the seat. She picked it up, staring at the person yelling on the other end before handing it to him.

He looked at his brother's face. Rex wasn't at the club anymore. It looked like he was in the limo.

"Hey. I can't talk right now."

"What the *hell* is going on?"

A loud whirring of engines in the air alerted him. "More everything," he said.

Al watched the drone take off after the Porsche. "Your little friend down there has some help."

"It's some random stranger," Georgie said. "We can't let her get in a car with a stranger."

"She just did."

They watched as the drone fired on the Porsche.

"Ohmigosh. Oh. My. Gosh! They're trying to kill her."

"I told you that would happen!" Al shouted back.

"I know! But—."

They watched as Jocelyn popped out of the sunroof and fired something. The drone exploded into thousands of pieces.

"That's right, you asshole!" Georgie was pissed. She turned on Al. "That was *righteous.*"

"May I never get you mad."

"Let's go."

"Are you sure?"

"Yes. She needs our help. She doesn't know where the getaway vehicle is."

"I think a bulletproof, missile-loaded Porsche trumps a Prius," Al said.

She was about to protest when she heard a voice call out.

"Wait! Wait!" Brittany ran up to the truck. "You left us! And you didn't answer your phone," Brittany yelled at her.

"I got this," Georgie told Al, rolling down the window.

"Listen." Georgie leaned over the window of the truck. She spotted the drink in Brit's hand. Her mouth tasted like cotton. "Is that Diet Coke?"

Brittany offered up the soda. "Want some?"

"Yeah, thanks." Georgie sucked back half of it and handed it back. "Okay, listen. It's too dangerous for you to go on with us. We just saw this super high-tech military thing explode. Then Jocelyn parachuted in and nearly died, and some guy— who got to the bridge before us because we stopped at the diner to pee and get drinks—."

"Milk had to get pie. Otherwise, it wouldn't have taken so long. You know how she is with her pie. She has some kind of sugar disease. It was one of those pie moments. She thinks better after eating—."

"Okay," Georgie said. "But listen. Some guy in a Porsche was here before us, and she got in the car with him. Three drones came and shot at them, and one forced us back over the bridge to here. Then that drone was shot down. Based on my experience with Holliwell and their," she held up her fingers as quotes, "*training exercises*, there's going to be a lot of firepower coming this way any moment. So go back to the diner and call a cab or someone to pick you up."

"Aside from the fact that your story is mostly unbelievable, I think I should go with you," Brittany said. "They killed my aunt."

"If they kill you, what will happen to your mom?"

"What about your mom and dad?"

"I'm with Al. He'll watch out for me."

"You should get out of the truck," Al said.

Georgie ignored him. "I don't even know if we'll be able to catch up with her, but I have to try." She pressed the button to raise the window. "I'll text you when and if there's an update, or in the morning."

Brittany hit the side of the truck in frustration. Al sped away, and Georgie watched her friend in the side view mirror until her phone blew up with angry texts.

That was so wrong. I'm going to kill you. Do not get killed before that! Brittany texted.

Al glanced at her to see what was up. The phone lit up again. *Seriously. Don't get hurt. Tell Al not to speed.*

Georgie sighed. They entered the forest past the bridge. "Do you think you can catch them?"

"Probably not before Holliwell, but we'll try."

CHAPTER FORTY-NINE

Brittany stood alone *again* at the side of the road. A strange noise from the forest warned her of oncoming vehicles. She hid behind the trees at the edge of the bridge as four aircraft in diamond formation came up above the river and turned to fly over the Dam Bridge and down the road—right behind Al's truck. They were dark shadows under the lights of the bridge, and utterly lethal looking. She swallowed hard. Was this an exercise, a threat, or an execution? What had they stumbled upon? Was it the same thing her aunt discovered?

A pink moped pulled to a stop at the side of the road and watched the action. Brittany's mouth dropped as she recognized the black dress under a leather jacket and helmet.

"*Milk?*"

She flipped her visor up. "Brittany! I thought you found them and left me."

Brittany walked over to the moped. "Where did you get this?"

"I know the pie lady at The Dam Diner."

"Of course you do."

"Here." Lena pulled another helmet from the saddlebags. "Maybe we can catch up. I totally didn't think it was anything, but now there are *drones*. Can you believe that? Did the girl show up? Did we miss it? Where is everyone? I've seen drones before, but not that kind. Did you get a picture?"

Brittany realized she'd been completely unprepared. She checked her phone. At least she still had half of the battery left. She put it in her over-the-shoulder bag, grabbed the helmet, and closed the saddlebag, careful not to jostle the boxed pie.

"Al and Georgie went after the girl. I don't know much more than that, except she's in a Porsche."

"A Porsche?"

"Yeah."

Lena looked at the speedometer. "A Porsche going sixty-five for fifteen miles and a moped going forty miles on a shortcut will meet at—."

"Are you doing math?"

"Yes," Lena said. "And according to my calculations, experience on these roads, and the distance between us, them, and the next possible intersection—it will take about fourteen minutes to reach the truck. I'm not sure about the Porsche."

"There are a dozen drones chasing them as we speak," Brittany said.

Lena revved the little motorbike. "Chances are, they'll be stopped before the rendezvous."

Brittany hopped on the passenger seat. "We better get going then."

Dominique stood silently at the news three drones had gone down. Ice trickled through her veins. She wanted Sunday Cashus back. The girl proved more resourceful than planned.

"We need road blocks," General Martin commanded. "But I don't want casualties. Get some Hunter drones on the move."

"Sir, I can't. Something is locking the Hunter drones."

"Get me Hanger H. Now. And a visual," the General clipped.

"Yes, sir."

A visual of Hanger H surveillance came onto the screens, followed by curses. The entire Hunter drone fleet disintegrated before their eyes in a series of dramatic, systematic explosions.

"Shit." The General studied the fiery display. "Medina. Find him. Meanwhile, get the Predators on the move before he blows them up."

"Done, sir." A corporal in front of the command center responded.

"You lost her?" Dominique asked.

"Have a seat, Dr. Wicker. We'll get her back," the General said, terse.

"Hopefully, before the media circus begins."

"What do you mean?"

She lifted her phone. "Put on the local news."

A soldier flipped a monitor to the news. "Local news uploaded a video from the Dam Bridge on an unusual boating accident."

"Someone call the station and cut that off," the General cursed. "What's the word on Dr. Cashus?"

"He went straight to the heliport. Already in the air, sir."

"How much were those drones?" Dominique watched the news footage of the crash that covered the EmWAV and the drones. The reporter speculated on what the wreckage might be.

"Sixteen million apiece."

She winced. "That's gonna hurt."

The General scowled. "If you have nothing useful to add, Wicker, get out. Otherwise, shut up."

"Yes, sir. My apologies. I'll just sit here." She folded her hands on her lap and whispered with amusement, "Quiet as a mouse."

A call came over the communication system, and one of the airport patrolmen flashed on the screen with three others holding down a man in the background. "General, we have Medina. He's done some damage to the control tower." As if on cue, the control tower exploded behind the men. Medina got an arm free and flipped a man, nearly escaping before they were able to wrestle him back down with the help of two more soldiers who came onto the scene.

The General shook his head. He liked Medina and Sunnie. He should have never let Dr. Cashus get his hands on either one. Now both would be lost.

"Bring him in," the General commanded. *One down, one to go.*

The Porsche raced down the highway, hugging the corners with precision. Jocelyn was impressed. She didn't know there were non-military vehicles like this. Georgie had resources.

Graeme. She took a breath. She remembered him, all right. And he remembered her. And, she didn't think she would ever forget the heat of his hard body over hers just minutes ago. She swallowed hard. That discovery was badly timed.

She wanted to ask him a million questions. But the guy, Rex, was still on the phone asking a million questions of his own, and Jocelyn knew in another minute they were going to have bigger problems. She could hear the whirring of more drones closing in.

"Should I end the call?"

Graeme nodded.

Jocelyn pressed the red button just as a blinding spotlight covered the vehicle.

"What the hell?" He squinted, slowing down a little.

"More drones." She popped her head out the sunroof far enough to assess. "I can't tell how many there are with the lights on us. Maybe four."

"Four?" Graeme gave her a quick glance. "Did you do something illegal?"

"I don't think so. Well, I took the EmWAV, but I was trying to escape before they did more experiments on me."

He frowned at her, as if uncertain of what to believe.

"They are *a lot* more wrong than I am."

"*Stop the car, and no one will be injured.*" The audio boomed into the night.

The phone in her hand buzzed again. A wacky face showed on-screen with the name Rex.

"Accept the call."

"Are you sure? He yells a lot."

"That's what fear sounds like. Answer it."

She did, pressing speaker icon.

"Rex, Rex!" Graeme yelled over his brother's rants. "I need help. Listen. How can I immobilize a drone?"

"Seriously?"

"Rex, can you help or not, because there a few on my tail."

"Pull over."

Jocelyn shook her head vehemently, shivering at the idea of surrender.

"Not an option."

Rex looked like the veins on his neck were going to explode. "What kind of drones?"

"Predator X-Class. Fully armed," Jocelyn said.

Graeme repeated, "Predator X-Class."

"There is no X-Class."

"It's new," Jocelyn said. "Smaller, faster, easier to maneuver."

"It's new," Graeme said.

"I heard. All I can say is, you *really* know how to pick 'em."

"It looks like a mini-Stealth Bomber," Graeme said.

They raced around a curve.

"Even better," came the sarcastic response.

"Surrender now. You won't get far. Don't make it worse." Jocelyn recognized General Martin's voice booming at them.

Rex lifted a hand to his forehead, rubbing frantically. "Unless you have missiles, your best bet is taking out the cameras—typically, the cameras are pretty lame and low resolution. But they'll also have radar and other surveillance equipment."

Jocelyn nodded to Graeme that she understood.

"Do you know for sure they're carrying a payload?" Rex asked.

A warning explosion went off in front of them, shattering the darkness.

Graeme gripped the wheel tightly and swerved. "Yeah. Seems like."

Jocelyn touched his shoulder to get his attention. "Slow down at the next straightaway." She started to climb out through the sunroof.

"Where are you going?" Graeme shouted at her.

"To take care of the surveillance system."

She heard him curse as the car began to slow.

Then she jumped.

Richie sang along with Lena Horne, enjoying the peace of the night while cruising the mountain pass in his tow truck.

An explosion of light sparked up across the valley below.

He braked.

Trepidation filled him from toes to scalp. Slowly, he pulled onto an overlook, turned off his lights, and got out. He could hear a familiar sound echoing across the wide valley. It did nothing to reassure him. He hugged his arms over his belly, forcing back the shakes that threatened to overtake him.

There was a light on a vehicle—tracking it along the curving road.

He closed his eyes and swallowed. Memories of his last days at Holliwell shoved their way back into his consciousness. His mouth went dry. His stomach heaved.

He took a controlling breath. *Do not vomit. I'm not going back. I'm never going back.*

His mental reassurance didn't stop the tremors. He looked across the valley again.

He couldn't make out the car, but it moved with aggressive elegance in and out of the curves.

He swallowed hard. Those moves were a little *too* familiar. *Nellie.*

More lights in the air warned him. Three helicopters came over the mountain, then dispersed. One flew right toward him. He shook violently as it passed overhead.

They were closing off the roads.

"Can you go faster?" Georgie thrummed the passenger door with her fingers, impatient.

"Not on these roads, and not at night. Listen, if we get caught, tell them I'm your cousin picking you up from a bad date. We're driving back to Vesuvius—to my place, so your parents don't find out."

"Do you have a place in Vesuvius?"

"No."

"Got it. We'll worry about that part later." Georgie stuck her head out the window. The drones had passed them, flying a direct path, their focus clearly on the Porsche. Georgie didn't think she and Al would be able to offer much help—but it might be hard to take Jocelyn away with witnesses.

She shivered, considering that plan. It was anything but comforting.

Jocelyn needed to be quick and strong.

She leapt from the Porsche and slid over the top of the first drone, catching a wing. The drone dipped instantly from her weight, giving her an idea. She punched the windows where the two cameras were located. The force of it bloodied her skin to the knuckles. Without pausing for the pain, she kept going, aiming her attention on drone number two.

She moved with deadly speed, before the formation could be broken, making a mad leap from the first drone to the one on her left, deliberately landing on the inside wing, exerting as much energy as she could to focus it downward.

The wing tipped immediately before the drone operator could counter her force.

She fell down and hit the road hard, rolling to the edge.

The drone flipped out of control into its partner on the right. She heard the mid-air collision and curled into a ball, covering her head as the two drones crashed into the highway in front of her, first hitting the mountain, then tumbling forward and off the road.

That left one last drone with camera capabilities.

The Porsche screeched to a halt not far from the fallen drones. Graeme jumped from the vehicle looking around.

For her.

That was so sweet. She closed her eyes, taking a breath, judging the distance to the car.

They would destroy him.

"Sunnie, Sunnie!"

The floodlight from the last drone shone on them as he reached her and kneeled to touch her head. "Don't move. Are you injured? I'll get you to a hospital. I promise."

She opened her eyes at that word, her hand snatching his shirt with force and pulling him close until they were inches apart. "*No. More. Hospitals.*"

He stared back, still on his knees, and slipped an arm under her shoulders. "Okay. No hospitals."

"I'm fine."

"That's remarkable."

The voice boomed again in the night. "*Step away from the girl and you will not be hurt.*"

"Persistent assholes, aren't they?"

She smiled, amused he could be so calm under the threat. She could smell the heat coming off his body and the light scent of some exotic aftershave. She needed this moment to collect her energy, to refuel herself. He had a dimple on one cheek. She lifted her bloodied hand to touch it, and he caught it with concern. She thought he might say something about the hospital again, but thought better of it.

"Your eyes are the bluest I've ever seen."

"They're going to kill you." She thought it best to keep him focused.

"That would cause a national incident."

"They can still make your life difficult and torture you before anyone finds you." It hurt to the core to say the next words. "Don't be my friend." Her voice cracked, husky with emotion.

He shook his head. "Too late."

The booming voice sounded again with a final warning to step away from the girl.

"I'm going to make a run for it. Without you. They'll follow me. You can get away." She hoped he read the message in her eyes and didn't fight her on this.

Finally, he nodded, still gazing at her thoughtfully while he tugged her beanie back into place. She was reminded of Seth, but this was different. Some feeling of hope and heat spread to her chest. She didn't know what it was but desperately wanted it. He leaned down, his cheek grazing hers, his breath gentle and warm, tickling her ear.

"There's a gun under the seat of the driver's side with two magazines."

"Thank you."

"Anytime." He winked.

She rolled away from him and hopped to her feet before he did, kicking out hard and connecting with the side of his head. She kept her foot flat and prayed he just went down and stayed there.

He staggered back, and she moved quickly punching his lip. He would have a visible bruise. Their eyes met. It would need to be enough. She couldn't bring herself to hurt him.

He fell to a knee and didn't follow her.

She darted for the car under a warning spray of bullets, dove inside, slammed the door, and hit the gas. Reaching under the seat, she pulled out the box with the gun and steered with her elbows long enough to shove a magazine inside. She put the other in the bag with her meds, which she singlehandedly flipped back over her shoulder.

Rex called out frantically for Graeme from the face of the cellphone. She ended the call, threw the phone out the window, and shifted into high gear.

She needed to get rid of the drone. But she knew that wouldn't be the end.

CHAPTER FIFTY

Graeme rolled onto his back and stared at the sky. "What the hell just happened?"

He chuckled. A girl just decked him. "What the *hell.*"

The thrum of the Porsche and the whirring of the drone faded into darkness. All that was left were stars. It was a pretty damn beautiful night, considering.

He reached into his breast pocket and pulled out his gaming glasses. The frames were screwed up a bit, but they worked. He put them on. "Location." A map displayed, zooming in on his location, miles from nowhere. "The Dam Diner it is." He rolled to his feet.

Something rattled up the road and club music cued the caller. His phone! He could track the car with his phone. *Thank you, Richie.* Excited, he ran and answered the call. It was Rex again.

"I can't talk, but I'm okay."

"What happened to your face?"

Graeme touched the side of his mouth and realized there was blood coming from his lip. "I got punched by a girl."

"As long as that's the worst that happened tonight."

"Yeah." Graeme wiped his lip. "If only."

"What else?"

His phone was cracked but worked. He switched apps and activated the tracking system on the Porsche. "Nothing. I'm not really sure...."

"I'm on my way to the airport. I'll be there in four hours."

"I could use a lift home." He started walking the direction of the Porsche icon moving steadily ahead on the map's GPS.

Rex shook his head. "I don't even want to know."

"I have to make a call."

"Text me on the hour, each hour, so I know you're all right."

"Got it. Later."

"Love you. Be smart."

"I will. Love you, too."

Graeme hung up. His brother had to be stressed. He'd just told him he loved him. Even though their family spoke their affection aloud, Rex hadn't done so in years. "It only took lethal drones and exploding missiles, but at least that was a breakthrough."

Lights cued him to an oncoming vehicle. Nervous about more military, he ducked off the side of the road, then cursed after a big pickup truck drove by. He might have caught a ride.

Graeme tapped back to the tracker. Sunnie didn't waste time. His stomach clenched with nerves. Even with Nellie at her disposal, the roads were treacherous and the military determined. He didn't want Sunnie hurt. And as dangerous as it might be, he really wanted to see her again. At the speed she was going, the odds were diminishing.

He gave Richie a ring. With any luck, he'd be awake and could pick him up.

⁙

Brittany's teeth jarred as the moped bounced through the mile-long tunnel with only their headlight for illumination. The bone-chilling feeling of being surrounded by earth did nothing to ease her worry.

"Almost there," Lena called over her shoulder, as if knowing Brittany was stressed. Her words echoed off the walls.

Brittany shook from inside out. She had a bad feeling.

A moment later, the feeling was verified. A light blazed behind them in the tunnel.

"Train!" Brittany shouted.

Lena looked behind her, shocked. "Not possible! No trains tonight."

Brittany screamed. "It's a train! Go faster!" They still had at least a quarter of a mile to reach the end of the tunnel. Brittany glanced back again. The light came fast. And faster. She started to pray loudly in between shouting, "Go, go!"

Then it was upon them.

Jocelyn had to change her strategy. She couldn't outrun or outdrive a drone. She looked in the rearview mirror. It kept its distance—definitely in tracking mode. That meant there was something else on the way, either ahead of her, or in the air behind her. Maybe both.

She pulled the emergency break and spun the Porsche to a stop.

She'd just passed a small crossroads leading down into the forest and off the main road. She put the car in gear, zipped down, and turned again. The Porsche had agility where the drone didn't. It couldn't move in reverse, so it had to make full turns. She watched it turn, calculating her odds. Definitely in her favor. The drone flew toward her on the turn, lower to the road, coming closer, clearly trying to spot her.

She gathered her things and tossed them to the side of the road before unlocking her seatbelt. If she blasted back up the hill a little, and turned in time, she just might make it.

She was desperate enough to try.

She gassed it and went into gear as quickly as possible. It came sooner than she expected.

There was no way to prepare for jumping out of a moving vehicle. Doing it twice in one night—not recommended.

She turned the wheel. Opened the door. And ate dirt.

A violent collision exploded above her.

It hadn't been a deep drop, and she'd tumbled off the side of the road a fair distance before being jarred by a tree root. A whirring sound caught her attention, and she turned as a piece of one of the vehicles—the drone, she realized—impaled the mountainside next to her.

She gulped, then used the wing to pull herself up. She'd lost her beanie. Her head felt vulnerable, but refreshingly cool after the activity. She reached around blindly, a little dazed. Acknowledging her dizziness, she paused, took a breath, and assessed her body, her emotions, and her surroundings.

Heat pulsed to her shoulder where she'd hit the ground first. She recognized the self-healing mode and breathed deeply to support the flow of energy. She needed to stay calm and focused. She pressed her hands to the earth. It felt good. Alive. She relaxed her body and took it all in until she felt strong again.

Grateful her recovery was quick, she searched for her beanie. She spotted it near the top of the incline and made her way up. Recovered, she put it on her head, threw her bag over her shoulder, and listened intently to the sounds of the night. She was safe, but it wouldn't be for long.

She heard an engine. Not a drone. She ventured to the side of the road, her hand on the gun inside her bag. She'd never hijacked a car, but now might be a first.

She stepped on the road and held up a free hand to alert the oncoming vehicle.

The truck stopped, the lights dimmed, and someone jumped out of the vehicle.

"Jocelyn!" The girl ran to her, stopping a foot away.

She recognized the voice before her eyes adjusted. "Georgie of the RCC."

Georgie laughed. "Ohmigosh. You look like hell. Are you okay?"

Jocelyn waved a hand to the Porsche standing on its nose twenty feet below with the driver's side door torn off and hanging from a tree.

"What happened to the driver? I saw you get in the car with him and *freaked* out."

"I had to drop him off. Not safe. You didn't send him?"

"No!"

"He had missiles and a gun."

Georgie froze at that news, speechless. "Explain later. Let's go. We're fifteen miles from the rendezvous. I have a car and supplies waiting for you." Georgie hopped into the front of the truck and Jocelyn followed.

"Al, this is Jocelyn. Jocelyn, Al."

"Hi, Al." Jocelyn took one look and assessed him. He could be helpful and wouldn't panic under pressure. "Thank you for helping. It's kind of a mess right now. There are seven drones down, but there's something else on the way. The last one held back a lot, just tracking me. That means they're preparing something else."

"Got it," Al said. "I'm going down the road you just came from. It's narrower, but better tree coverage at the bottom. Vesuvius is just on the other side of the mountain."

Georgie pulled out a piece of paper with a map. "If we get separated, go here. It's a church parking lot. There's a blue Prius. The key is on the driver's side under the front wheel in a little magnetic case. There's a backpack in the trunk with a thin sleeping bag, a wig, some clothes, power bars, and $200 dollars. Sorry, that's all I had."

"That's amazing. I've never had money before."

"Really? That's totally weird." Georgie recovered. "We bought plane tickets with the rest of the money as part of our decoy plan."

"Don't let anyone get caught."

"I know," Georgie said. "Certain death."

"Are there any hiking paths to Vesuvius?"

"Yes." Georgie pulled out more papers from the glove box. "I printed these just in case." She handed them to Jocelyn.

Jocelyn studied them. "I think I can make it quicker on foot this way. The path is not far from here."

"We can drive you," Georgie said.

"No." Jocelyn knew Martin was closing in. It was too quiet. "There's going to be chaos soon. You can't be seen helping me."

"But—."

"Georgie." Al's voice was hard. "She's right. These are drones. This is not just a ticket and a suspension."

"I know." Georgie sounded ready to debate.

Al glanced at the map. "The hiking intersection is coming up."

Georgie took her hand and squeezed it. "Good luck. Be careful."

"I will. Thank you for all you've done."

They entered an open valley at the bottom of the road, and Al pulled into a picnic site for the state park. The hiking trails connected there, and other than the small picnic area, there were a lot of trees to make discovery difficult.

It was perfect.

Graeme's stomach dropped when the Porsche icon stopped moving. Sunnie had either pulled to the side, been caught, shot, or had crashed. His slow jog became a run. Only half a mile more. He ignored the stitch in his side, his throbbing head, and gnawing thirst.

The phone vibrated in his hand.

"Richie?"

"You're alive! Oh, man. I saw this crash on the road, and I thought...I don't know what I thought. I thought it was Nellie! And there are military copters all out and about. What are you doing? You in Charlottesville?"

"Uh, no." Graeme gasped for breath, keeping his pace. "I'm trying to catch up with the Porsche. Thanks for the tracker, by the way."

"*What?*"

"Can you pick me up? Add it to my bill."

"Where you at?"

Graeme paused to check the map. He gave Richie the highway and crossroads where the Porsche stopped. "Go there."

"I'm ten minutes away, man."

"Thank you. My lucky night."

"Not if you let something happen to Nellie," Richie shouted before abruptly ending the call.

Graeme picked up the pace. Luck was subjective.

Brittany screamed the longest scream of her life. Then she sucked in air and screamed again until they made it out of the tunnel.

Zooming over their heads, up and out of the tunnel, was an army of flying saucers, each fifteen to twenty feet in diameter.

Lena pulled to the side of the road, and they took a breath. Then she took out her camera, stood by the tunnel exit, and recorded what was happening before typing furiously.

"What are you doing?"

"Sending this to the news people and the Pie Lady. Now I'm uploading it to YouTube." Lena continued to type. "Hopefully there's a news crew there already. At The Dam Diner, I mean. I called earlier. It's harder to kill people with cameras recording. That's the one good thing about the media. Civilians can use it, too."

"I can't believe you have coverage out here."

"Portable cell tower in my bag." She held it up. "Better safe than sorry when going to dances that might really be secret missions." She kept typing. "Okay. Delivered. We should be intersecting close to Georgie and Al, just across this valley and up the road to the highway."

"And then what?" Brittany stared into the distance wondering how they would get past the drones. "There had to be a couple dozen of those things."

"Looked like a platoon," Lena noted.

"Exactly."

Lena revved the bike. "You coming?"

Brittany climbed back on, feeling completely unprepared.

"What can we possibly do, Milk?"

Lena encouraged her with a quick smile before putting on her helmet. "We can offer them pie."

Brittany shivered. Georgie and Al might be killed by a platoon of flying saucers, Milk was certifiable, and their best defense was pie? When did this operation go downhill?

Georgie was right to bail on her. She wasn't cut out for rescue missions.

They stood on the edge of a wide-open valley surrounded by tree-covered mountains. The cool air demanded they take cover soon, but Georgie didn't know the appropriate way to say goodbye. Even though Jocelyn could pack a punch, Georgie didn't like sending her off into the darkness alone, despite the girl's confidence.

"I run fast. I can get over this hill in minutes. Don't worry," Jocelyn said.

"It's more like a mountain, but okay."

Al offered his hand, and Jocelyn took it. She pulled away, and when he didn't release her, Jocelyn waited. Georgie saw that her cousin struggled with something.

"I have to know." He bit his lip. "I have to know if you ever saw or heard of a girl. Her name was Bonnie Hill. She was a nurse."

Georgie was shocked. The Bonnie he refused to talk about! Was this why he'd been kicked out of the Army? She turned to Jocelyn. Ohmigosh. She saw it on her face. Jocelyn knew her!

"Jocelyn?" Georgie prompted. "Tell us. It's important. Please."

Jocelyn's face looked distraught in the moonlight. She shook her head, as if not wanting to tell them.

"Have you seen her?"

"Sort of." She put her other hand on top of Al's. "I'm so sorry." The touch of sympathy made him release her and step back against the truck. "I saw her name when I...I had to know, too." Jocelyn spit it out. "She's in the morgue."

"Oh, God." He fell against the truck and put his hands over his eyes. "I knew it. *Those bastards.* I just had to know for sure."

Jocelyn touched his arm, as if trying to offer comfort. "I understand. My parents were there as well. I'm so sorry."

Georgie gasped. "Ohmi—."

Jocelyn added, "If it helps, the scientist in charge of her was Dr. Laurence Cashus. He's experimented on a lot of people. Me included. I'm sorry if your friend might have been one."

Al exhaled, his voice hoarse. "You'd best go." He motioned to the path. "Run as fast as you can, and don't look back. Don't make her sacrifice for nothing. Please."

Jocelyn nodded.

Georgie stepped forward and hugged her fiercely.

Jocelyn released her. "Thank you so much, Georgie of the RCC." Then she turned and left without looking back.

Georgie and Al stood quietly afterward in darkness. Al rested his forehead against the truck, hands on his head. Georgie didn't know how to comfort her cousin, but wanted to give him a little privacy to recover his tough guy composure. She hadn't liked hearing the broken chord in his voice or seeing how his body had crumbled, weak from shock.

It hurt.

Finally, she touched his shoulder. "Come on. I'll drive." She hopped in the driver's seat and flipped the engine on just as a loud buzzing noise caught her attention. Nervously, she shut down the engine and turned off the lights. Al heard it, too. He immediately reached to the narrow back seat, lifted the cushion, and loaded his gun.

"Al?" Georgie put the window down. "What is it?"

The buzzing got louder, reminding her of locust invasions she'd seen in the movies. She lowered the window and listened. The impending noise of the unknown caused her to shiver with fear.

Al hopped out of the truck. "Go, Georgie. Now. Into the trees. Keep the lights off." Al had a scary-looking rifle over his shoulder and a gun in his hand.

"Where are you going?"

"Divide and conquer."

"Don't be a hero, Al."

"Who, me? Not on your life. Just get away." He slammed the door shut. "I'll call you from prison."

Georgie couldn't speak. Her throat constricted from terror as she looked toward the sky behind Al. Over the mountainside, a wave of darkness rose up, blocking out the moon and stars before descending on them.

Al banged the truck twice for her to go.

She hit the accelerator.

She could have sworn it was a wave of locusts.

Until they separated and began to form a circle.

CHAPTER FIFTY-ONE

Laurence tracked the drones with the remote viewer from the back of the helicopter. The drones were fast, but he wasn't far behind.

Every nerve in his body blazed with fury. That she would lie to him, humiliate and betray him like this was unforgivable. He'd given her life! He was going to catch her and beat the spirit, memory, and personality out of her. She would learn what real drug therapy could do.

He wasn't going to lose everything now. Not when he'd finally reached the top. His research and contributions to every project they had prepared would win him Nobel prizes. He would be recognized for his brilliance. He wouldn't let little Sunnie ruin it all.

"Target every signature you have within a mile of the last drone takedown," he ordered.

"We don't know who's who, sir. We don't have visuals yet."

"It doesn't matter. You should assume anyone out there might be helping her."

"Yes, but—."

"This is a *billion dollar asset*. Anyone helping to steal this asset from the U.S. Government should be shot and killed on site. Is that understood?"

"We report to General Martin, sir."

"You won't be reporting to anyone if that creature gets away."

He saw the look one of the soldiers gave him. They didn't understand that Sunnie wasn't human anymore. She was his project to own and control. His anger doubled. He would not give her up.

Another officer reported over their communications channel. "We have Alien 7 on a moped. Two bodies in dresses. Alien 26 moving toward a pedestrian, Alien 27 on a large vehicle coming toward us on the highway—a truck."

"Stop all vehicles," General Martin ordered.

The report continued from Headquarters. "We have another signature, center of the valley, a vehicle moving up the forest scenic path, and another human signature potentially left behind."

"That last vehicle must be her. Shoot the tires out, then give her a scare if needed."

"What about the moped girls? They look harmless."

"No one is harmless. Is Project Sunday's tracker online yet?" General Martin asked.

The specialist in the helicopter next to Laurence responded. "No, sir. It was designed for close proximity tracking on missions, not hunting." The soldier looked at his monitor. "But based on the previous monitoring, we know she's in this area."

Laurence had no patience for waiting. He pointed to the vehicle on the scenic path. "Go there." He would have his property no matter what it took.

There was no outracing a drone. Not on a moped. Brittany thought the person controlling it must be laughing at them.

Lena kept driving, undeterred. She grabbed her phone from her pocket and handed it to Brittany. "Keep it on the drone. It's live feeding to a news truck at the diner."

"You're freaking brilliant, Milk. I'm going to buy you as much pie as you want next time we're there."

The brilliant floodlight from the drone illuminated them, making it hard to see the threat. Brittany lifted the cellphone and prayed some of what they were experiencing would be captured. If nothing else, perhaps their final words would be recorded so their deaths could be avenged.

Hopefully, it wouldn't come to that.

Graeme saw Richie's tow truck down the road and waved to get his attention. A moment later, a dangerous-looking flying saucer raced up to the truck and hovered threatening, causing Richie to brake hard. The tow truck and drone faced off.

High-tech. Not good. Graeme hoped he hadn't gotten Richie in trouble.

He ran to the side of the road for cover. A spotlight went on him as another drone zoomed up and hovered. He pressed record on his phone and held his hands up as directed. With any luck, there would be evidence of his imminent death that his mother could use to tear down this screwed-up government.

An instant later, the phone blew up in his hand. He covered his face, cursing as pieces sprayed around him, and recoiled his scorched limb. They weren't messing around.

He checked his palm. A red mark slashed across the middle, burning like hell.

"*Go to the center of the road.*"

Graeme touched the side of his glasses, hoping the record function still worked. A message triggered that it might, but the battery was low. He held his hands up to let them know there was nothing in them, and hoped for the best. "I'm a U.S. Citizen," he shouted. "I have a right to a lawyer. If you're accusing me of something, I'd like to know what it is."

"*Hands on your head. Knees on the ground.*"

He stood his ground. "Drones cannot arrest U.S. Citizens."

"*You're on Government Property.*"

"This is a U.S. Highway running through a National Park. It is owned by the citizens of the United States of America. I'm one of them. I pay taxes. Technically, you work for me."

There was a moment of silence before he heard, "*Hands on your head. Knees on the ground.*"

"Not gonna happen," Graeme replied.

A burst of light flashed across his legs. His body buckled from the blistering pain, and he fell hard onto his knees. He suspected it was the same kind of laser that hit his hand. He touched his jeans and felt the raw skin. The laser had disintegrated his jeans, blazing right through a layer of skin.

He sucked hard for air, then pushed himself back to standing. The next strike hit his stomach before he could get fully upright. He fell and curled over defensively, sucking air…and getting angrier by the moment.

He stared into the headlights. He knew Richie was there. He could see him. They would have to kill them both. Surely that was not in their best interest.

He hated bullies. And he definitely hated government assholes terrorizing citizens, using force to obtain power.

But if they were after him, that meant Sunnie was still free. That knowledge gave him intense pleasure.

This time, knowing it would hurt, he smiled as he got to his feet again.

Richie couldn't stop the shaking. He gripped the steering wheel, but the tighter he gripped, the more his body shook.

The drone guarded him.

All he could do was watch, jumping in his seat at each strike. Graeme didn't know better. He didn't know what they could do. What they *would* do. It wasn't fair. They shouldn't be doing this. *Just stay down.*

Richie was useless. He knew it. Once in the throes of a violent attack, it was impossible to stop. He reached into his glove compartment for a brown bag. Something hit his truck, shaking it. He gripped the bag and inhaled hard. He couldn't understand the voice shouting at him. He couldn't hear. The blood pounded so hard in his ears it hurt.

He rocked. Rocking helped. He closed his eyes, breathed into the brown bag, and kept up the back and forth motion.

Better. That was better.

In front of him, Graeme fell for the third time.

Brittany screamed as the phone blasted out of her hand. She screamed again at the pain, certain her hand had been shot off, or there would be fingers missing and she'd never sew another outfit again.

Lena pulled to the curb.

Brittany stopped screaming once she realized she was mostly okay. Her hand appeared intact, just torched by whatever she'd been shot with.

Furious, she screamed at the still-hovering drone. "I hate you!"

In return, it shot out both their tires, causing them to lose balance where they stood and fall over. Lena caught the bike and Brittany hopped off, tripping in the process.

Finally, the drone took off, leaving them stranded in the dark, except for the headlight of the moped.

"This is going to make things more difficult," Lena noted.

"No kidding." Brittany didn't even want to guess how many miles from nowhere they were. And the mountain air was cold, despite it being spring.

"Wait!" Lena pointed across the flatland to their right. "Brittany, look." The drones had tracked someone and had them under a floodlight. "I think that's Al and Georgie."

"I only see one person," Brittany said.

As she spoke, an explosion ripped through the trees. Al's truck flew up into the air under the spotlight of a drone and flipped over backward.

Georgie didn't think escape was going to be much of an option. She hadn't gotten far in the truck when a drone shot out the back tire on the driver's side. Next came the front tire. It threw the truck off kilter and made it hard to go uphill. She put the vehicle in reverse just as something shot from underneath.

She could have sworn she heard a timer ticking down to her death. She struggled to get out of the truck, pressing the window instead of the door unlock. She screamed for Al, desperate as she fumbled with the door and seatbelt simultaneously.

Then the explosion went off, obscuring her cries for help.

Jocelyn froze.

The cries were familiar, even from a distance. *Georgie!* That was the problem with super-hearing.

"Eyes on the prize, not the price. Eyes on the prize." She repeated the advice viciously, over and over. She had gotten this far. There was no going back. "Eyes on the prize."

She looked out at freedom in front of her—the sky shone bright with stars. The moon lit her way. She just had to go downhill. *Don't look back. Do not look back.*

The explosion sounded, followed by the crashing roll of a vehicle.

She ignored it, looking forward. She could make it. She was fast enough. Freedom. Her family. Hope. She would never get another chance. She couldn't give this up. If she went back, her existence would be wiped out forever. She knew it. She knew Cashus. No one would know who she was or that she lived. She would have no hope of ever seeing her family again. They would destroy every last part of who she was. She couldn't take that risk.

"I won't go back," she screamed at herself. "I won't!"

She ran toward freedom.

But tears made her stumble.

Richie stared at the drone. Slowly, he began to notice things other than himself. The drone could hover and move sideways. In fact, it used horizontal inducted fan technology. He had personally perfected that technique.

A swift dart of anger filled him. He wasn't going to be taken down by his own inventions. The bulletproof glass had protected him so far, and he had other tricks—his retrofitted hand missile for one. He activated the launcher and listened while the machine rose into place over the top of the cab. He didn't give the drone a chance to determine his intentions.

It exploded right in front of him, shrapnel hitting the windshield hard enough to make the bulletproof glass crack. Next he aimed at the drone over Graeme. He had their attention now. The drone turned on him and he hit the gas, screeching to a halt next to Graeme.

Richie pushed the door open. Graeme stumbled forward and he pulled him inside. "Shut the door!"

Graeme did. He didn't speak and looked a little pale.

Richie took off. So did the drone. It chased them and shot at them, threatening. Richie aimed the other mini-missile. He shot and missed.

The second missile must have been enough to let them know he meant business, because the drone took off.

Richie slowed the vehicle—just a little—the roads weren't safe. He grabbed Graeme's injured hand to confirm the laser damage. "First aid kit under your seat."

Graeme nodded, slowly taking off his glasses with his good hand. He reached under the seat carefully, every move uncomfortable.

"There's a balm for burns. Use liberally."

Graeme nodded again.

Richie kept driving.

Neither of them spoke.

Not even about Nellie.

The tracking system beeped encouragingly. "Got her!" The soldier alerted Cashus, "She's coming toward us."

"Excellent. Let her come," Laurence said. He would make her beg for forgiveness.

The truck rolled mercilessly.

Whatever they'd shot, it had acted like a giant explosion, sending the vehicle into the sky before rolling back nearly all the way to where Georgie had started.

She'd been hit hard by all the airbags and was certain she'd have a black eye if she survived the rest of the night.

The truck eventually stopped, cab side up miraculously, and Georgie took a calming breath—then several more. Her parts all seemed fine. Her heart raced painfully, but she was alive. She wiggled her toes, then her fingers. Yes, a miracle, other than the throbbing on her cheek.

She heard Al's voice calling to her. Next thing she knew, he practically ripped the door off getting to her.

"I just wanna borrow your truck Saturday night," she heard him grumble. "I'll have it back, safe and sound." He huffed for air, pulling at the airbags to get to her. "Before you even wake up." He unlocked her seatbelt and helped her out of the truck.

Her legs wobbled. "Sorry."

He pulled her out of the truck and held her close. She hugged him back tightly.

"Can you walk?" he asked.

The whirring of a helicopter landing close by did nothing to make her feel better, but it made her legs stronger. "Yes."

Al changed tactics, dragged her behind the truck, and lifted his semi-automatic rifle. "Stay down."

She saw six soldiers race from the helicopter, while two stayed back with a tall man in a wind blazer.

Al gave a warning shot to keep the others away.

The tall man lifted a megaphone. "Come out, and no harm will come to you."

Al shouted. "Harm has already come to us. Identify yourself and what you want."

"That's classified."

"Well, I'm sorry, but I don't have anything here that's classified. Just me, my friend AK, and several rounds of fun, so let's call it a night, and I'll forget this little mistake of yours."

"Sir, we really don't want to hurt you."

"Then don't come any closer, because I really *want* to hurt you."

Georgie saw one of the six soldiers holding the forward position lift his wrist as if to speak to someone. He stepped back but held his ground and sent the other five men moving in a sweep.

"Not good."

"What?" Georgie whispered.

Al lifted his gun. "We're about to be surrounded."

CHAPTER FIFTY-TWO

Jocelyn sprinted. She didn't have natural night vision, but she could hear the soldiers moving through the forest in formation. In and out of the trees she navigated, then she jumped.

She took the first soldier down with a chokehold. He had zip ties on him. Very useful. Did they think that would hold her? She zipped his wrists behind his back, then his feet, and removed his weapons before tossing him facedown. She checked his belt. Heavy dosage tranquilizers. Perfect. She loaded the gun with two and stuck the other two in her bag.

Two soldiers moved in on Al and Georgie in the picnic area, with a third just behind in the cover of trees. She saw Georgie huddled by the truck, frightened.

She needed to get out in front of Georgie and Al before the soldiers saw her coming. Following instinct, Jocelyn raced forward, then sprang off a large jutting rock jettisoning herself through the air.

She heard Georgie's shocked gasp as she flew forward and shot the second and third soldiers mid-air. She landed and rolled into a stand in front of the fourth man, their leader, and struck him beneath the chin with the rifle, knocking him out and catching his rifle as he fell. She spun and used the rifle to shoot the fifth soldier obscured by darkness, mere feet from Al.

"What the?" she heard Al say. "I'm on *her* side." He jumped up behind Jocelyn. Georgie joined them. Jocelyn turned back to them. "Thank you. You should stay back now."

Al nodded, liking her idea. He took up aim behind a rock while she loaded two more tranquilizers into the gun.

The drones left their other targets and circled the valley from high above. Jocelyn walked across the road and out onto the field toward Cashus. She held up her hands.

"If you leave these civilians alone, I'll come with you peacefully."

"No!" Georgie screamed from behind her. Jocelyn put a hand up to stop her, but Al already captured Georgie's struggling body. He pulled his cousin away.

Cashus smiled and tilted his head at her. He waved to the skies around them, as lights from the drones lit up their standoff in the center of the valley. "You're not really in a position to negotiate."

She shrugged. "I can shoot you right now, if you really feel that way."

The two soldiers flanking him lifted their rifles defensively.

Cashus shook his head thoughtfully. "Drop your weapons and remove that bag from your shoulder."

She slowly did as they requested, trying to block out Georgie's furious whimper. She even took off her beanie, subjecting her pale scalp to the moonlight.

"You've caused a lot of trouble and exposed the program," Dr. Cashus said.

"I haven't exposed anything yet. Just my wonderful fighting skills gained from years of military training. The General would be proud, even if you're not."

"Don't taunt me, Sunday. If you apologize nicely, and beg prettily, I might reconsider your punishment."

Jocelyn took a long moment, holding the gaze of the man who had been her only family for the last ten years. Finally, knowing what she had to do, she bowed her head and spoke slowly.

"I am sincerely sorry."

She looked up and saw him nod in approval.

She took a knee, put one hand to the ground, and held up the other in supplication. She felt the force of the earth move through her, within her. The energy of the land and forest fed every cell in her body as she breathed them in, unconcerned about the powerful wind coming toward her, swirling up around them. She let her natural radar take over. She could feel where everything and everyone was.

She closed her eyes, in acceptance, in a simulation of defeat.

"I am sincerely sorry that you wasted your time coming after me." Her uncle took a step forward to get his balance as the gust of air coiled about them. "That I didn't realize sooner how evil you are." She met his eyes. He looked like he wanted to spit with anger at her defiance. "And that I ever called you uncle."

"You——."

Jocelyn stood, lifted her hands out, and spun in a single motion, releasing the pent-up energy at her targets. The power jolted out of her like bursts of lightning through her palms. It was a relief to expel the force. She whirled, taking aim, and her aim was true. Every drone spun out of control and crashed around them.

Gasps and a few startled yelps followed her actions. The two guards looked on with shock. She swept up the tranquilizer gun, shot one guard while still on her knee, then sprung up to jump-kick the second one as he rushed her. Cashus backed away as she snapped up an extra weapon.

She heard the remaining man in the helicopter—the pilot. He reported to General Martin that backup was needed.

Jocelyn garnered the rest of her strength and focused on the aircraft, fighting the internal strain it required. With intense focus, she guided the energy through the center of her being and out her hand. Slowly, the helicopter lifted, then tilted back. She took a deep breath and released, sending the aircraft into the mountain until the rotors stuck in the earth, and its spotlights shot up into the sky. The pilot sent a new message. *Clean up crew needed. Urgently!* She heard General Martin over the receiver, cursing.

The effort took its toll. Jocelyn gasped for air to replenish her strength. She had to finish it. Just her and Cashus. She stepped forward in the darkness and aimed the gun at him.

Only, it felt too heavy.

It started to tilt and fall from her grip. Her body became uncomfortably light. Her vision began to fade, and despite her will, she fell hard to her knees. She tried to fight the intruding darkness and heard Georgie's cry as her brain became fuzzy.

Breathing was difficult. Her hand touched the earth, attempting to find needed balance. It didn't work. Her strength faded fast. She needed energy to transform the power around her. That was the risk.

Cashus stared at her, curious, his face transitioning to triumph as he walked to her and grabbed the gun from her limp hands, this time to aim at her. He pushed her over easily with one kick.

Jocelyn thought she might lose consciousness.

A shot fired from behind her.

Cashus backed off. Suddenly, Georgie was there, helping her to her feet. And Al. Big Al had her back.

"Drop it," Al said. "Mine's more lethal than yours."

Cashus reluctantly dropped the gun. Georgie ran and grabbed it.

Jocelyn swallowed. Air felt good. She could still see him. Cashus. Hatred flowed through her, and it was more powerful than she realized. She lifted a finger. Just like she had practiced, in the same spot where he'd shot her.

It took an act of will. Her body burned painfully from the strain, but until he was gone, she would never be free. She didn't care if she died in the process.

He squirmed. Then screamed.

She focused pure energy on him, forcing *him* to *his* knees.

Georgie touched her shoulder. "No, Jocelyn. This isn't who you are."

"You don't know who I am." Her voice was harsh from pain and memories. "No one does."

"I know you're good. Give yourself a chance. Please, Jocelyn."

Cashus writhed, unable to move under her control.

"I want to,"—Jocelyn gasped for air—"kill him." Her eyes burned from the pain it took to summon this last effort.

"I know. But it will change *you*, not him."

She felt Georgie's free hand touch her raised one. Georgie didn't force her to stop, but her touch humanized Jocelyn, connecting her to the future and to possibilities. Jocelyn dropped her hand and let out a breath, her body trembling with exhaustion.

Cashus swore, "You'll never get away. There are more coming, even now. If you think you're safe, forget it. I will—."

The tranquilizer hit him hard in the chest.

"Shut. Up." Georgie held the gun. She walked toward him and shot the second tranquilizer. "For good measure. Asshole." Then she kicked him a couple of times to make sure he was out cold and walked back to Al and Jocelyn. Al nodded his approval.

Jocelyn gazed at her new friends. She tried to thank them, but nothing came out. A numb sensation washed over her. She felt her body collapse but didn't have anything left to stop it.

Al caught her.

"Jocelyn. Jocelyn!" Georgie panicked.

"Check her pulse," Al said.

Georgie held her wrist. "I don't feel anything. Al!"

Al didn't waste time. He laid her flat on the ground and administered CPR.

"She can't die. She can't. Not after all this. It's not *fair*." Georgie took Jocelyn's hand and held it, her finger searching for a pulse.

Al shook his head and cursed. "Come on, girl. You heard her. Not fair." He pumped Jocelyn's chest and checked again. Then he cursed with frustration as nothing happened.

"Oh, God." Georgie cried. "Please wake up, Jocelyn. Please."

Georgie heard her name in the distance. *Brittany?* She looked up, and from out of nowhere, Lena and Brittany came running up the side road through the valley.

Georgie stood and screamed. "We need help! We need help!"

Georgie fell back to her knees next to Jocelyn. Al continued the CPR, but Jocelyn's body remained limp. Not breathing. No pulse. Georgie gasped harshly, her eyes burning as she held Jocelyn's hand.

"Please, Al. Please save her." The tears flowed freely down Georgie's face. "I know you can do it. I know you can."

"Shit, Georgie." Al shook his head in despair. Brittany and Lena came to a stop next to them.

"Please keep trying." Georgie's body heaved with sorrow. "*Please.*"

Brittany put a hand on Georgie's shoulder and squeezed. Al breathed into Jocelyn again, her body rising and falling with his breath.

"Come on, Al. I'll help." Brittany kneeled next to Georgie and took Al's place giving chest compressions. Lena counted to thirty, while Georgie prayed.

"Go," Brittany told Al. He gave Jocelyn two breaths. They repeated.

After all the noise in the valley just minutes before, the only sounds now were the group of friends desperately working together.

"Please God, please God," Georgie chanted.

Al looked at the slender girl on the ground. She was gone. It was only his little cousin who wouldn't believe it. She believed in happy endings, in people doing good for each other.

"Georgie," Al spoke softly, but she shook her head at him.

"I believe in you, Al. I believe in you. Please save her."

He cursed. His own chest hurt from emotion. "It was just too much on her."

"No! Save her." Georgie reached across and grabbed his shirt. Her voice calmed. "I believe in you, Al. I *know* you can save her."

He had tried and failed once before. He didn't need another failure to add to the list. "I can't save anyone."

Georgie slapped him. All three of them stared at her. She spoke, calm but firm. "Save her."

"Georgie! I—," Al cursed, anger and frustration filling him. Bonnie had died along with how many others? He hadn't saved them. He wasn't a savior. Now he had to look at his cousin and fail the last person who truly believed in him. He didn't think he could survive that. He cursed again, his mind racing through every possible lifesaving method.

He pushed Brittany. "Get back." He lifted his arm and struck his fist down on Jocelyn in a precordial thump. Her body bounced in response. He did it again. Brittany winced, but Georgie focused like she could make everything better again.

"One more time, Al," Georgie instructed.

Al knew it was futile, but for his cousin, he obeyed. He looked at Georgie. She smiled softly with encouragement. He prayed the super girl just needed a super punch, and he prayed that if there was still a God, He or She would take pity on them. He brought his fist down and hammered her chest one last time.

Please, wake up.

Lena had pulled out a flashlight and focused it on Jocelyn. They stared at her pale face in silence.

Then, miraculously, her chest moved.

A small gush of air came from between her lips.

The three girls gasped while Al covered his eyes with the same fists that had brought Jocelyn back. His throat constricted and he couldn't breathe.

Georgie reached for his hand, her eyes full of gratitude. "That was good."

Al nodded, then picked Jocelyn up in his arms. "We need to get out of here."

Georgie grabbed Jocelyn's beanie and another loaded tranquilizer gun. "Let's go."

Georgie wasn't sure how they were going to get Jocelyn to safety. The girl was still unconscious when they reached the road. They might have to all take the hiking trail to Vesuvius.

Lena and Brittany wanted to be filled in. "We saw the drones explode," Lena said. Then she looked around and saw the bodies littered around the truck. "Uh-oh. What did you do?" Then she looked at Jocelyn. "Or what did *she* do?"

"They're just in a really deep sleep," Georgie reassured her.

"We need a ride," Al said.

"They blew the tires out of the pie lady's moped." Brittany motioned to the moped on its side where they left it after spotting Georgie. She examined the mangled truck. "I'm thinking the truck is out, too?"

Al put Jocelyn down near the truck. "I'll call my buddy."

Lena and Brittany crowded around Jocelyn, curious and eager to help, but completely out of ideas.

Georgie used the light in her phone to inspect Jocelyn. She lifted one of Jocelyn's eyelids, but the whites of her eyes weren't white. They were laced with blue, her irises iridescent.

Brittany leaned back in surprise. "*That's* not normal."

"Jocelyn, can you hear me?" Georgie was worried. "Please be okay. Please."

"Uh-oh," Lena said.

"What?" Al looked up. "Oh man. *Really?* This is not going to look good." He quickly shoved his gun in the truck, but kept the smaller one in his back belt. He didn't trust anyone right now.

A squad car came down the road flashing its lights.

"Unbelievable!" Georgie said. "Jocelyn, please, wake up."

Jocelyn's eyes opened. They were a glowing blue in the moonlight.

"Okay. Not good. Close again." Georgie put a hand over them. Jocelyn's skin was white and blue in the moonlight, but she had a feeling the blue really was her skin and not the shadows cast by the night.

The cop parked, left his lights on, and called out to them in a deep southern accent. "You folks okay?"

No one spoke. It wouldn't be long before the officer noticed the fallen soldiers slumbering in the dirt around them.

Lena waved a hand and chimed up. "Yes, sir. But we need some help. We seem to have gotten in the middle of some sort of training mission tonight. And they didn't see us or something. Our vehicles got damaged, and uh, our friend needs a doctor."

"What's wrong with her?"

"Food poisoning," Brittany hurried to explain. "Bad allergies. Like, to everything."

The cop looked over and nodded, keeping his distance. He had his hand on his gun. Georgie thought he looked friendly enough despite his terrifying height and bulk. His uniform was tidy, and he even wore a hat. Then he flashed a light on them and around the scene beyond his headlights. Georgie swallowed hard as he surveyed the bodies of soldiers spread about the picnic area.

"The men are just resting," Georgie rushed to explain. "Uh, tranquilizers or something. I think like, um, they were on teams, and the winners let them sleep it off and wake up here the next morning. Military humor."

The cop tilted his head at her explanation. "Very funny." He flashed his light over in the distance and landed on something. "Is that a helicopter sticking out of the mountain?"

"Crazy, right?" Brittany said.

The others nodded their heads, agreeing. The cop smiled for the first time. "Crazy," he echoed. "Don't worry, I've been following the news. There's been lots of confusion about tonight's training mission. I'm sure we can sort it all out."

Georgie thought she heard a collective sigh of relief.

The cop went to a couple of the soldiers and checked on them, then came over to the truck and shone his light on Jocelyn's face. "You're right. She doesn't look good at all. Allergies, you said?"

"Bad allergies," Brittany repeated.

"Hold this." He handed Lena the flashlight then checked Jocelyn's vitals.

"She's cold," Georgie said. "I think she's in shock, or something."

"Seems like you have a bunch of weapons here."

"The soldiers left them," Georgie said.

"Just the same. Everyone stay real still."

Al held up his empty hands.

The cop pulled out a phone. "Someone want to call a tow truck?"

Lena handed the phone to Al. He dialed and left a message.

The cop lifted one of Jocelyn's eyelids—his stunned reaction obvious.

"Blueberry allergy," Brittany said.

"Blueberries?"

Everyone nodded enthusiastically.

"O-kay." He inspected Jocelyn's arms next, running his fingers over the skin.

It was weird.

"What are you looking for?" Georgie inched closer, her instincts warning her.

He stopped at the top of her left arm. "This." Then he gave Georgie a wink and whipped a three-inch blade from his belt.

"No!" Georgie threw herself over Jocelyn.

Jocelyn opened her eyes at Georgie's cry. Memory and terror hit at once. Ruben, her guard at Holliwell, held a knife over her. She pushed back, desperate to get away, while Georgie blocked defensively.

Another girl jumped on top, covering her, and all three tried to move away at once, stumbling and falling over each other in the process.

Al grabbed a rifle and aimed, but Ruben merely smiled and waited, hands in the air. Finally, he spoke to Jocelyn—in Russian.

"Sergei sends his regards."

She looked at the knife and spoke back in his native tongue. "If you're here to kill me, do it fast, but don't hurt them."

He smiled. "Sergei sends his thanks."

Her eyes filled. She couldn't help it. It upset Georgie, but she couldn't explain.

"Does he forgive me?" she continued in Russian. How could he? She'd destroyed his life's work, and possibly killed some of his friends and family.

"I didn't say that."

"Will you tell him that I ask for his forgiveness? I hope in time he can do that."

Ruben nodded. "I must remove the tracker in your arm. Be still."

That's what the scar was? Sergei had it, too. Is that what they did when you arrived at Holliwell? They tagged you? She swallowed the bile building up in her mouth. "It's okay," She told the group in English. "There's a tracking device in my arm. He's not going to hurt me."

"Ohmigosh." Lena looked at Jocelyn suspiciously. "You're not a Russian spy, are you?"

"She's not," Ruben spoke in English, his southern accent gone. He ran the blade over the skin of her upper arm then winked at the blonde girl before cutting. "But I am. Hold the light still, please."

There was a collective gasp at the news, and another as he made a slash into her scar and started digging around with the tip of the knife.

Jocelyn didn't move as dark blood slowly oozed out.

"Ugh. That's gotta hurt," Brittany said.

"Yep." Jocelyn took comfort in the pain being short-lived.

"That's Brittany," Georgie said introducing her to Jocelyn. "Her aunt was Nancy."

The girl with the flashlight shined it in Brittany's face. "Oh!" Jocelyn stared at her. "You have the same green eyes. I'm sorry for your loss. She was kind to me. I'm so sorry."

"Light," Ruben reminded them, getting the light back on her arm.

Brittany acknowledged the sentiment and knelt down next to her, supporting her back while Ruben continued to dig with his knife.

"That's Lena, and the big guy you met already," Georgie added.

"Hi, Lena," Jocelyn offered before wincing at Ruben. "Are you sure you know what you're looking for?"

"Do your eyes always turn blue like that?" Brittany interrupted her.

Georgie whacked her in the arm.

"Were you genetically altered?" Lena asked, openly curious. "That would explain it...sort of."

"What do you mean?" Jocelyn started. They were staring. Did she look sick? Would they think she was a freak? Or a monster? Or dangerous?

"Oh." Brittany understood. She pulled something out of her little purse. "Here."

Jocelyn looked in the mirror while Georgie held a small flashlight up from her phone so she could see.

Jocelyn gulped hard. She looked frightening. She was surprised anyone came near her. Her bald head and missing brows were bad enough, but now her skin looked white with a bluish tinge, especially around her eyes. Her eyes were the really scary thing. They were bluer than when she saved the people from the explosion. It scared her. What if they didn't go back to normal? There had been so many drugs, she didn't know what caused this. Perhaps it was a byproduct of harnessing energy? She touched her bare scalp and shivered. Her skin was cool. Unusually so, for her.

The scariest thing was that she didn't recognize herself.

"I'm not a monster." She tried to comfort the face staring back at her. She didn't realize the words had come out, or that a tear had escaped, until Georgie took her hand in comfort. "Could someone find my beanie?" She felt vulnerable and really, really tired.

"Here," Georgie said, pulling the beanie from her pocket and helping Jocelyn cover her head.

Brittany put the mirror away and knelt back down next to her. "Blue's a good color. Look at Milk. She's like an albino. That's way weirder."

Jocelyn saw Lena roll her eyes and realized Milk must be her nickname.

"Diversity makes for a good team, remember?" Georgie said. "Milk, coffee, blueberry...."

"Sounds like an afternoon snack," Ruben said as he pulled an ultra-thin wire from her arm. Everyone watched as he cut the hair-thin wire into pieces before crushing the miniscule pinhead.

"Bastards," Al said.

"I didn't know," Jocelyn said. She adjusted her beanie lower, protectively.

Satisfied, Ruben got to his feet. "Now, maybe you'll have a chance. Let's go. The media has helicopters trying to get into the airspace. I don't think there are any more drones to send, but we still have to get through a roadblock. What happened to Cashus?"

"He's asleep in the field."

Ruben nodded. "We have about ten minutes before the cleanup crew arrives."

"What about them?" Jocelyn eyed her new friends.

"They can come," Ruben said. "As long as they don't mind the back."

Ruben and Georgie helped her to her feet, but her wobbly legs would not obey despite her best efforts. "I'm sorry." She clutched Ruben for balance. "I don't have anything left. Sometimes food helps. And I'm thirsty."

"I have water in the truck. And a leftover sandwich." Georgie ran to the truck.

Lena patted her shoulder. "I brought pie. I had a feeling it would help."

CHAPTER FIFTY-THREE

General Martin stood in silence.

They had lost contact with Project Sunday. He hesitated sending any more tech to find her until they knew a way to locate and contain her. The team in headquarters waited in silence.

"Alert the roadblocks to look for her. Send a photo. Tell them not to approach."

Dr. Wicker stood up from her chair in the back and approached. "Someone needs to contact the SOI."

"Someone already has," Secretary of Information Ramstein said as he walked into the room with his entourage. "Anyone below General, get the hell out. Wicker, you can stay."

Scads of people scurried to the exit.

"Sir," the General said.

"We need clean up and we need it fast."

"Already on it, sir."

"I want every scrap of metal and debris from every vehicle, truck, helicopter, and drone collected and accounted for."

"And an EmWav," Wicker added.

The SOI nodded. "All details or mention of Project Sunday are to be destroyed."

Wicker gasped. "But—."

"You can keep the science, but her files need to be deleted, along with any connection to her past. If anyone asks about Dr. Laurence's niece, she died in a helicopter accident. Wicker, you can take care of the details since you are here. Include a death certificate."

"Yes, sir."

"You're dismissed."

Wicker hesitated, then decided it was best to follow orders at this juncture.

"Martin," Ramstein said, "I want my staff to have copies of all the video and photos of every person who came into contact with any Holliwell personnel or technology."

"Yes, sir." Martin swallowed hard, still waiting for the dress down. "Shall I continue the search for Project Sunday?"

"Perhaps I wasn't clear. Project Sunday is dead."

"Yes, but——."

"I'll be handling this personally from here on out."

"Yes, sir."

He eyed the General's stars. "And I'll be taking those with me."

Several army trucks blocked the Dam Bridge as there was a lot of maneuvering to clean up the road. The soldiers there were on "need to know" instructions and didn't seem to know anything about what was going on. Richie and Graeme took the one lane open and were waved past the roadblock after a cursory inspection and a few questions.

They pulled into The Dam Diner and a media frenzy—at least as much media as one could muster in the middle of the night far from a small town. But it seemed like reporters continued to arrive.

The media wanted to question them on what they had seen, and Richie gave an interview on the drones and the technology being used that went viral in minutes. It was as if he had intimate knowledge of them.

Even more amusing—the guy with no Internet presence instantly had one.

Graeme and Richie huddled over breakfast, coffee, and pie at The Dam Diner until they could go back for Nellie at sunlight. He called his brother and left a message that he would be at the airport by nine. There had been some strange and awesome footage coming from inside the valley about military maneuvers and a possible accident during exercises. He didn't want Rex panicking if he connected the dots.

He also prayed Sunnie wasn't one of the casualties. He had a feeling he might never know. It was all very hush-hush on the government side. And after last night, he knew he needed to keep a low profile. If they'd done facial recognition on him, which he assumed they did, then he might have really put his family in a difficult position—if not dangerous—but that didn't mean he would stop seeking answers.

Once traffic was allowed back over the bridge, they went to collect the Porsche. Richie crumpled at the site of Nellie. Graeme felt pretty ill, too, but stayed strong for the mechanic.

Richie had received additional service calls, so they picked up a truck and pink moped nearby. Richie towed them all back to his garage in mournful silence. He couldn't get over Nellie. To be fair, it *was* a hundred-and-sixty-thousand-dollar vehicle *before* Richie's upgrades.

As the morning sun hit the crumpled metal on Nellie's broken nose, Richie merely rocked on his feet, alternating holding his stomach and rubbing his hands over his face.

It was more than money to Richie.

Graeme put a hand on his shoulder. "I have to go."

Richie nodded.

A chauffeured car with his brother had arrived. Rex was going to make sure he was on the plane. His brother got out, and Graeme held up a hand to signal he needed a minute.

"The repairs are going to take awhile. And I'll definitely want all the upgrades. Those missiles actually came in handy. And the bulletproof glass," Graeme shook his head. "Who knew I attracted the kind of woman who needed bulletproof glass." He winked at the surprised Richie. "Am I right?"

Richie's eyes filled with emotion. He embraced Graeme in a long hug. "I just love her so much."

"I know, man. She's in good hands now."

Richie stepped back and shook his hand vigorously. "I won't let you down."

"*That* I know for sure." Graeme trusted Richie more than any friend he ever had. "I'll be in touch."

Richie grinned, already getting to work, lowering the Porsche from the truck. "Will do, boss."

Graeme headed to the waiting car.

"Hey." Richie tossed a container to him. "Apply three times a day. It will help prevent scarring from the laser burns. Sorry about that, by the way."

"Wasn't your fault."

"Well," Richie hemmed. "Sort of."

Graeme laughed. He'd like to know *that* story someday. Someday when Richie trusted him enough to tell him. "You're a talented man, Richie Dubois. And a good one."

Rex opened the door for him. "Is that *wreckage* what remains of the Porsche?"

"That's Nellie. Careful with your tone. She has excellent hearing."

"Nellie looks like she had a rhinoplasty that went wrong." He looked a moment longer. "Interesting new air vents."

Graeme shrugged and lifted his hands. No denying the array of bullet holes decorating Nellie's cobalt blue frame.

"She'll recover. Stronger than before." Graeme got into the car carefully. The burns on his body were agonizing, he lip was sore from Sunnie's punch, he hadn't slept in thirty-two hours, and he didn't know what positive or negative outcomes the past night might result in. The most maddening thing—he was just as far from understanding anything as he was before.

"And you?" Rex handed him a bottle of water with some ibuprofen.

Graeme took the offering. He was grateful Rex didn't ask about the girl. That would have been harder to answer.

"I'll recover."

He was going to miss the slightly neurotic mechanic. He waved out the window to Richie who waved a station rag in farewell. At the very least, he'd made a new friend.

＊＊＊

The police car flashed its lights and bypassed the line of traffic out of the hills. A young soldier flashed a light at them, and Ruben showed his badge while his partner continued to eat pie. She was halfway through a whole pie.

"Picked these kids up at a little party in the woods after hours. They should have stayed at the dance."

The soldier flashed his light on the four crammed in the back seat, three of them wearing dresses and a big guy in the middle. All looked shamefaced.

He smiled. "No worries."

The younger cop continued to eat the pie.

"What kind is that?"

"Coconut cream," she said, smiling from under her blonde hair, glasses, and police hat. "Want some?"

He laughed. "No thank you, ma'am. You folks drive safe." He pounded the car twice and instructed the soldiers at the gate to let them through.

Ruben gave him a wave.

They drove the rest of the way to Vesuvius, while Jocelyn devoured the pie.

At Lena's Prius, Georgie gave her the backpack full of supplies, and they all prepared to say goodbye. Ruben was going to take Jocelyn a little farther. The others would head home.

Georgie gave Jocelyn a long hug, and after a moment, Jocelyn hugged her back.

"Thank you for giving me freedom, Georgie of the RCC. Because of you, I have a new life."

Georgie felt her eyes fill with emotion. "Anytime. There's information in your backpack. Friends generally keep in touch," Georgie explained. Then she squeezed her again, whispering in her ear. "I'll see you in New York."

Jocelyn smiled and thanked the others before she and Ruben left.

The rest of them stopped for late night breakfast, got ice for Georgie's black eye, then took the long way back to Charlottesville around the mountains, as far away from Holliwell as possible. They arrived back home just after eight in the morning, Easter Sunday.

Georgie asked Lena and Brittany to drop her off at her house. She just wanted to be home. The sun was bright and clear, the dew still glistening on the lawns of the pretty, manicured street where she lived. It was almost like the activities of last night were a bad dream.

To Georgie's surprise, Al got out with her. Not to her surprise, her father opened the front door of their home.

He took in Georgie's black eye, rumpled clothes, and Al's protective arm around her shoulders. Georgie knew he wanted to yell, but she saw the panic on his face.

"Are you okay, baby?" Her father's voice, husky with concern, was her undoing. She ran to his open arms while the tears and raw emotion of the night freed themselves as she held her dad, grateful for her family and grateful to be alive.

"I'm fine. Al took care of me." She reached for Al and pulled him into the circle until her dad hugged him, too.

"Okay, okay. It's going to be fine. Let's get you inside."

Georgie entered the safety of her home.

Behind her she heard Al say, "Sir."

Her father paused a long moment before answering, "Son." Then he added, "'Bout time you came around."

She turned to see what Al would do. He smiled, nodded his head, and followed her inside. He looked as grateful as she felt to be safely home.

Jocelyn and Ruben didn't talk much as they drove. She asked a lot of questions, but he didn't give a lot of answers.

He did instruct her on survival and avoiding government surveillance. The administration maintained a stronghold on the public, even outside Holliwell. Anyone without a personal cloaking program to disrupt camera and sensing technologies could be found relatively easily—unless you avoided any kind of pattern behavior.

She had a lot to learn. If he'd wanted to keep her on edge, he'd succeeded.

They pulled into a truck stop outside Knoxville, Tennessee. Ruben gave her the backpack and told her to go change.

When she came out, he was gone.

Ten minutes later, so was she.

EPILOGUE

The sign said free meal to anyone who could eat a seventy-two ounce steak in one hour. It had a picture of a platter-sized plate, complete with baked potato, corn on the cob, biscuits, cranberry sauce, and a frosty drink.

Heaven.

It was late morning, and the restaurant had just opened for the lunch crowd. Inside, the décor was dark, cool, and cluttered with signs, animal heads, and flags toting the Lone Star state. For a restaurant in the middle of a dry desert landscape, they sure thought a lot about their state.

There was music playing. She noticed that almost everywhere she went—music. It filled her with pleasure, even this strange stuff about Bubba, his dog, and their truck. It was warm and folksy. As far away from the military, bombs, and mad scientists as you could get.

Heaven.

She walked slowly toward a strong-looking woman in her fifties watching her carefully.

"Can I help you?" the woman asked.

Her heart pounded in her chest. What if he wasn't here? She'd come a long way to fulfill a promise. She tried to comfort herself in advance that at least she'd had an achievable goal to get her moving and focused. If nothing else, he had given her that.

"Yes, ma'am. I was wondering...." She put down her small pack. "If there was a guy named Seth who worked here?"

"Nope." It came out short and fast, crushing Jocelyn instantly.

"Oh." *Oh, no. Don't cry. Hold it together.* "Are you sure?"

The woman looked affronted. "Yes, I am. I own this place, and I hire everyone who works here."

"Oh," she said again. "Sorry. I didn't mean to be disrespectful."

The woman relaxed a little. "You here to eat?"

"Yes, please. I heard about your seventy-two ounce steak deal. I came a long way to try it."

The woman nodded. "Hats off. Have a seat."

"Sorry?"

The woman eyed her head. "No hats—or beanies."

"Oh, sorry." Jocelyn didn't have her blonde wig on under the beanie. She instinctively pulled it tighter around her ears. The woman waited. She took a steadying breath and reluctantly removed the beanie, shoving it in her back pocket. She took a seat at the long, empty bar trying not to look at herself in the mirrored wall across from her. Her scalp was still bare, but her eyebrows had sprouted. She didn't look or feel as normal without the beanie. She could sense the woman studying her, which didn't help.

"Not many girls ask for the seventy-two ouncer," she said. "Sure you're up for that?"

"Yes, ma'am. With all the trimmings. If that's okay."

"You're the customer. How would you like that cooked?"

"Medium-rare."

The lady called loudly to the kitchen for one medium-rare seventy-two. "Something to drink?"

"Just a big water."

"Everything in Texas is big, miss. You don't have to worry about that." The lady winked, and Jocelyn smiled for the first time.

She brought water over and Jocelyn drank it down, enjoying the icy coldness. "Is there...." The woman filled her drink and waited. "Is there by chance an Andy who works here?"

"I got a couple Andys. You got a last name?"

Jocelyn gulped. Her heart sped up again. "Andy Dufresne?"

"Andy Dufresne!" She grinned. "Why yes, he did work here. Not anymore."

"Oh." Disappointment filled her again. "Did he leave a forwarding number or address? Or anything for Red?"

"You Red?"

She nodded. "One second." She went back into the kitchen. When she came back, she said, "There's a package. It'll be here shortly. Steak will be ready in about fifteen minutes."

"Okay. Thank you!" She tapped her foot excitedly. He'd left her something! She couldn't wait. Another song sounded through the empty restaurant, and she tapped her foot more—mostly with impatience.

A customer entered the restaurant. She continued to tap her foot...until her senses signaled danger. She didn't hear footsteps entering. Her body went to defensive mode, rattling the silverware behind her as she spun toward the figure silhouetted by the bright sunshine at the entrance.

He took off his beanie. "Two bald teenagers walk into a bar...."

She ran to him.

His arms went around her, strong and safe. He'd gained weight and strength. His brows were filled out, and long lashes framed welcoming brown eyes. She hugged him hard.

"Seth."

"Hey." He held her for a long time. "I can't believe you're here."

"Me, either." She tilted her head and grinned. "I have *a lot* of news!"

"I bet." He laughed and held her again for a long moment before bringing her to the bar. They both had ear-to-ear grins as two giant plates landed on the counter.

The proprietress smiled at Seth. "Old prison buddies?" They nodded. "Take your time. This one's on the house."

She didn't know what that meant until Seth explained it was free.

"Oh! Thank you!" Jocelyn couldn't stop grinning...or touching Seth's arm. She couldn't believe he was real.

"They didn't hold back on you, I see."

"Do I look bad?" Jocelyn asked.

He considered. "Naw. You've got inner sunshine. You could be bald, blue, and emaciated and still be beautiful. Which, by the way, you kind of are."

"Thank you." The food smelled delicious. "Wanna eat?"

He kissed her on her shiny scalp. "Always."

They dug in.

It was the best meal she'd ever had in her whole entire life. And it wasn't just the steak, or the cranberries, or the butter melting on warm biscuits.

This was a time unrushed, unguarded, and full of laughter.

They talked for hours, without restriction or fear or repercussion.

Jocelyn would leave soon to find her family. Georgie had given her an address. The desire to have a family—her real family—was powerful. She only had a few years left to be with Morgan and Ben. She wouldn't waste it. And she wouldn't let anyone stop her, not even the Rochesters.

She might never know the truth about what had been done to her and why. She didn't even know *what* she was at this point. Human, or something else?

The only thing she knew for sure was that she was someone who didn't leave her friends behind.

That would have to be enough for now.

Seth raised his soda and they clinked glasses. Jocelyn savored the moment, her life, and every energizing molecule of freedom she could absorb.

And slowly, her soul began to open to what it needed most—a glimmer of hope.

THE END
...for now.

Dear Reader,

I hope you enjoyed this book. Please visit my website: **www.triciacerrone.com,** if you would like to join my newsletter to receive occasional updates on my projects, promotional opportunities, read my blog, or just stay in touch. I'm also on most social media as Tricia Cerrone if you would like to connect elsewhere.

To leave a review of this book, please go to **Goodreads.com** or your favorite online retailer.

Happy Reading!

Tricia Cerrone

BOOKS BY TRICIA CERRONE

Glimmer

BOOKS BY TRICIA CERRONE WRITING AS TRISH ALBRIGHT

Siren's Song
Siren's Secret
The Time Keeper